Elle Newmark lives in the hills north of San Diego, California. Her father, the chef who inspired her book, lives next door. He's ninety years old, and still cooking. This is Elle's first novel. Visit her website at www.ellenewmark.com

The Book of Unholy Mischief

ELLE NEWMARK

Doubleday

LONDON · TORONTO · SYDNEY · AUCKLAND · JOHANNESBURG

TRANSWORLD PUBLISHERS
61–63 Uxbridge Road, London W5 5SA
A Random House Group Company
www.rbooks.co.uk

First published in Great Britain
in 2009 by Doubleday,
an imprint of Transworld Publishers

First published in the United States of America
in 2008 by Atria Books,
an imprint of Simon & Schuster, Inc

A CIP catalogue record for this book
is available from the British Library.

ISBN 9780385615372

Addresses for Random House Group Ltd companies outside the UK
can be found at: www.randomhouse.co.uk
The Random House Group Ltd Reg. No. 954009

The Random House Group Limited supports The Forest Stewardship
Council (FSC), the leading international forest-certification organization. All our
titles that are printed on Greenpeace-approved FSC-certified paper carry the FSC logo.
Our paper procurement policy can be found at
www.rbooks.co.uk/environment

Typeset in 12/16pt Giovanni Book by
Falcon Oast Graphic Art Ltd.

Printed and bound in Great Britain by
Clays Ltd, Bungay, Suffolk

2 4 6 8 10 9 7 5 3 1

Mixed Sources
Product group from well-managed
forests and other controlled sources
www.fsc.org Cert no. TT-COC-2139
© 1996 Forest Stewardship Council
FSC

For the teachers

If I have seen further (than other men),

it is by standing on the shoulders of giants.

—SIR ISAAC NEWTON

CHAPTER I

THE BOOK OF UNHOLY MISCHIEF

MY NAME IS LUCIANO – just Luciano. I'm Venetian by birth, old now and chained to my memories, compelled to return, link by link, seeking clarity. There's a matter about which I am sworn to secrecy, but times have changed since I took my oath. In my lifetime, I've witnessed man's emergence from centuries of darkness. Great thinkers have unlocked our minds, and great artists have opened our eyes and our hearts. Some are calling it a renaissance – a rebirth – and it will reverberate far into the future because of a miraculous new invention called the printing press. Perhaps, now, it would be a disservice to the advancement of knowledge to remain silent. Perhaps the pendulum has swung a full arc, and the time has come for me to speak. If I proceed with caution . . . well, those who have ears, let them hear.

The intrigue took place in my youth, when I served as an apprentice to the doge's chef in Venice. I first suspected some unholy mischief when the doge invited an uncouth peasant to dine with him in the palace. In the time-honoured tradition of servants everywhere, I assumed my post behind the slightly open service door to the dining room in order to spy, and I marvelled at the sight of them together: The doge, chief magistrate of the Most Serene Republic of Venice, gracious and bejewelled, sat with his guest, a bewildered *paesano* with calloused hands, dirt under his fingernails, and unwashed hair that had been hastily wetted and pushed off his face to show respect.

The meal began with clear calf's-foot broth served in shallow porcelain bowls so fine as to appear translucent in candlelight. The peasant offered the serving maid a sheepish smile and murmured, '*Grazie, signora.*' His rough voice clashed with his meek demeanour.

She snorted at his ignorance – the absurdity of thanking a serving maid – then bowed to the doge and took her leave. Out on the landing, with me, she mumbled, 'I hope that dumb *contadino* enjoys his free meal. The doge is up to no good.' She shrugged and went down to the kitchen for the next course, but she needn't have bothered.

The peasant stared into his soup bowl like a Circassian studying tea leaves. Having come from his world myself, I could read his mind: Surely, here in the palace, soup should not be gulped from the bowl as it was in his own dirt-floor kitchen. How should he proceed?

When the doge selected a large spoon from an array of filigreed silverware beside his plate, the peasant did the same. The shabby guest attempted to slide the soup silently into his mouth from the edge of the spoon, as the doge did, but gaps in his rotted teeth caused a loud, sibilant slurping. The man's bristled face reddened, and he laid his spoon down in defeat.

The doge appeared not to notice. He smiled – a glimpse

of gold winking from the back of his mouth – and generously filled a silver goblet with his private stock of Valpolicella, a dark red wine with a floral bouquet and bittersweet aftertaste. With a hospitable tilt of his head, the doge said, 'Per favore, signore,' and offered the goblet to his chastened dinner companion.

The poor man smiled timidly and wrapped two meaty hands around the goblet. He tried to drink his wine slowly, soundlessly, and this self-conscious attempt at delicacy allowed the wine to saturate his senses. Unaccustomed to such complexity of flavour, he drank the goblet down and finished with a lusty smacking of his lips. Flush with pleasure, he carefully placed his empty goblet on the lace tablecloth and turned to offer his thanks to the doge, but . . . *Marrone!*

The man's smile twisted into a grimace. His forehead knotted like a ginger root, and he clawed at his throat. While he choked and struggled, his eyes spilled shock and confusion. He fell sideways off his needlework seat and tumbled headfirst onto the Turkish carpet with an inelegant thunk. His eyes glazed over with a dead man's stare.

The doge, a feeble, syphilitic old man, dabbed the corners of his mouth with a linen napkin, then heaved his royal personage off the chair. He steadied himself on the table edge with one liver-spotted hand, knelt over the corpse, and reached into the folds of his robe to bring forth a vial of amber liquid. He prised open the dead man's mouth, tipped the vial to lips already turning blue, and carefully dribbled in his elixir.

With a grunt of disgust, the doge poked his finger into the fetid mouth, pressing on the tongue to make sure the fluid trickled down the dead man's throat. When the vial was empty, the doge released the sigh of a man who has completed a small but unpleasant task. He pulled out the lemon-scented handkerchief he always kept tucked in his sleeve, wiped his hands, and then pressed the handkerchief to his nose. He inhaled deeply, clearly relieved to be able, finally, to counter the peasant's stench.

The doge, clad in his cumbersome brocades and with his handkerchief pressed firmly to his nose, sat back in his chair and watched the corpse with small, critical eyes. Absently, he adjusted his sly red cap so that the blunt peak at the back stood up, like a middle finger pointed at God.

CHAPTER ✣ II

THE BOOK OF BEGINNINGS

THE DEAD PEASANT HAD BEEN an invited guest, but I, a street orphan, gained entry to the palace through the kindness of my maestro. I owe him, and all my teachers, everything. Without teachers, humankind would be sitting in a cold, dark, clammy cave, picking nits and wondering how Grandfather started his legendary fire.

I met my maestro when I was fourteen or fifteen, but how could I know my true age? I don't know the date of my birth, though it hardly matters now. The peasant's murder occurred many years ago, in the year of our Lord 1498, the year the chef saw me stealing a pomegranate from a fruit stall in the Rialto and rescued me from my squalid life on the street.

I remember that pomegranate well – the leathery red skin, the fleshy weight of it in my hand promising wine-sweet clusters of ruby fruit. As I lifted it off the pile, I imagined the satisfying crunch, the release of tangy perfume, the juices glazing my lips and running down my chin. Ah, that biblical fruit with its poignant umbilical tip, choice of the gods and food of the dead. I clasped it to my breast and ran.

But the chef stepped into my path and grabbed me by the ear, saying, 'That's not the way, boy.' He took away my pomegranate – indeed I thought of it as mine – and he returned it to the vendor. My disappointment was spiked with anger, but before I could react, the chef said, 'I'll feed you in the palace kitchen. But first you have to wash.'

Marrone. To eat in the doge's palace I would have washed every lice-infested orphan, every suppurating leper, and every diseased prostitute in every poverty-ridden *calle* of Venice. I mumbled, *'Si, signore.'*

'Andiamo.' He kept a firm hold on my ear as we walked through the Rialto. We passed a baker from whom I'd often stolen bread, and the man gave a self-satisfied grunt, no doubt thinking I was finally off to be punished. We passed the fishmonger from whom I'd recently stolen a smoked trout, and the man raised his scaling knife to show me its wicked edge. We wended our way through crowds of shop-pers who glanced at me and then nodded at the chef as if to say, 'Good. You caught one of the rascals.'

We passed some of my scruffy and begrimed compatriots, who watched us from shadowed corners with suspicious eyes. Being escorted off the street by a well-dressed man could be either very good or very bad. I might be headed for a warm meal given freely out of charity, or I might be in for some cruel abuse reserved for boys like me whom no one would miss. I winked at my friends to suggest that I'd run into a bit of luck, but I wasn't nearly so confident as I was hungry.

In a back courtyard of the palace, I undressed and washed with harsh lye soap in a wooden tub of cold water. As I sat shivering in the tub, the chef lathered my matted hair and shaved my head. He said, 'There's no place for lice in my kitchen.'

'As you wish, *signore*.' I remembered his promise of food.

I recall a moment of panic when, as I sat naked and shaved in the wooden tub, he touched the dark brown birthmark on my forehead. He followed its outline too lovingly, and his hand lingered on my face a moment too long. Having encountered men who enjoyed the company of boys in intimate ways – and having more than once twisted out of their sweaty hands – I drew my head back sharply, afraid, but ready to be belligerent. I searched his face for a hint of the predatory mien I'd learned to recognize on the street, but no, it was an open face with intelligent eyes, mild as milk.

The chef withdrew his hand and resumed a businesslike air. 'Scrub,' he said. 'Behind your ears and between your toes.' He burned my clothes right there in the courtyard and stamped out the embers, saying, '*Boh*. Filth.' He gave me clean woollen pantaloons and a coarsely woven tunic of white cotton. The feeling of clean clothing on my freshly washed body made me squirm with pleasure as he led me inside.

The palace's busy kitchen was redolent of bay laurel and thyme, and it had three fireplaces, each of them large enough to hold a grown man standing upright. The chef ordered me to sit on a three-legged wooden stool in a corner, and he gave me a slab of yellow cheese and a slice of fresh bread with a thick, chewy crust. It had been a long time since I'd eaten cheese without spots of mould or ragged edges chiselled by a rat's teeth. I sat on the stool with my shaven head bent low over my food as I gobbled it down. Marco always said, 'If you get a free meal, eat fast before they take it away.' I crammed my mouth full; my cheeks bulged like melons so that I could barely chew. Still, I stuffed in more.

The chef touched my shoulder. 'Slow down, boy,' he said. 'Everything has its own time.'

As I gorged, I scanned the kitchen. Perhaps I could find something to steal on my way out – some tasty bit to take to my friends Marco and Domingo, a spoon to slip under my shirt and sell for a few coppers, or maybe an onion to trade for a slice of meat. But the precise choreography of a well-run kitchen captured my attention. A corps of about a dozen cooks in immaculate white jackets moved about the room with grace and purpose. That kitchen buzzed like a hive of efficiency – clean and fragrant and well lit by daylight flooding in from high windows on two sides of the long room. The nimble cooks stepped around scarred wooden chopping blocks heaped with vegetables and bearing ceramic bowls of meat marinating in pungent liquids.

The baker, who I later came to know as Enrico the Gossip, kneaded a raisin-studded dough as flour puffed up around him, a culinary wizard in a magic cloud. Enrico worked near a brick oven with an arched top, and that day he used his long-handled wooden paddle to pull out a shiny golden loaf with an intense perfume so intoxicating I had to stifle a moan.

Of course, Giuseppe was there, too – that mean, churlish, round-shouldered drunk – and he sneered at me as he swept the floor. I knew him from the Rialto; he was the brother of a fishmonger widely respected for the high quality of his product. I ignored Giuseppe that day just as I did in the Rialto, not yet understanding how bitterly he resented my presence in the kitchen.

I turned my attention to a fireplace with rows of glistening game hens turning lazily on rotisseries. Even with my stomach comfortably full, my mouth watered at the sight of so much meat, rubbed with spices, browning and dripping fat. The seductive sight of poultry roasting and the smell of bread baking blended with sounds of knives chopping, pots bubbling, and pans sizzling. The sensory glut verged on erotic.

In another fireplace, an iron pot, hanging over the fire, sent up twisting wisps of steam, and I wondered what culinary masterwork simmered there. I imagined thick white-bean soup or savoury rabbit stew or fresh vegetables tumbling in burbling chicken broth, dishes I'd heard of but had never tasted.

At the far end of the kitchen, a steep, narrow stairway led up to the dormitory where I would sleep – although, sitting on that stool, frantically devouring my bread and cheese, I never would have dreamed it. I assumed the chef was a kind man who fed street orphans from time to time, and I expected to be sent on my way at any moment.

As I sucked the last bits of cheese from my teeth, I noticed a stone cistern near the back door. Before my tenure in that kitchen expired, I would carry hundreds of sloshing buckets to that cistern. The adjacent wooden door led out to the courtyard where I'd bathed and from there out to the carnivorous city. It struck me as odd that a simple door was the only thing that stood between the kitchen's world of plenty and my own world of want.

On the other side of the cistern there was another door – closed that day – which I would come to know as the door to the chef's notorious garden, an assemblage of queer plants that spooked the cooks and contributed to my maestro's reputation for eccentricity.

The chef's modest desk faced the length of the kitchen, allowing him to survey his domain at a glance. In coming days, I would observe him at that desk, writing menus and planning banquets. Always the *artiste*, adept and original, he seldom consulted a recipe from the crowded bookshelves behind him. The books were dusty with disuse, but my maestro, a guardian of knowledge, loved to collect them. That day he stood near his desk, hands on his hips, monitoring the kitchen and calling greetings to the maids and charwomen coming and going through a swinging service door.

He said, *'Buon giorno*, Belinda,' and a dishevelled girl hauling a pail of sudsy water smiled at him; *'Come stai*, Teresa?' and a grey-haired chambermaid, slack faced and worn as an elbow, shrugged as she shuffled by.

As I watched the parade of uniformed women lug mops and trays in and out the door, the majordomo interrupted the drab procession with a fabulous entrance. He swooped in with his head thrown back at an imperious tilt, his prominent chin thrust forward, one soft hand holding out his gorgeous satin robe and the other swishing a silk fan with a fussy flourish. He wore beaded slippers with curled toes. Oh, those calamitous shoes.

The majordomo's theatrical presence held me spellbound, but the cooks, accustomed to the grand sight of him, paid no attention. Only one cook, Dante, paused while salting the aubergine and attempted a wry little smirk, but his heart wasn't in it. I would soon discover that the majordomo appeared in the kitchen almost every day, and the cooks were impervious to his glamour. That day, he wore delicious robes of peacock blue embroidered in salmon and trimmed in gold braid. As he swept past me, I found myself enveloped in a strong scent of lilac. The majordomo clucked a question at the chef – something about that day's sauce or soup; I don't remember, so dazzled was I by the sight of him – then pursed his lips and fluttered his fan while he listened to the reply. He chirped, 'As you wish,' and made a grand, slightly indignant exit, as if to punish the rest of us for being ordinary.

With the majordomo gone, the chef turned his attention to me. I picked the last crumbs off my shirt, wishing I were invisible so I might linger in that safe haven, but when he saw that I'd finished eating, the chef brought me a brown lumpish thing he called a potato. I'd never before seen that exotic New World vegetable, but I immediately liked its solid heft and its earthy smell. He gave me a utensil I came to know as a peeling knife, showed me how to use it, and told me to get to work.

And so it was. I peeled, swept, carted away rubbish, carried water (extraordinary amounts of water), stacked wood, stoked the fires and scoured heavy pots, all in return for food and a straw pallet in the servants' dormitory. It took several days to comprehend the miraculous fact that the chef – his name was Amato Ferrero – had taken me for his apprentice.

Giuseppe, the disgruntled sweeper, understood my good luck before I did. As an apprentice I outranked him, and the miserable *ubriacone* couldn't bear it. Whenever he passed by me, he whispered, *'Bastardo,'* or shot me the evil eye with his index finger and pinky stabbing in my direction. Behind the chef's back, he tripped me with his broom, scattered my neatly stacked wood, threw vegetable peelings on my clean dishes, and carried rubbish back into the kitchen to make me look lazy.

Still, I ignored him. For the first time since infancy, I ate three meals a day and slept indoors every night. I would become a cook, but it would not have mattered to me if the chef had been a cobbler or a fisherman. He fed me and offered to teach me a trade; it was more than I had expected from life. Seduced by luxury and afraid to offend, I dared not complain about Giuseppe or inquire into the chef's motives. I did his bidding and ate his food, and I counted myself blessed.

However, I did miss Marco, and I struggled with guilt for the inexplicable fortune that had favoured me and excluded him. At first, I hoped there might be work in the kitchen for both of us, but it soon became clear that I had secured the only job to be had. I redeemed myself by stealing food for him at every opportunity. Early each morning, before the cooks arrived, I gathered leftovers that wouldn't be missed, wrapped them in oilcloth, and hid them behind the cistern until late in the evening, when I took out the rubbish. Marco sometimes waited outside the courtyard, hungry and anxious, and when he wasn't there, I left the package behind a rubbish pail. It was always gone the next morning.

I also fed scraps to my faithful cat, Bernardo, who had grown fat and sleek since I rescued him as a starving kitten. After my first week in the kitchen, Marco brought him to me, saying, 'Here's your pesky cat. You can't expect me to feed him.' Although Bernardo often disappeared, in the mysterious way of cats, he always came back to eat and to sleep under my arm in the dormitory. Chef Ferrero tolerated him for my sake.

In those early days, I flattered myself that Chef Ferrero chose me because he thought me exceptional, because he saw the signs of a keen mind or appreciated the deftness of my quick, pickpocket fingers. Now, so many years later, I know that his choice had more to do with his faith in the human capacity to transcend adversity, as well as his wish for a son and his need for an heir – especially his need for an heir.

And the chef's timing was not capricious. In those days, a rumour was exciting Venice like a tickling sea breeze from the east. Everyone from the servant classes to the aristocracy was whispering about an old Byzantine book said to contain the formulas of ancient sorcerers. It was told that the book, thought to have been lost in antiquity, was actually hidden somewhere in Venice. I would eventually come to understand how the urgency created by this rumour spurred the chef to take an apprentice.

The rumours enthralled everyone. I recall one conversation, overheard early in my apprenticeship, that catapulted me into a feast of fantasies involving the object of my desire, *la mia bella* Francesca. One afternoon, Enrico huddled near the brick oven with the vegetable cook, Dante. They held their heads canted towards each other at a tense angle and stood with their arms folded tightly across their chests. Enrico whispered out of the side of his mouth, and Dante appeared captivated. Teresa – Enrico's gossiping counterpart and the palace's other conduit of news – loitered within earshot.

Always mindful of new developments around me, I busied myself stacking wood in their vicinity so I could listen to their conversation. Having lived by my wits on the street, eavesdropping seemed as natural as breathing, and every bit as necessary.

Enrico said, 'The book could have a formula for turning lead into gold.'

'*Boh.*' Dante sounded mildly disappointed. 'Alchemy is a myth. Anyway, the ones who want that book are already rich. No, it must have to do with manipulating people. Formulas for controlling minds or melting hearts.'

'Melting hearts? You mean a love potion? *Boh.* What good is that?'

Dante raised an authoritative finger. 'A man will tell his deepest secrets to a woman who befuddles him with desire.'

He nodded knowingly. 'There's no better spy than a temptress. A man in love is at a disadvantage.'

Enrico thought this over, then said: 'That's true. To be besotted is to be vulnerable. But there must be more than a love potion. Otherwise, why would the old doge want the book? Maybe there's a formula to prolong life.'

'For ever?'

'Who knows?'

Dio mio. The idea of a love potion that I might share with Francesca left me cockeyed and bedevilled. Of all the spectacular secrets attributed to the fabled book, I believed a love potion would certainly be its most valuable.

Everyone believed the book held whatever he or she wanted most. Francesca was the only thing I wanted, but other people wanted other things. Love, riches and immortality – these were the lusts that would lead us into imbroglios of mistrust and disaster.

The web of secrets began with the peasant's murder, which I did not hesitate to report to the chef. He knew that I spied on the doge, and he approved. He felt it could be instructive for me to observe noble behaviour and polite customs, particularly at the table. He always said, 'Tell me how you eat, and I'll tell you what you are.'

For him, the preparation of food was a tool to illuminate the mysteries of life. I can still see him whisking a froth of egg whites in a copper bowl held in the crook of his arm. He hummed to the tinny rhythm of his stroke until the viscous slush transmuted into a mound of snow. 'You see,' he said, waving his whisk like a wand, 'magic!' He pointed the whisk at me. 'Never forget, Luciano: animals feed, but men dine.' He spread his meringue on a buttered parchment, saying, 'That's why we call men of refinement men of taste.'

Under Chef Ferrero's tutelage, I began to glimpse the

value of refinement. Among other things, it seemed to lend a man the power to attract a certain type of woman, like the chef's well-bred wife, Rosa. I was curious about women, but I'd never been with one because the street girls all demanded money for the tiniest of favours. Marco was as curious as I, but he pretended not to care. Marco, who was bitter about the mother who had abandoned him and kept his twin sister, often said, 'Women, *boh*! A necessary evil.'

I didn't think women were evil, just inaccessible. My beloved Francesca lived in a convent, cloistered and untouchable, and yet I clung to hope. Francesca had been relegated to the convent by circumstance, but I could tell by her brazen curiosity in the Rialto and the careless way she allowed strands of blond hair to escape her novice's veil that she did not take her novitiate seriously. Indeed, I would soon discover that under her habit she was lush as a plum and saucy as sin. My youthful optimism allowed me to believe she would leave the convent and marry me if I could offer her a gentrified life.

But my transformation from street urchin to prospective husband would take time. The gritty cunning of the streets was embedded in me. It showed in my furtive walk, my rough speech, and my wary eyes. Eager to become a gentleman worthy of Francesca's notice, I observed palace life surreptitiously and catalogued my discoveries. On my weekly half day off, I entertained Marco and Domingo with pantomimes of the highborn. I dabbed the corners of my mouth with an imaginary napkin and I pranced over bridges with my shoulders thrown back and my chin thrust out. I executed a flamboyant bow to Domingo, saying, 'By your leave, my lord.' I flapped my hand at Marco, saying, 'Bring my gondola, boy.' For them it was a game; for me it was a rehearsal of my future life as a gentleman chef.

However, first I had to serve my apprenticeship to Chef Ferrero's satisfaction. After I saw the doge pour his amber fluid into the dead man's throat, I ran down the service stairs, two at a time, anxious to tell the chef about the murder. To my surprise, he didn't gasp or clutch his chest or even widen his eyes. He sighed and sat at a well-floured table carelessly pressing his elbows into a mound of dough.

'Are you sure, Luciano? Was the man truly dead?'

'Yes, Maestro.'

'Other states can be mistaken for death.'

'Maestro, he was poisoned. I saw his eyes. Dead as stone.'

'Oh, *Dio*.' The chef put his head in his hands. 'It's begun.'

CHAPTER ✤ III

THE BOOK OF LUCIANO

MEMORIES SPAWN MORE MEMORIES, and recalling those early days with the chef always pulls me further back to a time of wider possibility – indeed, time now feels like a cone of narrowing possibilities. My earliest memory is of a broad, coal-black face framed by gold hoops swinging from elongated earlobes. The whites of her eyes were yellowed, but her teeth were dazzling white. She had big teeth, and big bones that bulged under the scuffed black skin of her knuckles and elbows, the rough knobs of a hardworking woman.

La Canterina – The Songstress – was not her real Nubian name, but rather the name the girls gave her for the way she sang her moody African *canzoni* as she worked. La Canterina made the house run. She cooked the meals and scrubbed the floors and boiled the stained linens. At night, she put on a fresh blue turban and a clean apron to serve wine to the men in the *piano nobile*, where they drank and laughed with the girls. She tidied the bedchambers after each use, emptied the cloudy water in the washbasins, and poured fresh water into the pitchers. La Canterina brought the girls steaming hot rose-hip tea when they woke at noon. She took her breakfast much earlier, in the kitchen with me – hot tea for her, warm milk and bread slathered with honey for me.

I don't know how old I was when the nun brought me to the brothel, but La Canterina said a big man could have held me in one hand. I often begged for the story, and I can still see her briskly folding bedsheets while she recited it for me. 'Your legs were still bent up like a frog's, your cry was no more than a kitten's, and you flailed your tiny arms like a blind man.' At this juncture she would tsk and shake her head. 'Scrawny. Pathetic. Another burden in this heavy life.'

Sometimes she'd pause and lay down a half-folded sheet, and her voice would soften. She'd say, 'I couldn't send you back.' She'd straighten her shoulders and snort righteously as she whisked the wrinkles out of the sheet. 'Not that the *strega* would have taken you back anyway.' *Strega* – witch. Sometimes La Canterina rolled the *r* – *strrrrega* – curling the bow of her thick upper lip with contempt. She'd snap the sheet and go on. 'Her *strega* face was pinched and small, like her heart. The *strega* said, "We'd hoped it was a girl for us to raise in virtue. But it's a boy, *boh*." The *strega* dumped you in my arms and dusted off her hands. She said, "They all end up here sooner or later, so here he is." And she calls herself a Sister of Charity. *Strrrrega*.' La Canterina would snort one last time and walk off with the laundry, her high buttocks swinging in time to some lugubrious Nubian ballad.

La Canterina talked tough, but when one of the girls gave birth to a baby boy and left him, naked and squirming, on the kitchen table, La Canterina swaddled him in a soft towel and hummed to him as he sucked on the tail of her milk-soaked apron. When she saw me watching, she smiled and said, 'He's ours now.' She named him Bernardo – who knows why – and she doted on him for the one week of his life. When she discovered him dead in the drawer that served as his cradle, her wails brought the girls to the kitchen. The dim-witted young mother took her baby from La Canterina's arms and shook the limp little body. When he didn't respond she dropped him into the rubbish pail and went back to work. La Canterina unwound her turban to wrap the little fellow, and I will never forget how stricken and vulnerable she looked leaving by the back door, bare headed and clutching the shrouded bundle to her breast.

When I was big enough to pull a chair up to the cupboard in order to reach the jar of sweetmeats she kept on a high shelf, La Canterina started putting me out every day after breakfast, like a pet. She said, 'You can't blame the girls. They say, "Take in one, take in twenty" and this isn't an orphanage.' She shoved me gently out the back door, saying, 'The less they see of you the better. Anyway, you need to learn how to take care of yourself.' She touched the birthmark on my forehead and traced its uneven outline with a fingertip. The birthmark covers one quarter of my forehead above my left eye, and to this day it's still a deep nut-brown. She muttered, 'Dark skin, even that little patch, is an omen of sorrow. You might as well know it.'

The first time she put me out, I huddled outside the back door and whimpered all morning. When I became hungry, I picked through the brothel's rubbish pail and found fresh food scraps wrapped in oilcloth, just enough to quiet my belly. I ate, and then I curled around the pail for my nap. La Canterina let me go on that way, day after day, always making sure there was a wrapped meal tucked into the rubbish pail.

Soon, I began letting myself out. I wandered the streets in widening circles, curious about the world. I was not the youngest on those streets crawling with cats and orphans, and I was more fortunate than most because after dark, while the girls were busy with their customers, La Canterina took me inside to sleep in her bed.

She promised me a cherry tart for my birthday, a date she had chosen at random and traditionally celebrated by baking something special. I remember my selfish disappointment when I found her too weak on that birthday to rise from her bed to bake my tart. Soon after that, I came home one night and she was gone. A new woman with thick finger pads and rancid breath shooed me away from the door. That night I slept outside the brothel's back door. The thing I recall missing most was La Canterina's scent, a warm mix of baking and fresh ironing and womanhood – a distinctive blend I would not encounter again until I met Francesca. The following day there was no food wrapped in oilcloth.

I grew up on streets swarming with merchants of every stripe and sailors from every country. Venice has always been an international port of fevered comings and goings, and never more so than in those days. It was a clearinghouse for the goods of the world. The Far East supplied bolts of brocaded silk; Egyptian merchants sold chunks of alum for dying wool; Muslim traders brought brilliant violet dyes made from lichen and insects. In the Rialto you could buy sturdy iron implements from Germany, tooled leather from Spain and luxurious furs from Russia. Goods streamed in from every part of the known world: spices, slaves, rubies, carpets, ivory . . . In little Venice, improbably afloat on a cusp of the Adriatic, all the treasures of the world were on display, and everything had a price.

I loved to dally on the docks and dream about stowing away aboard the biggest ships. I watched them glide out to sea, their sails plumped with a hopeful wind, their hulls full of goods to trade in far-off places. I imagined myself in the hold, tucked snugly between soft sacks of Florentine wool and rocked to sleep by the waves. Living out-of-doors, I didn't know yet that dark, enclosed spaces made me uncomfortable.

My dreams were sculpted by blades of sea wind and the sharp smell of salt air, by flapping gulls and brawny sailors singing high up in the rigging, by water slapping at ship hulls and impatient cart horses stamping on the cobbles. It was in that time and place of unlimited possibility that I met Marco. He was older than I by a year or two, an impressive difference to a small boy. I clung to my ragamuffin mentor and imitated his streetwise manner of swagger and bluff. The chef became my maestro, but Marco was my first teacher.

Marco taught me the art of bumping into a woman preoccupied with thumping melons and dipping my light fingers into her purse. He taught me how to slip my small hand into a gentleman's pocket while barely skimming the fabric, catch a coin between two fingers, and slide it out, all in the course of walking by. We made a good team at the food stalls – one of us distracted the merchant while the other made off with a loaf of bread or a wedge of cheese. Marco taught me all this and more, but above all he taught me that when you see the *Cappe Nere* you walk away no matter what prize you have to sacrifice. The *Cappe Nere* – the Black Capes – were the secret police of the Council of Ten.

The existence of the *Cappe Nere* was no secret – they strode around Venice in distinctive short black capes that concealed stilettos and pistols – but no one talked openly about their casual cruelty and their far-reaching power as henchmen of the all-powerful Council of Ten. Even the doge answered to the Council, and everyone knew that if the *Cappe Nere* knocked on your door, those ten ruthless men had unpleasant business with you. If you were foolish, you fell on your knees and begged for mercy. If you were sensible, you flew out of your back door and boarded the first ship out of Venice.

Ironically, a *Cappa Nera* once provided Marco and me with a stroke of luck. We had lifted a ball of mozzarella from a cheese merchant's barrel, a slippery trick, and success made us greedy. We once tasted bread with green olives baked into the crust, and eating it had been the epicurean experience of our lives. Unfortunately, olive loaves were long and unwieldy, impossible to hide under clothing and difficult to manoeuvre through the crowded Rialto at a dead run. But we knew a one-eyed baker whose handicap gave us an advantage, so we decided to tempt fate by stealing an olive loaf to eat with our cheese.

I strutted up on the side of the baker's good eye, frankly appraising his bread. I examined his loaves with an insolent smirk, critically inspecting wares I could never buy. While the baker kept his good eye on me, Marco sneaked up on his blind side, snatched an olive loaf and bolted. But the baker must have heard something – perhaps the susurration of shifting loaves, or maybe a shopper's gasp. He turned at the last second and saw Marco pushing through the crowd with the olive loaf under his arm. The baker hollered, 'Thief!'

Shoppers looked up, but we darted around them, fast and agile. Laughing in wild anticipation of our banquet, we recklessly ran smack into a tall *Cappa Nera* with outstretched arms. He appeared out of nowhere. They did that. We froze.

His face was a hard mix of sharp angles: a prominent brow, a cleft chin and thin lips. Marco, the quick thinker, offered him our precious olive loaf. I prised the ball of mozzarella from my grimy pocket and proffered that as well, but the big man laughed and said, 'Bold little bastards.' He gripped us each by the back of the neck, hauled us over to the baker's stall, and levelled a look at the one-eyed merchant. He said, 'Generous of you to give these two your bread. You're a charitable fellow, eh?'

The baker's one good eye hardened in comprehension and outrage. He said, 'Sì, signore. I always give to the poor.' The baker shot us a cold look that conveyed his wish to kill us. Amazing what he could do with that one eye. He tightened his lips and said, 'Enjoy it, boys.'

The *Cappa Nera* kept hold of our necks. 'Thank the man, ingrates.'

We mumbled nervous thanks. The baker, anxious to be rid of us all, said, 'Signore, allow me to give you a fresh panettone. Feel. It's still warm.' He held up his prized sweet bread. 'Take it. Please.'

The *Cappa Nera* barked a brittle laugh. He let go our necks and cuffed the backs of our heads, saying, 'Get out of here.' We ran clumsily, hugging our food and glancing back to make sure no one followed. We kept running until we reached a quiet, rubbish-strewn cul-de-sac, where we sat against a sooty wall, panting and trembling.

I looked at Marco for confirmation that we had indeed survived a skirmish with a *Cappa Nera*. A tentative smile crept onto his thin, dirt-streaked face. He said, 'We did it.'

It was hard to tell under the grime, but Marco had freckles and red hair. Whenever the sun lit a rusty halo around his head, as it did that day, Marco's hunger-pinched face somehow looked simultaneously angelic and sly.

That time we ate our fill, but even with well-honed skills and the occasional bit of luck, there were too many hungry days. Vendors and shoppers alike watched for boys like us. Most merchants chased us off on sight. Once, as we crept up behind a fat lady at a fruit stall, her arms shot out and she grabbed each of us by the hair without even missing a sniff of the white nectarines. She said, 'Not today, boys,' and gave us a shove that sent us sprawling.

Some days we rummaged through rubbish heaps, fighting with the other urchins for scraps of anything remotely edible. On one of those lean days Marco and I had our first argument. Sifting through a pile of waste, I found a litter of new kittens, all dead but one. I cradled the little survivor in my hand, and it pointed its tiny face at me and mewled. I remembered La Canterina's description of me as a newborn and felt an unexpected surge of affection. I lifted the kitten out of the rubbish and ignored Marco's look of contempt as I put it in my pocket.

That day I took the great risk of snatching an entire pail of milk from a dairyman's stall. It was an awkward thing to steal, and I left a trail of spilled milk that anyone could have followed. The dairyman chased me, but he was reluctant to leave his stall unattended for too long. When he gave up, I still had more than half the pail full. I found a quiet spot behind a neighbourhood church and hunkered down to soak the tail of my shirt in milk and coax the toothless kitten to suckle. Marco fumed. 'You're feeding good milk to a *cat*?' His eyes were round with disbelief. 'Give me that miserable thing, you cabbage-head. I'll make short work of it.'

'Don't touch him!' I moved the kitten behind me. A dangerous sneer was forming on Marco's face, so I said, 'You can have half the milk, your fair share. What I do with my half is none of your concern.' Marco flicked the underside of his chin, but he backed down.

For two days, I fed the kitten, drop by painstaking drop, until the last of the milk soured and I finished it off myself. As I watched the helpless thing feed, something inside me softened, but not too much. On the street, you have to be careful about getting soft. I named my kitten Bernardo after La Canterina's lost baby, and I whispered all my secrets to him, all the soft things that I dared not share with Marco.

After a few weeks, Marco tired of calling me a fool and contented himself with a snuffle of disgust whenever I took a bit of chewed fish from my mouth and let Bernardo lick it off my fingertip. One morning, Bernardo disappeared to forage for himself, and Marco said, 'Good riddance.' To his disappointment – and my relief – Bernardo found us that night and every night thereafter. All cats have a homing instinct, but Bernardo was especially talented that way.

Bernardo, who had grown into a skinny ginger cat, hunted at dawn and dusk, the feline witching hours, but he always found me after dark, purring and rubbing against my leg. I cuddled him to my chest and the newly softened thing inside me responded as much as I would allow. Bernardo accepted whatever morsels I saved for him, and then he let me pet him and coo into his small, pointed ear. He slept nestled under my arm, and I took comfort from the living warmth of him against my body. I ignored Marco's frigid stares and caustic remarks. After all, poor Marco slept alone.

Marco and I would never discuss anything so feebleminded as the love of an animal. We limited our conversations to scheming and bragging. The most intimate thing I confessed to Marco was my wish to stow away and sail to Nubia. I didn't have the faintest idea where Nubia might be, but, remembering my honeyed mornings with La Canterina and her soulful *canzoni*, I thought the place would be worth finding. Stowing away had always been one of my favourite fantasies, until Domingo, the taciturn, pimpled boy from the Spanish port of Cádiz, described the fate of stowaways in lurid detail.

CHAPTER ❖ IV

THE BOOK OF DREAMS

DOMINGO ALWAYS STOOD WITH his arms crossed and his hands tucked into his armpits. Self-consciousness made him stare at his feet when he spoke, and he didn't speak so much as mumble and shrug. One afternoon, Marco, Domingo and I found a bag of barely nibbled chestnuts in a rubbish heap and we shared them happily while we strolled along the docks, admiring the ships. I mentioned my plan to stow away, and Domingo dug his hands deeper into his armpits. He said, '*Boh!*' Marco and I looked at him.

Domingo mumbled, 'I was nine, maybe ten, when I hid on a Spanish galleon. It was bound for Constantinople with a stop in Venice. On the second day at sea, a sailor found me hiding inside a coil of rope. He pulled me out, and the sailors shoved me around.' Domingo shrugged with one shoulder. 'They were laughing. I thought it was a game. Then one of them hit me.' He scowled at the harbour. 'They forced me to carry the slop buckets and fed me from the rubbish. I hauled rope until my hands bled and scrubbed the deck with salt water that ran red from my cuts and blisters. Some of them kicked me every time they saw me. I don't know why they did that, but I learned to move fast.'

Domingo's dull eyes came alive and his face, normally placid and flat, twisted with a surge of rage. 'There was a rigger . . . a hairy animal with rotted teeth who . . . who . . .' He swallowed hard and bit his lip. 'One night he caught me while I hung over the side retching from the motion of the sea and . . .' Domingo squeezed his eyes shut. 'He held me over the side and ripped off my pants . . . he did it right there! *Right there!*'

As suddenly as it had come, the animation in his face disappeared, and his voice returned to its usual monotone. 'I don't remember the rest of the voyage, but when we docked in Venice they threw me off the ship.' He kicked at the ground. 'Venice is no worse than Cádiz. I can pick pockets here as well as there.'

Marco and I exchanged a look, and then Marco gave him a friendly jab. 'I'm glad you're here, Domingo. When my whore mother disappeared I was, what, about five? I would have starved without you.'

Marco always called his mother a whore. Of course she was, but that's not what bothered him. The fact that she had abandoned him and kept his twin sister, Rufina, was the thing that stung. She kept the girl because a shock of red hair would bring a high price on the street. He'd never seen either of them again, but Marco thought that if he could find Rufina, he could save her from a life of degradation. 'That stinking *puttana* left me for dead and made Rufina a whore, but I'll show her. I'm not dead and I'll get Rufina back. You'll see.' Marco could barely feed himself, much less a sister, but that didn't stop him from dreaming. He regularly accosted red-headed prostitutes with a hopeful 'Rufina?' and often got slapped for his trouble.

The thing we never spoke of was that street prostitutes did not live long. The fact that Marco had never seen his mother or Rufina after that last day was ominous. It had been ten years and we all knew prostitutes dropped like flies from diseases, hunger, abuse, drink and despair. There were few old whores in Venice, only young ones and dead ones. We all knew it, but no one acknowledged it in Marco's presence.

When Marco's mother left him crying on the docks and walked away with Rufina, it was Domingo who sat next to him and gave him a crust of bread. Domingo said, 'You were a sorry sight that day. Weeping, shaking, wailing, "Rufina! Rufina!"'

'I wasn't crying.'

'*Boh.* You were sobbing your eyes out. And when Rufina broke away, the two of you flew into each other's arms and held on so tight your mother could barely pull you apart. When she dragged Rufina away the girl was screaming, "Marco! Marco!" You were both pitiful.'

Marco's lip quivered. He mumbled, 'We were only five.'

'I know. That's why I fed you.'

Domingo taught Marco to survive on the street, just as Marco later taught me. By the time Domingo was about twelve, his dour, pimply face had become familiar around the harbour, and a fishmonger allowed him to clean his stall in return for fish heads and bread. Domingo performed his chores reliably, and the fishmonger, who liked his quiet way, took him as an apprentice.

That was good for Domingo, but it enraged the fishmonger's brother Giuseppe, the same wreck of a man who swept the doge's kitchen and hated anyone who ran into a piece of luck. Giuseppe always stank of wine and sweat; he was lazy, slovenly and malicious. His hair was streaked with grey and he walked with a slight stoop. His chances had come and gone, and he knew it.

Giuseppe was one of those sad men so befuddled by drink that they've given up and are content to sit back and blame the world. He was pathetic, but too spiteful to inspire sympathy. He flaunted his failures as if they were a licence to make his way by any underhanded method he could. He lived a perfect reversal of the chef's philosophy of personal responsibility.

The chef tolerated Giuseppe for the sake of the fishmonger, a decent man from whom we often bought the daily catch. Giuseppe had a reptilian face with slit eyes and a hooked nose blasted by broken veins, but his brother looked more amphibian – froggish and friendly. The fishmonger was a peace-loving man, but he couldn't curb Giuseppe's bitterness about Domingo's apprenticeship. Giuseppe often gave Domingo a mean kick to the shin or a hard twist of the nose behind his brother's back. He called Domingo 'bastardo'.

Marco once asked, 'Why does Giuseppe hate you so much?'

Domingo shrugged and looked away. 'That's Giuseppe.'

The only subject that made Domingo talkative was the New World. He loved to repeat stories he'd heard on the docks of Cádiz. He said, 'The New World is full of golden people who wear nothing but blue feathers in their hair. They live an easy life in a lush green land. Ripe mangoes fall at their feet, and fish jump out of the water into their arms.' Domingo sighed. 'Imagine whole days swinging in a hammock, snacking on sugar dates.' He gazed dreamily out to sea.

Marco reached into his imagination and wove embellishments to titillate. He said, 'Women in the New World dance naked and they have three breasts.' Domingo gave him a sceptical look, but Marco went on. 'The shores are littered with gold nuggets, and the forests are filled with supernatural creatures who grant wishes.'

Domingo looked at his feet and laughed quietly Marco said, 'It's true. I've talked to sailors, too.'

I knew better because I knew Marco. He wanted to entice me into becoming a seaman and sailing to the New World with him, and he often talked of taking Rufina there to start afresh. But poor Marco didn't have to tax his inventiveness to tempt me. I'd already fantasized about a glorious existence beyond the horizon. I believed that in the New World I could leave behind my ignominious beginnings and create a perfect life with Francesca. My dreams always included Francesca.

The first time I noticed Francesca in the Rialto, I thought she was alone. Then the crowd shifted and I saw her massive Mother Superior standing at the stall of a spice merchant, picking through a sack of peppercorns, her nose twitching like a rabbit's, her face set and ready to do battle over the price. Francesca waited nearby, swinging her market basket and smiling at passersby. That sweet smile snagged me, held me, and wouldn't let me go. She had all her teeth and they were white, so white, and her face was clean and sunstruck.

A dog, small and wiry, sniffed the hem of her robe, and she knelt down to pet it. I heard her cooing and the dog nuzzled into her arms. She glanced around to be sure Mother Superior wasn't watching, then quickly took a sausage from her basket and fed it to the dog. He bolted it down greedily and then looked up at her with naked adoration. She laughed, and her laughter made me think of a field of wildflowers.

Francesca pulled a square of lace from her sleeve to wipe the sausage grease from her fingers, and I had the fleeting thought that I'd never before seen a nun with such a fine lace handkerchief. But that thought vanished with the sight of Mother Superior rising up behind her.

The older nun stood over her, shouting. 'Don't you know better than to touch a stray animal? I swear, you're hopeless, girl. Hopeless.'

The light went out of Francesca's face. She moved off behind the older woman but looked back at the little dog and rolled her eyes. She waved goodbye and her fingers moved like butterflies.

I was dumbstruck. Struck utterly dumb. I thought with a proper job I could rescue her from that oafish woman and the dreary life of a prisoner. I could marry her, buy her a dog, and take her to the New World.

Oh, but what a long, *long* time it would take to become a seasoned sailor. Judging by the sailors we saw in port, Marco and I would have to become men with gravelly voices, stubble on our faces and muscles bulging in our arms before we could secure a berth on a good ship. Then we'd need two, maybe three years of experience to undertake the perilous voyage to the New World. We had both noticed some light fuzz growing above our upper lips, a hint of definition in our gangly arms and fine hair sprouting on our bodies, but malnourishment made us appear stringy and younger than we probably were. Once, in a despondent moment, Marco said, 'You know, Cabbage-Head, we might be more than twenty years old before we get to the New World.'

'*Marrone.*' I said. 'Already half-dead.'

He glanced at the ragged denizens of the streets and added, 'But there's nothing to stay here for.'

'I guess not.'

'It's something to live for.'

'I guess so.'

Our visions of the New World – which included Marco and Rufina, the triumphantly reunited twins, and me and Francesca, the euphoric lovers – kept us going through long days scavenging on the street and nights spent huddling in doorways. Now and then we tried to earn honest money, but by the time we eased the ache in our bellies, there was only enough daylight remaining to carry off a pail of flyblown offal for some butcher or sweep the wilted leavings out of a grocer's stall. Sometimes they paid a few coppers, sometimes they paid nothing, and we could not escape our hand-to-mouth existence. We were dirty and gaunt and pitiable, nothing like the hearty seamen we saw climbing in the riggings of the best ships. Neither of us wanted to say it – that would give it power – but our dream became more improbable with each passing day.

One morning, we pilfered a dry, shrivelled salami from a Spaniard's sausage cart and sat in a church doorway to enjoy our feast. Meat always put us in an optimistic mood. Marco said, 'You know, Cabbage-Head, we could stay in Venice and claim that reward.'

'The reward for the book?' I wiped greasy hands on my pants.

'Why not?'

'You turnip.' I gave him an elbow in the ribs. 'We can't even read.'

'*Boh*. We can keep our eyes and ears open better than anyone.' Marco leaned back in the doorway and crossed his ankles. 'I could buy Rufina a new dress. Hey, I could buy her a house. It's nice to think about, isn't it?'

We'd been hearing talk about that book on every street corner. We heard merchants chatting about it with customers, servants gossiping in doorways, and prostitutes whispering in the dark. Once, we saw a naked man being escorted out of a gaming house, holding his private parts and begging to have his pants back. The man dragging him by the arm said, 'We'll soon have all your pants – and your home, too.'

'I'll get your money,' the naked man whimpered.

'Ha!' His tormentor regarded him with contempt. 'You'd have to claim the reward for that book to pay what you owe.'

The book's legend had resurfaced when a Turkish seaman, in port only long enough to stir the pot, had bragged his way up and down the docks. We saw him one night outside a tavern, addressing a bunch of sailors and toughs. He was tall and swarthy, with a heavy moustache and wild black hair. His chest was bare, and he wore a wide leather belt to hold up his ballooning pants. 'My ancestor brought it here,' said the Turk. 'He was one of those who smuggled St Mark's bones into Venice from Alexandria.' He slapped his bare chest with a flat hand. '*My* ancestor!' Then his voice turned wily. 'The bones and the book were hidden in a shipment of pork. Pork, eh? The Muslims would never search that. The bones and the book came here together.'

As proof of his story, the Turk pointed to the Lion of Venice, a gilded and winged creature holding an open book over the doors of St Mark's Basilica, where the saint's bones were interred. The Turkish sailor asked, 'Why is the lion reading a book?' His eyes bulged as he searched the crowd for an answer. He spread his arms wide and shouted, 'It's a clue, of course!'

After the Turk went back to sea, talk of the book made its inevitable way from the sailors' bars to the shops of the Rialto. From the shopkeepers, the rumour jumped sideways to the servant class and slipped into the homes of the gentry via service doors. It climbed up back stairways and entered the drawing rooms of the aristocracy. Eventually, it fell at the feet of the doge, who immediately ordered St Mark's bones disinterred and the grave site searched.

No book was found, but given that no other city enjoyed more traffic with Byzantium than Venice, the doge and everyone else remained convinced that the legendary book must indeed be hidden somewhere in our Most Serene Republic. The doge offered a small fortune to anyone who brought it to him, and criers walked the streets ringing bells and announcing the lavish reward. Stories spread and lusts grew.

For us, the lowest of the low, the book and the reward were topics for idle chatter. We didn't know how to read and wouldn't have known the scriptures from a grocer's list. The book was an unlikely quest for Marco and me, especially because we were already well occupied with staying alive from one day to the next. Still, we amused ourselves with gossip about the book and musings about the New World. One evening, after a dinner of orange peels and fish tails, we sat with our naked feet dangling in a quiet canal and shared fantasies of our future lives as men of wealth.

Marco said, 'After I get the reward money, I'll buy a grand palazzo in the New World, and Rufina will be a respectable lady. My servants will dress her in silk gowns and me in red robes, like a senator. I'll have a big stable of horses, and a cellar full of fine wine, and a pantry stuffed with more food than I can eat.'

I said, 'When I get to the New World, I'll send for a Nubian woman to sing to me. They sing well, you know. But she won't be a servant. She'll eat breakfast with Francesca and me and have her own room. Someday, I'll come back to

Venice and give the Sisters of Charity a purse of gold to tell me who my parents are.'

Marco stiffened. 'Parents? *Boh*. What a cabbage-head.'

'Well, I don't mean your mother—'

'The whore.'

'But wouldn't you like to find your father?'

'Why should I?' The anger in his eyes startled me. 'My father cared nothing for me. Yours, too.'

'You're right.' Marco's sudden intensity frightened me. 'I don't care.'

'We don't need parents.'

'Right.'

'We don't need anyone.'

'I need you, Marco.' I blurted it out and then held my breath. It was important to beware of that soft place inside. What if I had spoken too hastily?

Marco sat back and considered me, his long brown eyes calculating. 'That's true,' he said. 'Tell you what, we'll be brothers.'

Marrone. I'd never imagined anything so extravagant as a brother.

Marco said, '*D'accordo*, spit in your hand.'

We both spat and shared a slippery handshake. Marco said, 'I'm older, so that means you do what I say. *Bene*?'

I gazed up at my older brother. '*Bene*.'

'Parents. *Boh*.'

'*Boh*.'

The canal blushed in the sunset, then deepened to lustrous black. We leaned back on our elbows and kicked lazy patterns in the water. I felt something akin to peace that night as I sat beside my big brother, but my contentment was disturbed by questions I dared not ask aloud: Had my mother comforted me and kissed my toes as I'd seen other mothers do with their babies? Had my father held me with the clumsy tenderness I'd seen in other fathers? Had I been taken from them, or had they given me away? Had my birth caused my mother's death, or was she alive and looking for me? Was my mother comely or ugly? Was my father charming or crude? Had they wanted a better life for me than they could give, or had they been superstitious people, frightened by the dark birthmark on my forehead?

The treacherous soft place inside me opened and deepened and would not close up. It worried me. If I wasn't careful, if I let myself feel too much, I'd begin to feel the ache that was always lurking. I wasn't as tough as Marco. I did care. I cared *molto*.

CHAPTER ✣ V

THE BOOK OF HEIRS

I STOOD OVER CHEF FERRERO as he sat at the floury table with his elbows in the dough, and I begged for an answer. 'Why did the doge kill the peasant?' I held my hands in an attitude of prayer and rocked them under my chin. 'Please, Maestro. What has begun?'

The chef sighed, then stood and brushed past me waving his wooden spoon, the sceptre of his culinary monarchy. 'Those are no concerns for a youngster.'

A youngster? My childhood ended with La Canterina's death. Some would say I had a brief, unhappy childhood, but a happy childhood is overrated. I had a useful childhood. And now, *marrone*, now I had soft hair sprouting on my upper lip. I followed the chef around the kitchen, pestering him like a gnat. 'Was the peasant a criminal? Was it an experiment? Was the amber fluid an antidote? A potion?'

Chef Ferrero threw up his hands. '*Madonna!* Luciano, have mercy.' His outburst silenced me. He straightened his toque and then, in a conciliatory tone, said, 'How would you like a lesson in cooking?' He only meant to distract me, but the chef always did things in the kindest manner. For an apprentice, a cooking lesson from the chef is a great opportunity.

An apprentice must earn the right to move up in the kitchen hierarchy, and I was not yet permitted to learn the tricks of the trade. The cooks turned their backs or sent me away when it came time to select the herbs for a stew or add the deciding splash of wine to a sauce. Those were well-kept secrets learned only after serving a proper apprenticeship and moving, station by station, up the ranks. In that kitchen, only drunken Giuseppe was lower than me because he was not on a path to better things.

I was willing, even eager, to work hard because I needed the stature and respectability of a tradesman to win Francesca. Also, I was grateful to the chef for taking me off the street; I didn't want to disappoint him. Even the business of cooking was beginning to grow on me. The transformation of bloody flesh into toothsome dishes seemed an appealing skill. Plants yanked raw from the earth and turned into appetizing concoctions suggested a fascinating alchemy. I began to see that there was more to cooking than met the eye.

So I served my time. I stayed in the kitchen long after everyone else left, washing pots in a tub so large I had to stand on a stool and take care not to fall into the soapy water. I arranged the clean pots on a wooden rack and trudged back and forth, lugging pails of heated water to rinse them. After that I swept up vegetable peelings and spilled salt – all that careless Giuseppe had missed – cleared off work tables, swabbed chopping blocks, burned sugar and vinegar to dispel any lingering odours, and lastly, checked on the slow night-simmer of the stockpots. If the fire was too high, the stock might boil over, but if the fire went out, the stock would sour. I became very good at finding the perfect simmer and banking the fire to maintain it.

My most arduous chore was making sure there was no standing water left in the kitchen overnight. One of the chef's eccentricities was a horror of stale water; no one understood why, but it was one of his most stringently enforced rules. Every night I had to pull the plug at the bottom of the cistern and allow it to drain into a trough used only for watering the garden – never for drinking or cooking. The chef even insisted that I wipe the water buckets with clean rags after I emptied them and leave them to steam dry near the fire. All of this meant that I had to refill the cistern every morning. It seemed pointless, but it was a strict rule. By the time all my chores were finished, I was the last to fall into bed at night, and the first one back in the empty kitchen before dawn.

But a cooking lesson! I said, '*Grazie*, Maestro.' I bobbed my head with humble enthusiasm but, privately, I maintained the opinion that I could still wheedle out some information about the doge and the peasant. In those days I suffered from an inflated opinion of my own opinions.

Chef Ferrero said, '*Bene*, we begin.' He rummaged through a basket and selected a large, golden onion with unbroken skin. 'The onion,' he explained, 'is the queen of vegetables. It lends colour and enchantment to food, and its fragrance as it caramelizes in the pan is a promise of delight.'

'*Sì*. Delight. That reminds me of how delighted the peasant looked with his wine. That is, until he died.'

The chef picked up a chopping knife. 'When time permits, handle an onion with reverence. Notice the burnished skin.' He held the onion up and turned it slowly. 'It is the rarified colour of old sherry when light passes through the glass.'

I nodded and tried to remain respectfully silent, but . . .

'That colour reminds me of the fluid the doge poured down the dead man's throat.'

The chef closed his eyes for a moment. Then he carefully slid the tip of his knife under the topmost layer of skin. 'When you peel the onion, don't rip away the underlying flesh. Take a moment to loosen only the paper. Old onion skins come away easily, but young ones can be stubborn, eh?' The chef gave me a pointed look that I pretended not to understand. He removed the skin and held it out in the palm of his hand. 'Look at the skin, Luciano. Observe its delicacy, its colour and texture, like translucent shavings of copper and gold.'

'Gold! Now, there's a motive for murder.' The rash words seemed to leap from my mouth before I could stop them. 'I understand punishing a thief. But why pour drink down a dead man's throat?'

The chef rolled his eyes. Without looking at me, he pushed the papery skin into a little pile at the edge of the cutting board, and when I moved to gather it up he stayed my hand. 'Leave the onion skins, Luciano. They provide inspiration.'

'Inspiration.' I nodded slowly and, with abashed persistence, asked, 'I wonder what might inspire the doge—'

'Look at the naked onion, Luciano. She's newly stripped, and no one but you has ever seen her before. Her colours are virgin white tinged with spring green. Handle her gently. For the first cut, slice cleanly down the centre and behold what you've exposed.' He parted the onion to show me its concentric design and smiled. 'Lay open the intimate centre and admire the perfect nests within nests.' He mused over the onion's structure and murmured, 'There was a Greek teacher named Euclid who made some interesting observations about the geometry of circles . . .'. He must have noticed the confusion on my face and he added, 'That's not important right now.'

He picked up the onion and his voice turned brusque. 'Inhale the aroma, the soul, but take your time. The art of cooking, like the art of living, must be savoured for its own sake.' He wafted the onion under his nose and inhaled deeply. 'No matter that the food we prepare will be eaten in minutes; the act of creation is everything.'

He laid half of the onion flat on its cut surface and sliced it across, cocking one ear to the board. 'Listen to the crisp sound of each cut, Luciano. Hear the music of freshness.'

My eyes watered from the onion fumes, and the stinging tears diverted my curiosity. I asked, 'Why do onions make us cry?'

Chef Ferrero shrugged as a tear slid down his cheek. 'You may as well ask why one cries in the presence of great art, or at the birth of a child. Tears of awe, Luciano. Let them flow.'

I wiped my eyes, but the chef let tears roll freely down his face. A tear dripped from his chin as he scooped up the diced onion for the stockpot. His awe would season the soup.

'But the doge—'

'*Basta!*' The chef slammed the knife into the cutting board and turned on me with arched eyebrows. 'Leave it alone, Luciano. Everything comes in its own time, and your time has not yet come. Your lesson is over. Back to work, and not another word.'

I backed away twisting my fingertips at my lips as if turning a key in a lock. *Stupido*. I'd forgotten how easily I could be sent back to the streets. I grabbed my broom and busied myself sweeping goose feathers into a corner where I would stuff them into sacks for the maids. The goose itself was already browning nicely on the spit, and I planned to fish the neck and gizzard out of the stockpot the next morning when they'd be nice and tender – a special treat for Marco and Domingo.

The chef's outburst had been loud and uncharacteristic. I glanced around the kitchen to check the reaction of the cooks, but no one acknowledged me, and I assumed that I'd temporarily become persona non grata. Only Giuseppe caught my eye in order to shoot me one of his poisonous looks. My phenomenal luck as the street urchin turned into a chef's apprentice had indeed made me the object of his brooding, implacable hatred.

My busy young mind jumped from Giuseppe to the chef to the doge and the dead peasant and back again. I jammed fistfuls of goose feathers into coarse sacks, readying them for the maids who would sort out the fluffy down for pillows. Preoccupied with my thoughts, I allowed too many feathers to float over my head and drift into the fire, where they winked away with a quick sizzle. While the feathers flew around me in a soft blizzard, I plotted a way to discover what the chef knew about the peasant's death.

I knew where the chef lived. On Sundays, the one day he stayed home and let Pellegrino run the kitchen, the chef had occasionally taken me to Mass with his family at the church of San Vincenzo and then to his house for Sunday dinner. The hour of unrelieved tedium in church was the price for my inclusion in the chef's family, and I paid it gladly. I bathed carefully and put on fresh clothing in preparation for those Sundays when I sat in a church pew with the gentry rather than standing at the back with the beggars.

The service bored me, but I took consolation in the fact that the chef also seemed disinterested. His eyes wandered during the offertory; he examined his fingernails during the sermon; he sighed every time he had to kneel; and while the choir intoned a sonorous Gregorian chant, he stared into the distance and tapped an impatient foot on the padded kneeler. Once, I inquired into how he felt about attending Mass, and he said, 'It's a matter of form. One doesn't wish to attract the wrong kind of attention.'

After Mass, I was thrilled to sit at his dinner table and eat from a porcelain plate with a silver fork, like any member of a respectable family. Those meals were a revelation. The family talked about a world completely foreign to me – school, church, dressmakers, relatives and neighbours. I listened and spoke only when spoken to, and I never looked too long at any of his young daughters.

I didn't understand why the chef took me into his home on Sundays. Why not his sous-chef Pellegrino or Enrico or Dante or any other of the senior staff? But I didn't ask, in case questioning my good luck might somehow put an end to it. I kept my head down and wallowed in the deliciousness of belonging. I wrapped myself in borrowed familial warmth and pretended to be the only son in the chef's family.

The chef was madly in love with his family. His wife, Rosa, was his anchor; his eldest daughter, Elena, a fair-haired girl of ten, was his pride; his eight-year-old twins, Adriana and Amalia, mirror images of each other, were his wonder; and his little five-year-old, Natalia Sofia, with her extravagant mass of dark curls and a temperament as sweet as her face, was the tiny empress of his joy.

While Chef Ferrero encouraged me to eat up – 'Mangia, Luciano. Mangia' – Signora Ferrero passed the pasta without looking at me. She was not unkind, but her cool demeanour advised me to keep my portions small and my mouth shut. I didn't mind. I understood her attitude better than the chef's. What right had I to sit at her table? Neither she nor I seemed to know.

On the last Sunday that I would ever be allowed to dine with that family, we sat back, stuffed with our fine meal of chicken in rosemary sauce. We relaxed over fontina cheese and green grapes while Elena described her confirmation dress. I'm glad I didn't know then that the conversation would lead to the end of my Sunday dinners with the family. If I had, I might have wept into my chicken.

Elena's cheeks flushed as she chattered about her white dress, about the softness of the China silk and the intricacy of the Belgian lace. The chef listened while a wistful smile played over his face. Elena described the elaborate monogram she would embroider on one sleeve of her dress, and at the mention of the monogram the chef's smile sagged. He put down the grape he'd been about to pop into his mouth, and it rolled across his plate. He said, '*La mia bella* Elena. Today your confirmation; tomorrow your wedding.'

'*Sì, Papà.*' Elena's blush deepened.

He sighed. 'In time, you'll all sew lace on your wedding dresses and leave your *papà* behind. You'll embroider your husband's monogram on tablecloths and bedsheets, and the name Ferrero will be forgotten.'

Signora Ferrero slapped her napkin on the table. 'Don't, Amato.'

'I'm sorry, my love. It weighs on me.'

'It's God's will.'

The chef looked at me and seemed about to say something, but—

'Amato.' Signora Ferrero's voice was even and careful. 'Don't.'

The chef stared at the grape on his plate. 'He's a good boy, Rosa.'

'I won't listen to this.' She stood with stiff dignity. 'Camilla,' she called. 'Clear the dishes.'

Old Camilla rushed in from the kitchen, alarmed by her mistress's sharp tone, and began stacking plates. Signora Ferrero spoke with pinched lips. 'Amato, I would speak with you, please.'

As the chef followed his wife into the hallway, he smiled at his daughters and passed his hand over little Natalia's curls. In her agitation, Signora Ferrero failed to pull the door completely shut behind them, and we could all hear the urgent edge in her voice. Camilla cleared more slowly than usual. Natalia covered her mouth with a dimpled hand, and the girls stole apprehensive looks at each other. We all listened.

'Amato, you delude yourself.'

'Rosa, *cara*, you should see him in the kitchen. He works hard, and he's smart.'

'I don't doubt he's smart. He's a street boy who made his way into the palace.'

'He's not like other street boys. He has the instinct to be better. Like I did.'

'*Basta*. You pity him, and your wish for a son confuses you.'

'Rosa, he was stealing a *pomegranate*. Not mouldy bread to cram into his mouth with no thought. A pomegranate must be carefully peeled and eaten seed by seed. It takes time. Attention must be paid to eat a pomegranate.'

'What are you talking about? He stole a pomegranate because he could. He comes from the street. He has unsavoury companions. He's a conniving thief and you bring him into our home? You introduce him to our daughters? No! I won't have it. He'll cause trouble, Amato. I feel it.'

'*Cara*, don't upset yourself. I simply need an apprentice.'

'But why a thief? And why is he in our home?' Her voice

turned plaintive. 'I have a bad feeling about him, Amato. Why him? Why is he here? What are you up to?'

There was a pause. Then the chef's voice turned grave and faintly apologetic. 'Rosa, my love, I have something to tell you. Long before I met you, there was someone—'

A hand – whether it was the chef's or his wife's I'll never know – a hand pulled the door until it clicked fully shut, and the chef's words were reduced to a muffled garble. Was that when he told her his suspicions about me? Was that when he directed her attention to my birthmark? Was that when he gave her reason to think I could threaten the peace of her home? It would explain why that was my last dinner with them. She never even returned to the table that day.

I was saddened by Signora Ferrero's low opinion of me, but I was also touched and amazed by the chef's interpretation of my stolen pomegranate. It was a pleasing notion that anyone might take me for a thoughtful boy who would *choose* to steal a pomegranate, and then pick out one glistening seed at a time, savour the taste, and fastidiously blot my lips. I imagined myself eating like that – I who crammed food in my mouth as fast as I could – and I had to smile. I wondered whether anyone could change that much. Could there be refined instincts inside me without my knowing it? I had a thrilling moment, thinking I might become the sensitive, genteel boy the chef thought I was, but . . .

The moment passed, and the dismal truth asserted itself. If I'd been allowed to keep that pomegranate I would've ripped away the skin with my teeth and gorged on the fruit, crunching through full mouthfuls, tasting almost nothing, oblivious to the juices smearing my cheeks and dripping off my chin. I was *hungry*.

Still, the chef's remarks about the pomegranate reminded me of his approach to chopping an onion. Did paying attention to food really change the experience of eating it? I eyed the green grapes and the buttery fontina on the table, and I wondered whether a grape would taste any different if attention *were* paid.

I picked off a single grape and observed it: the colour was something like that of a green apple, but with a fragile translucency and a dull sheen. I turned it in my fingers, pressed lightly, and felt the firm, plump surface give under my fingertips. I said a silent *grazie a Dio* before placing it on my tongue, and then I rolled it around in my mouth, postponing the bite. The anticipation reminded me of Francesca – when would I see her again? The thought of her made me bite down hard. Still, I forced myself to take note of the way the skin offered a teasing resistance. The grape split and flooded my mouth with a flavour so delicate it was almost an aroma. I closed my eyes and sucked on the burst grape, enjoying the opposing textures of skin and pulp. I chewed slowly and allowed the nectar to saturate my palate. It seemed as though I'd never before eaten a grape quite so exquisite as that one. I looked at the bunch of grapes on the table and thought about eating them all that way, one at a time, paying attention, each one a perfect little miracle. I frankly found the prospect exhausting, but I chewed my grape with reverence for a long time, and it felt like eating all the grapes in the world at once. It was just a grape, but somehow it felt like a beginning.

Still, Signora Ferrero had been right. I'd stolen the pomegranate because I could. If mouldy bread had been handier, I'd have taken that instead. The chef was a naturally generous man who allowed people the benefit of the doubt, and, as his wife observed, his wish for a son may have confused him. She was more realistic, like most women, more practical. She spread her motherly warmth over her family like a brood hen on her nest, but her wingspan did not reach far enough to touch the likes of me. She loved her family and I was a threat to their innocence. She knew perfectly well that street boys were not noble in the face of hunger, and though this was a sad fact of life, my base character could not be allowed to taint her daughters.

Despite their differences, the chef loved her unconditionally – and he respected her as well. He respected all women. I remember his remarks on the subject, one afternoon in the kitchen when work was slow and the staff languished in an uncommon lethargy. Pellegrino and Enrico were lounging by the brick oven, complaining about their wives. Wishing to join them – wishing to act like a regular member of the staff – I remembered Marco's cynical refrain about women and thought to make them laugh over it. I smiled crookedly, imitating Marco's sardonic bravado, and said, 'Women, *boh!* A necessary evil.'

'How dare you!' The chef marched over, roaring. 'I will not have disrespectful talk about women in my kitchen.' Pellegrino scurried off to his chopping block, and Enrico busied himself with a bread paddle. In a lower voice the chef said, 'A woman is no trivial matter, Luciano. Choose well and you'll have a complete soul.'

'Forgive me, Maestro,' I answered meekly. 'I know you're right.' Then I told him about Francesca.

He said, 'She's in a convent?'

'Yes, Maestro. But she doesn't want to be.'

'How do you know that?'

'I can tell.'

'Oh, *Dio*.'

'But I love her!'

He rubbed his chin. 'Does she love you?'

'Not yet, but she might.'

'Oh, *Dio*.' He walked away shaking his head, mumbling to himself. 'A nun in the marketplace. *Dio mio*. Boys.'

At that time, I'd been in the kitchen about a month and I'd spoken to Francesca once, in the Rialto, on a shopping trip for the chef. But before that, I'd worshipped her from afar many times. I had often stood at a distance – ashamed of my ragged clothes, but besotted and yearning – and watched her walk in the sunlight behind Mother Superior. I studied her face, so soft and full of rosy light, and I was bewitched. I knew her name because the older nun often reprimanded her: 'Francesca, stop dawdling.' 'Francesca, don't daydream.' 'Francesca, did you hear me?' Mother Superior's nagging managed to dim the light in her face but did not extinguish it. Francesca would look momentarily chastened, but as soon as the older woman turned away, she lit up again and resumed gobbling up the sounds and sights around her.

Mother Superior billowed through the market in a starched white wimple and voluminous robes, like a ship sailing into port, while Francesca followed with small, chaste steps, carrying a wickerwork basket and sneaking looks at everyone and everything. Francesca wore the simple brown habit of a novice, with a rope tied around her waist. She dressed like a nun, but anyone could see her heart was not in it. A veil set carelessly back on her head allowed a glimpse of pale blond hair brushed away from her tawny brow, and a few loose wisps always danced joyously around her face. She had the wide eyes of an antelope.

I'd seen eyes like those on a hunting tapestry in one of the palace's public rooms, and the chef had told me what the animal was called. In the tapestry, hunters with eager faces pursued the graceful animal on horseback. The antelope seemed, like its name, a gentle creature, and I didn't understand the hunters' passion to kill it. The doomed animal looked out from the tapestry pleading for rescue, and the eyes disturbed me so much that I learned to walk past it with my head down.

Lost in the memory of Francesca's antelope eyes, I started when a maid tapped my shoulder. She'd come to collect the sacks of goose feathers, and seeing the light flurry of down still settling around me she pulled a face and wrenched the last sack out of my hands. She muttered, 'Wasteful boy.'

'Sorry.'

'*Boh.*' She gathered up the other sacks and stalked off.

Her contempt brought me back to the kitchen. Most days, I thought about Francesca obsessively, but on that long, strange day, after I'd witnessed a murder and peeled an onion, curiosity about the doge's motives consumed thoughts of Francesca like goose feathers in the fire. I was keen to understand what the doge had done, and it came to me like an epiphany that the chef would confide everything to the other half of his soul – his wife, Rosa. It wasn't every day that the doge poisoned a peasant at his table, and I felt confident the chef would tell her about it. All I had to do was go to his house that night and eavesdrop.

One errant feather tickled my nose like a warning, but I brushed it off and made my plans.

CHAPTER VI

THE BOOK OF CATS

IT ASTOUNDS ME NOW THAT the doge's palace, which was already venerable when I was born, retains its original elegance; the patina of youth still blooms on the ancient stones. It's a massive palace, taking up an entire side of the vast Piazza San Marco, yet it looks fragile. An arcade of fluted white pillars supports upper storeys of rose marble pierced by the keyhole windows of Byzantium. Now, as an old man, I sometimes visit Venice simply to marvel at that precarious balance of strength and delicacy. But on that seminal night so long ago, young and consumed by curiosity, I raced to the chef's house, blind to glorious architecture and ignorant of so much more.

I had to wait until the last cook hung up his apron, wished me *buona notte*, and walked out with a leftover lamb shank wrapped in oilcloth. It was *my* lamb shank. Or at least the one I'd intended for Marco and Domingo. I had put off claiming it and now it was gone. The chef's constant admonition echoed in my mind – *Pay attention, Luciano*.

When I felt sure no one would return, I shed my apron and escaped. In the Piazza San Marco, I glanced at the clock tower and saw that I'd probably arrive just in time to listen in on the chef's dinner conversation. That clock also shows the date, the phases of the moon and the position of the sun in the zodiac; astrology was then, and is still today, a serious science employed by the upper classes. I'd heard that we lived in the Age of Pisces, an age of mystery and becoming, and that it would be another five hundred years, a new millennium, before we entered the Age of Aquarius, the apocalyptic age of upheavals and revelations. The Age of Aquarius sounded like an interesting time to be alive, and I felt vaguely disappointed that I would not see it.

I loped along the Grand Canal, feeling the night's damp breath on my face. Behind the palace, I turned onto a side street leading to the Bridge of Sorrows, a marble arch that spanned a canal to join the secret passageways of the palace to the inquisitors' dungeons. Over that bridge, the *Cappe Nere* conducted criminals and heretics to dark underwater caves where the poor wretches lay chained in dank cells listening to the plash of oars as gondolas passed freely overhead. Shivering and starving, they waited for apish louts to drag them off to the rack or to the bloodcrusted spikes of the Iron Maiden. The prisoners' despair upon taking their last look at the sky had given the bridge its name. That night, the Bridge of Sorrows was deserted but for a cat slouching in the shadows.

There have always been too many cats in Venice. In moments of fanciful speculation, I regard the cats of Venice as a death motif. Everyone knows the myth of nine lives, the bad luck associated with black cats, and their reputation as familiars for witches. Cats and their dark myths are so much a part of the city that we've built fountains with small indentations, like tiny stairs, to make it easier for them to climb up for a drink. Cats and all they suggest are thoroughly Venetian, and I wonder: should all these cats remind hedonistic Venetians of their mortality? Should the nine lives make us ponder the concept of resurrection? Do these cryptic creatures hint at the possibility of magic in the world?

I paused briefly on the bridge to note the reflection of stars twinkling in the canal's black water; the white marble bridge appeared suspended in a starry night sky with pinpoints of light glittering above and below, and only now do I ponder the ominous implications of a city that floats in darkness. That night I crossed the bridge propelled by the exuberance of youth. My long days in the kitchen had made me dull, but that night the old thrill of risk quickened in my chest. Joking, I gave the lurking cat a warning that mothers used to subdue unruly children – 'Watch out! The *Cappe Nere* will get you.' The cat hissed its own warning. I laughed and ran on.

I've often revisited Venice since my youth, if only to smile at the irony, the enduring illusion of her nobility. The water still whispers tales of death as it laps against decaying *palazzi*. Men in capes still appear out of the darkness and dissolve back into it. Venice has always been a perfect setting for secrets, seduction and the melancholy thoughts of a poet. Tainted by iniquity, Venice invites moral surrender not with a playful wink, but with the understanding that she is, and always has been, sluttish under her regal disguise.

Venice is a city of illusions, and only one raised on her streets can find his way through her dreamlike convolutions in the dark. Having explored her thoroughly when I lived by her grace, that advantage was mine. It took only minutes to find the narrow *rio* of the chef's house.

It was a tall home with a blue front door, arched windows and a long stone balcony running the entire length of the *piano nobile*, that middle floor comprised of a dining room, kitchen and sitting room. As was typical, the ground floor was used for washing and storage, and the topmost floor was made up of bedrooms. Each bedroom had a middle-sized balcony with a potbellied iron railing that overlooked the cobbled footpath and the green canal. Stone steps led from the chef's front door directly into the water, where his private gondola, moored to a striped pole, rocked easily. It was a comfortable home, appropriate for a respected citizen like the doge's chef. It was exactly the sort of home I wanted for Francesca and me.

I paused in the deep nightshade of the *piano nobile*'s long stone balcony and my excitement waned with the advance of guilt. Until then, I'd always come to that house as a welcome guest. The chef had put a paternal arm around me, fed me, smiled on me, and welcomed me into his family. Now, prowling like a criminal, I felt the pinch of disloyalty. I thought about leaving, but I was young and burning to know . . . *everything*. I crept up the stairway to the *piano nobile* and slithered along the balcony's smooth stone floor, careful not to disturb the flowerpots lining the wall, until I reached the brightly lit window of the dining room. Blood pounded in my ears.

Adolescent ignorance regarding the natural complexity of life led me to imagine that the chef and his wife would be conveniently situated, near enough to facilitate my eavesdropping, but not near enough to detect my presence. Of course, they'd begin discussing the doge the moment I came within earshot. I anticipated the chef telling his wife all that had happened, explaining the reasons and consequences in clear detail, and signalling the end of the story by going directly to bed. Ha!

I snatched a look into the cheerful dining room and saw that it was warmly lit by at least a dozen chunky beeswax candles. The chef and his family sat around their long chestnut dining table, bathed in mellow candlelight, relaxed and chatting after their evening meal. Pressed against the wall, I listened. Smells of lamb stew and fresh bread wafted out to me, and I remembered that I'd not eaten my own evening meal. My stomach contracted, and I willed it to be quiet.

Signora Ferrero spoke of an altercation with the butcher. She never referred to him by name, but called him *il ladro* – the thief. She said, 'It's not my imagination. He cheats my sister, too. The man has a fickle scale and a heavy thumb.'

The chef murmured something vaguely agreeable.

The daughters spoke of teachers and school friends. As members of the gentry, the girls would never become fluent in Latin and Greek like aristocratic children, such as the pope's daughter, Lucrezia Borgia, but they'd learn to read and write and do their sums. Elena said she wanted to study astrology, but the chef said, 'Better to study the work of that young teacher from Poland, Copernicus. He has an interesting theory that the earth revolves around the sun, although you shouldn't bring his name up in public, eh?' The room went silent, and I peeked in. Elena stared at her father with a perplexed look, and little Natalia laid her cheek on the table and yawned. The chef said, 'Never mind. We'll talk about Copernicus when you're older.'

I listened to the mundane details of the family's day and waited for the chef to mention that there'd been a murder in the palace, but he only sympathized with his wife's complaints and listened to his daughters' reports. After a while, I realized he was, of course, waiting to be alone with his wife. What father would discuss murder in front of his young children? The girls would go to bed, and then he would tell her – *everything*.

Eventually, I heard the scraping of chairs, the clink of forks, and the clash of dishes as Camilla cleared the table. I pictured the old servant's bony hands piling up the plates, her long dour face with its humped nose, her thin grey hair twisted into a diminutive knot on top of her head. I'd watched Camilla clear that table many times. Once again, guilt intruded. How could I spy on these people? Apart from La Canterina, they were the only family I'd ever known. Shame on me. If I crept away immediately, it would be as if I'd never come. I started to back away from the window – and that's when they began to sing.

Spontaneously, the girls launched into a loud, vigorous rendition of 'Cielo Luna' while they helped Camilla stack dishes on a tray. I heard the chef's solid tenor join in for the chorus, and then I heard Signora Ferrero's soprano. Even old Camilla chimed in with her wheezy voice. Whenever some one went flat, they laughed, and soon the song became ragged with laughter and friendly jibes and the happy clatter of plates and cutlery.

They never sang when I was there.

When I was there they were sedate and polite. When I was there, they behaved in a manner appropriate for Sunday visitors – outsiders. But that night, without me to inhibit them, they were a real family, stuffed with lamb stew, tripping over each other's voices, laughing and singing . . .

I listened in the dark, alone and hungry, and I understood. I wasn't a member of the family at all. They had never accepted me; they had tolerated me. The ache of exclusion made me resentful, and slowly, I worked up enough anger to seal off the soft spot. My guilt slipped away unnoticed.

When the singing died down, Signora Ferrero whisked the girls upstairs, and I chanced another peek in the window. The chef sat alone at the table, fiddling with the stem of a half-full wineglass. His high spirits had vanished with his family, and he stared morosely into his wine until his wife called him up to bed.

At the edge of my vision, I saw the dining room lights wink out as the chef doused the candles, and then I heard his shoes scuffing the stairs. I craned my neck and leaned back over the stone banister to look up at the bedroom windows. At first I saw nothing, but after a moment, I caught a scant glimpse of the chef and his wife silhouetted in candlelight behind the muslin curtains of their balcony door. I straddled the banister, held on tight, and leaned out at a precarious angle to get a better view.

The chef ran his fingers through his hair, and then he made agitated chopping gestures with the edge of one hand into the palm of the other. Signora Ferrero stilled him; she laid her palms on his shoulders and began a slow massage. She whispered in his ear until his posture relaxed, and he wrapped her in his arms and buried his face in her hair. They talked, but I couldn't hear them. I needed to get up there.

The long stone balcony of the *piano nobile* was lined with clay pots and urns of different sizes, all filled with cheerful red geraniums. The largest of them was about three feet high, and I thought that if I stood on it and stretched my arms overhead, the extra three feet might be just enough for me to reach the floor of their small bedroom balcony. I stepped onto the rim of the clay pot and steadied myself before reaching up for the slate floor. I lengthened my spine and extended my fingers. The pot rocked underfoot, and my heart speeded up as I swayed to catch my balance. After I righted myself, I managed to get my hands on the bottom of two wrought iron spindles above me.

As I pulled myself up, the flowerpot again wobbled under my toes, tipped, rolled, clattered over the floor, and crashed down the stairs to the cobbled street below. A few pot shards splashed into the canal. I held my breath and hung there, dangling between the two balconies. The muscles in my arms burned as I tightened my fingers around the iron spindles.

The chef rushed to his balcony doors. I heard the creak of a rusty hinge, and he called out, 'Who's there?'

Marrone.

Signora Ferrero sounded unconcerned. 'A cat probably knocked over some geraniums.'

'*Dio*. Cats.'

'I'll send Camilla to the flower stalls tomorrow.'

My wrists ached, my hands had begun to slip, and I felt the weight of my body pulling away from my shoulders. But dropping back down would make too much noise, and I might be seen running away. I hung there.

The chef stood at the open door and huffed. 'Venice. Nothing but cats and sinners.' I imagined him shaking his fist at the night. 'But there's a nice breeze tonight.' He left the door open, and his footsteps receded.

The muscles in my arms quivered as I pulled myself up with raw hands, taking care not to grunt by keeping my lips pressed hard together. I swung one leg up to the slate floor and the scraping sound made Signora Ferrero say, 'I think that cat's on *our* balcony now.'

The chef clapped his hands and yelled, 'Shoo!' Signora Ferrero laughed, and her laughter covered the sound of me hoisting my body over the railing. I crouched in the recess beside their open door and leaned my head back against the wall while my breathing slowed and the cool night air turned my sweaty face clammy.

The chef and his wife moved about the room, preparing for sleep. Like all good Catholics, they put out the light before they undressed down to their underclothes and slid modestly into bed. But once they were under the sheets, I heard murmurs and kisses and the easy whispers of casual intimacy.

I couldn't believe that *that* night, of all nights, he would blithely make love to his wife as if nothing unusual had happened. I heard the swish of bed linen, a yawn, and a pillow being plumped . . . then nothing. What were they *doing*? I resisted the impulse to knock my head against the wall in frustration. But wait – they hadn't yet bid each other good night. Surely they wouldn't go to sleep without that pleasantry.

The chef whispered something, and as I strained to make out his words a scarred and scabby cat leapt silently from the next balcony, jumped down from the railing, and sauntered along the slate floor. It hopped onto my lap and brushed its tail against my face. I pinched my nose to hold off a sneeze and shoved the presumptuous animal off me.

Signora Ferrero's sleepy voice floated out the door. ' . . . so he poisoned a peasant. It's despicable but hardly his first murder. Why do you care so much about this one?'

'*Cara*, he tried to revive a dead man.' The chef made a disgusted sound through his nose. 'First he kills him, and then he pours something down his throat to bring him back. Insanity! I'm sure it has to do with that book. It's all this mad talk about formulas for immortality and alchemy . . . Everyone's going crazy. Some scheming alchemist probably duped the doge into buying a potion to defeat death. I just hope he was clever enough to get out of Venice before the doge tried it. The old man probably paid a fortune for a vial of cat piss.'

'A potion to defeat death? Is he so great a fool?'

'He has syphilis and doesn't want to die. People believe what they want to believe. But if the doge starts killing to find that book, people will panic, and the rumours will get wilder. The doge is bad enough, but imagine the carnage if Landucci or Borgia become interested.'

'*Boh.*' Signora Ferrero loaded the word with contempt. 'Landucci is vile. And Borgia, calling himself pope – he's a disgrace. Do you know he has more than twenty bastards? No wonder they call him the father of Rome.'

The cat beside me arched its back and spat, but not at me. Another cat had alighted on the railing, and they stared at each other with feline scorn. Both reared back and raised their hackles. I thought, *Oh*, Dio, *not a catfight.*

Signora Ferrero spoke through a yawn. 'Landucci and Borgia are too smart to be bothered by silly rumours. The doge is just desperate. He may not live long enough to find his chamber pot in the morning, much less that book.'

The chef mumbled something I couldn't hear, and his wife's voice turned consoling. 'Amato, calm yourself. Even if the doge finds this book, what difference would it make? There are no magic formulas. It might be best if someone did find the book and put an end to the gossip.'

'It's not that simple.'

'Why are you upsetting yourself? There's no alchemy, no immortality. As for love potions . . .'

I stopped breathing.

Her voice turned coy and teasing. 'Come here, *amore.*' She murmured something, the bed linen rustled, and she laughed girlishly. My heart hammered in my chest, pounded behind my eyes, and throbbed in the tips of my fingers. I knew I should leave, but – did they have a love potion?

She said, 'Our potion is no use to the old doge, but for you and me . . . come here, *amore*.' I heard another shifting of bedclothes, another whisper, and a low giggle. 'The girls are asleep, eh?'

'I have things on my mind.'

'So serious,' she purred. 'A tiny sip will make you feel better.' There was more rustling of bed linen, the sound of a drawer sliding open, glass clinking on glass, liquid being poured, and then a strange smell seeped out to the balcony: smoky and nutlike – it made me think of burnt chestnuts – a strange, dark aroma that was somehow bracing. I heard the lady's provocative hum, like a woman eating a delicious fruit. She said, 'Shall we indulge, *amore mio*?'

Meanwhile, the cats faced each other with arched backs.

The chef said, 'Not tonight, Rosa.' There was a pause, then more movement in the bed.

'Amato' – she sounded surprised – 'you're really turning away from me?' I heard the chink of a glass being set on the night table.

'I'm sorry,' said the chef. 'I can't stop thinking about . . . there's more to that book than you know.'

'What more?' A moment passed. 'Amato? What is it?'

As I waited for his answer, I pressed my back hard against the wall to stay clear of the cats. The fur on their backs stood straight up, inflating them to twice their size. They bared pointy white teeth, one spat, the other hissed, and then they sprang. I didn't know which to fear more, being injured in the war of claws or being discovered by Chef Ferrero. Their shrieks tore through the night, and the sound was raw and bone-chilling, like the screams of tortured babies.

From the bedroom, I heard, '*Dio*. Now what?' The chef

rushed to the door and pulled it wide open. I felt his presence just inches from me, peering out into the darkness, and I pressed my back harder against the wall, my eyes shut tight like a child who thinks if he can't see, he can't be seen. Sweat prickled at my hairline.

The chef said, 'Get out of here!' A slipper sailed out of the bedroom and hit one of the cats squarely on the head.

Immediately, the screeching subsided and I opened one eye. The cats had backed off to skulk in the shadows, eyeing each other, canny and vicious, sizing up the next assault.

'Dio,' said the chef. 'Maybe we should get a dog.'

I saw his bare foot advance from the recessed doorway and my stomach turned over. At the same time, Signora Ferrero said, 'Come back, Amato. Tell me about this book.'

He hesitated, then said, 'Sí. I think they're finished.' The foot retreated. The chef went back to his wife, and silence fell on the bedroom. Water lapped at the chef's gondola, and the cats issued muted warnings.

After a minute, the chef said, 'Rosa, you're my touchstone.'

'Such drama. What is this about?'

'This bizarre murder is significant. I believe the time has come to tell you about the book. But you can never repeat what I say – not to anyone. And if there's trouble, if ever I don't come home from work, you must go immediately to your sister's house. But don't stay there long. As soon as you can, go to your father in Aosta. He can hide you in the mountains.'

'Now you're frightening me. Amato, please, what is this about?'

The bed creaked as the chef moved closer to his wife. I inched nearer the door, cupped a hand to my ear, and struggled to hear. He said, 'Rosa—'

One cat rose vertically into the air, like a sorcerer's

marionette, and hurled itself at the other. Howls ripped through the night. The cats were only an arm's length away, and I saw claws tear across a yellow eye. I squeezed myself into the corner between the wall and railing and raised my forearm to protect my face. There was a savage grappling accompanied by demonic screeches.

The chef yelled, *'Madre di Dio!'* and again leapt from his bed and came to the door.

'Amato,' called Signora Ferrero. 'Don't go out there. You'll get scratched.'

Another slipper sailed out and he yelled, 'Get out of here, spawn of Satan!' Then he slammed the balcony doors shut.

With a whine and a whimper, one cat slumped in a matted heap. It appeared dead, and the other cat arched its back and yowled its triumph. But no, the defeated cat rose again. Back from the dead, it leapt from the balcony and disappeared into the night. The victor curled up to groom its paws while its hackles settled.

I had pressed against the railing so hard that my ribs ached, and now, with the balcony doors closed, I could not hear what the chef told his wife. There was only a weighted silence until I heard Signora Ferrero's muffled exclamation, *'Madonna mia!'*

I stole another peek into the bedroom and saw Signora Ferrero clasped in her husband's arms, weeping.

CHAPTER ✤ VII

THE BOOK OF VISITATIONS

M Y MAESTRO SELDOM TALKED ABOUT himself. He had a reputation for being secretive and somewhat odd. People noticed curious things about him – small things by themselves, but together they made Chef Ferrero as enigmatic as the Hindu incense merchant in the Rialto, only half-visible behind his screen of scented smoke.

When the chef chatted with the cooks, he managed to combine friendliness with a restraint that went slightly beyond professional distance. When he worked, he was the consummate *artiste*, silent and serious, examining his culinary creations with a sophisticated palate and a discerning eye. When he prepared his personal recipes, the special ones he didn't share, his obsession with privacy was so complete that the cooks grumbled about the tall hat making some people self-important. Even the paternal pats he gave me felt covert, and he always walked away before I could respond.

He didn't react to things the way most people did. When

the doge disinterred St Mark's bones in his search for the book, the kitchen staff, along with the rest of Venice, exploded with indignation, but the chef made no comment. I asked him whether he thought the act was sacrilege, and his answer was strangely irreverent. He said, 'St Mark's bones aren't his legacy, they're just bones. Reminders of things to think about, but just bones.'

He also had the annoying habit of beginning a provocative sentence and then breaking off without finishing, and it was always about some odd new idea or outlandish theory. Once, while watching Enrico build up a fire in the brick oven, the chef said, 'You know, there are some who believe there's a way to harness the power of lightning . . . but never mind that now. Temper the fire, eh?'

People alleged that the chef could prepare meals to influence people's behaviour (which was true), and rumours circulated about his improbable garden. He cultivated exotic plants no one had ever seen or heard of, and he knew how to use them in some of his most elegantly nuanced dishes. He grew love apples rumoured to be poisonous, knobby root vegetables, and serpentine vines with green pods dangling like claws. No one knew where he got his seeds or cuttings. The cooks always said a prayer and crossed themselves before they harvested the diabolical plants.

One of the most peculiar things about the chef was the people who visited him. One time, a well-known historian from Padua came to the kitchen carrying a clutch of folios, and he sat with the chef in hushed conference for an hour. Later, the chef said the folios were a rare collection of Far Eastern recipes compiled by a cook who had accompanied Marco Polo on his journeys. The explanation was accepted with nods of disinterest born of having seen too many such visitors over the years. Only later did I wonder how a simple cook in the thirteenth century might have learned to read and write, or how an insignificant thing like a recipe collection came to be preserved for centuries. When I asked Enrico about it, he said, 'I don't know, but don't ask him. Chef Ferrero doesn't like that kind of question.' Then he pulled his eyelid.

Another time, a copyist-monk, renowned for his skill as a translator of ancient languages, visited the kitchen and sat with the chef for hours over a single piece of vellum covered with markings that looked, from a distance, almost like the sheets of paper I'd seen in the doge's music room. That time I wondered how the chef himself had become erudite enough to consult with scholars.

After the monk left, I watched the chef stuff the vellum into one of his books and my curiosity got the best of me. I approached his desk, bowed respectfully, and asked where he'd learned to read and write. He shuffled his papers without looking up.

'School,' he said. 'Where else?'

'But why do you read all these old manuscripts?'

'I find history interesting.' He tried to wave me off.

I scratched my neck. 'What's so interesting about the writings of the dead?'

He stopped shuffling his papers and looked at me, surprised, as though the answer were painfully obvious. 'Luciano,' he said with exaggerated patience, 'if we don't know what happened before we were born, how can we know whether we're making progress?'

Marrone, it *was* obvious. 'I never thought of it that way before.'

The chef sat forward, elbows on his desk, and steepled his fingers. 'Let me tell you a story. There was once a vast library – you know what a library is? Good – the Great Library of

Alexandria. An Egyptian king required all residents and visitors to surrender every book and scroll they possessed to be copied for the Great Library. Some copies were so precise that the originals were kept for the library and the copies were delivered to the unsuspecting owners. The king also purchased writings from all over the Mediterranean, including the original scripts of Aeschylus, Sophocles, and Euripides—'

'Who?'

'Wise men with something to say that was worth hearing. The Great Library may have had as many as one million scrolls and codices – history, science, art, philosophy – the greatest collection of human knowledge ever assembled.'

'Are those the books you study, Maestro?'

'No.' He smiled sadly. 'While wise men acquired knowledge, lesser men made war, and parts of the Great Library were lost from time to time. The final assault came when a Muslim general conquered Alexandria and decided any writing that agreed with his Koran was not needed, and any writing that disagreed with it was not desired. "Therefore," he said, "destroy them all." It's believed that the books were burned to heat bathwater for his soldiers, and there were enough books to provide six months of fuel for the baths.'

'Why, that's . . . that's . . .'

'Disgraceful?'

'Stupid! It's just stupid, isn't it?'

'Yes, Luciano. And I'm glad you think so.' The chef motioned me forward and lowered his voice. 'But the good news is that the keepers of knowledge were not defeated. They devised other ways, craftier ways, to preserve what knowledge came their way. They went underground, assumed disguises, and learned to pass their legacies in code.'

'What kind of code?'

The chef sat back and knitted his fingers across his chest. 'I think we'll talk more about that another time. But tell me, what have you learned?'

'That it's a terrible thing to burn books.'

'Excellent. Go on now. I believe Dante has beets to peel.' He went back to his papers without another word.

There were no more stories that day, but in the following days there were many peculiar visitors: a linguist from Genoa, a librarian from the Vatican, a local calligrapher, and a priest purported to have ties to the heretic monk Savonarola. One time, a printer with inkstained fingers brought the chef one of the so-called quick-books fresh from his *stamperia*. The chef said it was the latest cookbook from Florence, and he added it to his overstuffed bookshelf.

For me, the most memorable visitor wasn't a scholar, but the chef's own brother, Paolo, who came only once, unexpectedly, from the family farm in Vicenza. Paolo visited a few days after my failed attempt to eavesdrop on the chef and his wife. It was early in my apprenticeship, and I was still insecure about my position in the kitchen; I worked silently, with my head down, and endeavoured to be invisible. Perhaps that's why the chef and his brother conversed within my hearing, as if they didn't see me.

Paolo first appeared at the back door, twisting a well-worn peasant's cap in his calloused, big-knuckled hands. He stopped just inside the door and stretched his neck, peering around the room, trying to locate his brother, and then he stepped into the humming kitchen, looking up at the high windows and sideways at the white-jacketed men around him. He moved awkwardly in his thick farmer's body. As he made his bashful way through the room, Paolo left a rush of whispers in his wake, and that slight shift in the normal workday buzz made the chef turn, with a sauced fingertip at his lips and a critical furrow in his brow, judging a cook's béarnaise. When the chef saw Paolo, the furrow disappeared. He smiled and shouted, 'My brother!'

Paolo's face lightened. The brothers threw their arms around each other, and the chef announced, 'Everyone, meet my brother, Paolo.' Paolo smiled shyly and twisted his cap. The cooks offered a nod or a polite smile and then turned back to their work.

For privacy, the chef and his brother walked to the back of the kitchen to converse at a discreet distance from the cooks. The chef poured two glasses of red wine and they sat at a table near the cistern, almost directly in my path as I, the invisible apprentice, carried water buckets in and out of the back door. Due to the chef's fetish about standing water, I emptied half-full buckets and hauled in fresh ones all day long.

After the customary pleasantries, they spoke of Paolo's family and the farm, of a new son, a new calf, his wife's indigestion, and an unusually smooth batch of homemade wine. When the conversation seemed to have exhausted itself, Paolo put a hand on the chef's shoulder and said, 'Amato, I didn't come to tell you about the farm. I came to tell you our mother has died.'

The chef's lips parted slightly, whether in surprise or from a wish to speak I don't know. Then my maestro put his head in his hands, and the brothers sat in silence while Paolo stared at the floor. Finally the chef said, 'May she rest in peace.' He made the sign of the cross and kissed his thumbnail. 'Thank you for coming to tell me, brother.'

'But of course I'd tell you.'

'I'll try to visit her grave.'

'*Bene.*' Paolo began twisting his hat again. Having

reported on the farm and delivered his news, he seemed to have no more to say. He twisted the cap mercilessly, and a nervous tongue darted out to wet his lips.

Seeing his brother's discomfort the chef said, 'You must be anxious to get back to your fields. Of course you are. But I have some beautiful veal. You'll take some home. So white, you won't believe your eyes.'

The chef started to rise, but Paolo pressed his shoulder, and the chef sat down again. Paolo said, 'There's something else.' The tip of his tongue flicked over dry lips.

The chef faced his brother with an expression partly perplexed and partly expectant, as though he might know what was coming. He said, 'About Giulietta?'

Paolo hung his head. 'And your son.'

My ears perked up. His son? Chef Ferrero had four daughters, but no son.

'Aha.' The chef nodded.

Paolo didn't look at him. He said, 'Giulietta died. The child didn't.'

'So. I *do* have a son.'

'I'm sorry, Amato.' Paolo opened his hands in a gesture of helplessness. 'You know how Mamma was. After Papà died, she did as she pleased.'

'My son lived.' The chef stared at him. 'Tell me everything.'

Paolo shrugged. 'There's not much. I came in from the fields one day to find Mamma and the infant gone. Later, I couldn't make her talk. I tried. I really did. She told me the child had died and she'd buried him, but I didn't believe it. He was a healthy boy – strong. I didn't know what had happened, and I didn't know what to tell you.'

'I believe you, Paolo. I remember you couldn't look at me when she told me they both died. You couldn't meet my eyes once that day.' The chef shook his head. 'But she lied to my face. And after the way she treated Giulietta . . . you know that's why I stopped visiting her.'

'I know. But don't judge her too harshly. She had such hopes for you.' Paolo lowered his voice. 'And she really believed the child was cursed. You know why.'

'*Sì*. The mark.'

A mark? I touched my forehead. A mark like mine? What if . . . but no, that's silly. How easily I could succumb to wishful thinking. Birthmarks were common enough.

Paolo said, 'I don't believe the nonsense myself, but she—'

'Ah, Paolo.' The chef wagged his head. 'Our mother did more injury than you know.'

'I understand.' Paolo squeezed the chef's shoulder. 'A man has a right to know his son, his immortality.'

The chef barked a laugh with no joy in it. 'It's not a matter of vanity, Paolo. A male heir would have made a difference to me. There are things at stake. You don't know.'

Paolo took his hand off his brother's shoulder and sat back. His bushy, mismatched eyebrows lifted in surprise. 'What are you talking about? You have four daughters. Come on, Amato. You're not a king, eh?'

'*Sì, sì*. Of course you're right. Forgive me. I'm not myself.'

Paolo lowered his eyebrows and waved as if to erase what he'd just said. 'I understand. It's a terrible blow.'

They sat a moment longer, once again sensing the end of their common ground. Then they stood and embraced. The chef said, 'What's done is done. Thank you for coming, brother.'

'*Niente*.'

'The veal?'

'I have to go.' Paolo was twisting his hat again.

'*Bene*. Go with God, Paolo.'

'Goodbye, Amato. I'm sorry.'

At first I felt only shock. There was a woman other than Signora Ferrero? A son? I couldn't imagine my maestro with anyone but his beloved Rosa and their daughters, but I heard what I heard.

After Paolo left, the chef sat at the table, looking blank and deflated, and my heart clenched for his loss. Losing his son through his mother's deception seemed worse than more ordinary kinds of loss – it was less natural than death, more personal and malicious than an anonymous twist of fate. I poured a stream of fresh water into the cistern and a rush of sentimental memory overwhelmed me: the chef's generosity in taking me off the street; the patient way he instructed me in my duties; the naked, unconditional love he showed for his family. He deserved to have known his son, and I wished I could comfort him. I wished I might replace the son he lost. I had a mark, perhaps like his son's; maybe I reminded him of this lost child. Maybe he considered me . . .

Then, the musical gush of water streaming into the cistern reminded me of how happily his family had sung when I wasn't there, and I remembered my place in the world. *Stupido*. He didn't want comfort from me. He was the maestro, and I was the apprentice. If he wanted to find his real son, he'd look for him.

The idea that he might look for his son disturbed me. Could he find the boy? How long had it been? What age would he be? Where would the chef start? How would he know him? Paolo mentioned a mark. What mark? And if he found him . . . *Dio*, what if he found him? A real flesh-and-blood son would surely take my place in the chef's affection, and what else might he take? My job? My future?

In a span of minutes, I went from sympathy for the chef to worry for myself. I caught sight of my face in the icy water of the cistern – frightened eyes and a grim mouth distorted by ripples in the water. Ugly. I glanced back at the chef, who hadn't moved, and my heart opened to him again. His suffering moved me, and I felt an urge to pray. I looked up, because that's what people do, and I thought: *Please, let him find his son.*

As I went out to refill my bucket, I remembered something the chef had said to his brother, exactly the sort of remark that contributed to his reputation as a mysterious figure. He'd said, 'There are things at stake. You don't know.'

But I wanted to know. I wanted to know everything. I was a true child of Venice, weaned on her mysterious beauty, her watery light shifting like magician's mirrors. Venice had seduced me with her female anatomy, with her liquid channels and her maze of voluptuous temptations. Venice excites a desire to know what is hidden, a lust to penetrate her charms, a wish to know all her darkest secrets.

Paolo's visit fed the flames of curiosity lit by the peasant's murder and fuelled by my spying on the chef's balcony. My Venetian lust to know *everything* stoked the bonfire that eventually consumed us all.

CHAPTER ✤ VIII

THE BOOK OF AMATO

IT WAS THE VERY SAME hunger to know everything that led me, many years later, to seek an interview with Chef Ferrero's own mentor, Chef Meunier. In all the time I worked in the palace, my maestro remained an enigma and offered few particulars about himself, nothing more than a name here or an anecdote there. I would be well grown before I found an opportunity to persuade Chef Meunier to supply the connecting pieces.

I had met Chef Meunier several times when he visited my maestro in the doge's kitchen. He was a bon vivant and a lover of good food who had travelled from France to Italy to learn how to cook, then decided to stay in *il bel paese*. Chef Meunier was short and stout and avuncular. Smiling and effusive, he always bounded into our kitchen, embraced Chef Ferrero, and then made himself at home, testing sauces with a fingertip, offering friendly advice and lavish compliments. '*Magnifique*. Just a leetle more cream, *non?*' He walked with a hop in his step, and everything amused him.

However, his round, rosy face had a chameleon-like ability to make an unsettling shift. The warmth in his blue eyes could drain away and his smile could go cold and fixed – but only for an instant. Immediately, the chill would be displaced by a hearty laugh or a slap on the back, and I always went away thinking it had been my imagination or a trick of the light. Now, I think not.

On each of his visits, Chef Meunier walked the length of our kitchen dispensing friendly nods and chattering. *'Bon. C'est bon. Délicieux.'* After everyone relaxed and forgot he was there, the two chefs would sit together with glasses of red wine, perhaps a dish of almonds, and talk in low tones.

Long after the events of this memoir, I returned to Venice, and Chef Meunier recounted my maestro's personal history. The gregarious Frenchman had aged into a stooped old soul, wrinkled as a walnut. At first he didn't want to receive me. He said, 'Why do you ask an old man to recall painful events?' He stood hunched and shivering in the doorway of his home. The day was raw and overcast with rain clouds low on the horizon, and he kept shaking his head and trying to close the door in my face. But I put my foot in the doorway and begged; I reminded him that we both had loved Chef Ferrero.

When he relented, he let out a long slow breath and then took me to a small room furnished with a writing table and two shabby chairs facing each other in front of a paned window. Between the chairs there was a rickety tea table bearing an unlit oil lamp, and there were books everywhere – hand-copied books, illuminated books, even a few of the new quick-books made on a printing press. Some of the books appeared to be pristine, but most were weathered and shabby. Books lined the walls, stood stacked in precarious towers, lay scattered over the writing table and piled under it. No wonder the house was so ordinary and the furniture so spare; Chef Meunier had clearly spent every spare copper on books. There were even some scrolls on the writing table – mouldering things the colour of tea.

Chef Meunier called for hot mulled wine, then sat in one of the chairs covered in a worn fabric that might once have been green; he gestured impatiently for me to sit in the other. After he pulled a knitted woollen shawl around his shoulders and laid a heavy rug over his lap, he looked shrunken in his tattered wrappings. His voice had aged to a wavering rasp, and he cleared his throat noisily again and again. His wife had died years before, and he had the look of an elderly, unkempt hermit. His servant, a shuffling old woman, brought in a covered clay pitcher of mulled wine and filled two cups. After she left, he pulled the lap rug up over his little paunch and began.

'Amato Ferrero was born in Vicenza – you've heard of it, *non*? It's a village of feudal farmers just outside Venice. His birth became one of those stories that is told and retold in families. One morning, his heavily pregnant mother excused herself from her work in the fields earlier than usual. When her husband and young son came in for their midday meal, they found bread and salami on the table and the woman in bed nursing her newborn. She said, "His name is Amato."'

I heard tapping on the window and saw the first drops of rain spatter the glass.

'When Amato was eleven, his father died of apoplexy.' Chef Meunier frowned. 'That man liked his wine too much.' He muttered under his breath as if remembering something unpleasant. 'After he was gone, tradition dictated that the little farm go to the older son, Paolo. So Amato's mother arranged for her second son to do menial work at the Inn of

St George. You know it, eh?' He put the wine cup to his lips and peered over the rim.

'I do know it, *monsieur*.' Indeed, everyone knew it. The Inn of St George still stands along the Grand Canal next to a square stone building, the Fondaco dei Tedeschi, a warehouse for German merchants. At that time in Italy, almost anything German was synonymous with barbarism, and Venetians were relieved to have the Germanic traders neatly segregated, grateful to be spared the pain of mingling and the spectacle of indelicate Teutonic customs.

But, as Chef Meunier explained, those social distinctions were unknown to Amato's mother. He said, 'The poor woman had to hug herself to contain her happiness when she told her son his little job had been secured. Amato told me she danced around her kitchen singing, "Venice! You're going to Venice!" He said she smiled so broadly you could see all six of her teeth.'

The old man chuckled, and I caught a glimpse of the young chef who used to visit our kitchen. Then he sighed. 'Amato was still a child. He didn't want to leave home. He told me that while his mother danced around the kitchen, he stared at the floor so she wouldn't see his tears.'

The rain on the window thrummed louder, and the light in the room dwindled, but the old man seemed unaware.

'Amato liked his mother's rough bread, he liked collecting chestnuts in the autumn, and he liked the smell of apples and homemade wine that seeped up from the cellar. He even liked sleeping with the cows and goats in the winter to keep from freezing – he told me the crackle of hay and the thick, tangy animal smells made him feel secure. Why would he want to leave all that for a big city full of sinister men in black capes?'

Chef Meunier raised a gnarled hand. '*Mais oui*, even in

little Vicenza people knew about the Council of Ten and the *Cappe Nere*. The boy told his mother, "I could sleep in the barn. I could eat less." Ah, *le pauvre enfant*.'

He sipped his wine in a melancholy pause, and rain pelted the window; by the time he resumed, the light in the room had gone grey and gloomy. He said, 'That leathery little peasant woman had ambitions for her clever son. She pointed to her hovel with its length of burlap for a door and said, "You can be better than this, Amato. Be better than this." The boy tried to argue, but she poked his forehead with a stiff finger. She said, "You have *brains*. Be better than this."' Chef Meunier pushed out his lower lip and nodded. 'She knew Venice was the place for a boy with quick wits.'

Amato quickly learned about the inn, and about the Venetian contempt for Germans. His job offered him many opportunities to talk to Venetian suppliers who made their disdain bitingly clear. Chef Meunier said, 'A butcher who supplied pork hocks and pigs' feet once dumped his bloody delivery in the courtyard, winked at Amato, and said, "God bless the Huns. They pay me for my rubbish."' He chuckled merrily. 'True story.'

I knew it was true. I had often heard Venetian merchants exchange horrified descriptions of the inn's patrons and their filthy habits: grunting diners with grease-smeared chins who gnawed on huge joints of meat; odiferous, foamy beers guzzled out of cups fashioned from stag's feet still hairy above the cloven hooves; bedchambers made noisy and foul by flatulence from the great quantities of cabbage consumed with every meal; and the slovenly German custom of an annual bath, which was particularly disgusting to the fastidious Venetians, who bathed as often as twice a week.

Chef Meunier adjusted his shawl. 'Most of the cooks at the Inn of St George were German – you know, trained to smoke pig flesh and marinate cabbage. *Ach!* Culinary heresy!' I smiled, but he appeared not to notice. 'A few Venetians worked there, too. *Naturellement*, they were unhappy to be there but a job is a job, eh?'

I sat forward, nodding vigorously, ready to describe how grateful I'd been to carry water and haul wood for my room and board, but the old man turned to the window and exclaimed, '*Mon Dieu!* The angels weep!' The rain came down hard and steady, and I heard the far-off rumble of thunder.

Chef Meunier sipped his wine and patted his mouth with his shawl.

'There was one at that inn, a pointy-faced soup cook who felt especially above it all. I don't remember his name. He kept a haughty silence, and he refused to eat or drink with his German colleagues. On his private shelf, he kept a bottle of Chianti and a goblet made of Murano glass – no doubt stolen from his former employer. He even kept a fork in his apron pocket.' The old chef shook his head in amazement. 'Imagine that. A fork.'

Chef Meunier smoothed his lap rug and marvelled at the notion of a soup cook in a second-rate kitchen having such an expensive implement. '*Oui*, while the Germans ripped meat away with their teeth and washed it down with beer, this fellow sipped Chianti from his goblet and wielded his fork with his little finger out like this.' The old man picked up his wine and crooked his pinky at an effeminate angle.

'That fellow refused to speak anything but Italian. He pretended not to understand even a simple *ja* or *nein*, and he advised Amato to do the same. He said, "Amato, you're still young enough to escape the barbarians".

'And Amato listened. *Mais oui*. In time, even Amato – remember, he was still a child, a peasant, and the son of a wine-besotted serf – *oui*, even Amato developed enough Venetian arrogance to make him look down on those he served. Day and night he watched for an opportunity to "escape the barbarians". That's what Amato wanted – an escape to something better.' The old man stared out of the window, transfixed by the grey sheets of rain lashing his house.

'How did he manage it, *monsieur*?' I asked.

'*Quoi?*' He looked surprised, as if he'd forgotten I was there. '*Ah oui*. One night, a German trader brought a Venetian nobleman to the inn. The Venetian was impeccably dressed in a satin doublet and a deep-red velvet cape. Amato said it was the colour of Bordeaux wine. I can imagine that fashionable man wrinkling his nose when he entered the inn – that place always smelled of sweat and beer.'

The knobby finger came up so suddenly I flinched. 'Amato saw what was going on. He was a sharp boy. His mother was right about that.' The old chef wagged the misshapen finger at me. 'He knew the Venetian had come reluctantly to finalize a deal. Of course he knew.'

The crabbed hand disappeared under the shawl, and the sound of rain surged as thunder boomed in the distance.

'Amato watched the two men negotiate over hollow stag hooves slopping with foam. He said that the German proposed a toast and drank his beer, but the Venetian only touched his lips to it. Why would anyone drink beer when they could drink wine, eh? Beer. *Mon Dieu.*'

I saw that Chef Meunier's attention could easily wander. Old age and the loss of too many loved ones had subdued him and made him ruminative. 'What did my maestro do, *monsieur*?'

'What? Oh. Amato ran to the kitchen and swiped the soup cook's Chianti and his goblet. He was a bold one. *Audacieux.*'

Chef Meunier bobbed his head, bestowing approval on my maestro's daring. 'Back at the table, the Venetian was looking grim and pale. Well, who wouldn't? The man was staring at congealed fat on a pig's foot. Ach! Amato set the wine and goblet before him, offered a sympathetic nod, and backed away. *Oui.* Just so.

'That man was Ercole d'Este, and I' – the finger shot up – 'I was his chef. Este called Amato aside as he was leaving the inn. He asked, "Can you cook?" Amato said, *"Sì, signore."'* Chef Meunier smiled and bobbed. '*Oui.* He said it just so, no hesitation. *"Sì, signore."'* He slapped the arm of his chair and laughed so hard he started to cough. It sounded as though he might be choking. I stood over him and thumped his back. After he caught his breath he looked up at me and smiled. He said, 'That boy couldn't cook anything. *Rien!* But he became my apprentice.'

I sat back in my chair and marvelled at how small turns – a glass of wine to cut the oleaginous taste of a pig's foot, or even a stolen pomegranate – can lead us onto unimagined boulevards. I warmed my hands around my wine cup and inhaled the scented steam.

Chef Meunier took a napkin from the tea table to blow his nose with a loud honk, and then he mopped his face. 'It was one of the finest houses in Venice. *Oui.* In the House of Este, Amato discovered the world of privilege.' The old man clutched the shawl tight around his shoulders, and there was something proud in the way he did it.

'I remember that house well – always hushed. Quiet talks over tisanes and cakes, silk dresses rustling in the halls. Every room had bowls of fresh roses, and in the evening candle-light glinted off the silver and set off little sparks in the crystal. It was a pleasure to be called to the dining room for a compliment. *Vraiment.* Nothing but the best in that house.'

The rain abated briefly and allowed me to hear the raspy old voice, which had gone soft and low with his reminiscing. 'It was all new for Amato. *Complètement nouveau*. I believe the boy was overwhelmed, so submerged in luxuries that it seemed to him the great house and everyone in it comprised one noble entity. In that house, he heard the murmurs of important men blending with chords from the family harp. *Mais bien sûr*, even the children loved music in that house. Amato observed lazy afternoons and listened to the gushing of *les jeunes filles en fleur*. Ah, those girls – every room flooded with the perfume of the gardenias they tucked into their bosoms.

'The grand family spent their days in pampered leisure and floated through nights in high canopied beds. The maids scented the pillows with fresh lavender and warmed the linens with heated bricks swaddled in Florentine wool. Ah, the House of Este . . .' His head drooped and he mumbled reveries into his chest.

I listened to the rain drumming on the roof and imagined my maestro as a young rustic in the House of Este, gawping at the easy extravagance and wanting to be part of it. Then the shutters banged, and the rain intensified, hammering the window, rendering it opaque and darkening the room. The old man went on. 'Every Sunday, Amato's day off, he rose long before dawn and rode to Vicenza on a dairyman's wagon. He came back after dinner on a fruit cart. He travelled six hours each way to spend an hour or two on the farm.'

His eyebrows pinched together. 'He was a good boy. He wanted to visit his mother, but I could see what was happening. *Oui*. It was inevitable. Amato began to notice the sour smell of his mother's kitchen, the rawness of her wine, and the overripe cheese that was too precious to discard.' He nodded slowly.

'After watching the Este's maids spread sun-bleached sheets on plush featherbeds, it pained him to see the flea-infested straw mattresses that lined the walls of his family hovel. He would have given his mother money if he had any, but as you know apprentices earn no wages.'

'Indeed. I remember a time—'

'One Sunday, Amato came back from Vicenza upset, *très vexé*. The boy had chastised his mother for her low habit of kicking the chickens that strayed into her house. *Oui*, and for the way she hawked up phlegm and spat into the fire. He spent that entire week feeling guilty. He was useless in the kitchen. The following Sunday he apologized to her, but she shrugged him off. His life was proceeding exactly as she had hoped, but for him the visits became uncomfortable. He began to stay away from home for two and three weeks at a time. She didn't mind; she wanted him to learn.'

The old chef leaned forward, and his voice went crafty and confidential. 'Amato learned this: even though he'd been born a serf, he could become a member of the gentry, like me, a master chef. He could have his own home, a gentle lady for a wife, educated children, and a respectable profession to pass to his son.' He smiled and nodded – a contented old man. '*Oui*, passing it on is what gives our lives meaning, eh?'

'Yes, *monsieur*. Passing it on is everything.'

He leaned back in his cosy chair, looking satisfied. 'Amato's profession was his permanent escape from the barbarians. *Naturellement*, he threw himself into his work. He became a sauce cook at the age of eighteen. Impressive, *non*?'

'Indeed, *monsieur*.'

'*Oui*. I was proud of that boy. But at nineteen he met Giulietta.'

Chef Meunier poured another cup of wine with a shaky

hand. He wafted it under his nose, slurped, and snuggled into his shawl. 'Giulietta came to the House of Este as a serving girl. She was fifteen – *une enfant*. Her complexion glowed; her hazel eyes were clear and innocent. *Charmante*. The first time Amato saw her, his face opened like a flower, and he dropped his ladle. It was one of those moments when time stops and after it begins again nothing is the same. *Un coup*.

'Giulietta was *très petite*. Slim hips. *Diminutive*. Once, I heard Amato wondering aloud whether he could encircle her waist with his hands.' The old man produced an offended grunt. 'That was no way to talk in my kitchen, but he was under her spell. He used to say that light on her black hair made him think of moonlight on the Grand Canal. *C'est ridicule*, eh?'

I thought of Francesca. 'Not for a man in love, *monsieur*.'

'*Boh*. They were children.' Chef Meunier made an impatient noise from the back of his throat. 'One day, Amato allowed a cream sauce to curdle, while he flirted with Giulietta – in *my* kitchen! *Intolérable!* I could see that Amato's plan had changed. He wanted that girl more than he wanted to be a chef. But allowing a sauce to curdle? *Mon Dieu*, it was too much.

'I lost my temper that day. I banged on that pot of lumpy sauce with my wooden spoon, like so.' He smacked his chair arm twice. 'I hollered, "*Non! Non!*" I tell you, the way those two carried on violated the sanctity of my kitchen. But that wasn't the worst of it. *Non*. Amato worried less about my anger and more about what impression the scene would make on Giulietta.'

The old man sighed heavily and shrugged under his shawl. 'A man is helpless in the face of love, especially a young one, eh?'

'Oh, yes.'

'The affair proceeded from daily flirtation to one night – oh, that must have been a night to remember – the night Amato learned that, *oui*, he could encircle her waist with his hands. After that, it was hopeless; it was obsession. Everything else – his sauces, his mother's dreams, his own ambitions – everything evaporated in the heat of their passion.' Chef Meunier shook his head and sipped his wine.

He looked out at the pounding rain and squinted as if trying to see the incident he wanted to recall. 'One morning, Amato requested an interview with me. When I saw his face lit from within, I knew what was coming. *Oui*, Amato wished to marry Giulietta.'

'Had you spoken to him about the book?'

'Not yet.' He wagged his head. 'But I shouldn't have waited so long. I should have told him sooner that marriage would interfere with my plans for him, that it would make things *très difficiles* for us both. I said, "Amato, you still have much to learn. *Beaucoup*."

'He said, "A married man can learn as well as a bachelor." *Boh*. I made a face like so.' Chef Meunier cocked his head to one side and knitted his brow in a sceptical knot. 'I told him, "We must talk. Come to my house tonight, eh?" Amato was annoyed, but he said that he would come.'

Chef Meunier looked around his book-cluttered room. 'That night we sat right here, Amato and I. It must have been strange for him to see me so serious. Ah, *oui*, I know. In the kitchen I played the merry elf, rushing from one station to the other. Everyone thought me genial, *très clément*, even comical. *Oui*, I know.'

I remembered how Chef Meunier's little belly used to bounce when he laughed, and how his tall white toque seemed to be almost a third of his height – a merry elf indeed.

'But that night, Amato saw this.' He leaned forward again and screwed up his face; a deep worry line appeared between his eyebrows and long creases bracketed his mouth. 'I told him, "Amato, I have a legacy and I need a wise and moral man to be my successor."'

'What?' I sat up straight. 'You told him . . . about us? Just like that?'

The lower lip jutted. 'Not all at once. You know how it's done.'

I leaned back. 'Yes, I know how it's done.' The ebb and flow of the rain reminded me of my own convoluted journey, of the unexpected twists of fate that led me into a life of shadows and secrets.

Chef Meunier smiled. 'Amato was *très* confused. He said, "As fine as your recipe collection is, I hardly think you need a saint to inherit it." Ach! He knew nothing, *absolument rien*. I used a grape and a raisin to explain how knowledge can be altered.'

I recalled a day, walking in the sun with my maestro, when he carried a bunch of grapes and a pocketful of raisins. I said, 'He initiated me with the same method, *monsieur*.'

He shrugged. 'It's standard.' His old face grew abstract. 'I explained to Amato that some of us devoted ourselves to the accumulation of knowledge, to becoming teachers. He wanted to know more, but, of course, first he had to accept.'

I nodded. 'It was the same with me.'

'Of course it was. Stop interrupting me. Isn't it enough you make me remember what happened to my beloved apprentice?' He sniffed. 'I told Amato that if he accepted what I offered, it must come before everything else – his wife, his children, his country. He asked, "Before God?"' The old chef threw his head back and laughed. 'I told him, "God is another conversation."'

'Indeed,' I said. 'God is many other conversations.'

He snorted. 'I put it to him bluntly; he had to give up Giulietta. Ah, *sacré bleu*! You would have thought I had asked him to give up both his arms, to cut out his heart, to lay his head on the block. He said, "I *love* her."'

Chef Meunier looked tired, and I didn't know whether it was from the effort of remembering or from the memories themselves. The room had become so dim that his face had darkened into planes and shadows. I lit the oil lamp on the tea table and poured myself another cup of wine. It was no longer hot, but I settled back in my chair, comfortable in the warm pool of light that encompassed us. Wind and rain battered the window and slammed the shutters against the house, but Chef Meunier, caught up in his memories, seemed oblivious.

He said, 'I gave him enough information to make his decision. Then he left. He later told me that he walked the dark streets all night with his head down and his hands clasped behind his back. He listened to the echo of his foot-steps on the cobbles, thinking and thinking. *Oui*, as we all did, I suppose.

'He didn't come to work the next day. When we spoke again, he told me he was honoured by my offer, but he thought it unfair.'

Chef Meunier raised his palm to stop my surprised retort. '*Oui*, unfair. Amato was standing on the threshold of a perfect life with Giulietta and he felt ambushed. *Embusqué!* As I said, he understood nothing.' The old man closed his eyes and murmured in French. When he opened them again, he looked sad. 'In the end, Amato persuaded himself that he could have it all. He didn't give her up, he asked her to wait. *Sot!* But he kept this from me until it was too late. He waited a full year to tell me about it. By then the tragedy was *un fait accompli*, too late to do anything.

'Without my knowledge, Amato had arranged a rendezvous with Giulietta in a secluded piazza. He said they sat on a bench holding hands, and she asked why Amato had missed work. He gathered his courage and told her their wedding must wait. She wrenched her hand away and asked, "How long?"

'He feared that if she left him he wouldn't be able to watch her go. But she didn't leave. She wept, then she pleaded, then she raged and beat his chest with her tiny fists. She accused him of having another woman. There were more tears, more accusations, and then, suddenly, she capitulated. I can imagine her straightening her little girl shoulders and saying, "Fine. I'll wait." Amato had no idea that Giulietta had scheming instincts. Many women do, you know.'

'*Sì.*' Francesca. Again.

'*Oui.* She intended to wait only as long as it took to become pregnant, which was not long at all. But when she came to him – with a thicker waist and her wedding dress already sewn – she was astounded to learn that Amato still wouldn't marry her.' The old chef picked at his shawl as rain pummelled the roof. 'Perhaps if he had come to me then . . . Ach, I flatter myself. The damage was done.

'Giulietta's pious family threw her out. That was to be expected. So Amato took her to his mother's farm to wait out her confinement. He visited every week – although, at the time I thought he was only visiting his mother – and every week Giulietta complained to him. His mother didn't want Giulietta's pregnancy to interfere with her son's ambitions. The two women resented each other, and Amato felt pulled between them.'

'A tight place for any man.'

'Amato tried to reassure Giulietta. He took her for long walks across farm fields smelling of cut grass. They hid in the honeysuckle, where they made love and then lay in each other's arms listening to the crickets. It hurts me now to think of it.'

Crashing thunder caused him to fall silent, and I struggled to imagine my maestro as a young fellow swooning in a patch of honeysuckle. I had known him as a middle-aged man with a respectable family. But we're all young once . . .

Chef Meunier shifted in his chair as if his bones ached. I was afraid discomfort might make him cut the story short, and I offered to fetch more hot wine, perhaps a pillow, but he said, 'It's only old age. Not important.

'Every week, Amato rushed to his mother's farm, eager to lay his hand on Giulietta's belly and feel the life stirring there. As her time came closer, he always burst into the little hovel expecting to hear the thin wail of a newborn. But he only found Giulietta, moving ponderously with one hand cupped under her belly, and his mother, thin-lipped, busy at the fire, and of course his brother, Paolo, watching the two women.

'One day, when Giulietta was past her time, Amato arrived to find only his mother and Paolo. He said his mother delivered the news with a stone face while Paolo looked away and fidgeted with his fingers. Slim-hipped Giulietta had died in childbirth, and the infant, a boy, had died as well. She said Giulietta hadn't been made for childbearing and that the child was cursed.'

'Cursed?'

'*Mon Dieu*, I'll never forget his face when he came back to Venice that day. Pale. Broken. *Choqué*. Amato dropped into a chair as if he'd been punched in the chest. He sat there, splay-legged and staring, too stunned to weep. That would come later. That was the day he finally told me what he'd done, all of it, from the beginning.'

I had long suspected that this so-called curse had to do with the reason my maestro took me off the street, but I wanted confirmation. 'How was the child cursed, *monsieur*?'

'A dark birthmark on the forehead.' Chef Meunier made a distracted gesture at my head. 'I suppose it was much like yours; they're common enough. But Amato's mother thought Giulietta had caught the evil eye. Peasants, eh?'

'A birthmark like mine?'

'I don't know if it was like yours. It was a birthmark. Not the most handsome of features but certainly not a curse.'

I nodded. I'd rarely thought of my birthmark as handsome or not handsome. Most people had some unique feature and mine was a birthmark. I did not grow up with mirrors at my disposal and I only knew the thing was dark brown because La Canterina told me so. Having a handsome face was not something to which street urchins gave much thought, but I had sometimes wondered whether the mark might be a curse. Of course that was in my youth, before I grew beyond superstition.

'Amato said Giulietta's grave was ordinary, a neat mound of freshly dug earth with a simple wooden cross and a posy of wild daisies. But the baby's grave was crude, nothing but a patch of barely scratched earth, and it was unmarked. They knelt at Giulietta's grave, and his mother mumbled a rote prayer. Amato asked, "Aren't we going to pray for my son?" She muttered, "That child was cursed. He's already in hell." *Alors, c'est fini.* Amato never visited his mother again.

'Each year, Amato observed the day of Giulietta's death and his son's birth by falling to his knees and begging forgiveness. *Naturellement,* the more he learned from me, the more he questioned who or what he was petitioning.'

'I know how that goes.'

'We all know how that goes. But Amato needed absolution for the selfishness that had made him hold on to Giulietta. *Mais bien sûr.* Isn't that why people need their gods? To grant wishes, to give assurances, to offer consolation, to mete out reward and punishment? Someone should be in charge, *non*? So Amato prayed. He kept track of how old his son would have been, and he found himself scanning the foreheads of boys that age. He admitted that he felt foolish doing it, but he couldn't help himself.

'A few years later, he became a sous-chef and married Rosa, a young gentlewoman from Aosta. She had fierce brown eyes, a tiger, that one. *Piemontese* women are *durables;* I think it's the hard winters in those mountains. *Oui.* Rosa had a jaw that showed fortitude and a character that promised loyalty. Those two were good together, and they adored their daughters.'

'Yes, they did.'

Thunder crashed overhead and lightning flashed in the window, causing us both to start. Chef Meunier said, '*Quelle pluie torrentielle!* I hope the woman has set out the water barrel.' Chef Meunier shared my maestro's obsession with fresh water. He huddled in his shawl and watched the rain sheet his window. He didn't need to say any more; we had come to the part of the story that included me. By the time Amato Ferrero became chef to the doge, he had achieved everything he'd wanted and his escape was complete. There was just one thing missing.

He wasn't yet forty when he caught me pinching the pomegranate and rushed me to a tub of cold water, eager to scrub my face and see whether the dark-brown smudge on my forehead washed off or not.

CHAPTER ✤ IX

THE BOOK OF DESIRES

AFTER THE CATFIGHT ON THE chef's balcony, I raced back to the palace to finish my evening chores. I washed the dishes in a fever, splashing the floor with suds and fumbling a wineglass, barely catching it before it shattered on the stone floor. I perspired as I banked the fires under the stockpots, then swept the floor like a storm at sea, all the while mumbling under my breath.

Signora Ferrero had talked about a love potion, and I'd smelled it – smoky and foreign, something like burnt chestnuts, but liquid. I'd heard her pour it and offer it to her husband. My blood boiled with the kind of excitement that's only possible in youth when everything is felt rather than understood. Oil lamps swinging outside the windows created a wavering light and gave the kitchen a dreamlike quality well suited to my mood on that confusing night of revelations. When Bernardo emerged from under the chef's desk I raised my broom like a victor's sword and announced, 'The chef knows a love potion!'

Marco used to ridicule me for talking to Bernardo, but in the palace, I saw the doge himself converse openly and at length with his cats. He named them after precious gems, calling them, 'My Emerald. My Sapphire. My Ruby.' He coaxed them to eat costly tidbits, petted them, and crooned to them. Oftentimes, he put his corrugated lips to a velvet ear and whispered like a besotted lover. Watching the doge, I realized that cats make a perfect audience – they don't laugh at you, they never contradict you, there's no need to impress them, and they won't divulge your secrets. I said, 'Think of it, Bernardo – Francesca in my arms.' I embraced the air and clownishly kissed my own biceps.

My stomach rumbled, and I remembered that I hadn't taken my evening meal. I ripped off half a loaf of Enrico's onion bread, then ladled out a bowl of beef stock and settled myself on the hearth. After I dipped a corner of the bread in my bowl, I remembered the day I had paid attention to eating a single green grape at the chef's table and the strange pleasure it had afforded me. The smell of savoury stock and fresh bread made my mouth water, but I stopped my hand short of my lips and forced myself to look at the bread. It was saturated with appetizing juices and flecked with caramelized onion. I wafted it under my nose and let it brush my lips. The bread's proximity to my mouth was excruciating, but I liked the idea that this manner of restrained, mindful eating somehow made me a better person. I wanted that.

I nibbled the soup-drenched crust, chewing slowly, with closed eyes, and let the soft bread slide down my throat. I felt it land in my stomach, warm and satisfying, and tried to pay equal attention to the next bite, but the scraps of conversation I'd overheard on the chef's balcony distracted me.

My mind wandered. I pulled it back to my supper, and it wandered again. It was no use. I abandoned my meditative effort and examined the situation with Bernardo.

I said, 'The doge is looking for this book because he thinks he can defeat death. All right, that's nonsense. But the love potion is real. The question is, does the love potion come from the secret book? If the maestro knows something about this book, he could be in danger.' I finished off my dinner with a few more thoughtless bites and slurps, but I left a puddle of broth in the bottom of the bowl for Bernardo. While he licked it clean, I stroked his back. 'We can't let the doge become suspicious of the chef. Everyone thinks the doge is senile, but he's not. He's putting on an act because of what happened to Doge Faliero.'

The Council of Ten always elected weak old men as doges. They tolerated no opposition to their power, and they wanted nothing more from a doge than the ability to make public appearances without drooling. Doges were not even allowed to open their own mail.

But once in a while the council misjudged; Doge Faliero had been one of their more spectacular mistakes. I'd often walked through the Hall of Doges and felt spooked by the black curtain hanging over his portrait. When I asked the chef about it, he said, 'That fellow was too ambitious. He plotted to overthrow the council and have himself proclaimed prince of Venice. But they found him out and had him beheaded.' The chef's mouth turned down in disgust. 'They displayed his body in the Piazza San Marco with his head between his knees. It was a warning to future doges, eh? And it worked. No doge ever tried it again, and that was more than a hundred years ago.'

Our doge seemed more typical – very old and slightly addled, or so he appeared. Having had opportunities to observe him alone, I knew that a conniving mind hid behind that pretence of senility. The Council of Ten referred to the doge as *il vecchio idiota* – the old idiot – and they were so certain of his ineptitude that they never took a moment to look beyond the trembling hands and quivering chin (which held steady enough when he dined alone). They never troubled to look him in the eye, though if they had, they would have seen a cunning that belied everything else. I imagined our doge slipping out of his withered skin like a snake, emerging newborn and voracious, sliding silently into our midst and striking without warning.

With my stomach full, a wave of exhaustion came over me. I leaned back against the hearth, and the fire's warmth and fluttering light lulled me into gentler thoughts of Francesca. I closed my eyes and saw the beloved face dominated by wide-set antelope eyes. Her eyebrows arched like the wings of a swan, and the whites of her eyes, almost bluish, made a startling contrast to her caramel skin. I later learned that her great-great-grandmother had been kidnapped by slavers in Turkey, brought to Venice, and then sold to a German trader. It was a common story in Venice. Francesca's more recent ancestors had been German and Italian, and the result was a mix of northern ice and Mediterranean warmth.

Francesca's upper lip curved in that sensual way that caused jealous Muslim husbands to veil their wives' faces. Her smouldering Levantine beauty contrasted with her silver-blond Teutonic hair, shockingly fair next to her dusky complexion and the sultry hint of Byzantium flashing in her dark eyes. Her nostrils were shaped like perfect teardrops.

I stretched out on the hearth and recalled speaking to her for the first time, about a week earlier, while shopping for the chef in the Rialto. I'd watched her many times before when I lived on the street, although I'd never dared to show myself in my filthy, lice-ridden rags. But after the chef washed me and dressed me and my hair had grown back, I felt my clothes and manner bespoke a decent young man with respectable prospects, and I decided to approach her. I had adored her from afar for more than a year, desperately wishing to feel those antelope eyes turned on me, and one day, in the street of greengrocers, I found my opportunity.

Mother Superior had plunked a large cantaloupe into Francesca's basket and the unexpected weight caused the girl to drop everything. The older nun stood with her fists on her square hips while Francesca scrambled to retrieve fallen turnips and escaping apples. The heavy melon rolled up to my foot – obviously divine intervention – so I picked it up and returned it to her basket with a reverent dip of my head.

The scent of soap in her hair and the fragrance of fresh-baked bread lingering in her woollen habit unleashed a memory of La Canterina, and I became light-headed in her aromatic presence. I noticed a frill of lace tucked into her sleeve and briefly wondered how she came by such extravagance. But no matter, for then our eyes met and I blinked. She murmured, 'Grazie,' in a voice like the low note of a lute, and sweat broke out at my hairline. I wanted to make her smile – a smile on that face would have been a bestowal of grace – and I strained to think of a witty remark. But, overwhelmed by her scent and intimidated by her closeness, I was struck dumb. I rescued the last apple and held it out. My tongue felt swollen and my mouth parched. When she took the apple, her fingertips brushed mine. A shock ran through my hand, burned up my arm, heated my neck, and flared like a match behind my eyes. I even felt an embarrassing tingle in my groin, which rendered me frozen as well as mute. Again, she said, '*Grazie.*'

I wanted to say 'It's nothing', or 'It's my pleasure'. I wanted to appear casual and well mannered, to bow like a gallant and say 'At your service, my lady'. But I was confused by her touch and lost in her scent.

I said, 'I love your nostrils,' then clamped my mouth shut in horror.

Francesca laughed, which made Mother Superior leave off inspecting the lettuce and glare at me. That bear of a nun grabbed Francesca's arm and dragged her off into the crowd. I watched her go, knowing that she probably thought me simpleminded. In fact, I did feel stupid and doltish, and I despised myself the whole day.

Sitting alone on the hearth, the excitement of eavesdropping on the chef's balcony dwindled, and the shame of my encounter with Francesca came back in a painful rush. The memory of my humiliation erased all thoughts of doges and secret books, and even the promise of a love potion. What good would a love potion do me when Francesca would probably never look at me again? I hauled myself up the back staircase to the servants' dormitory and tiptoed past rows of snoring servants.

Curled on my straw pallet, I hugged my knees to my chest and felt my face tighten as a hot tear slipped out of the inside corner of one eye, trickled across the bridge of my nose, and slid down the opposite cheek. That night's exhilaration over the chef's love potion dissolved in the acid memory of my mortification. I'd introduced myself to Francesca as a dunce, and it would take a miracle to redeem me.

The next morning, Chef Ferrero bustled into the kitchen without his usual smile. We all waited for his hearty shout of *buon giorno*, but it never came. A few cooks offered a greeting, and he responded with an absent nod. He slapped three packages wrapped in oilcloth onto a table, then unwrapped a gorgeous cut of prime veal, a mound of freshly caught red mullets, and a heap of still-wriggling spider crabs, all purchased before dawn in the Rialto. He made no comment about the promising whiteness of the veal or the remarkable clarity of the mullets' eyes. He pulled a freshly starched white toque onto his head without his customary self-satisfied grunt, and he unlocked the spice closet without engaging in his ritual sniff of cinnamon.

That day's great task was to prepare a dinner for a special guest from Rome – Loren Behaim, the pope's astrologer and alchemist, one of the most learned men in Europe. It would be an elaborate meal and preparations began early. The chef ordered a cook out to the kitchen's strange garden to snip fresh lavender and marigold blossoms. The other cooks exchanged worried glances and the chosen man stalled at the garden door until the chef gave him a threatening look. Before stepping out into the garden, the hapless cook made the sign of the cross, took a deep breath, and balled a fist behind his back, protection against the evil eye.

That day, the chef was more exacting than usual. He instructed Enrico to prepare a quantity of spongy dough, saying, 'Remember, warm hands are best for kneading.'

Enrico swelled with indignation at the unnecessary reminder.

'Pellegrino,' said the chef, 'slice the veal thin and against the grain.'

Pellegrino huffed under his breath, 'How else?'

The chef ordered the fish cook to put the spider crabs

into the leather salt-water tank. He patted the threshing crabs, saying, 'They'll be sweeter if they enjoy their final hours.'

'Of course,' the fish cook muttered. 'Who does he think he's talking to?'

With chores assigned, the chef pulled a neck chain out of his collar and unhooked a small brass key. He walked over to a row of copper sauté pans hanging from an iron rack and removed the largest one. Hidden behind that gleaming pan was a small oaken cabinet, which he unlocked with his brass key. Very quickly now, he removed something from the cabinet, secreted it in his trouser pocket, and then relocked the cabinet. He turned, saw me watching, and cleared his throat. 'Have you resigned as my apprentice, Luciano?'

'No, Maestro.'

'Are you a saint then, waiting for a sign from God?'

'No, Maestro.' I grabbed two wooden buckets and ran out to the courtyard. Cold water gushed into my bucket while I replayed the sight of the chef withdrawing something from his private cabinet – but what was it? I thought I'd seen a glint of green like the glass used for wine bottles. Or maybe it was more of a greyish green, like a dried herb. It had been such a fleeting glimpse. I closed my eyes to recapture the image, but all I could see was the chef's closed hand slipping into his pocket.

I lugged my water buckets into the kitchen just in time to hear the chef announce that he would take personal charge of the veal sauce. 'It's a fragile sauce and can't be fussed over by too many hands. It's sensitive to disharmony.' The cooks had already taken note of the chef's mood, so they simply nodded. But when he began ladling stock into a saucepan, uncorking wine and assembling ingredients with the intensity of a virtuoso, the sauce cook pulled his eyelid. There he was again, the haughty *artiste* whose privacy no one dared to disturb.

That evening, it fell to me to carry a great tray laden with porcelain dishes, solid gold chargers, crystal goblets and silver cutlery up to the dining room. Chambermaids trained in the art of table arrangements would lay the table with hand-tatted lace cloths and a huge bowl of white lilies. Footmen would use pulleys to lower a massive chandelier so that the maids could light its one hundred tapers.

My breath came hard as I struggled up the circular stairway with the heavy tray. I pushed open the service door with my back, lugged the tray into the opulent dining room, and set it down on a marble sideboard. The doge stood in the middle of the room with two of his thick-necked guards. He'd been speaking quietly – all their faces bore a sombre expression – but when I entered, huffing and puffing, he'd cut off abruptly. All three men watched in silence while I unloaded the tray. I took my time, handling each piece with care, hoping the doge would continue talking in my presence. But before I finished, he waved a veiny old hand my way and said, 'Get out.' I bowed and backed out of the room. After closing the door, not quite all the way, I crouched to peek through the keyhole.

The doge said, 'I want you both ready tonight, over there.' He pointed down the room. 'Behind the portrait of the Ugly Duchess.'

The two guards looked down the length of the dining room, but my view was limited, so I abandoned the keyhole and nudged the door open just enough to see the far side of the room. On that wall hung an eight-foot-high portrait of the blue-eyed Duchess of Tyrol. A bulbous nose squeezed between jowly cheeks and close-set eyes had earned the poor woman the popular title of the Ugly Duchess. The artist, in a valiant attempt to distract attention from her unfortunate face, had tried to soften and obscure his subject amid swirls of pink satin, pounds of pearls and a towering hairdo. He was clearly a skilled painter, but no one is *that* talented.

They walked to the painting, and I understood how two men could hide behind it when the doge pulled on the gilded frame and the entire painting swung open on concealed hinges. It revealed a dark passageway, no doubt one of the many secret galleries that led to the Bridge of Sorrows and across to the dungeons.

The doge showed the guards how to slide back a small panel behind one of the lady's blue eyes. On the floor inside the passageway were wooden steps high enough to bring a man's eyes up to the eyes of the portrait. The doge slid the panel back in place, and I saw that the trick eye was a masterpiece of *trompe l'oeil*. The doge turned his back to the painting and instructed his guards to watch the dining table that night for his signal. He said, 'When I do this' – he curled his forefinger in a lazy, come-hither gesture – 'come out and take him.'

One guard asked, 'To the Leads, my lord?' He referred to the upper-prison cells directly under the lead-tiled roof, which made the cells hotter in summer and colder in winter. The Leads were reserved for prisoners of rank to inhabit while they mulled over their options. Though they were spartan and uncomfortable, the Leads were infinitely better than the dungeons, a warren of pitch-dark, rat-infested caves with low, bolted doors and special chambers in which subhuman men tortured their prisoners. Some nights, shadowy figures could be seen rowing a lumpish sack out of a water gate and heading out to sea where no one could hear the splash.

The doge thought for a moment, then said, 'I don't have time for the niceties. Take him directly to the dungeon.'

The guards exchanged a quick look, and the one who had

asked about the Leads cleared his throat and said, 'With respect, my lord, Herr Behaim is said to be a close friend of His Holiness.'

The man's impudence surprised me. I thought the German astrologer must indeed be powerful to embolden a guard to question the doge. The doge's rheumy eyes narrowed into that shrewd look that so few ever saw. He moved closer to the guards and his voice dropped to a conspiratorial hush. I prayed the heavy service door wouldn't creak as I eased it open another inch to hear him.

The doge said, 'There are plots against our Most Serene Republic. We must protect her, even from Rome.'

The two guards were typical of the men in the doge's small personal guard. They were rough, uneducated young fellows with a taste for fighting and strutting about in crisp uniforms. In time, they would leave the doge's service, marry wholesome girls, and become bakers or blacksmiths or fruit merchants. They had nothing in common with the hand-picked *Cappe Nere*, who worked alongside Inquisitors and were well trained in brutal interrogations and merciless executions. Many heretics facing the auto-da-fé had looked down from the stake and seen the pyre lit by an impassive *Cappa Nera*.

The council's secret police were killers who wore the black cape for life, but the doge's guard was comprised of an ever-changing bunch of feckless young ruffians. That's why the two ignorant boys in the dining room, thinking the doge had taken them into his confidence, huffed in unison to demonstrate their appreciation for the doge's trust, as well as their offended patriotism.

The doge nodded like a disappointed sage and shrugged as though the matter were out of his hands. 'I'm hoping Herr Behaim will talk to me like an honest Christian over a civilized dinner, but if not, well, we do what we must. For Venice.'

The guards mumbled, 'For Venice.' They bowed stiffly and disappeared behind the portrait of the Ugly Duchess. With a swish of wood on canvas, one of the lady's blue eyes turned brown.

I raced down to the kitchen, leaping the last four steps in one go, and burst through the door. All the cooks turned to look at me. Dante raised a questioning eyebrow, and Enrico put down his bread paddle. Giuseppe, slumped over his sluggish broom, glowered at me while I whispered my report to the chef.

The chef barely glanced at me, nor did he pause in his preparations. He added wine to his saucepan, whisked the mixture, and said, 'Plots against Venice, eh?' He smiled, then dipped a fingertip into the sauce, touched it to his tongue, and closed his eyes to test the undertones. When he opened his eyes he said, 'You're still here?'

'But, Maestro,' I said, 'the doge is going to kidnap the pope's astrologer.'

The chef pinched a few grains of salt from a dish, sprinkled it into the sauce, and whisked again. 'You're very good at spying, and that can be useful, but don't be a nuisance.'

'But, Maestro—'

'Bring in more wood. I have a dinner to prepare.'

CHAPTER X

THE BOOK OF NEPENTHES

THE CHEF WAS RIGHT, OF course. I was good at spying because I'd spent most of my young life at it – not only as he'd done, to learn correct manners, but for survival. Marco and I had spied on the merchants in the Rialto, waiting for the moment one would turn his back long enough for us to grab his wares and run. While looking for Rufina in the Campo San Cassiano, we spied on the prostitutes, who smelled of wine and musk, fascinated by the quick, crude couplings we saw in dark *calli*. Once, we watched a woman pressed against a wall with her skirts bunched at her waist and her legs wrapped around a grunting man who groped her breasts and bumped rudely against her hips. She squinted in the lamp-light and counted her coppers behind his head.

We spied on old women paying for sardines with shaky hands, hoping they'd fumble a coin. Outside gaming houses, we watched noblemen stumble out, always on the lookout for the one too drunk to feel our fingers in his velvet purse.

We spied on well-dressed sons of princely houses and were astonished at the way they sauntered along, carefree and sure of themselves, as if the world were a safe place, as if there were not dangers in every step and disasters lying in wait. We could tell that those boys felt no hunger and that their teeth didn't ache, because they smiled for no reason. We wondered why God granted them the advantages we lacked. For myself, I believed, as La Canterina had predicted, that the birthmark on my forehead had sealed my fate. But I couldn't see what was wrong with Marco.

After joining the palace staff, I spied on cooks who wasted food that I later wrapped and took to Marco and Domingo. I spied on other servants, on the chef and his family, and on the doge – indeed, all the days of my life were strung together by a slippery thread of watching and calculating. Spying had been my means of learning about the world and surviving it. Spying had kept me alive, and I saw no reason to give it up.

During state dinners, my job as an apprentice afforded me wonderful opportunities for spying. I ran up and down the spiral stairway, cheerfully carrying each new course and hauling off the dirty dishes from the last. I handed loaded platters and steaming tureens to maids who waited on the landing, and I caught glimpses of the dining room as the women went in and came out with the trays. The maids left the door ajar so they knew when to serve more wine or bring in the next course. That slight opening was just enough to allow the voices of the doge and his guests to carry out onto the landing. Between courses, I lingered there with the maids while I kept one ear trained on the doge's conversations.

On the night of the dinner for the pope's astrologer, I watched through the cracked-open service door as the doge and Herr Behaim entered through the grand double doors on the other side of the room. One brown eye of the blue-eyed Ugly Duchess followed the doge and Herr Behaim as they walked to the table and seated themselves. Herr Behaim praised the room's elaborate Byzantine decor, the silk-clad walls and coved ceiling, and I noticed that his Venetian was accented with a Germanic growl. The doge sat facing the portrait of the Ugly Duchess, and Behaim sat at his right hand, the hand that might give the fatal signal.

The meal began with asiago cheese rolled in herbed breadcrumbs and grilled just to the point at which the breadcrumbs acquire a golden hue. It was a tricky dish because it had to be grilled only to the edge of melting – one second longer might cause the cheese to bleed through its crispy coating and ruin the presentation. Still sizzling, it had to be rushed to the table before it could cool and solidify. The cheese was accompanied by a cold bottle of Foianeghe Rosso from the doge's cellar, a full-bodied wine with the character of an overture.

The doge cut through the delicate crust and into the soft, warm cheese. Herr Behaim held up his fork and admired the shimmering reflection of candlelight on silver. 'This charming implement you Italians invented, tell me again what you call it.'

'A fork.'

'Of course! Why can't I remember that odd little word? I hear it's becoming a fad in the French court.'

'The French? I doubt they can master it.'

'Be merciful, my lord. Venice sets the style; the rest of us can only follow.'

The doge smiled, placed a forkful of cheese in his mouth, and closed his eyes as it spread over his tongue, herb crusted and butter-luscious. Before I ran off for the next course, I heard him purr.

For the *primo piatto*, the chef had chosen to serve a dish he called gnocchi – small dumplings made with potato flour. It was an unusual dish as potatoes were a rarity from the New World and largely unknown. The gnocchi were simply dressed in browned butter and sage and then dusted with freshly grated Parmigiano-Reggiano. It was a plain presentation with no garnish, and it was accompanied by a white table wine of no special distinction.

My mouth watered as I carried the gnocchi up to the dining room. I'd tasted one dumpling in the kitchen, and I loved the earthy flavour as well as the way it resisted when I sank my teeth in. The butter and sage coated my mouth so that the taste lasted even after I swallowed. I liked the way it felt in my stomach, solid and nourishing, and I looked forward to learning how to make it.

When the maid placed the two plates of unadorned gnocchi on the table, the doge arched one white eyebrow at her. 'Dumplings?' He turned to his guest. 'I apologize for the commonness of this food. I'll send it back at once.'

But Behaim placed a hand on his arm. 'Please, my lord. Your chef's reputation is well known. I'm sure these dumplings are delicious.'

An embarrassed smile crept over the doge's face. 'I'll admit it; I love dumplings.' He snickered. 'Under our noble clothing we have the stomachs of peasants, eh?'

They shared a smile, less polite and more authentic than earlier, and dived into the gnocchi. I heard little hums of pleasure as their teeth sank into the lumps of buttered potato pasta. Behaim murmured, 'Perfect. And as I suspected, not ordinary.'

The doge spoke around a full mouth. '*Sì, sì, al dente*, and, yes . . . different.'

Polite conversation ceased while they ate their peasant food. I heard wet chewing and silver clinking unceremoniously on china. They washed their food down with the unpretentious wine, and both of them mopped up stray drizzles of butter and cheese with the last pieces of gnocchi. Camaraderie replaced courtly manners and friendliness joined the table like a third diner.

The doge sat back and knitted his fingers over his belly. 'So, we've eaten dumplings together. I won't mention it if you won't.'

'A secret I'll be happy to keep if I may rely on being invited to do it again.'

Hearing the word 'secret', I moved closer to the door and strained to catch every word.

The doge said, 'If one wishes to learn a secret from a friend, one must offer that friend a good reason to share it.'

'My lord understands the ways of the world.'

On the landing, one of the maids slapped the back of my head and whispered, 'It would be easier to hear the conversation if you joined the doge at his table. Shall we set a place for you? Or will you, perhaps, honour us by bringing up the next course?' I started down the stairs, chased by the sound of clucking tongues.

When I returned with the fish course, the maid whisked the two plates out of my hands and pushed the door open with her hip. As she stepped into the dining room, the doge was leaning towards his guest as if about to speak confidentially, but seeing the maid he sat back in his chair and blotted his lips with a napkin.

After the simplicity of the gnocchi, the fish course was astonishing. Pellegrino had spent the entire day preparing the two red mullets. He had partially removed the heads and cleaned the fish through those small openings, leaving the bodies intact. Then he massaged each fish to loosen the flesh and bones, which he painstakingly removed without breaking the skin. The mullet flesh was combined with chopped spider crab, cream-softened bread, finely minced shallots and a whisper of garlic, thyme, nutmeg and butter, and then carefully stuffed back into the skin. Pellegrino returned the heads to their natural position and patted each fish into its original shape. He surrounded the stuffed mullets with vegetables and herbs and sealed all of it in parchment to poach gently in its own flavourful steam.

On the plate, they looked like simple baked mullets surrounded by a frill of lemon slices. The maid set a plate before each man, and the doge said, 'More plain food?' But when his first cut revealed the unexpected medley inside, he laughed out loud.

Herr Behaim said, 'Your chef has a sense of humour.' He took a bite, held it in his mouth, and rolled it on his tongue. Pleasure suffused his face. '*Mein Gott im Himmel*, I don't know what I'm eating, but it brings me closer to God.'

The doge chewed thoughtfully. 'Crab?'

'Perhaps, but more. Appearances deceive.'

'As in life,' said the doge.

'Well said, my lord. You wouldn't believe the ridiculous things people expect me to know simply because I'm the pope's astrologer. They expect occult knowledge of every description. The groping of small minds; they embarrass themselves.'

The doge leaned towards his guest. 'My friend, we've eaten dumplings together. You don't mean for me to believe that your knowledge is limited to astrology?'

'Herbal remedies.' Behaim shrugged. 'And I dabble in alchemy, that's no secret.'

'All men have secrets.' The doge smiled.

'My lord, my secrets interest only my confessor. I think even he's bored.'

'Impossible.' The doge leaned closer. 'You're known as the most learned man in Europe.'

'Flattering, but absurd. As my lord has observed, things are often not what they seem.' Behaim lifted his wineglass and took a sip of the well-chilled Tocai, which the chef had chosen to bring out every nuance of the mullets' complicated filling. Behaim sniffed and sipped and held the wine on his tongue a second before swallowing. 'Ah, your chef is an artist.'

The doge tasted his wine and nodded. 'It's true. This Tocai compounds the mystery of the food. I admit I'm puzzled.' He drained his glass and smacked his lips.

'All puzzles should be so delightful.' Behaim chewed a mouthful of mullet with his eyes closed. He said, 'It's like listening to a symphony.'

'Hmmm.' The doge sat back in his chair. He raised his right hand and I saw one finger uncurling. I glanced at the portrait of the Ugly Duchess and saw her brown eye narrow in anticipation. But instead of giving the signal, the doge only summoned a maid to refill his wineglass.

The other maid slapped the back of my head. 'Do we have to beg for every course?' As I started down the stairs, she hissed, 'Too nosy for your own good.'

Chef Ferrero had taken charge of the main dish himself. Tender veal cutlets had been dipped in beaten eggs and seasoned flour, then lightly seared and served in a dark brown sauce. The presentation was completed with a sprinkle of lavender leaves and marigold petals – green and gold, like a spring morning – and served with a loaf of crusty bread rather than the customary glazed onions.

'Veal,' Behaim said. 'What a luxury. One wonders how many calves are torn from their mothers so that we might eat well.'

'That's the luxury. We ingest the innocence of childhood.'

Behaim swirled his fork in the glossy sauce. 'This sauce is uncommonly dark. It swallows the light.' He took a taste. '*Mein Gott*, what is that flavour?'

The doge took a bite and chewed slowly. 'I confess it's new to me. My chef is endlessly inventive.'

I kept the service door ajar with my toe and watched them eat the milk-fed veal tender enough to cut with a fork. They nibbled the marigold petals and soaked up the dark sauce with fistfuls of spongy bread. I watched the doge's index finger and waited for the gesture that would bring out the guards; the one brown eye watched as well, and it never blinked. The men raised their glasses and toasted innocence with a decisive, wood-aged cabernet.

Behaim said, 'This sauce is magnificent. I believe His Holiness would enjoy it.'

The doge leaned sideways and gave him an elbow in the ribs. 'If Borgia enjoys as much variety in his food as he does in his women, I'm afraid only one marvellous sauce will not suffice. Still, we try to accommodate . . .' The doge twisted in his chair and raised his hand. I thought: *This is it!* But he only called to the maid. 'Woman,' he ordered. 'Fetch this sauce recipe for my guest.'

She hurried out onto the landing and slapped my head again. 'You heard,' she snapped. 'Get the recipe.'

I found the chef assembling biscuits on a dessert platter, but before I could speak he asked, 'Are they eating the veal sauce?'

'*Sì*. They're polishing their plates with the bread.'

'Good. Good.' The chef seemed nervous; one might have thought he was serving the Council of Ten. He said, 'Keep your eyes open and tell me what happens.'

'Maestro, the doge wants the sauce recipe for His Holiness.'

'The sauce? Are you out of your mind?' The chef shook his head emphatically. 'I'll be happy to prepare my Sauce Nepenthes for His Holiness, but I cannot divulge the recipe. If everybody could cook like Amato Ferrero, what value would I have?'

I relayed this answer to the maid, who brought it to the doge. Upon hearing that the chef had declined to share his recipe, the doge hit the table with a fist. 'Insolence!' he roared. But again Behaim restrained him with a diplomatic hand on his arm.

He said, 'Your chef is right. An artist must protect the secrets of his trade. Perhaps you'll allow him to come to Rome and prepare the dish himself for His Holiness.'

'Of course. But . . . what were we talking about?'

Behaim sat back, sipped his cabernet, and knitted his brow. 'Sauce Nepenthes. Odd name. I believe Nepenthes was a Greek god – the god of sleep? No, that was Morpheus. Was Nepenthes the god of remembrance, or forgetfulness?' He gave a futile wave. 'I can't recall.'

The doge stared absently at the portrait of the Ugly Duchess and said, 'What would I know of Greek gods? You're the scholar.' He blinked quickly, then looked around the room and sighed. 'Strange. I never noticed that the Ugly Duchess had one brown eye.' He slumped back in his chair. 'Perhaps I've had too much wine.'

Behaim glanced at the portrait and wagged his head. 'I don't know the colour of that lady's eyes. I've never been inclined to look too long at any of her portraits.'

'Understandable.'

The meal finished with spiced wine and a platter of oblong biscuits. The ends of the biscuits had been dipped in another dark brown sauce, which had somehow hardened.

The doge said, 'We call these biscuits bones of the dead.' He held one up and rotated the coated end to examine it. 'But I've never seen them with this . . . what is this?'

'Your chef is an artist with a sense of humour. He serves the bones of the dead dressed in mourning.'

The doge lifted the spiced wine. 'We'll eat the bones of the dead and toast life.'

Behaim drank the toast, then selected a biscuit and took a bite. His face transformed like a saint in rapture. 'Mmmm. The coating on this biscuit is as erotic as the veal sauce was divine. It induces a lust for more.' He licked biscuit crumbs from his lips.

The doge bit the dark end off a biscuit, chewed, and muttered, 'One thinks of one's youth.' He swallowed. 'Amazing. Even after the taste fades, the pleasure lingers like a tickle in the brain. Delicious as sex.'

'Mmmm. Irresistible as sin.'

They chewed in silence and ate their way through the entire platter. This time the maids eavesdropped as intently as I, and no one slapped me. The older one mumbled, 'Sex and sin. *Boh*. Pigs.'

Behaim finished his spiced wine and sat back. 'So, my lord, we've eaten innocence and death and are content. What cannot be done in life has been accomplished at your table.' He pushed back and stood. 'I thank you for a memorable meal. My respects to your chef.'

The doge sat staring at the Ugly Duchess. 'I feel I'm forgetting something. But food and wine and old age will do that, eh?' Once more his hand came up, but only to rub his eyes.

He shook his head as if to clear it, then he stood and threw an arm around the astrologer. 'Convey my regards to His Holiness.' He chuckled. 'Borgia, that rascal.' They left the room laughing like the best of friends.

The brown eye of the Ugly Duchess followed them to the double doors. The eye blinked, swept the empty room, stared for a moment and then, after a subtle swish of wood sliding against canvas, turned blue and still.

I helped the maids clear the table, then rushed down to the kitchen and dumped the dirty dishes into the soapy tub without scraping them. The chef didn't seem to notice; he motioned me over with an anxious gesture. 'So,' he asked, 'did he arrest the astrologer?'

'No, Maestro. Just when I thought he would, they began acting like friends.'

The chef's face relaxed. He sat down on a stool and said, 'Bene.'

'But, Maestro, it was strange. What did you feed them?'

He looked at the floor for a moment and then at me. 'Food has power, Luciano. Each dish works its own magic, a kind of alchemy that changes our bodies and our minds.'

The chef put a hand on my shoulder. 'Consider the effect of melted cheese. Soft, warm, comforting, so easy to eat you barely need to chew. It makes a man relax. Then came the dumplings. Plain, common food to inspire trust, to awaken a sense of shared humanity and the enjoyment of simple things. Dumplings breed camaraderie.'

I said, 'They agreed to keep their love of dumplings a secret.'

'Sì?' The chef smiled. 'Then Pellegrino's surprising mullet made them reflect on the folly of judging by appearances. The doge expected Behaim to know something based on his reputation, but the fish made him question his assumptions.'

'What did he expect Behaim to know?'

He waved the question away. 'The important thing is that if he was mistaken, the doge would look foolish.'

Mentally, I slapped the back of my own head. *Stupido*. The book. The doge expected Behaim to know something about the book.

The chef continued. 'The veal is obvious. No one can eat veal without thinking of innocence. I served it with bread instead of onions because bread is more human. Animals can dig onions out of the ground and eat them raw. Only humans settle down to grow grain. That means planning for the future, milling the flour, adding the magic of leavening, and careful baking. Bread reminds a man that he's civilized.' He chuckled. 'It also helps them eat all the sauce. I wouldn't want them to miss the sauce.'

'They wiped their plates clean.'

'By the time dessert comes, hunger is tamed and the satisfied diner settles back to consider the human condition. Eating bones of the dead inspires thoughts of immortality. A mysterious and delicious black sauce suggests facing the unknown and loving it. It leaves nothing to fear. Taken together, the elements of this meal conspired to relieve the doge's suspicions and leave him satisfied.'

'That's ingenious, Maestro.'

'Well then, what have you learned?'

'That food can manipulate men's hearts and minds.'

'Very good. Now finish those dishes.'

But the chef had omitted an explanation for his greatly praised Sauce Nepenthes, the high point of the meal and the turning point of the doge's attitude. I asked, 'And the veal sauce, Maestro?'

'What about it?'

'Well, after they ate the sauce—'

'That's enough.' The chef adjusted his high white toque so that it sat low on his forehead, never a good sign. 'You can't learn the secrets of the maestro without first doing the work. Wash the dishes. And next time, scrape them first, the way I taught you.'

Marrone.

I was impressed with the chef's skill, but it was clear that he would not share his secrets easily. I'd have to earn his trust, so that night I decided to take this matter of cooking into my own hands. I would make a grand gesture. How hard could it be? If you combine nothing but good-tasting ingredients, the result would *have* to taste good. It seemed like simple common sense. I would make something so delicious, so original and extraordinary, that the chef would beam with pride, call me a culinary virtuoso, and promote me on the spot. After I adjusted the fire under the stockpots for the night simmer, I fired up Enrico's oven and planned my strategy.

Meat was out of the question because I didn't know the secrets of seasoning and roasting. Vegetables were a bit tricky as well, all of them needing delicate preparations unknown to me. I started with a wedge of triple-cream cheese because that seemed like a rich and elegant base that would need little embellishment. I cut a large slice of cheese and stripped off the skin, leaving only the voluptuous centre, which I set into a clean bowl. I had noticed that wine went into the best dishes, so I added enough claret to thin the cheese to a mixable consistency. As I beat it together, I watched the pure white turn a murky shade of rose, and the sharp smell of wine overpowered the milky fragrance of cheese.

Although such a dramatic change in colour and aroma was unexpected, I decided it was not a fatal blow to the plan.

The chef had once said that the cornerstones of culinary art were butter and garlic, so I cheerfully whipped in a knob of softened butter and pressed a large clove of garlic. I whisked it all until it was smooth, tested it with a fingertip, and judged it to be not bad. But not bad wasn't good enough for a grand gesture. I stood before the brick oven and pondered what might elevate this concoction from an oddly flavoured cheese to something that would make the chef raise his eyebrows with appreciation.

The brick oven reminded me of Enrico, who often bragged that his lightly sweetened breads and confections were everyone's favourite. He once said, 'Meals are only an excuse to get to the dessert.' I wasn't sure that was true, but I had noticed that people usually greeted the dessert course with smiles, even though they had already eaten their fill. Confections always found favour, and so I poured a golden stream of honey into my mélange.

After it was well blended, it was rather pretty – smooth and thick, luscious looking, like pudding or custard. I'd even got used to the raw veal colour caused by the wine, and I thought the whole thing might really work, but my next taste was jarringly unpleasant. Something was off, out of balance, just plain *wrong*, but what?

I recalled Pellegrino adding raisins to frumenty with the remark 'Any pudding is improved by fruit'. In desperation, I tossed in a handful of raisins and stirred. Now I'd lost the silky texture, and the raisins looked a bit like small dead roaches, but I hoped that the magic of cooking would plump the raisins, make the batter cohere, and meld the flavours. I poured everything into a square pan and slid it into the hot oven.

The kitchen immediately filled with the smell of garlic, which was normally a good thing but not, I suddenly realized, for a dessert. Still, honey and garlic were both fine ingredients by themselves, and perhaps I'd stumbled upon a new and wonderful combination. I watched bubbles appear around the edge of the pan, and the mixture became pockmarked with tiny wells of bubbling butter. Next, the raisins swelled up, covered in a cheesy film that looked like white scabs. The whole mess glistened under an oily layer of melted butter and bore a sickening resemblance to chunky vomit.

I couldn't bring myself to taste it. I scraped it into a dish and offered it to Bernardo, but after one sniff, he looked at me with narrowed eyes and glided away with his tail in the air. I went to bed puzzled but not defeated.

CHAPTER ✣ XI

THE BOOK OF LANDUCCI

I DIDN'T PRESS THE CHEF further about the doge for fear of being cast back out on the street; Venice is an uncommonly painful place to be poor. To be poor in Venice means deprivation amid staggering wealth; it means scavenging rubbish heaps in a city bursting with delicacies imported from all parts of the world; it means shivering in the shadow of marble palaces that are breathtaking in their opulence.

There was only one week in the year when all Venetians might feel cared for and carefree. In midsummer, Venice celebrated La Sensa, the doge's symbolic marriage to the sea. During La Sensa the city fathers provided food and drink enough for all Venetians to make merry for eight uninhibited days. During La Sensa, the sea, on which Venice depended for her prosperity, became the symbolic bride of the doge in a dazzling display unequalled among Venetian celebrations.

For us – orphans, drunks, prostitutes, mental defectives

and all the other outcasts of Venetian society – the excited chatter started weeks in advance. We sat in exuberant groups on the docks and in crumbling piazzas, bragging about how many chicken gizzards we'd devour, how much cheese we'd shovel down, how many litres of wine we'd swill. We vowed to gorge and sing and dance until we fell unconscious. Ruined men, toothless, malnourished, and stinking in their lice-infested rags, promised to ravish every woman in sight, humble or noble. The women, equally scabrous and filthy, tittered like flattered girls.

The great day dawned with a procession of boats festooned with rose garlands and packed full of senators dressed in scarlet capes. Citizens crowded into the Piazza San Marco and jockeyed for a favourable position from which to watch the doge, the resplendent groom in golden robes, as he emerged from the ducal palace and boarded the *Bucentaur*, which was ablaze with crimson banners waving from her masts. The *Bucentaur* led a flotilla out of the lagoon; the sun flashed on hundreds of oars while a choir of two hundred men chanted onshore and all the bells of all the churches pealed continuously.

A contagious giddiness swept over the city when we saw the doge stand at the bow of the *Bucentaur* to intone his vow. He raised his arms and proclaimed, 'We wed thee, O sea.' Then he cast a gold wedding ring into the Adriatic. The crowd cheered, and the flotilla swarmed round the *Bucentaur*. Trumpets sounded, guns boomed in salute, and the people raised their voices in a cacophony of jubilant shouts.

Gondolas bearing aristocratic coats of arms bumped alongside gondolas full of courtesans blowing kisses and baring their creamy breasts. Every piazza burst to life with acrobats, bird callers, magicians, jugglers, dancers, singers and musicians plucking pear-shaped lutes or banging tambourines. After dark, countless bonfires reddened the night sky, and a torchlight procession wound through the streets like a river of flame.

The first day was always joyful, but after that it was simply too much for too long. People with homes to go to did so and continued the celebration as it suited them. We in the streets did what we'd promised – we gorged and guzzled to the point of sickness and beyond. As the days passed, people sagged under the weight of too much cheap wine, not enough sleep, and the burden of relentless merriment. In the heat and throng, people fainted, vomited, quarrelled and flew into hysterics. Somehow, most people forgot this aspect of the festival from one year to the next, but not me. I found the excess stupefying. It was a mad, congested mass of men and women and children and horses and dogs and donkeys and cats and chickens (yes, chickens), a gluttonous, raucous, drunken clamour that went on for eight long, loud days and nights, leaving me crushed and gaping.

But I believed that my first La Sensa in the palace would be different. In years past, I had watched the dignified senators and their polished ladies disappear into the palace, and I was sure their celebration would be far more measured and refined than the chaos in the streets. I fantasized about serving at a stylish gala given by the doge for his court, regal ladies and gentlemen enjoying themselves with grace and decorum. There'd be no stepping in puddles of urine or slipping in vomit, no jealous wives tearing the hair of other women, no brawling drunks falling into the canals, and no pitiful babies crying in baskets while their young mothers drank and danced, tipsy and oblivious.

I looked forward to participating in an evening of fine food and gentle music that would leave my sensitivities unmolested. I planned to wrap two packages of the finest leftovers in oilcloth, tie them with a bow, and present them the next day to Marco and Domingo. It didn't matter that Marco took everything without thanks. It would be a display of my own largesse, a demonstration of how gracious I'd become as a result of my proximity to the highborn. I didn't need his thanks.

Domingo, on the other hand, was always grateful. Once, as he thanked me too effusively and too long for a dry rind of Parmigiano, I cut him off. '*Niente*,' I said, motioning dismissively at the cheese.

He said, 'Not only for the cheese.' He put a hesitant hand on my arm and then quickly withdrew it. He looked down at the pavement and spoke in his quiet way. 'You're a good friend, Luciano.' His pimples glowed red.

I mumbled, '*Boh*, it's nothing.' But we both knew that for boys like us, friendship was indeed something.

As the morning of La Sensa dawned, I was surprised to see that there was no unusual flurry in the kitchen. In fact, the pace seemed lethargic. I asked the chef when we'd begin our preparations for the feast, but he said, 'Watch and learn.' He smiled and walked away.

My first taste of reality came after the ceremony in the lagoon. Our frail old doge collapsed the moment the palace doors closed behind him, and he had to be carried up to his rooms by two burly guards. The old man had fallen prostrate from exertion and heat, and his court was nowhere in sight. The chef wagged his head and said, 'Every year this ridiculous thing becomes more strenuous. One of these times we'll have another one dropping dead.'

'Another one?'

'The last doge. On his very first La Sensa – "his day", as he called it – he ate too much melon while he sat bareheaded in the garden under a scorching sun. The old fellow turned red as a radish, foamed at the mouth, and died on the spot of apoplexy.' The chef shrugged. 'They're not meant to be very smart or last very long.'

But our doge was more prudent than his predecessor. He simply retired to his chambers to recover quietly from the one essential duty Venice required of him. That evening he ordered a cup of cold soup and ate it while propped against pillows in his high, canopied bed.

I was disappointed that the doge's court would not be in attendance, but at least the Council of Ten and the senators would dine in the palace that evening, and I looked forward to my first good look at that powerful group of men. I'd seen only one of them before – Maffeo Landucci, who had the unusual habit of appearing in the kitchen unannounced.

Once, Signor Landucci had arrived while the chef was consulting with a papermaker and a calligrapher about menus for a banquet. Landucci entered the kitchen and stood just inside the service door, wrinkling his nose and dabbing his brow with a grey silk scarf. He reeked of good health and old money. While he waited for the chef, he stared at Giuseppe, who was sweeping up after breakfast, and a look passed between them, but it had no meaning; both men, after all, were something to behold, each in his own way.

The chef rose to greet him, but Landucci waved him down with his silk scarf and waited in the doorway. After the chef finished, Landucci politely introduced himself to the papermaker and asked technical questions about his process. Next he inquired into the names and locations of the best calligraphers in Venice. He listened carefully, his head cocked and a small, polite smile fixed on his face. He thanked the craftsmen and left as casually as he had arrived.

The chef was inexplicably irritated for the rest of the day. He banged around the kitchen short-tempered and dissatisfied with everything and everyone. At the time I attributed his mood to having too many intruders in his kitchen. Now I know he understood Landucci's questions only too well.

Matteo Landucci appeared another time while the chef was chatting over a glass of wine with an antiquarian bookseller. The chef had professed an interest in a rare, hand-copied book of recipes from North Africa, said to have been collected by one of the cooks who accompanied Scipio at the defeat of Carthage. Although the originals were long lost, the bookseller thought he might know where to find one of the few copies still in existence. The men were discussing cost when Landucci appeared. Landucci introduced himself and then peppered the bookseller with questions about his sources for antiquarian books. When he left, the chef's mood once again turned dark.

I asked Enrico about the chef's foul moods following Landucci's visits. Enrico, always enthralled by gossip, virtually twinkled at the prospect of relating a succulent story. 'The chef despises that man,' he said. 'Haven't you heard about Landucci and his son? I thought everyone knew.'

'I don't.'

'Oh-ho.' Enrico rubbed his hands together. His face was brick-red from the heat of his oven, and his eyes sparkled. He said, 'There were two boys, eight years old, playing at hanging, and one was accidentally killed. The dead boy was Landucci's son.'

'Poor man!'

'*Boh.* You mean poor boys. Landucci cut out the other boy's liver, then had it cooked and served to his father. They say just as the man swallowed the last bite Landucci told him what he was eating. The man started to gag, but Landucci stabbed him in the heart before he could vomit. Said he deserved to die a cannibal.'

'I don't believe it.'

Enrico puffed up like one of his own yeast loaves. 'I have unimpeachable sources. Anyway, the story is well known. Ask anyone.' Offended, he disappeared behind an enormous mound of dough.

That evening, I carried only one tray of dishes and cutlery up to the dining room, enough for only three place settings. It seemed that while Venice spun itself into an overheated frenzy, the doge would sip cold love-apple soup under his bed canopy, and only three councilmen would come to the palace to eat a sensible meal of the same soup, cold chicken and chilled cantaloupe.

I felt cheated.

When the double doors of the dining room opened, Landucci entered first. As I recalled Enrico's gruesome story, the sight of him striding across the Turkish carpet gave me a horrible thrill – and yet there was nothing horrible about his person. In fact, he looked quite the distinguished gentleman. His face was stiff as wood and his mouth thin as a splinter, yet he was handsome in a sharp, flinty way. He had eyes of an indeterminate colour, shifting to blue one moment, then to green, and then settling into grey. He was tall and dash-ing, and he moved with patrician grace. He had the pale skin of one who lives a pampered life indoors. Only a thin, blue vein, pulsing slowly at his temple, suggested warm blood under his skin.

He must have been a vain man. His hair and beard were short and precisely trimmed, his clothing was fashionable, his fingernails were manicured, and he had a habit of flick-ing off dust motes with his silk scarf. He brandished the scarf to add emphasis to his words, and he held it to his nose whenever a servant approached. He dressed in ambiguous shades of grey – muted, elusive colours that matched his eyes.

Signor Castelli entered next. He was a large, square man, serious and capable. He pulled out his chair with one efficient move, sat erect and cleared his throat, ready to do business. Behind him came Signor Riccardi – known affectionately as Old Riccardi – shuffling along with a walking stick and smiling gently. Old Riccardi's face was so wrinkled it looked like candle drippings, but the smile creased his eyes pleasantly. I asked the maid about the rest of the council members, and she said, 'They're at home, *stupido*, like every year. This year, for some reason, Landucci wanted a meeting.'

In previous years, after the senators and their ladies entered the palace in stately assemblage, the festivities I had envisioned took place only in my mind. In truth, the high-born took refuge in the doge's palace only to avoid pushing through the unruly mob in the piazza. They left discreetly through back doors and made their way home through small streets and narrow *rii*, undisturbed by the crowd. They may have stayed for one polite glass of wine, but there had never been a feast with music and powdered ladies whispering behind Chinese fans. And that night, there would be only a dull business meeting over an equally dull meal.

I'd put on a clean apron, washed my face, combed my hair, and hoped that the boisterous revelry in the streets wouldn't interfere with the formal celebration in the palace. But now, as I watched the three men mumble greetings and settle into their straight-backed chairs, the festivities in the street struck me as gay and inviting.

The men were impeccably dressed in summer silks – grey for Landucci and cool jewel tones for the other two, the blues and greens of the sea. As men of stature, all three wore hats. Stout Signor Castelli wore a circular flattop hat with a round brim, like a cake on a plate. Old Riccardi wore an arrangement of gauzy white cloth cleverly wound around his head so that it fell in graceful drapes to keep the sun off the back of his wrinkled neck. Landucci wore a voguish hat of starched grey silk with a neat brim. But in spite of the smart clothing and the music carrying in from the street, the mood at the table was subdued. The men sat far apart at the long table, as if making room for the aura of power that surrounded each one. All three wore beards, a feature that makes some men look wise but only made them look more formidable.

We served love-apple soup first. Love apples, sometimes called tomatoes, were believed to be poisonous, but the chef grew them in his garden and knew the secret of rendering them harmless. He used them for soup as well as for a number of zesty sauces that greatly enhanced his reputation. Landucci sipped properly from the side of his round spoon. Old Riccardi slurped and dribbled into his white beard. Signor Castelli seemed to have little appetite.

Unsurprisingly, the love-apple soup turned the conversation to the art of the poisoner, and Castelli told a favourite story of revenge. He'd once poisoned a bishop, a political rival, and then had the body squeezed into a child-size coffin and put on display in the man's own church. He chuckled at his own wit and said, 'Of course, the sweetest story of revenge belongs to Landucci. That business with the boy's liver.' Castelli laughed, first a dirty little chortle, then louder with head thrown back, mouth agape, and tongue extruded.

'That was not revenge.' Landucci gave his grey silk scarf a sharp snap, and a dark flush crept up his neck. The vein at his temple pulsed. 'That was justice.'

Castelli lost his smile at once. '*Scusi*, Landucci, I only—'

'I *loved* my son.' Landucci's pallor ripened to a plum colour, and another vein bulged in his neck. 'Justice, Castelli. To sin against me so grievously required nothing less.'

'Of course,' Castelli blustered. 'God's own justice. Absolutely.'

Old Riccardi sighed. 'When did such things become proper conversation for the dinner table?'

The men sat in silence while the maids served cold chicken on clear glass plates – oval medallions of white meat nestled amid simple greens and fresh herbs suggesting a sunny summer meadow. A garnish of thin lemon slices and paper-thin rounds of cucumbers added crisp textures and cleansing flavours. A cooling-down seemed appropriate at that moment, but the dish failed to mitigate the impressive colour Landucci's face had achieved.

A maid leaned over Landucci's shoulder to refill his glass. She had, of course, heard the account of his double murder and, finding herself so close to the murderer, she began to tremble. The wine overflowed the glass and spilled onto the table. Flustered, she pulled the carafe back too quickly, and more wine sloshed into Landucci's plate, onto his chest, and into his lap. Terrified, the woman put down the carafe, seized a napkin, and tried to blot the wine from his vest while she whispered frantic apologies. As she mopped up, she steadied herself with one hand on the table.

Landucci sat back, surprised. He looked at his stained vest and his chicken floating in wine. He murmured, 'Clumsy slut.' He grabbed his fork in a tight fist and made a vicious stab into the back of her hand. Then he bore down until the prongs penetrated fully. After he let go, he pulled a lace-edged handkerchief from his vest and dabbed away bubbles of saliva from the corners of his mouth.

The woman stood still, her mouth wide open but making no sound. She stared at the fork handle that still quivered from Landucci's thrust as blood pooled around the prongs embedded in her hand. Her face turned waxy white. She gasped once and, very slowly, sank to the floor, staring at her hand in disbelief.

I stared, too, and tasted bile on my tongue.

Old Riccardi sighed again. 'Landucci, for God's sake, are you intent on ruining my appetite tonight?'

Castelli pushed a chicken medallion around his plate and said nothing.

Landucci nodded humbly. '*Scusate, signori*. That was an unfortunate lapse of manners. I beg your pardon.' He gestured at the maid on the floor and said, 'Someone get that out of here. And get me another fork.'

The two other maids on the landing said nothing, and their faces betrayed no emotion. One of them took a clean fork from the service tray and brought it to Landucci before helping the swooning woman off the floor.

The injured woman's face remained a wax sculpture of horror until she reached the service door. Then her body convulsed, and finally tears sprang to her eyes. But when a sob escaped her mouth, the other maid clamped a hand over it and led her away. The fork handle bobbed grotesquely as she walked and left a spotty trail of blood on the stone stairs.

Landucci pushed aside his wine-soaked chicken, and a strained quiet came over the table. The other maid should have rushed in to clean up the mess, but she and I stood on the landing, temporarily immobilized by the sight of the bleeding woman hobbling down the stairs. In that still moment, the singing in the piazza rose to a joyous crescendo, and I felt a sick nostalgia for my old friends. The maid cuffed the back of my head, a signal to get on with the meal, and then she hurried into the dining room to take away Landucci's plate.

I brought up the tray of sweet melon in a daze of shock and handed it to the maid, who took it without looking at me. Her face was blank, and I wondered whether she'd seen this kind of thing so often it no longer surprised her, or whether she knew better than to show that she'd noticed anything.

Each slice of melon had been dressed with a few drops of Modenese balsamic vinegar to bring out the sweetness of the fruit and garnished with fresh mint leaves. It was served on alabaster plates, the swirling insubstantial white of thin clouds. I looked at the carefully arranged plates thinking that if I had to put anything in my mouth at that moment my throat would close in protest.

Old Riccardi wiped his forehead with a napkin and said, 'I'm hot. Let's finish our business and go home.' He speared his fruit and brought it to his mouth with a tremulous hand. He chewed with great care, like a man whose teeth hurt. 'I'm too old to waste time,' he said with a full mouth. 'I'd prefer not to die at this table, eh?'

Castelli began to choke. He coughed, drank some wine, and coughed again. His face reddened, and his eyes watered.

Old Riccardi asked, 'Are you all right?'

Gasping for breath, Castelli nodded. 'I'm fine.' He coughed again, then caught his breath and said, 'Maybe you don't have to die at all, Riccardi.' He paused to clear his throat and take a sip of wine. 'Maybe the doge will find that book with the formula for eternal youth. What do you say, Riccardi? Would you like to be young again?'

'Not particularly.' Old Riccardi wiped his perspiring face with a napkin.

Landucci, whose high colour had subsided, said, 'Eternal youth. *Boh.*'

Again, Castelli demonstrated his ability to lose his smile in an instant. 'Of course I was joking. I know that's nonsense.'

Old Riccardi held up an arthritic finger. 'Why so sure? If medicine can banish illness, why couldn't there be an ultimate medicine to banish death? And what about the other formula – alchemy?'

'Come now, Riccardi.' Castelli offered him an indulgent smile.

Old Riccardi continued unfazed. 'My jeweller says bronze is made from a formula. Just because we don't know a formula for gold doesn't mean there isn't one.' Old Riccardi looked around the table, his faded eyes gone sly and amused. 'Imagine the doge making enough gold to buy the *Cappe Nere* and getting rid of us. Eh? Eh?'

'*Boh!*' Landucci threw his napkin on the table. 'If that book holds anything of value, it will be those gospels that discredit Rome. And they're probably not all in one book either. There could be many volumes, and surely there are copies. But if we could get our hands on just one, we could use it to control Borgia. Or' – his eyebrows shot up as if he'd just had a brilliant thought – 'we could have copies printed in one of the new *stamperie*. We could have the thing read aloud on every street corner.'

'A popular revolt against Rome?' Old Riccardi's voice was quiet and calm. 'Then what, Maffeo?'

Landucci shrugged. 'We might weaken Borgia enough for us to take the Papal States. Then France would court an alliance with us instead of Rome. We could unseat Rome and make Venice an empire.'

'And you the emperor, Maffeo?' asked Old Riccardi.

'Why not?'

Old Riccardi pushed the last piece of melon around on his plate. 'If Borgia finds those gospels, he'll destroy them.'

'That's why we have to find them first.' Landucci leaned forward. 'I want to double the doge's reward.'

'Sì,' said Old Riccardi. 'We could do that. But then the doge might triple his. Where would it end?'

It was then that I noticed Castelli fiddling with his beard and keeping his head down as if some engrossing spectacle were taking place on his alabaster plate.

Old Riccardi said, 'Out with it, Maffeo. What else do you want?'

Landucci's eyes flashed like quicksilver. 'This information has been protected for a long time, and many people must know many things about it. I propose we have the *Cappe Nere* pay visits to all the monasteries in Venice and the Veneto and bring us their copyists. I propose they also visit universities and libraries. Bring us the historians, biblical scholars, booksellers, translators, papermakers, calligraphers, illustrators, librarians, antiquarians, bookbinders, engravers, printers . . . Castelli, can you think of anyone else?'

'No.' Castelli continued his study of alabaster.

Old Riccardi stroked his white beard. 'What will we do with all these people once we have them?'

'Question them, of course.'

'And you expect them simply to tell you what they know about writings that have been successfully protected for centuries?'

Landucci started to twist his silk scarf from opposite corners. 'They'll probably need an incentive.' The plum flush had begun to rise from his collar again.

Old Riccardi smiled. 'The reward?'

Landucci stood and began to walk slowly around the

table. He held one corner of his scarf in each hand, twisting as he walked. He said, 'Certainly we'll offer a reward. But we both know any successful campaign must persuade those less likely to be swayed by greed.' The vein at his temple had begun to pulse.

'Ah. So you mean torture and murder.' Old Riccardi was nodding. 'The torture and murder of our finest minds. You would kill all of them, Maffeo? Where would that leave us? Again I ask, where would it end?'

'When I have my leverage over Borgia.'

Castelli tried to intervene. 'Riccardi, be reasonable. We must beat Borgia to it if Venice is ever going to get out from under Rome's thumb.'

Landucci had made his way around the table and now stood directly behind the old man. He said, 'Power isn't for the squeamish, Riccardi.'

'Why did you invite me here tonight, Maffeo? You knew I'd never agree to this.'

'Out of respect, Signor Riccardi. To give you the opportunity to agree.'

'I see.' Old Riccardi looked at Castelli, who had by then taken up the study of cutlery. 'Everyone else has already agreed, then?'

'I'm afraid we have.'

Castelli murmured, 'Please, Riccardi.'

'No.'

As Landucci slipped the grey silk around Riccardi's neck, the old man closed his eyes, but they flew open when Landucci jerked the scarf tight. Landucci grimaced as he executed a brutal twist and held it firm. Old Riccardi's eyes bulged, his mouth opened, his body bucked, then bucked again, and finally, *grazie a Dio*, he sagged. Landucci lowered the old man's forehead gently onto his last slice of sweet melon.

After Landucci slipped the silk scarf out from under the dead man, he sighed. 'Pity,' he said. 'Old Riccardi has succumbed to the heat. But he had a long life. It was his time, eh?' When there was no response, he looked at Castelli and spoke more slowly. 'I said, it was his time, eh, Castelli?'

Castelli tore himself away from the contemplation of the table linen. 'Yes,' he said. 'It was his time.'

Landucci returned to his place and gulped down his wine without bothering to sit. 'I'll arrange to move a cooperative senator into Riccardi's place on the council. After a decent period of mourning, we'll offer the vacant senate seat along with double the doge's reward for information about the book. Meanwhile, we'll dispatch the *Cappe Nere* as planned.'

Landucci rang for the footmen, and as soon as they opened the doors, Castelli rose and left without a word. Landucci addressed the footmen, who stood staring at Old Riccardi's limp form, his cheek lying on the melon. He said, 'Signor Riccardi has succumbed to the heat, may he rest in peace. Remove the body and inform the doge.' He tucked his scarf into his wine-stained vest and walked out.

Memories can play us false, and I know I didn't really hear the clatter of cloven hooves as Landucci left. But if I were a dreamer or a poet, I might describe the thump and slap of a ropy tail, the odour of sulphur, and the hat betraying a glimpse of horn. Yet, Landucci, a cold-blooded murderer, truly loved his son. When Castelli had mentioned the boy's death, Landucci's face clearly showed a father's grief. The murderer could feel love. At the time I wondered how it was possible to harbour both God's love and Satan's evil in the same heart. Now I think God and Satan have nothing to do with it.

After the footmen carried Old Riccardi away, I helped the maids clear the table and listened to the festival roaring in the street. My dear compatriots, so full of life – my *paesani* with their friendly lice, brown teeth, and honest black earth under their fingernails – at that moment, they seemed decent and solid people all.

But instead of rushing out to join them, I ran to the kitchen to tell the chef about Old Riccardi's murder. To my disappointment, the chef had already left for the day, and Pellegrino would be in charge of the kitchen for the entire week of La Sensa.

In no mood for celebration, I retired to the servants' dormitory and occupied myself with turning over the events of that evening in my head. I had many questions about what I'd heard. As for secret gospels to discredit Rome . . . well . . . I had heard that word – 'gospel' – before, but I had no idea what it meant.

CHAPTER ✦ XII

THE BOOK OF FORBIDDEN WRITINGS

I SUFFERED THE WHOLE WEEK of La Sensa, fretting through distracted days and restless nights, disturbed by the commotion in the streets, by discordant music, drunken shouts, ugly laughter and sudden screams. I twisted on my pallet enduring half sleeps tortured by dreams of fork-stabbed women and strangled men. Fortunately, no unusual challenges arose at work; the palace was quiet as the doge and other aristocrats remained sequestered during La Sensa, insulated from the frenzy in the streets, waiting quietly for the hilarity to run its course. Pellegrino ran the kitchen with ease, and I performed my duties in a sleep-deprived daze.

On the eighth morning, when the city lay in ruins from the festivities, I staggered down to the kitchen as exhausted as I'd ever been from any La Sensa. My gut burned, and the dry grit of sleeplessness scratched my eyes. I felt terribly alone with the horror I had witnessed, and I ached to confide in someone. When the chef arrived and sat down at his desk, I stumbled over and blurted, 'Landucci killed Old Riccardi, and he's looking for the book.'

The chef straightened his toque and looked at me a long time, his jaw tightening and releasing. He said, 'I know. Everyone knows.'

'Oh . . . I just thought—'

'Pellegrino,' the chef called, 'bring me a bunch of grapes and some raisins, eh?' Pellegrino brought the fruit, and the chef said, 'Let's take a walk, Luciano.'

'A walk?'

'Andiamo.' He left the tall hat on his desk, pocketed the raisins, and strode towards the back of the kitchen swinging his bunch of grapes. I followed obediently.

We walked through the courtyard and out into the dishevelled city. The chef shaded his eyes and peered down a canal varnished in morning light, then up at a Gothic spire soaring into a cerulean sky. He popped a grape into his mouth and said, 'Nice day, eh?'

'*Sì*, Maestro.'

'Grapes?' He broke off a small cluster and held it out to me.

'*Grazie.*'

We walked in the general direction of the Rialto, strolling across stone bridges and down cobbled *calli* littered with debris from La Sensa. Sweepers pushed broken glass, paper buntings and rotting food into the canals. The water swallowed the rubbish and added it to the decomposing sludge that winter storms jostled out to sea. Venice seemed able to digest unlimited amounts of decay.

The chef stopped in front of a small church and pointed up at a stained glass window. 'That glass is made right here in Venice.'

I had no idea what game we were playing. I nodded.

'Do you know how glass is made, Luciano?'

I'd seen Venetian glassblowers with long tubes pressed to their lips. They blew a pliable bubble of molten glass, which hung off the end, wobbly and malleable, and then they lopped it off and shaped it into bowls and vases before it cooled. But I didn't know anything about their formulas or techniques. I said, 'Not much.'

'Glass is two parts wood ash and one part sand that's heated to melting.' He smiled. 'Combine sand and fire and human ingenuity and achieve this.' He gestured at the stunning window blazing like a cache of gems in the morning sun. 'Amazing, eh?'

'Sì, Maestro.'

The chef pointed to the glass saints clad in robes of sapphire and amethyst. He said, 'You add cobalt to make blue, manganese for purple and copper for red.'

'Sì.' I was lost.

He gestured at the window. 'Saints and virgins; that's all they allow. *Boh*. What a waste of talent.' He lowered his voice. 'There are ancient cave paintings in France, astonishing things. With few strokes and little colour, they show the beauty and terror of nature – lines so fluid you expect them to move. Those paintings mark the birth of art, but very few know . . .' He glanced around and cleared his throat. '*Basta*. We'll save that for another time.' He continued walking, kicking aside an empty wine bottle here, a half-eaten fig there, and I scrambled along. 'So sand becomes glass; add a mineral and it glows with colour. Would you call that alchemy?' He offered me more grapes.

I took the grapes, thinking, *Ahhhh, so* that's *it*. 'Is alchemy the secret in the book?'

'Is that what you want it to be?'

'What? No. I mean . . . I don't care.' I ate a grape and remembered Old Riccardi talking about a formula to make bronze and asking, 'Why not gold?' I said, 'Is alchemy possible?'

'Many brilliant men dabble in alchemy.'

'You mean—'

'What do you know about this book, Luciano?' The chef stopped and faced me.

I scratched my neck to stall while my brain whirred, searching for the right answer. I wanted to ask 'What do *you* know?' But I said, 'The doge and Landucci want it for different reasons. But no one seems to know exactly what's in it. I've heard talk of alchemy and an elixir for immortality—'

The chef threw back his head and laughed so heartily I saw the horseshoe shape of his upper teeth. 'An elixir. How completely they miss the point. What else?'

I kept my voice even. 'A love potion?'

'*Boh.*'

Merda! He was lying. I willed my face to go blank. 'But, Maestro, I think love potions *are* known to some people. And I, for one, would find a love potion very useful.'

He raised one eyebrow. 'Would you now?'

My blank expression collapsed, and my voice acquired an urgent edge. 'I told you about Francesca. She's in a convent, and I've embarrassed myself in front of her. Now I need a miracle to win her.'

'*Dio*, Luciano. She's a nun. Don't be a fool.'

I felt pressure behind my eyes, and I blinked fast. 'Please, Maestro. Don't ridicule me. I thirst, and she's like salt water. The more I see her the more I want her. I suffer for her. She's the light of my life.'

The chef sucked at his teeth and considered me. He said, 'I'm sorry you suffer, but you're mistaken. The light of your life is within you.'

'What?'

'*Basta.*' He fixed me with a stern look. 'This book. What else have you heard?'

I decided to try out the words that had meant so much to Landucci. 'I heard something about secret gospels.'

'All right.' He nodded. 'What about them?'

'Nothing. Only that Landucci wants to use them against Rome.'

'You can call that nothing?' The chef pulled a hand through his hair. 'Are you out of your mind?'

'Maestro, what's a gospel?'

His mouth dropped open a little. 'Of course. How would *you* know the gospels?'

I winced at the slight emphasis he put on 'you'. How would *you* know? Everyone in the world would know the gospels, but not Luciano, the *stupido*. I stuck out my chin to demonstrate my indignation, but the chef seemed not to notice.

He said, 'I'll tell you about the gospels, but you mustn't go around repeating what I say. You could get into serious trouble. Can I trust you to be discreet?'

'*Sì.*' Stealth had long been my way of life. 'I'm good at keeping secrets.'

'*D'accordo.* You once asked why I was interested in the writings of the dead. In time, I'll teach you to read and you'll begin to understand. For now I'll just tell you that some of those writings are gospels – stories about the life of Jesus. Of course, you know who Jesus was.'

'*Sì,* Maestro. Everyone knows Jesus is God.'

'*Boh.* Jesus was a teacher.'

I wasn't versed in theology, but this sounded heretical. 'Not God?'

The chef sighed. 'They talk about three gods in one or one

in three, depending on who you ask.' He rolled his eyes. 'What a tale. God arranges to torture and kill his son, who is also himself, in order to forgive sins not yet committed. It makes no sense. If a compassionate God wanted to forgive, why not just forgive? I'll tell you why: there's not enough drama in that. No blood, no pathos, it's flat. But human sacrifice to atone for sin is a compelling idea borrowed from paganism. It's primitive and emotional. It's an old favourite.'

It was too much information thrown at me too quickly. I said, 'I don't understand three gods in one.'

'Of course you don't. No one does. The church says it's a virtue to be satisfied with not understanding. Questions are a nuisance.'

I scratched my head.

'Luciano. Pay attention.' The chef plucked a grape from the cluster and held it up. 'This is a grape, eh? Smooth outside, juicy inside.'

'Sì.'

With his other hand, he dug a raisin out of his pocket and held it next to the grape. 'A raisin, eh? Wrinkled and dry.'

'Sì.'

'As sand transforms into glass, a grape withers into a raisin.'

'Sì. Like magic.'

'No.' The chef gave me a warning look. 'It's a natural process. Take a handful of sand, a grape, or a gospel, then add something or leave something out, subject it to time or men's meddling, and change is inevitable.' He ate the raisin and the grape and seemed pleased with himself.

I said, 'The gospels have been changed?'

'Sì.' The chef picked a piece of raisin from his teeth. 'The gospels have been fought over, copied and recopied, translated and mistranslated. *Madre di Dio*, I wouldn't be surprised if they'd been wadded into balls and kicked around for sport.'

It seemed to me all that tampering would make them worthless. 'How do you know what to believe?'

'Exactly!' The chef raised a stiff finger, and his eyes blazed like the glass saints. 'Always examine what you believe. Christians call Jesus a god, as if that's an original idea, but pagans have half-human gods all over the place.' He shifted his jaw as if someone had struck him. 'Personally, I think creating gods in our own image is arrogant.

'And that business about a virgin mother? Ha! All the pagan gods had virgin mothers. But, ask yourself, why is a virgin better than a natural mother, like my Rosa?' He sniffed. 'As if women are polluted by men. It's insulting. But Jesus knew better. Some of his closest disciples were women. God is inside *all* of us.'

'Really?' *Marrone.* If God was inside me, it meant there was hope for me. I said, 'I like that idea. Why should it be a secret?'

'Power.' Chef Ferrero clenched his jaw. 'Now we get to the heart of it. Let's sit.' He walked to the canal and swept a scrambled mass of paper streamers off a bridge's stone step. He sat there and gestured for me to sit next to him, which I did with a sense of unease – he looked pensive and grim.

The chef rested his elbows on his knees and said, 'I want to tell you a story. Hundreds of years ago, a man named Irenaeus condemned most of the writings about Jesus as heresy, and they were driven underground. He chose four gospels he liked and devoted his life to creating a church around them. He called it the Catholic Church.'

'But the condemned gospels were saved?' I felt a twitch of understanding. 'They're in the book?'

'Some saved, some lost, some, we think, still hidden and undiscovered. We call them the Gnostic gospels – Gnostic means "wisdom", eh? – and what matters is their message. They tell us that we don't need a church between us and God.' The chef locked eyes with me. 'God is inside you.'

'Me?'

'You, me, all of us. Embrace yourself, Luciano. You're better than you think.'

'But if the gospels have been changed, why should we believe the Gnostic gospels any more than the others?'

'If you're going to believe anything out of a book, use your head.' The chef pointed to my forehead and raised his eyebrows. 'The Gnostic gospels, and even three of the approved gospels, say that Jesus was a man who carried God inside him, just like the rest of us. Jesus wanted us to look within and see that part of ourselves. His message was not about some kingdom *out there*; it was about enlightenment *in here*.' The chef laid the flat of his hand on his chest. 'That message is repeated in many texts, but that "Son of God" business is not. So, if you use your head, you can see that it makes more sense to believe the thing that is repeated and corroborated rather than the thing that is not.'

'Sì, but . . . Irenaeus is dead.' The chef had given me permission to think for myself and I was suddenly full of questions. 'So, if the Gnostic gospels make sense why are they still secret?'

'Irenaeus may be dead, but his church isn't. The idea that we need priests to intercede for us is convenient for a church that governs with absolute power. In fact, the beginning of the Roman church came about through a political power play. When Constantine, the first Christian emperor, moved his court from Rome to Constantinople, he left a supervisor in his place. That was the first pope.'

'A Roman supervisor?'

'*Sì*. It was a matter of the emperor keeping control over Rome.' The chef made a fist and clenched it so tightly his arm trembled. 'It was an iron control that brought centuries of intellectual darkness when men who dared to think freely did so at their own peril. The church will do anything to maintain control. They've even waged bloody wars under the banner of religion, simply to hold onto their power.'

'*Marrone.*'

'History is instructive, but the church's history . . . well . . .' The chef slumped a bit. 'As you learn more – and you will because I'll teach you – try not to let it make you bitter.'

I nodded. 'I'll try, Maestro.'

'Do you understand now? The Gnostic gospels have political power because their message undermines the church. Those gospels interest dangerous men, and you shouldn't meddle in things you don't understand. For Landucci and Borgia, this is about politics and power. For the doge, it's personal, but it's still risky to get in his way.'

'How do you know all this, Maestro?'

He gave me an odd smile. 'A teacher has a responsibility to get his facts straight.'

'A teacher?'

'Just remember, churches are man's invention.'

I couldn't help thinking about all the decent people who flocked to church every Sunday and fell on their knees. I said, 'But people truly *believe*.'

'*Sì*. Blind faith is what allows churches to manipulate them.' The chef grabbed my shoulder and squeezed. He looked angry and his eyes pinned me in place. 'Never believe blindly, Luciano. Never!'

I was fascinated by the chef's passion, and a little frightened too. I said, '*Sì*, Maestro.'

He let go of my shoulder, and we sat for a while watching the canal. Eventually he murmured, 'Poor Jesus. He was a good Jew, and he preached a decent method of living. Someone should try it sometime.'

'Jesus was a Jew?'

He nodded. 'A devout Jew all his life. Jesus had no intention of starting a new religion. He obeyed Jewish law and preached only to Jews. He never told anyone to take his message to the pagan Greeks, but Paul did anyway. That's how Greek myths got mixed in with Christian doctrine. What a mess. Like adding the wrong spice to a pot of soup. It changes the flavour, and not always for the better, eh?'

I thought of the Venetian Jews I'd seen in the Rialto, mysterious people in sombre clothes, a people apart herded into their secluded ghetto and forbidden to come out after dark – and those restrictions imposed by Christians? I wondered what other ideas history had twisted. 'What else is in the book?'

'Science, art, philosophy, history, animal husbandry . . .' The chef raised a hand and inscribed circles in the air as if the list was far too long to recite. 'Even a little cooking.'

'*Marrone*. That must be a big book.'

He nodded. 'A teacher named Socrates said that knowledge is the source of good and ignorance is the source of evil.' He gave a sad snort. 'They killed him, too. People hate having their beliefs challenged. But trust me, there's more to know in this life than church doctrine. Human potential is . . . well . . . maybe Jesus wasn't the only one who could work miracles. Maybe we all can.'

I grinned. 'Now you're joking.'

He gave me a queer half smile. 'Human beings have untapped potential. But they're easily led because they don't trust themselves. That's why the church calls them sheep. Learn to trust yourself, Luciano.'

For the first time, I saw that accepting anything without examining it was not virtuous and I wanted to ask a question that, until that moment, had seemed vaguely blasphemous. 'If we're not supposed to think, why would God give us brains?'

The chef smiled. 'Very good, Luciano.' He stood up and dusted off his pants. 'I knew you'd understand.'

Seeing my maestro in good spirits comforted me. Perhaps the situation at the palace was not so dire. Perhaps the murders and machinations signified nothing more than individual men manoeuvring to hold onto their power. Perhaps the real power lay in the chef's secret knowledge.

Feeling reassured, my empty stomach began to overtake my interest in history, and I wanted something more substantial than grapes. We were in the Rialto, and the wheels of cheese, bushels of apples and baskets of fish sharpened the hollow feeling in my stomach. I hoped the chef might buy us a bite of breakfast.

When Chef Ferrero stopped at the stall of a German baker, my stomach purred. Although the Germans were disparaged for their rough manners and greasy food, when it comes to bread they have always been the masters. I almost groaned at the sight of lustrous rye breads infused with honey, a braided egg-bread sprinkled with toasted almonds, and a savoury batard with flecks of dill in the burnished crust. The aroma made saliva well up and pool under my tongue.

The chef purchased a cinnamon sweetbread, and then we went on to the stall of a greengrocer, where he bought two blood-red apples. We took our breakfast to a small, quiet piazza and sat on a public bench in the shade of a neighbourhood church. Before breaking bread, the chef asked, 'Do you know much about making bread, Luciano?'

'A little.' At that moment I only knew the smell of it was driving me mad.

'Bread is one of man's greatest feats of alchemy. Flour, water, yeast, a bit of salt, the right technique, and *presto* – bread.'

'I understand, Maestro. You alter something, and it becomes something else. Are we going to eat that?'

To my great relief, he broke the loaf and handed me half. I bit into it gratefully. While we chewed, we watched a squadron of old women in black dresses hobble into the church for morning Mass. One of them gave a mean kick to a drunk passed out in the church doorway, a victim of La Sensa. She hissed, '*Ubriacone*,' shot him the evil eye, and scurried inside. The chef said, 'You can't escape the church. It lives inside people.'

With bulging cheeks and bread crumbs on my lips, I nodded politely. I'd had enough talk about the church for one day; I was more interested in the fact that some new bond of trust was being forged between the chef and me. I said, 'Thank you for confiding in me about the Gnostic gospels. I feel privileged, Maestro.'

'And what have you learned?'

'That the gospels are powerful and worth preserving.'

'And?'

'I have God inside me?'

'*Bene.*' The chef bit into his bread and chewed thoughtfully. His Adam's apple bobbed as he swallowed, then he said, 'What I've told you is controversial, and talking about it could be dangerous. So keep your mouth shut, eh?'

'*Sì*, Maestro.'

'You may decline to know more if you wish.'

Me decline to know more? Not likely. Very carefully, I asked, 'Maestro, do you have the book?'

The chef screwed up his mouth as if I had posed a difficult philosophical problem. 'It's not that simple.'

'It's not?'

He bit off a corner of the bread and chewed slowly. 'Let's say I share certain information with others.'

'You could be in danger.'

'That depends.'

'On what?'

'Perhaps on you.'

'Good. Then there's no danger. I would never betray you.'

'That's my hope.' The chef put a hand on my shoulder and squeezed. 'You are my hope, Luciano.'

I thought of his daughters – Elena, his pride; the twins, his wonder; Natalia, his joy. And I was his hope? Like a son? 'Maestro,' I said. 'I'm honoured.'

'Good.' He took his hand away. 'You should be.' He proffered one of the apples and asked, 'Do you know the story of Adam and Eve?'

'The one about the first people?' I took the apple and polished it on my sleeve.

The chef nodded. 'It tells of the creation of Eve from Adam's rib.'

'That's a strange idea.' I couldn't think of any woman I knew who would appreciate that. I bit into my apple with a wet crunch.

The chef took a bite of his apple and then held it out to appraise the white flesh. He said, 'The story of Adam and Eve isn't supposed to be taken literally.'

'No?' I chomped down happily.

'No.' The chef watched me eat and said, 'That story is a parable, like Jesus's stories.'

I worked my way around the apple, thinking, *Marrone,* the chef really knows how to choose well.

'Your ribs are right here, over your heart.' Lightly, he tapped the left side of my chest. 'Some of my writings say Eve's birth from the region of Adam's heart speaks of spiritual awakening. That this spiritual awakening marks the beginning of humankind.'

'That's a better story.' I was down to the apple core, and out of long habit I began to eat it.

'Sì, a better story. But people may choose to embrace their spirituality or not. So there's also a story about a fruit tree, the tree of knowledge.'

I nodded as I finished off the apple core, seeds and all.

'Adam chose not to eat from the tree, but Eve, his spiritual side, persuaded him to taste the fruit of knowledge. You see? Knowledge, Luciano – that's how they awaken to the fullness of their humanity.' He watched me wipe apple juice off my mouth with the back of my hand and added, 'The fruit they ate was an apple.'

'An apple?' My hand stalled at my mouth. My lap was covered in bread crumbs, but nothing remained of the apple. I felt the weight of it in my stomach, already becoming part of me. If I had ever wondered how closely my hunger for knowing *everything* might bind me to the chef, I knew the answer in that moment. I'd eaten the whole apple, and there was no going back.

That night, as everyone slept, I crept down into the kitchen to make another attempt at a dish to impress my maestro; I wanted him to know his faith in me was not misplaced. I fired up the brick oven, reminding myself that garlic has no place in a confection and butter becomes a layer of oil floating atop the cheese. I felt confident and excited; this time I would get it right.

I helped myself to the triple-cream cheese (still convinced it would make a delicious base) and then added a dollop of honey to sweeten it and heavy cream to thin it enough for my whisk. Since my last endeavour, I'd noticed that wine was primarily used in sauces and stews, and so, in a moment of blind inspiration, I added, instead, a splash of almond liqueur, which I hoped would add subtle flavour without changing the creamy colour of the cheese. Instead of the roach-like raisins, I threw in a handful of chopped almonds that I imagined would provide a satisfying crunch and harmonize with the liqueur.

I beat it all to a smooth batter and poured it into a square pan, intending to cut rectangular slices after it cooled. I slid the pan, hopefully, into the oven. Once again, I watched the edges bubble and noticed, with satisfaction, that instead of an overpowering smell of garlic there was a warm seductive hint of almond in the air. The bubbles turned to a froth that danced over the entire surface, and I assumed this was a sign of cohesion. My creation would come out of the oven like firm custard with undertones of almond and an unexpected crunch. The rectangular servings would make an unusual presentation – neither cheese nor pudding nor custard, but something completely new and unique.

The bubbling froth subsided to a gently bumpy surface, and to my horror those damnable pockmarks began to appear with oil percolating in the tiny craters. The nuts completed the disruption of the creamy texture and gave the whole thing a crude curdled look.

If only this cross-breed concoction would cohere, it might yet be cut up into squares and served on a plate with some appealing garnish, perhaps strawberries and mint leaves for colour. I took the pan out and stared at it as it cooled, willing it to stand up, pull itself together, *be firm*. When the pan was cool enough to touch, I dipped my spoon into the mixture and it came out dripping and coated in something with the consistency of buttermilk. It didn't taste bad at all, in fact I licked the spoon clean, enjoying the balance of sweetness and almond, but it wasn't anything I could present to the chef. It was like a sweet, cheesy soup into which someone had accidentally dropped nuts. Why was the cheese breaking down? Why wasn't it holding together like cake or custard?

Discouraged, I didn't even try to interest Bernardo in this latest disaster. I dumped it into the rubbish pail, noticing that honey had scorched the bottom of the pan, forcing me to scrape and scrub with a stiff brush, and I went to bed angry. This one had been promising. It had tasted good; I had come so close. Somehow, I had to find out what would make it hold together.

CHAPTER ✤ XIII

THE BOOK OF MARCO

THE FOLLOWING MORNING DAWNED CLEAR and cool, and the chef decided to send me to the Rialto to buy pears and Gorgonzola. It was a culinary test, and I was ready. I'd accompanied him on other shopping trips when he instructed me on how to judge pears by scent and colour and touch. They must be bought at the absolute peak of ripeness, with no hint of green or bruising. They must be firm, though not hard, and well perfumed, ready to be eaten the same day but overripe the next. The cheese must be *dolce*, not *piccante*, because it would be served with the pears for dessert. The ripeness of Gorgonzola is more forgiving than pears. Already veined with a pungent mould, it will last a good while, although even moulded cheeses have their limits. When I lived in the streets I once scavenged Gorgonzola with worms peeking out of their crumbly blue caves.

Chef Ferrero gave me a handful of coppers to buy two dozen pears and two kilos of cheese. It was a show of trust in my honesty, as well as my ability to select correctly and negotiate well. I dropped the coins in my pocket, grabbed a market basket, and bounded down the length of the kitchen. Near the back door, I picked up a bulb of fennel for Domingo and hurried out through the courtyard. I was eager to get to the Rialto and catch a glimpse of *la mia bella* Francesca.

The Rialto has always been the great marketplace of Venice, her thumping commercial heart. The docks of the Grand Canal are always jammed with ships, and the quays are crowded with porters. I loved to watch the bustle of buying and selling – spices and gold, oil and emeralds, tigers and teakwood – the constant hum of haggling and barter, the swarm of languages, the people talking with hands and feet.

And the colours! Since most of the people in the Rialto were foreign – or illiterate like me – craftsmen hung out multicoloured signs in picture language: a cluster of purple grapes for the vintner, green bottles for the apothecary, a gilded unicorn for the goldsmith, a stippled mare's head for the harness maker . . . the marketplace was a gaudy picture book come to life.

In addition to the shops of craftsmen, the greater Rialto spread out through a tangle of narrow alleys lined with food stalls. In the butchers' quarter, slaughtering was done on the spot and blood dried in the sun amid piles of offal swarming with iridescent flies. That was my least favourite area. I felt slightly nauseated by the lowing of frightened animals and by the butchers with bloody smears on their hands and clothes. Sometimes, even their hair was matted with brown clots of drying blood. Ugh. It was almost enough to make me lose my taste for meat. Almost. My maestro transformed meat into appetizing creations that bore no resemblance to those doomed animals.

The other stalls were cheerier. Near the harbour, fish merchants presided over tables heaped with black mussels and silvery fish from Brittany glittering on ice. In December, great blocks of snow were brought from the Alps packed in straw and then stored underground in thick-walled ice houses where they easily kept for a year or more. Domingo's fishmonger was never stingy with his ice, which is why his catch stayed fresh and brought him some of Venice's wealthiest clients, like the doge's chef.

As I ran past the fishmongers, Domingo waved and called out, 'Hey, Luciano. *Ciao*, eh.' He nudged the fishmonger. 'There goes Luciano. My friend.'

I felt too hurried to stop that day. I threw him the bulb of fennel and called out, 'Eat it with trout.'

At the poultry stall, geese honked and gabbled, and I flapped my arms and honked back. Amputated chicken feet (excellent for soup) hung in bunches, and ducks with trussed legs squawked in twig cages. Sometimes I tossed stale bread crumbs into their cages. The duck merchant loved that; fatter ducks meant fatter profits.

Even the narrow canals around the Rialto teemed with floating shops – a small barge piled with jumbled green grapes, a boat heaped with oranges and limes, and another listing under a mountain of melons. I jogged along, drunk on all the colours and smells of the known world: pyramids of blood oranges from Greece, slender green beans from Morocco, sun-ripened cherries from Provence, giant white cabbages from Germany, fat black dates from Constantinople, and shiny purple aubergines from Holland. I hurried through this edible maze, my old home, fighting the urge to pinch something whenever a vendor turned his back. I no longer needed to steal food, but habits of survival die hard.

I passed a stall offering pears picked that morning on the mainland; they were still warm from the sun, their leaves still fleshy and alive. I noted the location for later, after Francesca.

A popular cheese merchant stood in his stall behind a barrel of hand-tied balls of mozzarella floating in buffalo milk. He called to passersby, 'Come, *signori*. Smell my perfectly aged Parmigiano. Look at my beautiful Manchego, just in from Spain. Try some. You'll fall in love.' But his great wheel of Gorgonzola *dolce* overpowered the aroma of everything else. I'd come back for it after I bought the pears. First, though, I'd find Francesca.

At that time of the morning, I'd often seen her in the street of olives, so I took a shortcut through the dark, smoky street of copyists. The copyists, who served as secretaries for the illiterate, were solemn old men sitting in straight-backed chairs with wooden writing boards laid across the chair arms. Many wore long beards and girlish curls along the sides of their faces. Some wore skullcaps on the backs of their heads; others wore prayer boxes strapped to their foreheads; a few wore fringed shawls and amulets around their necks. But they all looked alike to me. The copyists were Jews. Forbidden to own property, Jews turned to merchandising, money lending and academics. The copyists were some of the most scholarly men in Venice.

Their implements lay spread out before them: a razor for scraping crude parchment clean, a pumice stone to smooth it, a long narrow ruler, and a boar's tooth for polishing the finished product. Each writing board held ox horns with different coloured inks to dip their well-seasoned quills into, and all the copyists kept a basin of hot coals at their feet to dry the ink. Those braziers created the dense, smoky air that made me hold my breath as I ran a zigzag around their little islands of literacy.

When I lived in the streets, I seldom went near the copyists. I only used their street as a shortcut or a place to hide. The sooty air scratched my throat, and there was nothing to steal but an occasional scrap of gold leaf that, with gentle handling, might be traded for bread, but more often disintegrated in my sweaty fist. Near the end of the street of copyists, a figure ran towards me at high speed. His shape and gait were familiar, and then I spotted the red hair – Marco. He'd stolen something and was running for cover, as we'd so often done together. We saw each other at the same moment, and instinctively I ran with him into a cul-de-sac full of waste and alive with rats.

We squatted next to a heap of rubbish and Marco, breathing hard, looked me over. He let out a low, sneering whistle and said, 'You look softer every time I see you.' He pulled a carrot from under his filthy shirt and ignored me while he devoured it. There were rings of dirt around his neck, his oily hair stood out from his head in russet clumps, and an open sore festered on his arm. His eyes were red rimmed and oozing something sticky. The sight of him made me feel guilty and slightly ashamed of my clean clothes.

That morning, preoccupied with seeing Francesca, I'd only grabbed the bulb of fennel for Domingo, knowing I'd pass his stall. I hadn't expected to run into Marco. I sat back and let one protective hand fall over the pocket weighted with the chef's coppers. A fly buzzed my face but I didn't swat it, fearing the sudden movement might alert Marco to the jingle of coins. Food scraps were good, but money would be much better.

Marco finished eating his carrot and then rummaged

in the rubbish heap. He asked, 'Did you bring me anything?'

'Sorry, I have nothing today, but I'll put something out tonight.'

He pulled a heel of bread from the waste, brushed off a coating of dirt and mould, and then bit down, but it was too hard. *'Merda.'* He threw the hunk of bread at a wall and it clunked against the brick as if he'd thrown a rock. Then he turned to me and brightened. 'Hey, I might have seen Rufina last night. There was a girl about the right age with red hair, just like mine, right outside the brothel where my mother worked. But she went inside with a sailor before I could talk to her. I'm going back tonight.' He hitched up his baggy pants. 'Why are you out of the kitchen?' He appraised my shopping basket and then said, 'You're going to the Rialto, aren't you? You're shopping for the chef. Do you have money?'

I barked a short incredulous laugh and hoped that a grain of truth would make the whole story believable. Crouched together as we were, his face was close to mine and I forced a look of boredom. 'Money? Do I look like the king of Spain? I'm going to the street of olives to look for Francesca.'

'I don't believe you. What's the basket for?'

'To *look* like I'm shopping. I can't just stand around and stare at her.'

'A nun.' He shook his head. 'You're wasting your time.'

'What do you know?' I jumped up and flicked a contemptuous thumb off my front teeth. Too late, I heard the jangle of coins in my pocket.

Marco stared at my pocket. 'You *do* have money.'

'I have to buy pears for the chef.' I stepped back.

He jutted his chin in the direction of the palace. 'You're becoming like them.'

'I can't give you any money, Marco.' *Marrone,* I hated to

hear myself. I ate three good meals a day and slept warm and dry every night, and poor Marco still had nothing. I wanted to offer him something, anything, to ease my guilt and also to distract him from the money. I squatted back down, moved closer to him, and lowered my voice, 'Listen, I really can't give you this money, and I'm sorry I have no food today, but I'll tell you a secret.'

Marco sulked. 'I can't eat secrets.'

'I know something about the book.'

Marco flicked a grimy hand in dismissal, but a glint of interest flashed in his eyes. He said, 'Tell me how to get the reward. That's all the book is worth to me.'

'The book is more valuable than the reward. The doge is killing people to find it, and' – I paused for effect – 'Landucci wants it.'

'Landucci? Is he dying of syphilis, too?'

'There's no formula for immortality, Marco.'

'*Merda*. I know that. Why does Landucci want it?'

I would never repeat what the chef had confided, but gospels wouldn't interest Marco anyway. I knew what he wanted to hear. 'You were right, big brother. Old Riccardi said it might be possible to make gold.' I stood and leaned against the wall, crossing my arms with nonchalance and hoping to look worldly-wise. Marco and I would never see that reward, but if I couldn't feed his stomach at least I could feed his fantasies.

Marco jumped up and began pacing the cul-de-sac, kicking at bits of rubbish, clenching and unclenching his hands. 'I *knew* it! Gold is what this world is about.' He faced me and I flinched at the sight of his pink eyes inflamed with excitement. He said, 'We have to get it.'

'The book? Us?' I should have seen that coming, but it was preposterous. 'Marco, we can't even read.'

'You live in the palace. You can know what they know. As soon as they find the book, we steal it.' He dusted off his hands. 'Easy.'

Marrone. 'Marco, these are dangerous people. Landucci has the *Cappe Nere* out looking for this book. They're ready to torture and kill anyone – everyone. You want to steal from *them*?'

'It's worth the risk.' Marco was almost vibrating with excitement.

'No. It isn't. Listen, I don't know for sure that the book has the secret of alchemy. Old Riccardi only said it was *possible*. But it's too dangerous—'

'Selfish!' Marco moved his face close to mine, and I held my breath against his rank odour. 'You risk nothing bringing me scraps of food. But when it really matters, when you have something to lose, you're a coward. I took plenty of risks to train you, to keep you alive.'

'I know, but—'

'But nothing. You're one of us, not them.' Marco pushed his chin towards the palace again. 'Come on, Luciano. With you on the inside, we have a chance.'

'But the chef—'

'*Merda* on the chef. The chef keeps you for a slave.'

'No.'

'You're a fool. He'll never promote you. Why should he? What has he taught you – to wash dishes and haul wood? Why doesn't he promote you? What does he keep in that secret cabinet you told me about? How did he make that magic sauce? He's a strange one, your chef. People talk, you know. Maybe he's a sorcerer.'

'Oh, Marco.'

'Then why all the secrecy? I bet his secret cabinet could tell a good story. I'll bet he has all kinds of magic potions in there.'

'You're crazy, Marco.' But he'd hit a few nerves. First, I did still wash dishes and haul wood. My one cooking lesson had been slicing an onion. Useless. I performed my chores well and faithfully, but he hadn't even mentioned a promotion. The gospels were interesting, but they really had nothing to do with me. Second, the chef did keep a secret cabinet, and he did refuse to explain his Sauce Nepenthes. Third – most grievous of all, and something Marco didn't even know about – the chef had lied to me about having a love potion. When Marco mentioned potions in the cabinet I remembered hearing Signora Ferrero pouring a drink in their bedroom while she giggled and teased; I remembered that rich, dark smell. Magic potions? Is that why he kept the cabinet locked?

A new thought presented itself: Maybe the chef was trying to distract me with talk of reading and secret writings so that he didn't have to promote me.

Marco smiled his sly, brown-toothed smile and slumped back to the ground. 'Believe what you want about your chef.' He lounged against the wall and knitted his fingers behind his head. 'But if you want to get that nun out of her convent, you'll need plenty of help. Some say that book has a love potion. We both know that without a love potion or a pile of gold, she'll never look at you. I bet some rich cardinal already has his eye on her.' Marco knew how to get to me.

He spotted the uncertainty in my eyes and he pounced. 'We could be rich, Luciano. You could have Francesca. We could all go to the New World. Tell me, how could our happiness harm your chef. How?'

Marco saw my growing confusion and milked it. 'As it is, with her in a convent and you so scared . . .' He shrugged.

'Who said I was scared?'

'You did. You won't take a risk. Not even for Francesca and

the New World. You're a big disappointment, Luciano. I didn't think you were such a coward.' Marco picked at his scabby arm.

Riddles about secret gospels suddenly seemed completely irrelevant. What did the manipulations of priests and politicians have to do with me? How *could* my happiness hurt the chef? Why *hadn't* he mentioned a promotion? But still . . . 'Marco, we'd better think about this. First of all, we can't even read.'

Marco's voice turned cajoling. 'What's become of you, Cabbage-Head? We're smart. We can learn to read. We can do anything we set our minds to.'

He was right. We'd never let anything stop us before. Maybe I *was* getting soft. I'd promised never to betray the chef, but the love potion had nothing to do with his secret gospels. I was only slightly surprised to hear myself say, 'I suppose I could keep my eyes open.'

'That's my little brother.' Marco smiled and jumped up. I clamped a hand over my money-filled pocket, but he laughed at me. 'Don't worry. Why would I take a few coppers from the little brother who's going to help me get the formula for making gold? Go do your errands, like a good slave. *Ciao*, Luciano.' He waved, and then he was gone.

I lingered in the foul cul-de-sac, biting my bottom lip and trying to understand what exactly had just happened. By the time I walked out to the street of copyists, Marco had disappeared amid the overlapping pillars of smoke.

I had stayed too long with Marco and I couldn't spare the time to look for Francesca in the street of olives. The sun was high, and I consoled myself with the thought that Francesca, who shopped in the morning, had probably gone back to the convent by then. I imagined her tatting lace handkerchiefs, her slim fingers manipulating thread and needles – lucky needles. I plunged my hands into my pockets and grumbled a string of curses as I retraced my steps to the fruit and cheese stalls.

I chose my pears carefully, examining each with eyes and nose and a light touch. I selected only the plumpest and rejected one with a faint blemish that the vendor tried to hide in his palm. I congratulated myself on my keen eye, knowing my maestro would be impressed. And it *would* matter because I was *not* a slave and he *would* promote me.

I bargained with the cheese merchant and watched closely as he cut a large wedge of Gorgonzola. When he weighed it, I stood near his scale so that he couldn't cheat. Grumpily, he wrapped the cheese and dropped it in my basket. The cheese was ripe, the pears were perfect, and a few coppers still clinked in my pocket.

I should have been happy, but I walked back to the palace brooding over Marco's insidious words. Slave? *Boh*, what did he know? I'd get my promotion, and if I learned anything about alchemy along the way, fine, I'd share it with him. As long as I didn't betray the chef there would be no problem. It wouldn't be hard to keep Marco away from the chef; he never came to the kitchen because he envied my job, and it galled him to see me there. Marco always waited for me to come to him. Marco would never cause a problem with the chef. Marco was . . . *right there*?

There he stood, in the courtyard, right next to the kitchen door, bold as day, waiting for me. He stepped into my path, saying, 'Looks like a feast tonight.' He massaged his concave stomach and I heard the growl of that solitary carrot being digested. 'Or do you eat like this every night?'

'Stop it. Here, take a pear.'

'Only one? You eat three times a day.'

'*Marrone*. All right. Take two.'

Marco plucked two rosy pears from the top of the basket. I said, 'Marco, you shouldn't be here.'

'Why not? You owe me. Do you have any money left?'

Marco had the look of all street boys, a mingling of fear and defiance spilling from deep, hungry eyes, and I remembered the desperate feeling that went with that look. 'In my pocket,' I said. 'I have a few coppers left. Take them and get out of here.' I felt him dig the coins out of my pocket and I knew the chef would be furious. He'd think I'd been too stupid to pay the right price.

Marco closed the money in his grimy fist. 'I knew I could count on you, Luciano. You're not so soft. Together, we'll get that book.'

'Marco—'

'I'll be back tomorrow.'

CHAPTER XIV

THE BOOK OF SUSPICIONS

I ENTERED THE KITCHEN LIKE a backward sneak thief, intending to leave booty rather than take it. Quickly and quietly, I unwrapped the pears and Gorgonzola on a side table, hoping to bring in wood before the chef noticed I was back. Later, after he'd counted the pears, I'd feign my well-practised innocent look while I claimed that I'd left two dozen pears and a handful of coppers on the table. I'd scratch my head and wonder out loud what might have happened. Maybe I'd nod towards Giuseppe and pull my eyelid. But as I turned to make my getaway, I found myself facing Chef Ferrero.

He stood with his head cocked at a sceptical angle, and he aimed a rigid index finger at the pears. The finger jabbed in time with his count: '*Uno. Due. Tre. Quattro. Cinque* . . .' He counted to twenty-two. 'Didn't I tell you to buy twenty-four pears, Luciano? I know you can't read, but I myself taught you to count.'

'The other pears were no good, Maestro. Bruised. Ugly.'

'In the Rialto, where mountains of fruit come from every corner of the world, you found only twenty-two good pears?'

'Sì, Maestro.'

'Hmm. Where's my change?'

'I have no change, Maestro.'

'I see. Pears have suddenly become very dear.'

I nodded. 'Very dear.'

The chef regarded me with philosopher's eyes for what felt like an eternity. He said, 'You have hungry friends out there, don't you, Luciano?'

'No! I mean . . .' I felt sweat blooming under my arms. I couldn't lie to him. I would take my punishment. 'Yes, Maestro. I do have hungry friends. I gave away two pears and the few coppers I had left.'

'They weren't yours to give.'

'I know and I'll make amends. Tomorrow, I'll steal two pears to replace what I gave away.'

'No, you won't.'

'I had to do it. If you saw his face . . . Have you ever been hungry, Maestro?'

'Yes, actually, I have been hungry. Not for a long time, but I remember. All right. Pears have become dear, and we're lucky to get the last good ones, eh?' He ruffled my hair and passed his hand over my birthmark. 'You have a good heart, Luciano. And you told the truth. That's worth more than pears. Now bring in the wood.'

'What?'

'Are you deaf?'

'That's it? That's all?'

'What do you want? A medal for your kindness? Get to work.'

I walked away amazed. Chef Ferrero's readiness to forgive

was too far evolved for my suspicious, streetwise young mind to comprehend. In my world, we called people like him fools, yet I knew he was no fool. I simply couldn't comprehend the scope of his kindness.

Marco, on the other hand, was easy to understand. Marco would be furious if he ever suspected I'd cheated him, and he wouldn't care a whit that it had been done for charity. And why should he? No one needed charity more than he.

I identified more closely with Marco than I did with the chef, and that's why Marco's corrosive words worked on me as I loaded firewood into a bucket. I muttered under my breath, 'I'm *not* a slave.' But why was I still peeling potatoes and carting rubbish? I'd been working for the chef for almost three months by then, the normal tenure for an apprentice. I'd mastered my tasks and performed them reliably. Why hadn't the chef mentioned a promotion? And Marco was right about the secrecy, too. What did he keep in that little cabinet, and why was it locked and hidden behind copper pans?

Marco's suggestion that I would always be a slave ate at me, eroding my trust a little more with each backbreaking load of wood. I stacked firewood in neat piles next to each fireplace, fitting the split logs together like a puzzle. Eventually, the rote motion quieted my thoughts enough to catch the whiff of a tense undercurrent in the kitchen, a murmur that filled the spaces between the ordinary sounds of a regular workday. I smelled the distinctive scent of gossip in progress, so I picked up my broom and positioned myself to hear more. I swept nonexistent dust near the feet of Enrico, who was pretending to assist Pellegrino in stirring the frumenty, a thick, rich pudding of almond milk, egg yolks and saffron. The frumenty would be served with the venison steaks that were marinating in a dish of assertive Burgundy.

Grey-haired Teresa stood nearby, humming and pretending to polish silver while she listened.

Enrico whispered as he stirred. 'Not only the dungeon. They killed him.'

'Are you sure?'

'*Boh*. It wasn't a cat squirming in that bag.'

'You saw?'

'Eduardo saw. They hauled a big, lumpy bag out of the water gate and rowed out to sea. When they came back' – he raised one eyebrow – 'no bag.'

'*Cappe Nere?*' Dante's voice was barely audible.

'With the *Cappe Nere*, no one sees anything. These were just the doge's men.'

'But are you sure it was—'

'Yes, the Spanish alchemist. Everyone is talking. No one has seen him, and his stall is chained up.'

'He must have sold the doge some potion that didn't work.'

'Maybe an aphrodisiac.'

'For the doge? Ha! Even the Spanish alchemist has his limits.' Enrico moved closer to Pellegrino. 'I heard it was a failed potion to revive the dead. Remember the peasant?' He pulled his eyelid.

I hadn't heard the chef approach. He grabbed Enrico by the arm and whirled him around so forcefully the cook dropped his spoon, splattering frumenty all over the floor and onto his shoes. The chef's eyes went hard. 'If I wanted gossip in the kitchen I'd hire my daughters' friends.'

Teresa disappeared, Pellegrino wiped up the frumenty, and Enrico raised both his palms and bowed as he backed away towards his floured table. '*Mi perdoni, Maestro.*'

I, too, began to beg the chef's pardon, but he cut me off, saying, 'Back to work.'

That day I gladly performed my solitary and silent task of potato peeling. I sat on a three-legged wooden stool with a basket of dusty brown potatoes on my left and a clean empty bowl on my right. It was calming to strip off the rough skin, dig out the knots, and get down to the smooth white flesh. As the first dark strips fell on the floor between my legs, I regarded each one as a clue, reasoning that when I had enough of them, some kind of truth would stand out naked as a peeled potato. Four strips for the gospels, three for murders, two for formulas and potions, one for a locked cabinet.

The peelings rose in a solid pile between my legs, and the white potatoes mounded up like a sculpture in my bowl, but no matter how many times I rearranged my clues, they remained stubbornly separate. Damn the potatoes. Damn Marco. Damn the chef and his secrets. Indignation rose like the pile of dirty potato peelings, and I watched the chef with mistrustful eyes. Was he ever going to promote me? Would he ever share the love potion? Was he only distracting me with talk of secret writings? And what was he hiding in that cabinet?

The chef was busy preparing his special venison sauce, and he had announced that he wished not to be disturbed. He walked past the big spice closet the cooks used and approached his private cabinet. He removed the copper sauté pan and unlocked the little oaken door with his brass key. Very quickly, with the same furtive manner as the last time, he took something out, slipped it in his pocket and immediately relocked the cabinet.

At that moment, the locked cabinet embodied all my questions about Chef Ferrero and my future in his kitchen. I went back to peeling: one stroke, two, three and the white potato began to emerge from its brown jacket. I could see how the pattern of each strip of skin fitted into the last, all conspiring to cover the potato entirely. One stroke at a time, and eventually you see it all. But, *marrone*, I was seeing nothing.

Marco was right. We had always been able to do what we set our minds to, and that day I set my mind to getting some questions answered. Marco had taught me how to pick pockets, how to shoplift and how to open locks with a piece of wire. The night we broke into the shop of a Florentine wool importer to steal blankets, he said, 'You don't need eyes for this. Just a light touch and a good ear.' That winter, I slept warm on the street for the first time. I was accustomed to trusting Marco, but he had suggested that the chef was deceiving me, was perhaps even a sorcerer. That was ridiculous. Wasn't it? The cabinet was suspicious, but practitioners of black magic kept dried snake eyes, raven's claws, the desiccated noses of hanged men, rat entrails bound with hair, and the shrivelled umbilical cords of stillborn infants. The chef wouldn't keep anything so loathsome in his pristine kitchen. Would he?

Sauce Nepenthes was certainly questionable, as was the chef's habit of talking about obscure matters that had nothing to do with his profession. And, of course, there was the thorny matter of the love potion. Did he keep *that* in his cabinet? *Marrone*, what if the love potion had been in the kitchen, right under my nose, all this time?

Bene. God helps those who help themselves. It was time to take matters into my own hands. I took a peek at the lock on the chef 's cabinet and knew it would yield to my wire.

That night, I rose from my straw pallet and tiptoed barefoot down the servants' stairway with the wire in my hand.

Watery light wavered through the kitchen windows and cast moving shadows on the walls. I moved towards the chef's cabinet, thinking, *Just a quick look.*

But the shifting night shadows unnerved me. I decided to warm up to my mission by peeking into the big spice closet first. Unlocking the closet door didn't feel like a violation – it was left unlocked all day for the cooks. Going in there would merely give me a closer look at what everyone else saw every day. In fact, it occurred to me that, by then, I probably should have been given a tour of the spice closet already. That thought helped me to feel indignant and justified.

I inserted my wire into the lock and pressed my ear flat on the door to hear the muted clicks. When I pulled the tall, narrow door open, a barrage of smells assaulted me. First a sweet blend of cinnamon and cloves with earthy undertones of thyme and oregano, then a piney whiff of rosemary and a heady punch of basil. The pungent mix stunned me, and I stood still, letting it envelop me. Equally dazzling was the knowledge that many of those spices had come from remote parts of the world. They were precious commodities carried over deserts and mountains and oceans, too expensive for any but the richest kitchens.

My eyes bulged at the sight of a squat round jar of peppercorns so wide across I would need two hands to lift it – a rich man's ransom in pepper. A handful of peppercorns cost the same as a week's pay for a common man, and I'd often heard the expression 'dear as pepper'. Merchants sometimes inflated profits by mixing in false peppercorns made of clay and oil. I prised off the wooden lid and ran my fingers through the peppercorns like a miser revelling in his gold. Some were broken, and the sharp smell made my nose twitch. No clay in there – a fortune in a jar.

Above the jar of peppercorns, I noticed a silver box delicately engraved with birds and flowers. I picked the flimsy lock, then lifted the lid and stared in wonder at a hoard of ducats and coppers glimmering in the fragile light. That silver box held the kitchen's ready cash for small purchases. The chef made large purchases on the doge's credit, but I'd often seen the majordomo casually drop a purse on the chef's desk. The chef always emptied the money into that box without even counting it, and I'd never imagined there was so much. When the chef gave me or Pellegrino coins to run out for supplies, the coppers and ducats came from that box. He took out what he needed and tossed the change back in without making any calculations. It astonished me to think that what I considered a fortune was only petty cash, barely worth keeping track of.

I'd never touched a gold ducat before. I picked one up and felt awed by the weight of it in my palm. It was heavy and smooth and finely sculpted. All the coins were magnificent, and not only because of their value. They were mesmerizing to look at: gold and copper, illuminated by wan moonlight, glowed like the chef's onion skins transmuted to metal. Temptation twinkled for an instant, but no, I reminded myself, I hadn't come to steal. The chef had said I was better than I thought, that I had God inside me. I replaced the ducat and closed the box.

Sated, I stepped out, relocked the closet door, and squinted at the copper sauté pan that concealed the chef's private cabinet. Still, I hesitated. For one so curious I was curiously sluggish to get on with it. I looked around the kitchen for any chores I might've forgotten. I peeked into the stockpot to assure myself the simmer was holding at the right level, then I took up my broom to search for a missed lettuce leaf, a stray fish bone, a grain of salt. I concentrated on the floor . . . and yet, somehow, I kept seeing that copper sauté pan in my peripheral vision.

Bending to sweep under a chopping block, I noticed a beetle picking its way slowly over the uneven stone floor. I picked it up, saying, 'Sorry, Signor Beetle. The chef doesn't allow insects in his kitchen.' I carried the beetle out to the back courtyard and released it. Watching it plod away, I remembered tales I'd heard about Calabrese witches who made a mashed insect stew for people to smear on an enemy's front door. It was said to be a powerful curse with no antidote and in Calabria people always inspected their doors before entering their homes.

Thoughts of the occult made me recall stories about Circassian witches who concocted purees of dog tongues, fish eyes and goat intestines to ingest while they cast spells. Disgusting. The chef would never have anything to do with such filthy profanities. Perhaps the chef practised some form of harmless white magic. Perhaps . . .

Get it over with!

Aware that the shuddering shadows and my strained nerves were goading my imagination, I hurried to the cabinet and quickly removed the copper sauté pan from its hook. Excitement caused me to fumble the pan and it fell on the stone floor with a ringing clang. I looked around to be sure the noise had not alerted anyone, and then I slipped the wire into the lock. Instantly, it became slippery from the sweat on my hands, and I cursed as I wiped my palms on my woollen breeches. I forced myself to take a deep breath and begin again. My lips pressed hard together in an effort to concentrate. When the tumblers fell into place, the small door creaked open a teasing finger's width. I heard a sharp intake of breath and felt a surge of panic before I realized the sound had come from me. I gripped the door handle with trembling fingers.

At that time, I was ignorant of the story about Pandora's box, of the idea that prying could unleash disaster and that some doors should never be opened. But even if I'd known that tale, I doubt that I'd have retreated. Prudence disregarded, wisdom yet to come, and curiosity blazing away, I pulled the door open.

What a relief! Three shelves held common glass bottles and jars, the same as those used for the herbs and spices in the cooks' closet. Wonderfully dull. There were also a couple of small cloth pouches like those used for sleeping powders and smelling salts. Everything was neatly lined up and clearly labelled just as it would be in an ordinary apothecary shop. I opened a few jars and sniffed the contents – they all smelled like herbs and seemed to be culinary provisions. The chef's big secret was just an innocent little spice cabinet after all, a place to keep those ingredients that were too rare or expensive to let the cooks use wastefully, if they knew how to use them at all.

The green glass jars full of dried leaves sparked a memory of the chef removing something greenish to make Sauce Nepenthes. I opened one bottle and made note of the verdant aroma. I removed a leaf and bit a tiny piece off the edge. It tasted unfamiliar but not unpleasant. There was a grassy aftertaste; it was clearly a herb. Everything else in the cabinet seemed equally unexciting. No nail clippings, no coils of hair, no putrefied remains, no smoky potions smelling of burnt chestnuts, and no books. That cabinet contained nothing more than the secrets of a great chef, the makings of his reputation. I let go a sigh of relief, feeling reassured that I'd learn to use them, as my maestro said, when I was ready.

I closed the door but hesitated before locking it. If those herbs and spices were so rare that they had to be locked up, fit only for a maestro, a simple knowledge of them might impress the chef. He respected knowledge above all. If I could learn the names of a few of his treasured herbs, he might be impressed enough to promote me. After all, Francesca wouldn't wait for ever.

I imagined myself dropping the name of an uncommon herb into a conversation. The chef would smile and say, '*Bravo*, Luciano. I see you've been paying attention in the Rialto.' That kind of cleverness might secure my promotion and shut Marco up for good.

Of course, I couldn't read the labels. I studied the words and began to see them as designs, lines and loops, dots and crosses, like little pictures. I could copy pictures. If I copied the lines and shapes faithfully, I could get someone to read them for me.

I went to the chef's desk and removed a quill and parchment, but I left the bottle of ink alone, fearing I might spill it. Sitting on the hearth, with Bernardo curled at my feet, I mixed a puddle of black ink from ashes and water. By the faint glow from the embers under the stockpots, I painstakingly copied the shape of the letters from several bottles and one pouch. The quill skipped and blotched, and after it grew soft from my crude ink and heavy hand, I stopped to sharpen the tip with a paring knife. At one point, I drooled on the parchment because I'd unconsciously been working with my tongue sticking out of the corner of my mouth. I blotted it with my sleeve, but saliva had smeared two whole words, almost a half hour's labour. No matter. As Marco had said, I could do whatever I set my mind to. I sharpened my quill and went back to work.

I was astonished at what great drudgery the business of writing entailed, and I felt a twinge of gratitude to have been left illiterate. But the result of my effort was impressive. I said, 'Look, Bernardo.' I held up the parchment to admire the finished product – a clumsy, blurry list of primitively scrawled words. My opus.

I replaced the quill and bottles just as I'd found them and relocked the cabinet. Then, I crept upstairs to the servants' dormitory and secreted the stolen words under my pillow. As I waited for sleep and pondered my next steps, I realized that I didn't know anyone who could read the words for me. Drifting off, I had a semi-conscious vision of the pretty silver box and its cache of glittering ducats and coppers. Before sleep claimed me, I told myself that the money belonged not to the chef, but to the doge, that it was only petty cash and the modest price for the services of a copyist would never be missed.

CHAPTER ❖ XV

THE BOOK OF HERBS

T HE NEXT MORNING I BUSTLED DOWN to the kitchen earlier than usual, wire in hand. I opened the spice closet and helped myself to one ducat from the silver box before I started my morning chores. When the chef arrived, I met him at the door. 'Buon giorno, Maestro. It's a beautiful day, eh? Will I be going to the market again today?'

'Sì.' He pulled on his high toque. 'When I was there at dawn the peaches hadn't come in from the mainland yet.'

'I'll find you the best peaches in the Rialto.'

'Trying to make up for some lost pears, Luciano?'

I nodded. 'I want to do a good job, Maestro.' And I meant it.

'Ecco.' He disappeared into the spice closet and came out a moment later with a handful of coppers that he dropped into my jacket pocket. He said, 'Bring me twenty peaches that are gold as a sunset, big as a fist, and smell like heaven.'

'Sì, Maestro. And may I take an orange for my friend Domingo?' I'd learned that orange slices cleanse the palate pleasantly after a meal of fish. The chef tossed me an orange, and I stuffed it in my other pocket. I considered another orange for Marco, but . . . he'd made me doubt the chef. No orange for him.

I sneaked upstairs to collect my stolen words. Bernardo was there, nesting on my pillow, and I moved him aside, saying, 'Everything's all right now. I have a plan to impress the chef, and soon we'll be vegetable cooks.' I would buy the chef's peaches, and I'd buy wisely, but first there'd be a detour. I retrieved my parchment and headed for the street of copyists.

I passed the fishmonger's stall and gave Domingo his orange. As usual he gushed embarrassing gratitude. I barely escaped without him embracing me. At the entrance to the street of copyists, I fingered the ducat in my pocket and wondered how one selects a reader. Were some more educated than others? Could they all be trusted? I took slow, cautious steps through the murky street and studied their faces. It was the first time I'd ever really looked at them closely and individually. When I lived on the street, I usually rushed through, fleeing from irate merchants.

Some of the copyists sat in makeshift stalls; others simply placed a chair on the street and set a writing board across the chair arms. They were not all as old as I'd always thought. Some were quite young, perhaps only a few years older than Marco. Smoke from their coal braziers tinted their hair and complexions grey, and their pensive posture, with heads inclined over their work, made them look bent with age. The scholarly attitude of the copyists and the hushed ambience of the street were contagious; all around me, people spoke in whispers as if in a church. I became aware of the sound of my own breathing.

Certain streets in Venice contrive to play tricks with

sound. Some acoustical magic occurs when tall, crooked buildings lean over a curved and cobbled lane. Sound only penetrates at each end, while the middle remains quiet, insulated by old ghosts and layers of history. While neighbouring streets rang with the world's commerce, the street of copyists held its peace; it was quiet enough to hear the rustle of paper, the scratch of the quill, and the scrape of pumice stone against parchment.

One copyist sat idle with nothing on his writing board. He watched my approach, which in turn made him approachable. I laid my bleary list on his board and asked, 'Can you read these words and tell me their meaning?'

He looked me over, up and down and up again. I appraised him, too. He was ancient; his rice-paper skin was truly grey, his straggly beard sparse and white. A milky haze of cataracts overlaid his once blue eyes. I wondered whether he could see at all and then I realized those poor eyes must be the reason he had no work. The musty smell of old age seeped through his clothes and his left hand, knotted and crisscrossed with ropy veins, quivered in his lap. His voice was as tarnished and cracked as an antique mirror. He replied, 'Can you pay?'

I took the ducat out of my pocket and held it up. I had observed that others in that street paid only with coppers; gold ducats were rarely seen there, and surely more than most copyists were accustomed to getting. The rheumy eyes glimmered at the sight of gold, but when he reached for it, I clasped it in my hand and said, 'First you read.'

'How do I know you'll pay once I've read?'

It was a fair question. I placed the ducat on his writing board, but before I removed my hand I said, 'I'll leave it there, but read before you touch it.' He nodded and I lifted my hand. I thought I saw amusement in his face.

He said, 'Let's see what you have.' The old Jew lowered his head so close to the writing board that his beard brushed the parchment. He read the first word: 'Cacao.' Then he looked up. If there had been amusement in his face it was gone now. He said, 'This is a pod found in the New World. I've heard it can be made into a delicious confection, sometimes a drink.' He shrugged his bony shoulders. 'But only a small quantity exists in Europe, and it's owned by the king of Spain.' When I didn't reply, he bent over the parchment again and scanned the rest of the list. He took a breath, then asked, 'Where did you find these words?'

The question made me feel cornered and panicky. I said, 'I'm paying you to read, not ask questions.'

He stared at me another moment, then read the next word: 'Coffee. This is a bean from Arabia. They use it to make a drink that gives men unnatural stamina and energy.' He waited for a reaction. When he got none, he continued. 'Henbane – a simple herb. Gossip claims that it prevents ageing, but that's an old wives' tale. It makes a decent tea.' His finger traced the next word: 'Valerian. Another herb, a mild relaxant.'

Leaning over to peer at my own scribbling, I recognized that last word as the one I had copied from the bottle I thought the chef had used to make Sauce Nepenthes. I said, 'A mild relaxant? That's all?'

He looked up, annoyed. 'That's what I said, didn't I?' One bristly eyebrow lifted crookedly. 'Of course, if you take too much . . .' He rocked his head from side to side.

'What happens if you take too much?'

'I suppose it could affect your mood or put you to sleep. How should I know? I'm a copyist, not a herbalist. Do you want to hear the words or not?' He bent back to the parchment, and his trembling finger pointed at the next two words. 'Chrysanthemum and ginseng. The first is a flower grown in China for tea. Ginseng is also from China, but I don't know its precise use. I think it might be a flavouring.' Then, mumbling, 'Or maybe that's ginger.'

His head hung over the next word so long I began to wonder if he'd fallen asleep. Or died. I said, 'Go on.'

He looked up, blinking, and I noticed that the tremor in his hand had become more pronounced. I said, 'Well, what is it?'

He shook his head. '"Amaranth" or "amanita". It's poorly written, and the ink is smudged.'

'What are they?'

'Don't be impatient.' He stroked his flimsy beard. 'I've seen both those words in Greek texts. I think this word is "amaranth". It's a grain. The amaranth leaf symbolized immortality in ancient Greece, but I think amaranth is extinct. Hasn't been any amaranth in . . . who knows? Ha! How do you like that? The symbol of immortality died out. Ha!'

'Yes, very amusing.' I wasn't smiling.

The Jew said, 'Maybe the word is "amanita", a poisonous mushroom. But I can't tell. This writing is terrible.'

That carried an unexpected sting. 'I didn't ask for your opinion of the writing.'

'All right, all right.' He made an irritated gesture. 'The last word, then. This is interesting. The others all have some culinary use, but the last word is "opium".'

I'd heard of opium, a medicinal substance used to alleviate pain. Opium was sold in apothecary shops and it was sinfully expensive. I said, 'Are you sure?'

'That's what I said, didn't I?'

I thought opium must have some culinary use I knew nothing about. I said, 'What does opium do?'

'It's for pain, but . . .' He gave me a thin smile. 'Opium induces dreams, boy. When you ingest it, you have dreams so sublime that you're drawn back, again and again, even against your will.' He waved a quavering hand. 'Just as well you don't know.'

'Can you cook with it?'

'Cook with opium? There's a novel idea.' He stroked his beard again and his smile showed small, worn teeth the colour of old cheese. 'Well, why not? Ha! I suppose you could stir a bit of opium into the soup. That meal would give you sweet dreams all right. Opium soup. Ha!' He picked up the gold ducat. 'Anything else?'

'Why the rush?' I wanted to know more about opium. 'I don't see any other customers waiting.'

'Insolent brat.' He pocketed the ducat and waved the parchment at me. 'You've had your service. Get going.'

So there it was. They were simply rare and expensive botanicals used for confections, teas and bread. And opium, besides relieving pain, gave sweet dreams. You could put it in soup and . . . and . . . have sublime dreams that make you want more?

Suddenly I knew what the chef did with his opium. Everyone called his white-bean soup sublime, and once they tasted it they *always* wanted more. The opium powder must be his secret ingredient. White-bean soup was on that day's menu, and I took it as a sign that God was on my side.

It all made perfect sense. The chef kept his most fabulous ingredients secret to insure his reputation. As he said, what value would he have if everyone could cook as well as he did? Armed with my new knowledge, I decided to indulge in a celebratory peek at Francesca. I headed for the street of olives.

As I'd hoped, she was there, waiting behind the mountainous Mother Superior, who was engrossed in beating down the prices of the Sicilian olive seller. Francesca took the opportunity for what Mother called 'gawping'. Her cheeks were charmingly flushed, and her eyes moved restlessly over the crowd. Excited breathing lifted her small breasts under the brown habit, and the sight quickened my own breath as well.

Francesca had the unmistakable look of one of those girls who found themselves in a convent for lack of other options. Girls had three choices: marriage, the convent, or the brothel. A girl with no dowry could forget about marriage and thus, many girls found themselves reluctantly working for God or the Devil. I saw how hungrily she watched people, how the lively swirl of the market animated her face, and I wondered how she endured that silent black-and-white existence behind the high stone walls of the convent. I'd never been in a convent, but I imagined solitary nights in her cell and dull days on her knees chanting a repetitious rosary or reading from her breviary.

Reading.

The plan to ask for help in reading my 'shopping list' arrived in my head fully formed, but finding the courage to actually approach her was more difficult. I fell back on the old street sense that had taught me to grab the turnip and run. My legs moved towards her without the consent of my brain. To my surprise, she smiled and said, 'The cantaloupe boy. Come to praise my nostrils?'

Merda, she remembered. I said, 'I wasn't myself that day.'

She raised an eyebrow. 'Do you think you're the first boy I ever saw tongue-tied?'

'Um—'

'Don't worry. It was sweet.'

'Oh. Well, I have this . . . I work in a kitchen, you see, and I have this shopping list, but I'm having trouble reading it.' I held it out but I don't remember whether I specifically asked her to read it. I only remember the green-apple fragrance of her breath, the shock of her eyes meeting mine, and the magnetic current that pulled me to her. I remember the fan of her eyelashes as she lowered her eyes to read, and I remember the translucence of her fingernails, the pale pink nail bed and clean white rim, as she pointed to each word. And, of course, the beguiling scent of her. I caught the smell of soap and baking and, under that, a flowery musk, mysterious and exciting. Her scent conjured a dreamscape of everything I longed for.

Francesca didn't read as well as the copyist. She sounded out 'ca-ca-o' and 'cof-fee', smiled at me, and shrugged with one insouciant shoulder. 'Sorry, I don't know what they are.'

'That's all right.' I moved an inch closer.

'Henbane. That's for tea, but too bitter if you ask me.' She read the next word easily. 'Valerian.' Then she chuckled.

'What's funny about valerian?'

'Valerian isn't funny, but . . .' She ticked her head towards Mother Superior and rolled her eyes.

'I don't understand.'

'Valerian is something like weak wine. Mother nips at it in the pantry all day to calm herself. It makes her forgetful, and by evening, she's forgotten everything that vexed her during the day. Valerian is quite dear, but no one complains of the expense because it makes Mother easier to live with.'

'Chrysanthemum' and 'ginseng' proved difficult to pronounce, which afforded me an opportunity to move closer and hold an edge of the parchment as if I, too, were trying to make out the words. I manoeuvred my hand so that our fingers touched and, to my surprise, she didn't move away. For a moment I flattered myself that she enjoyed my touch, but when I stole a sideways peek at her face, I saw that she hadn't even noticed. Her eyes were narrowed in concentration. She read 'amaranth' aloud, and then, 'No, that can't be right. Maybe it's "amanita." Hmmm . . .' She tapped a finger on her chin.

'What's wrong?'

'I think someone made a mistake. Amaranth is a grain, but I've heard it hasn't grown since, oh, I don't know – a long time. And amanita is a poisonous mushroom; surely you wouldn't shop for that, either.'

'Hmmm.' I tapped my own chin. 'Someone probably made a mistake.'

Francesca read the last word and shook her head. 'This is strange. This word looks like "opium", but no one would put that on a cook's shopping list.' She moved closer to me, her glorious eyes alight with mischief and her scent making me light-headed. She whispered, 'Have you ever tried it?'

She was so close, so conspiratorial, so intoxicating. I felt my face begin to redden. 'No. Sort of. Well, I mean, it's only for soup.'

'Soup?' She stepped back and regarded me coldly. 'Are you making fun of me?'

'No! Never . . .' Oh, *Dio*, what had I done?

Mother Superior's voice rose above the crowd. '*How* much for garlic olives? Are you mad? You're already robbing me for the oil-cured!' She turned to Francesca with comically rounded eyes, shouting, 'Can you believe the gall of this thief?' In her anger she seemed not to notice me at all.

When the nun turned away, I said, 'I was only joking about the soup.' I wasn't about to go into a lengthy explanation of how the chef manipulated people with food. 'I wouldn't make fun of you.'

'Hmm.' After a moment she said, 'You're odd, you know that?'

'Well, I—'

'Never mind.' She handed me the parchment. 'I like odd.' She glanced back at the older nun and said, 'Mother says I'm odd, too, but that's only because I don't want to be like her. Look at her.' Francesca gestured at the ruddy-faced nun arguing with the beleaguered olive merchant. 'She knows how to get the best prices, and she says I should listen and learn. But how can I bother with the price of olives when there's so much to see? Just look at this marvellous city. Do you roam around all by yourself?'

'Yes, I suppose I do.'

'What fun!'

It didn't seem advisable to point out that scavenging food and sleeping in doorways hadn't been that much fun.

'You're lucky.' She made a sweeping gesture at the market and exhilaration suffused her face. 'Look at all this. Look at that red turban. Did you ever see such a rich colour? And look there, that black man with the ropes of blue beads around his neck. Isn't he beautiful? Mother says he's from a place called Africa. Oh, just the name . . . Ah-free-cah . . .' She closed her eyes and her teardrop nostrils flared. 'Smell that? It's the smell of life. It makes me want to shout and sing. If I were a boy, I'd hire out to sea and travel the whole world.'

I thought I'd never met anyone less suited to be a nun. I said, 'Why a convent?'

Francesca flipped back her veil as if it was a luxurious mane of hair. There was something cool in the gesture, and I feared I'd offended her. She said, 'Why a kitchen?'

'Sorry,' I said. 'I just wondered—'

'We take what we can get, don't we?' She fiddled with the

rope at her waist. 'My parents died a long time ago. You know how it is. My choice was nun or courtesan. But a good courtesan needs a protector. I didn't know anyone to mentor me, and a girl alone on the street ends badly. At least in the convent I might catch a bishop, maybe even a cardinal. Hey, what's wrong with you? Close your mouth, eh?'

Just then, Mother's voice rose to shriller heights, and I was grateful for the reprieve. Francesca seemed strangely casual about being a courtesan. Was she only trying to seem worldly? Surely my fresh-faced darling would have *some* reservations about prostitution. Wouldn't she?

The big nun screamed, 'How dare you try to rob a woman of the cloth?'

The olive merchant looked exhausted. 'Then go somewhere else, Sister, and see if another merchant is more respectful.'

By the time Mother Superior resumed a more civilized tone, I'd regained enough composure to manage a reply. 'You made the right choice.'

She shrugged. 'We'll see.'

I felt sure she was exaggerating her indifference. Carefully, I said, 'What if you met a man who asked for no dowry. Would you leave the convent to marry him?'

'What man worth having would marry with no dowry? I don't want to be a fishwife, eh?' She laughed. 'You really are strange. Who are you shopping for anyway? Are you an apprentice?'

'An apprentice. That's a good one.' It was a day for exaggerations, so I inflated my chest and said, 'I'm a vegetable cook in the doge's kitchen.' With my faith in the chef restored, I felt it wasn't so much a lie as a premature truth.

'I suppose that's not a bad job.'

'It's a great job. I'm going to be a chef.' Emboldened by my self-endowed status, I moved closer and extended a pinky finger until it brushed against her hand. She curled her pinky around mine and a delicious heat rushed up my hand and through my body. I stood beside her, linked by a finger-tip and paralysed by love. I looked down, wanting to see our fingers entwined, and I noticed the ruffle of lace protruding from her sleeve. I said, 'Do nuns always keep lace handker-chiefs in their sleeves?'

'Oh, this?' She pulled out the lace and held it up for me to admire. 'I made this.' The sun filtered through the open-work and cast dappled shade on her face. 'I love tatting lace. It gives me something to do in my cell, and I do so enjoy pretty things.' She gazed at the diaphanous cloth and a dreamy smile came over her face.

'I learned the technique from a Belgian, Sister Ninette. She died last year but she left me her bobbins, and the convent buys me fine silk thread because my designs fetch a steep price from wealthy ladies. Just last month, I finished a mantilla for a lady of the Spanish court.' She stood a little taller and pulled the intricate fabric taut. 'This is my newest design. You see? Dragonflies.' I looked closely and saw the outline of a fragile wing with gossamer veins.

'It's beautiful.'

'Thank you.' She admired it a moment longer, then poked it back into her sleeve. 'I'd go completely mad without my needlework.'

Mother concluded her bargaining with a final huff of dis-gust, and while the merchant wrapped her briny purchases, she glanced over her shoulder at us again. I was drunk on Francesca's touch, dizzy from her scent and encouraged by her friendliness. Mother's screech – 'Filthy boy!' – lacerated me. She turned on me like a mad dervish, sizzling and ruddy-faced, rosary beads rattling, robes whirling. 'How dare you touch her?' She pushed me out of the way with a meaty hand, grabbed her olives, and pulled Francesca away, saying, 'It'll be a long while before I bring *you* to the market again.' As the older woman dragged my love off into the crowd, Francesca looked back at me and winked.

I bought the peaches in a daze. The entire world looked gold as a sunset and smelled like heaven; I had trouble telling one peach from another, but I forced myself to concentrate and I chose well. Now that Francesca thought I was already a vegetable cook, I couldn't make a mistake that might delay my promotion. I walked through the Rialto under her spell, and the carnival of colour and noise didn't touch me. I existed in a bubble of enchantment. Nothing intruded on my ecstasy until I reached the kitchen courtyard.

As promised, Marco was there, leaning against the wall with his arms crossed cockily. I put down my peaches and dug the wrinkled and smeared parchment out of my pocket. I held it up to his face. 'Look. Last night I opened the chef's private cabinet and copied these words off the bottles in there. Today I had a copyist read them. They're nothing, Marco. Just herbs the chef uses for special recipes. Are you satisfied?' I picked up my basket of peaches. 'I'll leave some food out later, but now I have to get back to work.' As I moved past him, his hand shot out and grabbed my arm. I said, 'Get off me, you dirty turnip.'

'*Dirty* turnip? Well, pardon me, Signor Cabbage-Head.' Marco backed up with his hands in the air. 'Maybe I don't get a nice bath once a week like some people, but I taught you everything you know. You could keep a civil tongue in your head.' His mouth was sneering, but his eyes looked wounded.

'Look, Marco, I don't want to sneak around behind the

chef. I've changed. I'm not a thief any more. I'm going to be a better person.'

'*Boh!* No one changes.'

'Oh?' He was wrong and I wanted him to know it. I wanted him to know I had something good in me. 'Last night I had a chance to steal a lot of money, and I didn't do it. There's a silver box of coppers and ducats in the spice closet. It's ready cash that doesn't even get counted, but I didn't take any. Well, a ducat for the copyist, but nothing for myself. The chef is going to make me a vegetable cook. I'm going to earn my money honestly. You'll see.'

'*Boh.*' Marco scuffed his heel on the pavement. 'A vegetable cook.' He sulked and scratched his hollow belly. 'This doesn't change anything, Cabbage-Head. I still want that book.'

'Here,' I said. 'Have a peach.'

He took it in sullen silence.

'Like I said, if I hear anything about alchemy, I'll tell you.'

'You better.' Marco shoved his peach in a pocket and slouched away.

In the kitchen, I unwrapped the peaches, arranged them on an oval platter, with their blushes turned face-up, and presented them to the chef. He inspected them like a jeweller examining diamonds. He turned one over, sniffed, and smiled. 'Well done,' he said. 'Keep this up and you'll be cooking soon.'

'*Grazie*, Maestro!' But, I wondered, how soon? I decided it would be best to impress him with my new culinary knowledge immediately. Armed with the names of those rare herbs, I felt very close to my promotion.

I picked up my broom and swept my way across the kitchen towards the chef, who was sprinkling salt into a pot of his sublime white-bean soup. He stirred steadily, round and round, while the beans broke down and thickened the soup. When the mixture reached the right consistency, the chef added a handful of fresh spinach and recommenced stirring. He worked until the mixture was well blended, then crumbled in some dried sage and gave it a shot of ground white pepper. He dipped the tip of his little finger into the soup and touched it to his tongue. He rolled it in his mouth, and his eyebrows knitted. 'Not quite,' he murmured.

I stepped forward as if onto centre stage and cleared my throat. In that proud moment, I could feel my head already swelling with the thrill of being a vegetable cook. I leaned towards the chef so that no one else would hear the secret ingredient and whispered, 'Perhaps it needs some valerian.' The chef turned and straightened his high toque. 'What did you say?'

Stupido! Valerian was for the sauce. What a blunder. I looked around to be sure no one was listening and said, 'I mean opium. The soup probably needs more opium.'

The chef's face twisted into an expression of anger so intense it made me take an involuntary step backward. He said, 'Where did you learn those words?'

I couldn't think fast enough. 'From Giuseppe?'

'No, you didn't.' He seized my arm. 'Tell me, Luciano.' The kitchen fell into an audible silence.

I stammered. 'I don't remember.'

He released my arm and adjusted his toque again; it sat very low on his forehead, almost touching his eyebrows. I braced myself. He took a step forward, and I instinctively hopped back and raised a defensive arm in front of my face. I waited for the blow with eyes closed tight, but it never came. When I opened one eye, I saw the chef fingering the brass key around his neck. He glanced at his private cabinet and said, 'This is unacceptable.'

'Maestro, I—'

'*Silenzio!*' He circled me with his hands clasped behind him. He didn't raise his voice or make threats, yet he exuded menace. He said, 'You will not eat for the rest of the day.' He continued to circle, and I dared not move. 'We're serving roast chicken tonight. In the courtyard, there is a crate with twenty hens to kill and pluck and clean. You'll do all of it by yourself. Then you'll get down on your hands and knees and scrub up the mess.'

The entire staff gawked. No one had ever seen such a display of temper in that kitchen. They stared at us until the chef flapped a hand and said, 'Back to work. Everyone.'

I could manage a day without food, but the idea that my maestro, my benefactor, my *saviour* should be the one to impose hunger on me was a stunning blow. And twenty chickens to kill and pluck and singe and clean? *Marrone*, that was the filthiest, vilest task of all. Wringing their necks while they struggled and fought, chopping off the heads, and pulling out handfuls of slimy, stinking guts before hanging them by the feet to drain? I'd finish with blood congealing all over me, clotting between my fingers, drying in my clothes, and smeared over my face. Then I'd have to singe the pinfeathers – argh! Just the thought of that cloying stench made my throat close up. Beginning to end, it was an odious, disgusting job.

Even worse would be the humiliation of getting on my hands and knees to scrub the cobbles. Normally, the chef would call a charwoman to clean up that sort of mess. After I finished my foul task, scrubbing the pavement would add insult to injury. My two magic words, 'valerian' and 'opium', had moved me even further away from promotion. Now I was demoted to charwoman, and the chef was angrier with me than he'd ever been.

I killed and plucked and cleaned the first chicken, then hung the headless body by its feet. Blood ran down my arms, splattered my face, soaked into my clothes, and puddled on the floor. The stench was nauseating. I'd killed chickens before, but that day, after the chef's unexpected rage and seeing my clever plan backfire so completely, my stomach turned over and bile rose in my throat. I gagged and ran to the rubbish pail to throw up my morning meal. I came back, gasping, wiped my mouth with a bloody hand, and returned to my repugnant chore.

Nineteen more? Simply for having spoken two words? I only wanted a promotion, and what in the name of God was wrong with that? Rage swelled in my throat until I had to spit. I ground my teeth and hung the ghastly chickens by their feet. The pile of warm guts pulsed with a few still-beating hearts, and suddenly I hated that kitchen and everyone in it. In my confusion, memories of simpler times on the street with Marco and Domingo came back to me purged of hardship, as if it had been nothing but good times and camaraderie. In that unhinged moment, I thought Marco had the right idea after all. I should be using my place in the palace to nose out information about the secret of alchemy or find a way to claim that reward. At the very least I should get my hands on the love potion. The repulsive odour of scorched pinfeathers made me gag again, but I had nothing left to bring up. I mumbled, 'I've been a fool.'

With the last chicken cleaned, the entrails sorted and the organs rinsed for the stockpot, I got down on my hands and knees with a bucket of water and sponges and rags and brushes. I dragged myself through the ignominious chore: first soak up the blood with sponges, then change the water, then wash the cobbles, then fill the bucket with clean water and scrub between the stones with a soapy brush, then rinse and mop. I worked with my head down, and my tears dripped into the suds.

I knew where Marco slept. I also knew I could recover his goodwill and elicit his advice with a nice, fat leg of roast chicken.

CHAPTER ❖ XVI

THE BOOK OF THIEVES

BERNARDO WATCHED WHILE I WASHED off the chicken blood. I said, 'Looks like Marco was right. The chef doesn't want me to learn and he'll be sorry. Somehow, I'll get that love potion. Then we'll leave.' I stripped down to my small clothes (how mercilessly Marco would have teased if he knew I wore small clothes under my trousers), and I pumped cold water to sluice over my head and shoulders. As I pumped, I resented anew the many unnecessary buckets of water I carried every day – without complaint – to satisfy the chef's unreasonable mania for fresh water. I rubbed myself raw with lye soap and rinsed thoroughly, but the odour of chicken blood seemed to ooze from my pores even after I put on clean clothes. The foul smell of humiliation was indelible.

I wouldn't tell Marco about the chickens. I couldn't bear to see his look of smug triumph. I'd tell him just enough to explain my change of heart and draw out his advice.

Ironically, it was Marco himself who had taught me that only fools tell the whole truth. Marco said that lies could tip the scales in an unjust world and that it was only right that we create advantages for ourselves to make up for our meagre lot in life. Marco said we had a right to lie.

That night in the dormitory, I waited impatiently for the other servants to fall asleep. I felt simultaneous dread and eagerness for the meeting with Marco, and I distracted myself with fantasies of Francesca. I hugged Bernardo and thought about her green-apple breath, the silky feel of her fingertip, the way her remarkable eyes devoured the swell of life in the market. I stroked Bernardo, saying, 'I know I could make her happy.' Bernardo purred. 'She hates the convent; anyone can see it. If I had that love potion she'd come away with me and we'd both be happy.' Bernardo snuggled deeper into my chest. 'All I want is the love potion. He can keep his old writings. I won't betray him, even though he betrayed me.' I felt my eyes fill, and it made me furious. 'I'll show him. I *won't* betray him. I'll leave here and never say a word about those writings. Never. He'll know he lost a good man, and he'll be sorry.' My lips trembled, but I didn't cry.

When the moon peeked through a high window, I fished the stolen chicken leg from under my blanket and tucked it into my waistband. Oh, *Dio*, that aroma. It had been roasted to golden perfection, crisp outside and juicy inside, with a crust of coarse salt and crushed thyme. It made my mouth water and my stomach howl, but I resisted. I needed Marco's counsel more than I needed dinner. I shoved my shoes under my arm and ran down the stairs and out the back door, tugging on one shoe at a time while I hopped forward on the other foot.

That day, Landucci had announced his reward for information about the book, and even at that late hour, people were still out talking about it. I passed clumps of street people huddled in excited bunches. Lamplight glowed in the windows of modest homes where labourers should already be asleep, and prostitutes conferred on corners while potential customers passed them by. There was an unusual number of gondolas about as well, the gentry out visiting neighbours to discuss the big questions: Why a senate seat and small fortune for that book? What secrets might be in it, and where might it be hidden? Landucci had announced that the book contained secrets of state that must be kept from Genoa and Rome, but no one believed that for a moment.

I raced through the dark streets to the Church of San Domenico, and as I'd hoped, Marco still slept in the deep recess of the church's double front doors. The Gothic stone lintel sheltered him from wind and rain, and in the morning he sat directly in the path of early churchgoers whose piety inclined them towards charity. Once, an old woman gave Marco an entire loaf of fresh bread. Another time, a girl with a baby in her arms filled his hand with coppers and kissed his grimy cheek. It was a coveted location that Marco had, more than once, defended at the cost of bloody nose or swollen lip.

Others, mostly drunks, idiots and orphans, slept under rags in the shallower crevices of the old church, but I spotted Marco immediately by the blue wool blankets, torn and stained now, that we'd stolen from the Florentine importer. He'd appropriated mine when the chef took me off the street, and during the day, while he was out hunting food, he stashed them in a secret hiding place.

I pulled the chicken leg from my waistband, squatted down beside the mound of blue blankets and wafted it under his sleeping nose. With eyes still closed, he darted his hand out of the blankets like a lizard's tongue and grabbed my wrist. When he recognized me, he propped himself up on one elbow, pulled the meat to his mouth and tore off the first bite with the chicken leg still in my hand. While he chewed, he took the leg from me and held it close to his chest, like an animal guarding its kill.

He gobbled down all the meat, gnawed at the stripped bone and bit off the cartilage end before either of us spoke. When he began to crack open the bone with his teeth to get at the marrow I said, 'The chef's not going to promote me.'

'I know that.' He sucked out the marrow and licked the inside of the bone.

'You were right. Something funny is going on in that kitchen. He does have suspicious recipes that change men's moods.'

Marco wiped his greasy lips with the back of his wrist. 'That sauce?'

'Sì. Sauce Nepenthes and also a white-bean soup that makes people eat like pigs. They can't get enough, and I think the secret ingredient is opium. But you should've seen the chef's face when I mentioned it. *Marrone,* he was angry.'

'Opium? Interesting.' Marco pulled off a sliver of bone to pick his teeth. 'So, what do you want from me?'

'I tried to learn a few things on my own, and . . .' I looked down and muttered, 'He didn't like that.'

'I told you!' Marco pointed his sliver of bone at me. 'Nobody helps nobody for nothing. He just wants a slave.' Marco broke the denuded bone into pieces and sucked on them for any last traces of flavour.

I hugged my knees. 'I mentioned the names of a couple of special ingredients and he went crazy. *Pazzo!*'

'He doesn't want you to know anything important. But

this is good. If he uses magic and drugs, we can blackmail him for whatever he knows about that book.'

'And for the love potion.'

Marco put down his brittle remnants of bone. He said, 'The love potion. Sure. We'll get your love potion, too.'

'You heard about the senate seat?'

'Everyone's heard.' Marco snorted. 'The secret in that book is how to make gold. Has to be.'

I decided to broach the other thing that had been nagging at me. 'There was something in that cabinet called amaranth, but the copyist said amaranth doesn't grow any more. I don't think I miscopied it. But how could the chef have a grain that doesn't grow any more?'

'Good question.' Marco scratched lazily at the vermin in his hair. He said, 'You have to steal some of the stuff in that cabinet.'

'Steal from the cabinet? I don't know . . .'

'Just a little. Not enough to be missed. And some money, too.'

'I don't want to steal his money.'

'It's not his money, Cabbage-Head, it's the doge's.' He shrugged. 'Only enough to pay the Abyssinian. You said yourself a coin or two wouldn't be missed. We have to know what your chef's got so we know what we have to bargain with.'

'*Marrone*. The Abyssinian?' This was getting complicated. But after a moment I said, 'All right.'

The next day was an agony of ambivalence and waiting. I tended to my chores with my head down, wrestling with Marco's idea, and the chef took my subdued demeanour as a sign that I'd learned my lesson from the previous day's humiliation. I tried to catch his eye, hoping for a small smile, for some tiny hint of forgiveness. My anger had subsided and any gesture of kindness would have made me abandon Marco's plan. What I really wanted was a chance to talk to him, to ask him why he'd treated me so harshly. But throughout that long day Chef Ferrero addressed me as 'apprentice' or 'boy'. He ordered me about the kitchen with dismissive waves and never met my eyes. His coldness made me angry all over again. Worse, it hurt, and it confirmed the belief that Marco was right and I was, indeed, on my own.

After everyone left for the night, I faced the moment of decision. I toyed with the wire in my pocket and stared at the chef's cabinet. Once again I tried to postpone the act because this time I knew it would be nothing but straightforward stealing. I attended to my night duties slowly, with uncommon diligence, and the impending deed hung in the air like the odour of chicken blood.

With the last chore completed, I stood in the middle of the room looking for one more task, but the clean orderly kitchen had no need of further attention.

I removed the copper sauté pan and laid it on the floor, then faced the cabinet door and stared at it. I wanted to turn around and go to bed. If I opened that door I would embark on a path that did not include the chef. I felt sad and sick. My breath quickened, and I fiddled with the wire. There was an uncomfortable fluttering in my chest. To steal from the chef was a betrayal, there was no other name for it. But hadn't he made it clear that I would remain a slave? Hadn't I been forced to kill and eviscerate twenty hens and do the work of a charwoman simply because I knew two of his secret ingredients? How much clearer could it be that he had no plans to promote me?

The familiar lock opened easily. I took a deep breath and pulled the door open, exposing the shelves of neatly arranged bottles and jars. As I reached for the first jar, a voice froze my hand in mid-air.

Behind me, the chef said, 'Why, Luciano?'

CHAPTER ✤ XVII

THE BOOK OF GROWING

THE PHRASE 'CAUGHT RED-HANDED' probably originated with a murderer caught with the blood of his victim still on his hands. Nevertheless, I got caught red-handed and red-faced, drenched not in blood, but in shame and fear.

'I can explain,' I blubbered, having no idea how I might do that.

The chef sounded tired. 'Please don't lie, Luciano. What are you doing? Are you out of your mind? Why do you pry into things you don't understand?'

'I want to understand.'

'By stealing? I want to teach you something important, and you do this?'

'But you don't teach me what I need. And when I learn something on my own, you make me kill chickens.'

'Ah. The chickens.'

'Just because I knew the names of some secret spices?'

'Those weren't secret spices, and you weren't punished for

knowing them. You were punished for the way you learned them. You broke into my cabinet. I suppose you copied the words and had someone read them, eh?'

It gave me pause to know I was so transparent. 'I wanted to know about your magic recipes. I thought you had decided not to promote me.'

'Magic recipes.' He managed a sad smile. 'Surely you know better.'

'But—'

'A maestro doesn't need magic. What appears to be magic is knowledge. Remember the dinner for Herr Behaim? That was skill, Luciano, not magic.'

I remembered the dinner, all right. I also remembered his evasion about the Sauce Nepenthes. I said, 'Just because food has power and you have skill doesn't mean there can't still be magic.'

The smile drained from his face. '*Dio*, you try me.' As he locked his cabinet, my mind cast about for a place to sleep that night. I hoped Marco would let me share his doorway.

'I'm sorry, Maestro. Will I have to leave?'

'*Dio*. I don't know.'

'I wanted to be better, but I thought you gave up on me.'

'Me? You're the one giving up.'

'No. I thought I had to fend for myself.'

'That's what you're doing here?'

'I don't know.' And suddenly I didn't. The chef's hurt look made it seem like a terrible mistake, a gross misunderstanding. 'I don't know what I'm doing here. Please give me another chance. I won't listen to Marco any more.'

'Marco? This was someone else's idea?'

'No.' I wouldn't involve Marco. I was the one who sought him out. I squared my shoulders. 'No, Maestro. It was all me. But I was mistaken and I'm sorry.'

'Are you protecting someone?'

'No. There's no one else.' I took a deep breath and braced to take my punishment like a man. 'Do what you wish to me. I deserve it. But please know that I am truly sorry.' I felt my eyes fill and pretended to scratch my nose to wipe away a tear.

'At least you're willing to take responsibility.'

'Sì. It was all my doing.'

'It's important for a man to take responsibility.'

'I do. But it was stupid and I'll never do it again. You're like a father to me.'

'Oh, *Dio*.' The chef looked tired. 'I have to think,' he said. 'Go to bed.'

'You mean upstairs?'

'Should I wake the majordomo to prepare a guest room for you?'

'Thank you, Maestro.' I backed away, bowing as I went. 'I'm sorry, Maestro. Thank you. I'll never—'

'Oh, be quiet and go to bed.'

I was sincerely repentant, but he had asked why, and part of me felt I could have asked him the same thing. Why so many secrets? Why the parade of scholarly visitors? Why the locked cabinet? And what was the meaning of that strange garden? The chef's garden was a constant source of whispering, pulled eyelids and encrypted warnings to all who ventured there. Most of the garden was devoted to the usual things – lettuces, onions, cabbage and aubergine – ordinary ingredients for good, honest meals. But then there were the chef's other plants, the ones that made the cooks cross themselves and kiss their thumbnails whenever they were forced to handle them.

Take love apples, to start with. Their poisonous reputation was as well known as that of hemlock, and the cooks protested loudly the day the chef put in his seedlings. What if their roots contaminated the onions? What if their fumes caused swoons or fits? What if the odd, tangy smell of their leaves attracted disgruntled ghosts from the nearby dungeons? It took repeated assurances, the installation of a wire enclosure, and the fact that nothing catastrophic followed their planting to keep the staff from uprooting the love apples behind the chef's back. Even so, one cook left, and another developed a twitchy eye and started nipping at the cooking sherry.

After the love apples, the chef put in beans – another rarity from the New World – and then potatoes. Once, he tried something he called maize, but the plants failed, so instead he bought sacks of dried maize from an unknown source. In a giant stone mortar, he ground the dried maize down to a coarse yellow meal from which he made one of his exotic specialties – polenta.

I'd peeked through the garden door a time or two, but I'd never actually needed to set foot out there, for which I was grateful. The palace gardeners tended to the weeding and watering, and the cooks harvested what they needed. The chef himself saw to his collection of leafy freaks.

The morning after Chef Ferrero caught me with my hand in his cabinet, he didn't speak to me, and I worked in a limbo of apprehension, wondering exactly what my punishment would be. While finishing my midday *panino*, I stood at the threshold of the open garden door trying to enjoy the mingled smells of mint and rosemary wafting on a shifting breeze. But, waiting for the axe to fall, I couldn't concentrate on my food or the scented air. As I swallowed the last bite, the chef came up behind me and put a hand on my shoulder. I jumped, thinking, *Here it comes.*

He said, 'Would you like to see the garden, Luciano?'

The garden? *Marrone,* this would be worse than the chickens. 'No, thank you, Maestro.'

The chef took my elbow as if he hadn't heard me and guided me outside. We walked along neat gravel paths bordered in every shade of green. The gravel crunched beneath our shoes, and the chef named his strange crops as we went. When we came to the love apples – garish red globes, some oozing slimy red poison from split skins – I took care not to let the leaves brush against me. I watched in horror as the chef buried his face deep in their foliage and inhaled fiercely. Next to the love apples, malevolent beans crawled up tall poles, out-of-control mutations with curled tendrils like green fingers blindly reaching for passersby. I eased by them carefully.

I followed the chef to the circular herb garden with relief. Here were familiar plants with gentle smells: thyme, dill, mint, basil and others equally benign. He asked me to identify the ones I knew and gave me a brief dissertation on their uses: Dill was good with fish, thyme complemented veal, mint went well with fruit, and basil was perfect for the dreaded love apples. He plucked two large mint leaves with purplish undersides, placed one on his tongue, and gave me the other. We came to rest on a curved stone bench in the middle of the garden, and we sat there sucking on fresh mint, him enjoying the breeze, and me awaiting the judgement that must be coming.

He continued his lecture on herbs. He talked about the subtlety of bay laurel, the many varieties of thyme, and the use of edible flowers as garnishes. A hummingbird whizzed by and hovered; the chef grew abstract and said, 'You know,

there are those who believe men will someday be able to fly.'
He raised his hand to point at the hummingbird drinking
from a red flower, and I shielded my face. When no blow
came, I peeked through my fingers and saw the chef staring
at me. He looked like a man whose face had been slapped.
He said, 'I'd never hit you, Luciano.'

'Oh, I know. I was just, uh . . .'

He turned away from me and spoke quietly to some invisible listener in the sorrel. He said, 'My father used to beat me
and my brother, and even my mother. He drank, you see. He
was a very sad man. I hated him. I wrapped myself in hatred
for protection; I cradled hatred in my heart, and it was a bitter comfort.

'One day when I was old enough, big enough, I pulled
him off my weeping mother. He'd been beating her with a
stick, as if she were an animal. I was a child, but I screamed
at him. "What kind of man are you? You should be
ashamed."' The chef looked at me, and his eyes infected me
with his sadness. 'My father was gaunt by then, and always
filthy. He dropped his stick and slumped onto a chair. He
looked at my mother whimpering on the ground as if he'd
just noticed her, and you know what he said? He said, "I am,
son. I am ashamed."

'I'll never forget the moment my father admitted his
shame. It helped me to discover that there's freedom in forgiveness. We are better people for knowing how to forgive.'
The chef looked at me again. 'That's one of the reasons I've
decided to forgive you for last night. You knew you'd done
wrong and you took responsibility. You've earned another
chance.'

'Grazie, Maestro.' At the time I wondered how I could be
forgiven so easily. Now I think the chef knew I would carry
his mandate to forgive for the rest of my life.

He said, 'My father died soon after that incident. If he'd lived, he might've redeemed himself.' I must have looked doubtful because he added, 'No one is beyond redemption.'

'Giuseppe—'

'No one, Luciano. Unfortunately, some of us die before we get there. Of course, there are those who believe we get more than one life . . . but that's another conversation.' He went on in the neutral tone of a teacher. 'At first, I only wanted to be different from him. Better. I thought I only needed to achieve professional success and social respectability. Then I met Chef Meunier. You remember him, eh?'

'Sì, Maestro.'

'God bless his droll heart. I learned from him that the measure of a man is taken not only by his achievements, but also by his struggle to achieve, his will to do good, and the tenacity of his effort. I see that will in you, Luciano.' He stood then, and something in the deliberate way he did so made me stand as well. 'I have something to say to you, Luciano, and I'll say it plainly. I've given this much thought, and I've made my decision. I believe your occasional lapses are due to youth and your unfortunate beginnings. I believe you have it in you to be a fine man, and I want to help you. I wish to make you my protégé, the heir to my knowledge.'

Shocked at this blunt statement, I wondered how my effort to impress him had earned punishment, while my attempt to steal had earned forgiveness. I didn't understand it, but apparently my future with the chef was assured after all. I was the chef's protégé. I would have the opportunity to become a better person. The chef would help me transcend myself. Elated, I wanted to feel the word in my own mouth. I said, 'I'd be honoured to be your protégé.'

'Bene. From now on I'll expect more from you.'

I had many questions about what, exactly, a protégé did. I understood that it was better than an apprentice, but I had questions about new duties and privileges. I said, 'Now will you teach me to cook?'

'Certainly.'

'Will you tell me what makes custard firm?'

'Custard? Eggs, why?'

'It's one of those things that looks like magic. It goes in liquid and comes out firm. Eggs? How strange.'

'It's no mystery. Haven't you ever seen eggs firm up when they're cooked? They bind with the other ingredients and pull it all together.'

I smacked my forehead. 'Of course!'

'Custard. Sometimes you're a strange one, Luciano.'

'Not as strange as this garden. Will you explain these plants to me?'

The chef smiled. 'This garden is about greatness. Anyone can boil an ordinary pot of rice. What makes a great chef is skill out of the ordinary. That's what this garden is – it's not magic, it's just not ordinary.

'The first seeds for love apples came from the New World. They're not poison, Europe simply hasn't caught up with them yet. For now, only I appear to have the secret of rendering them into salubrious delicacies. People eat in amazement, and my reputation grows.' He laughed and pointed to a corner of tilled earth where nothing grew. 'When the season is right, I'll plant yams there. Then you'll see some magnificent dishes.'

'Yams?' I wanted to talk about protégés. I wondered whether a protégé might be allowed to learn the formula for the love potion.

'Yams are a type of potato, also from the New World. Long and slim with orange flesh, sweet as honey.' He bunched up his fingers like a rosebud and kissed the tips. 'I grow white potatoes, too, and keep a supply in the root cellar. Just wait, Luciano. In the root cellar you'll see things more interesting than love apples and beans.'

I could see that we would have to discuss culinary matters before I could broach the love potion. 'How do these strange things get to Venice from the New World, Maestro?'

'How does anything get to Venice? Strapped onto camels and horses and elephants, packed in the holds of ships, piled onto carts and wagons, tied on the backs of men.' He circled the air with one hand as if to say 'Who cares how they get here, as long as they do?'

'But so few have been to the New World.'

'You think so?' His eyes danced with a devilish glint. 'Men thought the earth was flat, yet Cristoforo Colombo sailed right through the horizon and showed us that the earth is round.'

'Maestro, men have been burned as heretics for saying the earth is round.'

'Well, I wouldn't say it to an Inquisitor. But in fact, the earth *is* round and always has been. So why assume that Colombo was the first to discover it? Muslim astronomers said the world was round centuries ago. And Norsemen were criss-crossing this round earth in overlapping arcs long before Colombo.'

'Norsemen?'

'Explorers and adventurers have brought us far more than what you see in this garden, or even what you can find in the hidden stalls of the Rialto. They've brought us ideas and divergent views of the world and its people. In the forests of Africa, there are tiny black men who have lived with nothing but the earth under their feet for thousands of years. In the Far East, high civilizations thrived millennia before Jesus. In the New World, nations rose and fell for centuries before the Spaniards arrived. Travellers before and after Marco Polo have been importing and exporting a steady stream of goods and knowledge. Knowledge is the most valuable commodity. Knowledge is the stepping stone to wisdom.'

The chef spread his arms wide to encompass his garden. 'What you see here is nothing. Over the centuries, hundreds of writings and scientific formulas have been added to the body of human knowledge.'

'Formulas? Like alchemy?'

'A formula's just a recipe, Luciano. Don't make too much of the word. What you need to know is that some of us have taken on the task of collecting, recording and protecting as much of this knowledge as we are privileged to learn. We save ideas worth thinking about, even when they're incon-venient, and especially when they're threatened. We keep the flame of free thought alive. We are the Guardians.'

'Guardians.' I looked at the love apples with new eyes.

The chef ruffled my hair. 'The world is bigger and older than you know, and we're all heirs to its accumulated won-ders. There are things you could never imagine. There's a vast land down in the southern sea where giant rodents stand on two feet and carry their babies in pockets. I'd like to see that.' He smiled. 'The Guardians believe we shouldn't discard our inheritance too easily. We can see farther ahead by standing on the shoulders of our predecessors. Civilizations are built on the bones of the dead.'

'What about God?'

'God?' The chef closed his eyes and rubbed his temple as though he'd suffered a sudden stabbing pain. 'That word is used to excuse some of humanity's most heinous behaviour. God is another conversation. For now we're talking about great teachers and the knowledge they've passed to us.'

It all sounded so grandiose that my voice came out in a whisper. 'You want to share this knowledge with me?'

'Everything in its own time. You have much to learn before you're ready for the secrets encoded between chicken broth and roast lamb.'

Chicken broth? Roast lamb? *Boh.* I wanted to hear about the grand ideas, the big secrets: alchemy, giant rodents and love potions. I said, 'But, Maestro—'

'Luciano, first things first. When the Guardians began, we needed a disguise. We needed a way to collect and save our body of knowledge without becoming a clear target, like the Great Library at Alexandria. Someone hit on the idea of being cooks. No one notices servants, eh?'

'That's true.' I remembered the chef and his brother chatting in my presence as if they couldn't see me walking back and forth right in front of them.

The chef continued. 'Cooks are among the few servants who have a reason to keep written records. We can collect writings from foreigners, and no one is interested in them. After all, they're just recipes, eh?' He chuckled. 'At first, we were only cooks. Later, it was decided we should become master chefs, because that path is long and arduous enough to allow a man time to ponder his commitment. Our recipes are codes, a way to save pieces of knowledge that might otherwise be lost or destroyed. But before you reach the rank of a maestro, you'll have to spend years studying and preparing.'

'Like a novice nun?'

'A nun? Ah. Are you still in love with the convent girl?'

'Yes, Maestro. I want to marry her.'

'There's plenty of time for marriage.'

'But if I'm too slow, she might marry someone else. I'd die if that happened.'

'You wouldn't die, but I understand your feelings. I loved a girl once . . . be assured, you wouldn't die.'

'I would *want* to die.'

'Luciano, marriage is a fine thing, and it will happen for you in time. For now, try to understand that I'm offering you something noble to live for.'

'Why me?'

'Aside from seeing potential in you?' He brushed the hair off my forehead and passed a thumb over my birthmark. 'I have my reasons.' He bit his lip lightly. 'Do you know anything about your parents, Luciano?'

'Nothing.'

'*Ecco*. It's not important.'

'But, Maestro, you choose me even though you know me to be a thief?'

'You can be better than that if you want to, and I think you do.'

The chef had more faith in me than I had in myself. It was true I wanted to be better, good enough to be a vegetable cook and a husband, but could I be good enough for *this*? I said, 'I don't know—'

'You hesitate. That's good. It shows you take it seriously. I hesitated, too, because I wanted an easier path. Also, because I feared there might be more of my father in me than I could overcome. Fathers and sons; a complicated business.'

'I don't even know who my father is. He might have been a criminal.'

'It doesn't matter. Each of us is unique, and growth is not a goal, it's a process. Develop the best in yourself. When we succeed in this, humanity advances. *Bene*?'

He made it sound grand and yet simple. I said, '*Bene*.'

We walked back through the garden in silence while I struggled to fit Francesca into the complicated future the chef had laid out for me. I was still wrestling with that when we came to the door of the root cellar and he heaved it open. Worn wooden steps disappeared down into an inky darkness; it reminded me of looking into a bottomless well, and I hung back. Cool, fusty air arose from deep underground.

The chef stepped down into the gloom, saying, 'Now you'll see something interesting.'

'I believe you,' I said. 'I don't have to see it. We can go back to the kitchen now.'

He half turned and looked up at me, his face perplexed, his legs already swallowed in the darkness. 'What's the matter?'

'I don't like cellars.'

'*Boh*. There's nothing down here but food. *Ecco*, take hold.' He reached out to me, and a combination of trust in him and fear of being seen as a coward made me take his hand. I followed him down the steps into the dark cellar; my palms went clammy, and my breath became heavier with every step.

The cellar smelled musty and alien, and I recognized very little in the shadowy sacks and barrels and crates stacked and piled along the rough-hewn walls. Sausages hung from the ceiling along with strings of onions and garlic. We pushed them aside as we walked stooped over, and the chef pointed out his treasures. 'Coffee beans, maize, sugarcane, saffron threads, dried mushrooms—'

'Are the mushrooms called amanita?'

The chef's face had become an indistinct chiaroscuro of angles and planes in that cave-like cellar, but I saw the one wry eyebrow he cocked at me. 'As you probably know, amanitas are poisonous. No, these are not amanitas.'

He went on with his inventory. 'Peanuts, cacao . . . ah, cacao. Now here's something close to magic. It gives sauces supernatural depth, and combined with sugar it makes a confection as intoxicating as wine.' The chef patted his sack of cacao; he fawned over it like it was a spoiled pet. He pushed aside a thick sausage and pointed beyond the cacao. 'That sack over there is amaranth. It's rare and hard to find but worth the search. It gives bread a nice nutty flavour.'

Everyone else thought amaranth was extinct, but apparently the chef had secret sources. Before I could ask where he bought his amaranth, a terrible pressure began to squeeze my chest and my thoughts turned chaotic. My skin crawled, and I felt an urge to run. I said, 'I don't like small, dark places.' My breath had turned fast and shallow. I gasped, 'Can we go now?'

'It's only claustrophobia and, perhaps, a fear of the dark.' The chef seemed unconcerned. 'It's basically a fear of death arising from dread of the unknown. It's the common but irrational fear that catastrophe will suddenly present itself for no other reason than you can't see it coming. Don't worry, you're not dying.'

'Fear of death?' An invisible weight compressed my chest; it felt like a vice.

The chef said, 'Most people fear death. That's why they love food that gives the illusion of cheating death. Love apples, bones of the dead, anything black.'

'I have to get out of here, Maestro.' I felt light-headed. I began to sweat and tremble. 'I think I *am* dying.'

'No. You're panicked by the closeness and the dark. There's no disgrace in fearing the dark. Many people do. A teacher named Plato warned us to beware only of those who fear the light.'

'What?' My heartbeat had escalated to an alarming gallop, my eyes watered, and my vision blurred.

The chef's voice seemed to reach me from a distance.

'Luciano. Pay attention. Right here, right now, there's no danger. Take a deep breath.'

'I can't.'

'Take one good breath, and we'll leave.'

'I can't.'

'Look at me.' He held my face in his hands, and his eyes steadied me. Even though my heart still raced, I managed one normal inhalation. Then the chef put his arm around me, and we walked out together. Safely out of the cellar, I sat on the ground until my heart slowed. I wiped the sweat from my face and asked, 'How did you know I'd be able to do that?'

'I only wanted you to try. Remaining calm in the face of fear is an important skill, and one you'll need. When we dig down into ourselves, we find unexpected strength. I want you to learn how to do that. That's how you'll grow.'

'Sì, Maestro.'

'Well then, what have you learned?'

'That I have untested strength in me.'

'Bene.'

For the second time in my life, I felt an urge to pray. I looked up, because that's what people do, and thought: *Please, let me grow.*

CHAPTER ✤ XVIII

THE BOOK OF BORGIA

ONE MORNING, THE MAJORDOMO GLIDED from the service door to the chef's desk, pursing his lips and holding his turquoise robes above silk-clad ankles. The glamorous, lilac-scented man delivered his message in a rush, fluttering his fan to ward off the kitchen's heat and dabbing the base of his throat with a snippet of lace. He chirped, 'The doge has been summoned to Rome. You shall accompany him and prepare your Sauce Nepenthes for His Holiness.'

'I'm honoured.' The chef executed an elaborate bow, perhaps too elaborate. 'I'll need my apprentice to assist.'

The majordomo waved a soft hand and trilled, 'As you wish.' He pirouetted on his beaded slippers and made his proud way back to the service door with quick, little steps.

'Maestro?' I stood motionless, holding a wet dishcloth that dripped onto my shoes. 'Me? In Rome?'

The chef motioned me closer and spoke quietly. 'You can be sure Borgia has some reason other than my sauce to invite the doge to his table.' The chef tapped the side of his nose.

'But to cook for the pope is still an honour, isn't it, Maestro?'

The chef smiled. 'It's time to begin your education, Luciano. You need to see Rome.'

All that day I paid special attention to every morsel of food left on every plate. I collected the leavings carefully and saved all the bones with a scrap of meat on them; I gathered a mountain of bread crusts and foraged for every stray rind of cheese. Once assembled, it looked like a pile of rubbish so I threw in some turnips and carrots, which were cheap and plentiful. I wasn't sure how long we'd be in Rome and I wanted to leave as large a parcel as possible for Marco and Domingo.

That night, when I took out the rubbish, Marco was there, waiting. His eyes lit up when he saw the oilcloth slung over my shoulder and bulging with food. 'What's this?' He grabbed the cloth, peeked inside, and his face fell. 'It's mostly bones.'

'There's some turnips and cheese, too. Give some to Domingo and tell him I said *ciao*.'

'Why the feast? If you're trying to apologize for getting caught and not getting anything out of that cabinet, it won't work. I still don't know how you could be so clumsy. You used to be a good thief. If you really want to apologize you could try again.'

'I'm not apologizing for anything and I'm not going to try again. I'm going to Rome, and I don't know how long I'll be gone.' I gestured at the oilcloth. 'This will have to last.'

Marco's eyes narrowed. 'Why Rome?'

'The chef has to cook for the pope.'

He sneered. 'Why does he need you?'

'I'm his apprentice.'

'*Boh.*' Marco shoved the oilcloth under his arm. 'I'm sure you'll eat well in Rome.' He turned to go. 'I'll just take my bones and get out of your way.'

'Marco, don't be like that.'

He looked back at me. 'Like what? Hungry?'

'Marco—'

'Have a nice trip, Luciano.'

And then he was gone.

The great cities of Italy are like different flowers in the same garden. Venice is a burst of pink azaleas turning brown at the edges, a carnival of decadence. Marble palazzi sink, centimetre by centimetre, while every winter, the sea floods the city ankle-deep and her citizens frolic and fornicate in her watery heart. Bacchus jeers at the Grim Reaper, and oblivious musicians in the Piazza San Marco play madly while a dried-up whore runs a lascivious tongue over her rouged lips.

After Venice, I thought I knew debauchery, but I wasn't prepared for the two-faced tawny opulence of Rome, the Venus fly-trap, an exotic beauty with a taste for flesh. Being much older than Venice, Rome had had centuries more to perfect the art of duplicity. While the rest of Italy sang folk tunes, Rome chanted in an ancient basso of contrived moral authority. The unchallenged image of a saintly Rome obscured the life-and-death power struggles festering beneath its gilded domes and embroidered vestments. If Venice was a slut, Rome was a murderer.

I've since come to believe that the illusion of Rome's sanctity is aided by the sirocco that blows two thirds of the year. It's a sultry southern wind that crowds the sky with low grey clouds. It makes mildew blossom in secret places, spreads leprous stains of humidity on stone walls, and makes people feel as if their heads and noses are stuffed with cotton so that they cannot smell the corruption under the incense.

Smell, always evocative, is the best way to describe some elemental differences between the Roman kitchen and ours. In Venice, Chef Ferrero hung leafy herbs to dry in the rafters, which tinged the air with a hint of the garden, and sea breezes swept mouthwatering aromas from one end to the other.

The kitchen in Rome was below ground, and no fresh air lightened the accumulated odours. Instead of herbs, Borgia's chef hung pungent Spanish hams covered in verdigris mould from his ceiling, and in one corner of the dim room, a sullen leopard huddled in its cage, gnawing on a hunk of raw meat. Its low, curdled growl and dull yellow eyes revealed no hint of the spirited creature it must once have been. Its demented pacing in that narrow cage depressed me and tweaked my claustrophobia. But Borgia often indulged his taste for exotic animals, and the leopard attracted little attention in that jaded kitchen. Aged meat and the leopard's stench made Borgia's kitchen reek of the wild and the dead.

Everything in Rome, even food, reached excesses unimaginable in other places. On our second day in the Eternal City, I accompanied the chef to the marketplace. I gaped like a rustic at a display of duck mousse and goose pâté sculpted over the carcass of a swan; it was garnished with quail feathers and roosted on a nest of ostrich eggs – five winsome birds killed and pillaged for a centrepiece. I studied a pale calf's head in aspic with a carnation in its mouth, one blue eye staring and the other closed – death, the clown, winking.

I contemplated tissue-thin prosciutto, the colour of diluted blood, pooled around melon slices the colour of flesh. In another stall, a vendor stood proudly over a bushel of truffles – big as apples and black as sin, warty lumps with a carnal musk, rooted out of the loamy soil of Périgord by pigs. I gasped at the mythic sight of fresh zebra meat, bloody slabs spread out on the animal's own striped hide in a display that seemed somehow pornographic. The zebra meat reminded me of Borgia's leopard.

I was eager to catch a glimpse of Borgia, the rich Spaniard who had purchased the title of Pope Alexander VI, but the chef told me to keep my head down and my mouth shut. I'd almost despaired of seeing the great man when Borgia's Castilian chef, annoyed at our presence in his kitchen, insisted that I make myself useful. He said, 'Why is that boy here? He's in the way.'

The chef nodded and snapped his fingers. 'Luciano,' he said, 'help the maids.'

I quickly relieved a maid of a luncheon tray and followed her up to the dining room. The Roman maids, mousy women with tense faces, were even more cowed than ours in Venice. Not surprising, really; after all, they worked for one of the most powerful and ruthless men in the world.

That day, Borgia would be dining with Herr Loren Behaim, and the maid nervously checked the tray twice before she carried it into the dining room. As was my custom, I hovered behind the dining room service door to listen and observe.

And in he came! The outer doors burst open, and Rodrigo Borgia barrelled into the room like a lusty stallion. He greeted Behaim in a booming voice, bristling with energy. Broad and muscular, in he came with his pugnacious walk, his cleft chin shoved out, still in his riding clothes, his crop in his hand, muddy boots ringing on the marble floor, and on every finger gold and precious gems. In he came, a man's man who liked horses and women – a swarthy, powerfully built man with square hands and a strong nose and nostrils flared open to life. A hirsute man with tufts of black hair sprouting on the backs of his hands, the perpetual shadow of a beard on his face, and a mass of springy hair greying obediently only at the temples. He had thick eyebrows over lively eyes, curious, intelligent eyes, hot brown eyes that could become suddenly penetrating. He flashed a dazzling, white-toothed smile – a pirate. In he came, laughing and easy, and why not? He was rich and powerful, and he filled the room like a charging bull.

Herr Behaim stood and dipped his head. 'Your Holiness.'

'Sit, Loren.' Borgia straddled a chair and absently raised a hand towards the service door. Immediately, the maid rushed out to him with a tray of bread and olives and a carafe of Spanish sherry. Borgia preferred the food and drink of his native land. He said, 'Tell me, Loren, how shall I use this old Venetian?' Borgia dismissed the maid, poured two glasses of sherry, and handed one to the astrologer.

Behaim accepted the sherry with a gentleman's nod. 'Your Holiness, the doge believes, or wants to believe, that the book holds a formula for eternal youth.' Behaim smiled.

Borgia put his sherry down and bellowed, 'But that's marvellous!' He laughed with his mouth wide open and head thrown back. He slapped his knee and asked, 'Does he even know about the Gnostic gospels?'

'I believe he's heard of them. But he's so haunted by his own mortality he doesn't grasp their import. Also, he believes there's only one book. There's no doubt that copies exist, as well as a significant number of people who know about them. Still, the doge obsesses about one book with a formula for immortality.'

'Wonderful.' Borgia looked astounded and delighted. 'How shall we proceed?'

Behaim leaned back in his chair and passed the sherry under his nose. 'You can simply condemn the book as blasphemy. Tell the people the book is being protected by heretics and Satanists. Then offer a reward the doge can't match. That will get his attention.'

'I don't know.' Borgia swirled his sherry. 'I can condemn anything I want, but people are harder to control than they used to be. It's those troublemakers in Florence stirring people up, giving them ideas, making them curious. People are getting bold, thinking for themselves. It's not like the old days. If the reward is too high, someone might actually find the damn gospels and try to use them against me.'

Behaim sat forward and lowered his voice. 'Your Holiness, as your astrologer, I assure you there's very little threat of exposure. This is the Age of Pisces, the age of secrets. Significant revelations are not likely to become public until the Age of Aquarius. For now, the secrets are ours to use and control.'

'And when will we see the Age of Aquarius?'

'Not for five hundred years, Your Holiness. A new millennium.'

'Perfect.' Borgia leaned back in this chair and laughed.

That afternoon, Rodrigo Borgia stood on his public balcony and denounced the notorious book as a volume of dark arts and heresy. He raised his brawny arms in blessing and proclaimed, 'Any man who brings me information leading to the recovery and destruction of this infamous book will be given a cardinal's hat with all the properties, privileges and monies that position entails.'

The crowd went wild with cheers, applause and incredulous laughter. *Anyone* could be a cardinal, and why not? Borgia had already given the tall hat to several of his bastard sons before their thirteenth birthday. He, too, loved his sons.

My maestro demanded privacy to prepare his Sauce Nepenthes, and Borgia's chef, a proud Castilian insulted at being displaced in his own kitchen, treated Chef Ferrero as a nuisance beneath his notice. He condescended to taste the sauce and then made a great show of spitting it out and rinsing his mouth with wine. He made an eloquent gesture of disgust as he left the kitchen.

That night, I stood behind the barely open service door of the dining room, alert and ready. I heard the customary pleasantries followed by the inevitable lip-smacking and praise for the food. The doge appeared clear-eyed and aware, no trembling hands or quivering chin. Over the soup course, he broached the subject on both their minds. 'Your Holiness has offered a generous reward to halt the spread of heresy. That book could be yours within the week.'

Borgia grunted, 'People are fools. The book is best kept out of their hands.'

The doge used his spoon to make figure eights in his bean soup. 'I imagine you've made inquiries all over Italy?'

'Sì.' Borgia slurped his soup. 'We questioned Savonarola for weeks before we hanged him. Infernal pest. The Inquisitor questioned him so thoroughly we had to hurry the hanging before he expired from the questioning. But sadly' – Borgia shrugged – 'nothing.' He picked up his bowl and gulped the last of his soup.

The doge sighed. 'I fear I, too, will end with nothing. I was outbid by my own council, and now, of course, no one can match your reward.'

'The reward is merely a distraction. Those who know anything vital won't surrender it for a reward. They're on some sort of mission. *Boh.*' Borgia ran a finger around the inside of his soup bowl and licked off the last of the bean soup. 'Only I and your Council of Ten have the resources needed to deal with that kind of fanatic. We have methods. If we can make one subversive talk, we'll have a trail to follow. Crack just one, and we'll get to the bottom of this . . . this book conspiracy.'

'By resources, you mean the *Cappe Nere?*'

'And my Swiss mercenaries.'

The doge caressed the stem of his wineglass. 'I have a proposal for Your Holiness.'

'Speak up.'

'We both know the book is probably in Venice, and it *could* come into my possession first. With all due respect, I have resources of my own. If I find the book first, I'd be willing to assist you in destroying any bothersome heresies.'

'In exchange for what?' Borgia smiled like the pirate he was.

'A gentleman's bargain. We agree that no matter who finds it, we'll share it.'

Borgia looked amused. 'If I find it first, why should I share it?'

The doge leaned forward and lowered his voice. 'I can provide enough intelligence for you to acquire Venice as the newest member of the Papal States. All I want from that book is anything that might be pertinent to my health. The rest is yours.'

Borgia shook his head as if he couldn't believe his good luck. He raised his wineglass. 'I drink to your health.'

The doge touched his glass to Borgia's, and they drank.

When the maids served the veal in Sauce Nepenthes, Borgia said, 'Ah, here it is. Now we'll see whether your chef deserves all the extravagant praise from Herr Behaim.'

The men ate with gusto, but after complimenting the dish and agreeing on its pleasing nuances, they became distracted. They started sentences without finishing them, drifted onto tangents, and allowed long, unsocial silences, each lost in his own befuddled reverie. Only when the subject of table manners came up did they converge onto a shared passion: their superiority to the French. Having invented the fork, the elite classes of Italy looked down on the vulgarians who still dipped their fingers in the gravy. Borgia chuckled, 'Last time I dined in France, King Charles crouched over his food like a gargoyle.'

The doge sniggered. 'Between courses, Count Dubois scratches his private parts.'

'I know.' Borgia bobbed his big shaggy head. 'And I had to ask his wife to stop sniffing my food like a stray dog.'

The doge choked on his laughter, and wine shot out of his nose. He caught his breath and said, 'They have to be told everything – "Please, *monsieur*, don't wear your toothpick in your collar like a bird carrying a twig to its nest."' He wiped a smear of Sauce Nepenthes from his chin with the back of his hand.

Borgia slapped his knee and roared. 'After blowing your nose, madam, please don't look into your handkerchief as if pearls had been deposited there.' He shifted in his chair to pass wind and widened his eyes in mock embarrassment. 'Bean soup, eh?' He roared with laughter.

They laughed until tears ran down their cheeks. They pounded the table and hooted while they recited a litany of boorish French traits – their terrible food, their dismal fashion sense, their sexual perversions – but they said not another word about the book.

I didn't expect to see another Venetian in Rome and so, when I arrived on the service landing the following day to help the maid clear, I was taken aback to see Maffeo Landucci sitting in the same chair the doge had occupied the previous night. Lunch was finished, but the men were still engaged in conversation.

Borgia said, 'You have an advantage, Landucci. The book is probably in Venice, and I know you already have the *Cappe Nere* combing the city and countryside.'

'We both know there must be copies in many places.' Landucci pulled the grey silk scarf from his sleeve and flicked it at a speck of dust on the table. 'Has Your Holiness checked the Vatican library?'

'Don't be ridiculous.'

Landucci shrugged. 'The first book will lead us to the rest. But Your Holiness will make a formidable opponent no matter where the first book is found.'

Borgia sat back and crossed his muscular legs. 'You may rely on that.'

'If my *Cappe Nere* unearth something first, it's quite true that I'll have an advantage, but it could be a mutual advantage.'

'You begin to interest me.' Borgia's posture was relaxed, but his eyes were steady and piercing.

Landucci perched his elbows on the table. 'If I find the first book, I'll make a public show of presenting you with it. You can do what you like with the thing, but you'll introduce me to the right people, in the right manner. I won't belabour the point, but I'm younger than you. Endorse me as your successor. Connect me. After that' – he shrugged – 'when the time comes for Your Holiness to claim your eternal reward, I could secure the papacy with a promise to make Venice one of the Papal States. I'll share the book in return for your support in the College of Cardinals.'

'And if I outlive you?'

'Then you will have lost nothing.'

Borgia sat back and regarded Landucci with a mixture of contempt and respect. 'Of course, you'd never try to hasten my departure from this earthly realm.'

'Your Holiness, I need your wholehearted endorsement.' Landucci seized his wineglass and raised it high. 'I drink to your long and healthy life.'

The two predators drank without taking their eyes off each other. After Landucci left, Borgia sat alone, hunched over his empty plate. Later that day I heard chamber-maids discussing the odd fact that the pope had spent the entire afternoon in the underground vaults of the Vatican library.

On our last evening in Rome, my maestro and I went walking along the Tiber. Chef Ferrero excused us from the kitchen, saying, 'I don't want to leave Rome without paying homage to her magnificent sights.' The Castilian chef waved him off like a bothersome insect. But I smelled a ruse – my maestro cared for food, not architecture.

As I suspected, the chef paid little attention to the fountains with lusty cherubs spouting and gushing, or to the cathedrals as ornate as wedding cakes. We waded through the extraordinary to-and-fro of Rome, the busy anthill life of the natives. Rome, like the Italian personality, has quick blood, a feeling of cheerful chaos. Housewives argued with vendors, young men preened for pretty girls, and children yelped and darted between people's legs. A well-dressed lady came out of a shop to check the quality of cloth in daylight while she wagged a warning finger at the shopkeeper. A man selling watermelons called to passersby: 'Good to eat and drink and wash your face!' We saw cobblers tooling leather, and we heard men singing, women chatting and the ironmonger's ring of metal on metal.

Borgia was evident or implied in everything. The Borgia family crest, a charging red bull on a gold background, hung on church doors, over balconies and in shop windows. The papal flag fluttered in the breeze and clapped against grey stone walls. Barrel-shaped nuns, Borgia's handmaidens, strolled in pairs, and Borgia's Swiss mercenaries strutted around in crisp, blue-striped uniforms with sabres clattering at their sides.

In every street, we saw Borgia's clerical army. First, a baptism: a priest in a lace surplice followed by altar boys with angel wings attached to their shoulders and the young parents carrying a squalling infant newly cleansed of original sin. Moments later, a funeral: prancing horses decorated with black plumes and silver ornaments drew a black carriage accompanied by a retinue of weeping relatives and, of course, the priest. The ubiquitous priests, Borgia's spiritual soldiers, escorted the faithful from cradle to grave.

At the Tiber, we sat on a grassy slope. The chef sat with his arms around his knees and stared at the river. He said, 'I've been wanting to talk to you, Luciano.'

'And I to you, Maestro. Did you know Landucci is here?'

He looked surprised, then annoyed. '*Dio*. I should have expected it.'

'He met with Borgia today. He wants to trade the book for Borgia's support in the College of Cardinals. He wants to be the next pope, but he told the council he wants to overthrow Borgia. He's playing both sides.'

The chef wagged his head sadly. 'See how they scramble over one another like rats after cheese? In the hands of men like that, civilization will perish like Atlantis.'

'What's Atlantis?'

'Another time.' The chef put a hand on my shoulder. 'Well done, Luciano. You're a worthy protégé.'

The chef seemed satisfied with my report, so I decided the moment was right to broach the subject of my promotion. 'Maestro, did your mentor promote you after he took you into his confidence?'

'Yes, he did.'

'With respect, Maestro . . .' I lifted praying hands to my chin. 'As your protégé, I beg you to promote me.'

A thoughtful look passed over his face, then he said, 'You're right.'

I wasn't sure I'd heard him correctly.

He said, 'When we get back to Venice, you'll be a vegetable cook. Dante will instruct you.'

I had expected some argument and could barely grasp the idea that I was really, finally, moving ahead. The thrilling thought of myself steaming spinach and stuffing artichokes overwhelmed me. When I found my voice, I said, '*Grazie*, Maestro, *mille grazie.*' The long-awaited promotion had been awarded just like that.

He said, 'When you took responsibility for breaking into my cabinet without laying blame on anyone else I saw your manhood. And today you've shown yourself capable of understanding how these *criminali* manoeuvre themselves into power. Yes, you're ready. You'll be a vegetable cook.'

'I humbly thank you, Maestro.' I inhaled deeply and even the sin-soaked Roman air tasted sweet just then. Feeling powerful, feeling that the life I'd dreamed about was truly beginning, I said, 'Maestro, if you knew a love potion that could help me win Francesca, would you share it?'

The chef swatted a bothersome mosquito. 'There are no love potions, Luciano.'

Merda! Why did he keep lying about that?

The chef said, 'We have more serious things to talk about. If you're going to move along in the kitchen, you must also move along in other areas. Tell me, what do you think of Borgia?'

I said, 'Borgia's powerful.'

'Powerful, eh? That's a small word for it. Borgia wields more power than any head of state in Europe. Kings are crowned by the pope – and toppled as well. His Swiss mercenaries are a formidable army – three thousand soldiers and four thousand infantrymen. His cardinals and bishops are vested with enormous estates and huge financial resources. Yes, he has wealth and military strength, but what do you think really gives Borgia his power?'

'With money and armies, what else does he need?'

'The people, Luciano.' The chef unhinged his jaw in a way that made him look cross. 'The church can lose money and land, but the faithful will always fight to get it back. Millions of people pledge Rome their unquestioning obedience. People think they need the church for their salvation, and the church wants to keep it that way.'

'I understand, Maestro.'

'Good.' He touched my chest lightly. 'Remember, don't look up; look in. Jesus said that. Lao-tzu and Buddha said the same thing.'

'Who?'

'Buddha and Lao-tzu were teachers long before Jesus. There have been many like them – Epictetus, Zoroaster,

Confucius, Aristotle . . . and they all wore sandals.' The chef stared at the river, and his eyes lost focus. 'It's curious, but when you see sandals, a philosopher can't be far off.' He blinked, and his eyes sharpened. 'The wisest teachers have all told us to pay attention and wake up. They mean for us to wake up to our own divinity. But imagine what would happen if people woke up to the idea that they don't need priests, that they only need teachers.'

'Are you sure of that, Maestro?'

'Absolutely. That's what the Guardians are – teachers. Not only do we collect and guard knowledge, we pass it on. So the next question you must ask yourself is whether you're willing not only to learn but also to teach. It's a grave responsibility. Some of the things we teach put us in the way of men like Borgia and Landucci.'

'Maybe the best way to teach would be to make all the writings public.'

'Not yet. The Guardians are too few, and our means too limited. I wanted you to come to Rome so you'd understand the power arrayed against us. Knowledge is our weapon. Some of us are working on a way to use the new printing process to turn the forbidden writings into quick-books, but it must be done in secrecy until the tide of knowledge is too strong to stop. Someday, perhaps, we'll be able to print books faster than they can burn them, but right now it's too slow, too dangerous. People get ugly when the things they hold dear are threatened, and these men hold their power very dear. Are you ready to oppose them?'

Marrone. Until then I hadn't understood I'd be opposing Borgia and Landucci, but the chef's passion was infectious. I said, '*Sì*, Maestro. I am.'

CHAPTER ✤ XIX

THE BOOK OF THINGS UNSEEN

WE RETURNED TO VENICE AFTER five gruelling days in a carriage, bumping over rutted roads. There were stretches when the road was so rough we got out of the carriage to walk in order to save ourselves injury from the violent jostling inside. On the way to Rome, anticipation had sustained me, but the return would have been no more than an uncomfortable trip if not for the chef's stories. He spoke of writings and illuminations saved from places as remote as Babylon and repeated the imperative to acquire knowledge wherever it might present itself.

Late in the evening, the horses clopped into the central courtyard of the palace, and I disembarked, weary and grateful to be home. I expected the chef to continue on to his family, but he climbed down after me, beating dust from his clothes and mumbling about seeing how Pellegrino had treated his kitchen.

We made our way to the back courtyard and I followed

the chef into the deserted kitchen. He lit an oil lamp and walked down the long room, nodding approval at the clean chopping blocks, surveying the well-swept floor. He checked the simmering stockpots and then wandered back to the cistern and peered inside. He shouted, '*Madre mia!* The water hasn't been changed.'

It was then that I noticed the buckets. Instead of being turned upside down near the hearth they stood behind the cistern, each partially full of fetid water – a blight in the otherwise pristine kitchen.

'Get to work, Luciano.' The chef pointed to the offending buckets and I gathered them up while he pulled the plug at the bottom of the cistern; it came out with a wet sucking sound and he watched it drain into the trough with a look of disgust. I hauled the buckets outside and dashed the stale water onto the cobbles. As always, it looked like perfectly serviceable water to me, and I grumbled to myself about the chef's unreasonable fetish. I longed to stretch out on my straw pallet.

Inside, I found him stacking wood in the fireplace that held the sturdiest swing arm. He pointed to a large round iron pot, saying, 'Fill that with fresh water while I build up the fire. No telling how long that water was standing. We'll have to scald the buckets.' He moved with heaviness in his arms, there was a strained, haggard cast to his face, and the dust of our journey was caked in his clothing. He looked as tired as I felt. I said, 'Maestro, can I do this in the morning?'

'No.' He pushed the iron pot at me with his foot.

I went out muttering and yawned while cold water gushed into the pot. Full to the brim, it was too heavy to lift by the handle, and I carried it in my arms, staggering under the weight. The chef helped me hang it on the swing arm, saying, 'We can't take any chances.'

'Chances on what?' I was breathing hard from the exertion.

'Aside from the fact that rats may have been pissing in that water?'

'Oh.'

The chef poked the fire and blue-tipped flames licked the bottom of the pot. He said, 'Have you ever heard the name Roger Bacon?'

'No, Maestro.'

He grunted. 'Of course not. No one remembers Doctor Mirabilis.'

'Doctor who?'

'It means Astounding Teacher. He was a possessor of forbidden knowledge – the rogue magician.'

'What has he to do with scalding buckets?'

The chef sat down on the hearth. He said, 'I'm going to tell you a story.'

Marrone. After five days in the carriage he wanted to tell another story? Now? But he was the maestro, so I sat and listened.

The chef said, 'Bacon was born three hundred years ago in England. He was a Franciscan friar, and as such, he was restricted from publishing anything without the approval of the church. Naturally, any studies that elevated science over theology were prohibited, and Bacon, who was a brilliant scientist, was prevented not only from publishing, but also from teaching.'

'A teacher who couldn't teach?'

'*Sì*, a travesty.' The chef opened his hands and crooked his head as if to say 'What can you do?' 'But Bacon had an ally. At that time, a French intellectual held the papal throne – Pope Clement IV – and they circumvented the restriction by having Bacon write his findings in the form of letters to the pope. He sent Pope Clement treatises on logic, mathematics, physics and philosophy. Those papers got to Rome but were never published. And when Pope Clement died, Bacon was arrested.'

The story sounded like some of the others I'd heard over the past five days; they always had the same theme – knowledge being squelched.

'They accused Bacon of witchcraft, and he was held in solitary confinement for ten years. Some thought he welcomed the chance to continue his research unmolested, but he told a confidant he went willingly only because they showed him the torture devices they would use if he resisted. He was a practical man. He planned to write a comprehensive encyclopedia but only fragments ever appeared, and after his death his name was quickly forgotten.'

'Then how do you know—'

'Bacon may have been confined, but he had to eat. One of the few people who had contact with him during those productive years was his cook, who, as you might have guessed, was a Guardian.

'The writings that brave chef saved are astounding, Luciano. Roger Bacon calculated the position and sizes of celestial bodies. He predicted flying machines and ships powered by steam. He explained the manufacture of gun powder before Polo brought it back from China. He studied optics and designed instruments to look into the heavens as well as into a glass of water.'

'What is there to see in a glass of water?'

'Bacon said there are tiny creatures, minute organisms too small to see or touch that multiply in standing water. These unseen demons can enter the body through the mouth and make people ill. They carry plague and pestilence and can even cause death. That's why I always use fresh water.'

I looked at the water buckets and imagined minuscule creatures wriggling in malignant glee, writhing over the bottom and slithering up the sides, oozing their loathsome humours. The thought alone made me ill, and my stomach convulsed.

'But,' the chef continued, 'Bacon's writings say that boiling water will kill the creatures and render the buckets clean and safe.'

The chef went on, elaborating on the marvellous ideas and theories hatched by this medieval genius, until we heard burbling from the iron pot and saw the first tendrils of steam rising.

As we scalded the buckets, I felt a palpable sense of relief. I pictured the vile little creatures disappearing in the steam, and for the first time, I upended the buckets with a sense of accomplishment rather than irritation at a useless chore. The chef said, 'Tomorrow, scald the cistern before you refill it.'

'Sì, Maestro.' I would do it gladly.

'And now, good night.'

He shuffled out of the back door and I sat on the hearth, marvelling at his knowledge. Someday, wise men would study the writings of Roger Bacon and build those flying machines and steam-powered ships and devices to measure the heavens and instruments to shine light on the infectious things squirming in water. They would benefit from Roger Bacon's brilliance because of his chef, a Guardian, and they would use that knowledge to remake the world. The realization that I might be part of this honourable society humbled me. The Guardians were . . . magnificent. They were *all* astounding teachers.

I wished for a fitting way to begin my training, to show the maestro I was worthy. Now, armed with what I'd learned from my culinary failures and knowing that the magic ingredients were eggs, I decided to attempt a recipe that would symbolize the Guardians themselves.

I would create a dish that looked ordinary, a simple thing that no one would look at twice. A deceptive dish that looked more innocent than it was, and it would be white as a cook's jacket. It would look plain, but in the mouth it would erupt with surprising texture and flavour. There must be a clear contradiction between the sight and the experience of it. Above all, it must be delicious enough to impress the chef and possibly be included in his book.

Included in his book? Perhaps I was becoming self-important. Still . . .

Excitement refreshed me and I prowled the kitchen, hunting up my ingredients. First, of course, I scooped out the triple-cream cheese. In another bowl, I separated four eggs and beat the whites until they were frothy and thick. I drank the yolks rather than take the chance that they might darken the cheese. I grated Indian cane sugar because it was sweeter than honey and I would need less, which in turn would lessen the chance of burning. For the unexpected undertone, the almond liqueur had been perfect, and I added it happily with a small congratulatory sip for myself. I added just enough cream to thin the cheese, then whisked it to a thick batter and folded in the beaten whites. I licked my wooden spoon and found it more luscious than it looked. Perfect.

Next came the camouflage. There would be no square pan, no need for clever rectangular slices announcing, 'Look! Here's something different!' This dish would not call attention to itself. I buttered and floured a round shallow pan, as I'd seen Enrico do with his most delicate confections, and then I poured in my creation. I banked the fire in the brick oven to a low even heat and set the pan on a high grate. I watched it closely and turned it every few minutes so that it would bake evenly. The egg whites did indeed make it expand and cohere. No bubbles and no pockmarks. The instant it began to acquire a hint of gold around the edge I took it out. After it settled and cooled, I turned it out onto a flat earthenware cheese plate and stood back to admire my masterpiece.

As I'd hoped, it looked like a simple wheel of cheese. No one would guess that a heavy rich cheese had been lightened with meringue, and that Indian sugar and almond liqueur were hiding in that innocent white disguise. I covered it with a clean kitchen cloth and left it on the chef's desk.

The next morning, I watched the chef furrow his brow as he lifted the cloth. 'Who left this cheese on my desk?' The cooks shrugged, and I said, 'It's not cheese, Maestro. Why don't you try some?'

The chef looked at me warily, then cut a wedge. I could see he was surprised at how easily the knife glided, how the 'cheese' offered no resistance. He brought the slice to his nose and said, 'Almond?' Then he took a bite, and his face opened as the fragile white skin gave way to something creamy, rich and fragrant in his mouth. 'Why this is . . . what is this, Luciano?'

I moved closer and lowered my voice. 'It looks ordinary, but isn't. Like the Guardians.'

The chef took another bite and closed his eyes while he chewed. 'You baked this?'

'I did, Maestro.' I was so eager for his verdict I caught myself shifting from one foot to the other. 'Do you like it?'

The chef chewed slowly and nodded. 'It's very fine, Luciano. I believe this is worthy of . . . saving.'

'*Grazie*, Maestro!' I wanted to tell everyone I had created a clever new recipe and what it signified; then I realized that was the one thing I could never do. That was my first indication of how it felt to be a Guardian.

The chef said, 'Later you'll tell me your method and I'll write it down. I have just the place to keep it.' A look passed between us and I knew I had pleased him. He said, 'What shall we call your sumptuous creation?'

'I don't know, Maestro.' I hadn't thought that far ahead.

'Something simple I think.' He took another bite and smiled. 'How about "cheesecake"?'

'*Sì*, Maestro.' A small part of me had hoped he would call my first culinary success something a bit grander, like La Magnifica Torta di Formaggio da Luciano. But I grudgingly accepted that that might defeat the purpose.

That afternoon, the chef assembled the kitchen staff and, like a king conferring a knighthood, announced, 'It's been more than three months, and Luciano has completed his apprenticeship. Now he's a vegetable cook.' He fitted a soft white toque onto my head. It felt like a crown, and I immediately tilted the hat at a cocky angle. I don't remember smiling – I remember feeling joy transform my face. I felt my eyes crinkle, my ears push back, my cheeks tighten, and my breath move over exposed teeth and gums. It must have been an alarmingly unbridled smile because the chef straightened my toque and said quietly, 'Moderation, Luciano.'

The cooks nodded and resumed their work: Apprentice to vegetable cook was the expected progression. Teresa put down her mop to blow me a kiss, and Enrico gave me a kindly smile, but when the chef turned away, Giuseppe raised a hand with the index finger and little finger pointed at me and jabbed the air. I ignored him and took my place at the vegetable station next to Dante.

That same evening, I made a naïve attempt to placate Giuseppe. I waited for him in the back courtyard and when he came out I smiled and opened my palms, saying, 'Giuseppe, what did I ever do to you? Come on, *paesano*, can't we be friends?' I should have stopped there, but in my eagerness, I missed the darkness gathering in his face. I said, 'Live and let live, eh?'

Giuseppe advanced on me until I could see the big, greasy pores in his face. Afraid to move, I cut my eyes back and forth, hoping to see someone coming out of the kitchen, someone who might stop a crazy drunk from snapping a boy's neck and throwing him in a canal. He hissed, '*Bastardo!*' The slurred word spattered my cheeks with spittle and his foul breath made me flinch.

'You and Domingo make me sick. *Boh*. No fathers, no name, you're nothing. But my fool brother and that fool chef treat you like sons. Like *sons!*' The sibilance produced a new volley of spit that made me blink. 'And now you're a vegetable cook? What's so special about you, eh?' Giuseppe grabbed my nose between two knuckles, gave it a hard twist, and held it. I clamped my teeth down so as not to sob. He held on for a minute, squeezing while I struggled against him, and then he let go as if he were shaking off something foul. He stalked off, muttering, 'Be careful, *bastardo*. Giuseppe is watching you.'

CHAPTER ✤ XX

THE BOOK OF FRANCESCA

'DID YOU MISS ME?' MARCO LOOKED surprisingly happy to see me, though he'd never admit it. 'How was Rome?'

'Corrupt.'

'So you felt right at home.'

'Worse than Venice.'

'Not possible.'

We sat alongside a canal on a quiet *rio* leading to the Rialto. After running my errands for the chef, I'd brought Marco a piece of cheesecake. I enjoyed the extravagant praise he heaped on my creation, but I didn't tell him I'd made it. I felt guilty for my increasingly good fortune compared to his misery, and I also didn't tell him I'd been promoted to vegetable cook; he was already envious enough.

Marco spoke around a mouthful of cheesecake. 'Listen, Cabbage-Head, I've been talking to people about the things in the chef's cabinet. You know that grain that's not supposed to grow any more? Well, it does and you can buy it right here in Venice if you have enough money and know where to look.'

'You mean amaranth? *Boh.* You're a turnip.'

'*Sì*, amaranth. Guess what it's for?'

'Bread.'

'He'd like you to think so. It's called the leaf of immortality. It's magic.'

'Marco, that's ridiculous.' But I squirmed, remembering the copyist laughing over the idea that the leaf of immortality had died out, and then seeing a sack of it in the chef's root cellar. Marco was right about amaranth being available; I needed to distract him. 'Guess what Borgia had in his kitchen.'

'Don't change the subject.' Marco shot me a contemptuous look. 'Listen, I've talked to a lot of people, and I'm telling you the old Greeks knew some way to use amaranth to extend life.' He gave me a mean jab. 'I bet your chef does, too.'

Dio. 'Marco, do you see any immortal Greeks walking around?'

His eyebrows perked up. 'How would I know if I did? Anyway, that's not all. Opium isn't for soup, Cabbage-Head, it's a strong painkiller. You can buy it in apothecary shops, but some people use it for pleasure and they can't stop and it kills them. Opium has no place in a kitchen.'

Damn. I'd always admired Marco for his enterprise, for the way he found things out, put them together, and made them work to his advantage. But now he was using his ingenuity to ferret out the chef's secrets and it frightened me. I said, 'You don't know what you're talking about.'

Marco leaned back on his elbows. 'Believe what you want. But your sneaky chef is up to something and I want to know what it is.'

'Marco—'

'Open your eyes! I think your chef knows something about this book, and he's going to get caught. The *Cappe Nere* are all over the place.' Marco made a slicing gesture across his neck. 'But us, we're invisible, Luciano. We're nobody. If we found the book, we could disappear with it. We might be doing your chef a favour. If he's buying opium, he's not innocent.'

My stomach churned. Francesca seemed to think opium soup was a joke, and the chef never did explain what he used it for. If opium had no use in a kitchen, why *did* he have it? Was it possible that the Guardians had a darker function than what he'd told me? Was he getting ready to spring some sinister purpose on *me*? I didn't know what he did with his opium but I couldn't let Marco see my confusion. I said, 'The *Cappe Nere* aren't interested in the chef, and neither should you be.'

'Big shot, eh?' He angled his head at me. 'Big shot knows everything the *Cappe Nere* are interested in. Listen to me good, Signor Big Shot. I'm getting that book with or without you.' He flicked his hand under his chin.

'Marco, I don't know what the *Cappe Nere* are up to, but it wasn't amaranth that I copied. It was amanita, just a mushroom. And the chef keeps opium for pain. He gets headaches.'

'I'm not falling for that. You're still trying to protect your chef, eh, slave?'

'Slave?' *Marrone*, why did he have to push me like that? 'For your information, I've been promoted to vegetable cook.' I regretted it immediately, but it was too late.

Marco picked at a scab on his arm. 'When were you going to tell me? I thought we were partners.'

'Marco, there's nothing to be partners for. The chef knows

nothing about alchemy. I know nothing about anything.' I avoided his eyes. 'You're impossible, you turnip. Leave this alone, eh?'

As I walked away, Marco called out, 'It's not over, Luciano. You still owe me.'

I was bursting with the need to tell Francesca about my promotion and I headed for the street of olives. Vegetable cook. How could she not be impressed? I wanted to see her eyes widen and that fetching smile spread across her face. Then I remembered: I'd already lied to her about being a vegetable cook.

I stopped in front of a carpet shop, trying to concoct some pretext for talking to her. I could hear the click of the abacus inside as the merchant calculated the price of a rug for a woman who stood by, stroking the richly patterned border. That merchant spoke to women every day because they wanted to hear about his carpets. What did Francesca want to hear about?

Life.

Stuck in that convent and starved for details about the world, she'd eat up gossip about the book – the doge looking for immortality, the *Cappe Nere* rounding people up for Landucci. And I could tell tales about my trip to Rome, where I'd seen Borgia himself and a leopard in his kitchen. I could weave stories to amaze and astonish her. I raced through the street of olives looking everywhere, scanning the people in front of each stall, but she wasn't there. Maybe she was shopping elsewhere that day. I elbowed my way past the fishmongers' stalls, where morning light made the sardines shine like silver coins. I picked through a shamble of vegetable stalls and fruit carts, where the air smelled like an orchard tinged with salt. The milling crowds of the Rialto combined Greeks, Germans, Turks, Africans, Arabs and Orientals, a compression of all Venice – but no Francesca. After running up and down a maze of *calli*, I found myself, once again, in the street of olives. Venice, the trickster, had had her way with me.

I dragged myself onto a rickety dock and sat watching a gondolier: his red-striped shirt bright against the blue sky, and his gondola cutting through the green water with a ruffle of water tickling the bow. Church bells tolled the call for mid-morning prayers, and I became aware of the time. I jumped up and hurried through the street of bakers, where I spotted Francesca's portly Mother Superior sailing along, sweating and fretting, with an unfamiliar pasty-faced novice behind her carrying a basket full with bread and rolls. Francesca was probably still being punished for her friendliness towards me.

My errands were finished, and I wanted to know where she lived. I decided to follow them home.

The convent was a medieval building with keyhole-shaped windows. It sat back off a quiet canal and hid behind a forbidding stone wall covered by cascades of jasmine, a profusion of dark green leaves and tiny starburst flowers, white as a bride's veil. The house had probably been built as a second home for some Turkish trader, and the small rooms of the harem had converted easily into cells for the nuns. The larger chambers, originally designed for pleasure, made ideal common rooms and chapels.

Mother Superior stepped up to the wrought-iron gate, and as she turned a massive key in the lock, I glimpsed Francesca through the scrolled ironwork. She was kneeling in the garden, pulling weeds with an air of ennui. She looked up at the sound of the gate opening and saw me, waving behind Mother. Before the gate swung shut, I pointed to a small, wooden side door, and I thought I saw the subtlest of nods before she bent back to her work. I wasn't entirely sure, but . . .

I couldn't take the chance of missing her and of losing the chance to speak to her alone. I sat on the ground under a mass of hanging jasmine and leaned against the old wall. I imagined her stealing out of the side gate to meet me and enjoyed a pleasant tingle of anticipation. Fearing discovery, we would whisper with our heads close together in delicious collusion.

Time passed and my excitement levelled out. The chef knew I had friends living in the streets, and I knew he'd allow me a little extra time as long as I finished my day's work. As a cook, I was entitled to a bit more freedom than an apprentice.

I made myself comfortable against the wall, stretching my legs out in front of me, and began plucking white blossoms. The combination of humid heat, the hushed lapping of water, and the heavy perfume of jasmine lulled me into a half sleep.

When the tolling of the noon bell from the convent jarred me awake, I found myself surrounded by a scattering of tiny white blossoms, and I looked up to see the sun directly overhead. I'd been gone from the kitchen for more than an hour, and anxiety made me restless. I walked to the wooden door and peered into the small rectangular opening cut out at eye level. No Francesca.

Should I stay and risk the chef's anger or leave and miss Francesca? I was a prisoner of hope and I paced while preparing a story about obstacles encountered during my errands – endless queues in the market, a church procession that blocked the street, old friends who stopped me to say hello. Within minutes, *grazie a Dio*, the small gate squeaked open just enough to frame her face, lovely as the dawn. She whispered, 'We get two hours for siesta. I can't sleep so I work on my lace, but I hate the silence.' She shot a fast look over her shoulder. 'Be quick, I can't get caught.'

I was instantly stupid at the sight of her. 'You risked this for me?'

She laughed, and it was a silvery sound, like the tinkling of small bells. 'I thought you had something important to tell me.'

Her cool amusement might have been a warning to a rational man, but . . . 'Oh, I do. Very important.'

'Well?' She wet her lips with a kittenish pink tongue.

Marrone – that tongue bothered me. 'Everyone's looking for a book with a formula to make gold.'

'Alchemy? *Boh.*'

She wasn't as easily impressed as I'd hoped. I said, 'Not only that, some say the book has a formula for eternal youth.'

Her face went very still, and then she laughed again. 'What nonsense.'

'No. I've been to Rome. I know things.'

'Rome?' She finally looked curious. 'What things do you know?'

'Everyone wants this book. Rewards have been offered.'

'I haven't heard about any rewards.' She pouted. 'It's like living in a tomb here.'

'The doge, the Council of Ten, even Borgia, they've all offered rewards. Money, a senate seat, even a cardinal's hat.'

'Those are big rewards.' She appraised me with new interest. 'What else do you know?'

Her interest made me reckless. 'They say the book has the secrets of alchemy and immortality and I'm looking for it myself. I already have some clues.' I squared my shoulders. 'If I found it, I could get you out of this convent. Would you like to get out?'

'Yes, but . . . What do you want from me?'

'I want to make you happy. Wouldn't you like to be rich? And never get old?' I felt a vague uneasiness about going too far.

Her mouth twitched. 'Now you truly *are* making fun of me. That's cruel, you know. Have you nothing better to do?' She adjusted her veil. 'Why are you making up these stories?' She sounded querulous, but there was hope in her eyes and hesitation in her voice. She wanted to believe.

'I'm not making it up. They wouldn't have offered those rewards if there weren't something very special in that book.' Her breathing had quickened – or was that mine? 'There really is talk of alchemy and immortality. Isn't it nice to think what you could do with all the gold you could ever want? And if you were immortal—'

'There'd be no hell.' Her eyes sparkled.

'No hell?' That had never occurred to me.

She opened the door wider and moved close enough for me to smell her green-apple breath and the soap in her hair. She whispered, 'Why have you come to me with this?'

'I've watched you. You're so beautiful . . . I want to take you to the New World.'

Her face opened. 'The New World? I've heard about the New World.' A complicit smile lifted her pretty mouth. 'That would be exciting.'

Then she stood back and looked me up and down, not the way the copyist had done, but carefully, slowly, deliberately noting every detail, every inch of me. Her gaze lingered on my birthmark, my shoulders, and my hips, examining, measuring, weighing, judging . . . It was excruciating. Eventually, she shook her head slowly. 'No,' she said. 'I don't believe you.' She looked over her shoulder again. 'I have to go.'

She tried to close the gate, but I held it open with my foot and leaned in. I said, 'I'm not making this up. You could come away with me. Think about it.'

She flashed a wicked little smile and said, 'Talk is cheap. Show me something.' Then she pushed me out of the way and closed the gate.

Show her something? I backed away from the door, enchanted and hopeful. If I could get the love potion, I could show her something. I walked back to work, tripping over cobbles and bumping into people, drunk again on possibilities.

When I entered the kitchen, the chef said, 'Took you long enough.'

'I stopped to see someone. A friend.'

He tilted his head and regarded me with suspicion. He said, 'Your face is flushed.' Then he flicked a jasmine blossom off my shoulder. 'You were at the convent. With that girl.'

'But . . . yes. I had to see her. I *had* to.'

The chef pulled his hand over his face and looked away for a moment. Then he said, 'I was young once, and I loved someone the way you love her. But, Luciano—'

'I know. I know. I won't see her again when I'm supposed to be working.'

'Oh, Luciano. Why a nun?'

'I'm going to change that.'

'*Dio.* Dante is waiting. I'm sure he'll let you know what he thinks of tardy cooks. Go on now.'

After Dante unleashed a string of caustic remarks about wasting his time on incompetent, undeserving boys, he dumped a mountain of onions in front of me with a warning to 'be quick and do it right, or else'. We settled into a rhythm of synchronized chopping.

Chop, chop, chop – 'Show me something.'

Va bene. Chop, chop, chop – I'd show her something.

That Sunday, I walked into the Church of San Vincenzo, washed and combed and determined to make a favourable impression. I refused to cower in the back with the urchins and beggars. I was a cook. Boldly, I walked down the centre aisle, feeling dwarfed by the Roman columns and Gothic arches, but holding my shoulders back and head high. I sat in a middle pew, in full view of the chef and his family. The well-dressed matron already seated in that pew looked down her nose at me, stood with a stiff back, and removed herself to another pew. I blamed my birthmark. I'd forgotten that without my cook's jacket and toque, I was just another motherless boy.

Stand, sit, kneel, sit, stand, kneel . . . I felt like a puppet. Did God really care so much about my posture? And why did the priest have to drone his incantations in a language no one understood? But I told myself: This is what respectable people do. Still, during my hour-long captivity, I prayed only for release. When the priest finally made his exit and the faithful heaved up off their knees, I darted into the aisle to intercept the chef's family.

Chef Ferrero stood in the pew helping his wife up, and when she saw me, she gave her husband a look that seemed to ask, 'Him again?' The chef said, '*Cara mia*, take the girls outside. I'll join you in a minute.'

'Of course,' she said through clenched teeth.

She stood in the aisle and motioned her daughters out of the pew. As they filed past their father, he caressed each little face trimmed in its lace veil. Signora Ferrero hesitated long enough to give me a look that scorched my eyebrows, but I assured myself that in time I could win her over. After Francesca and I were married, Signora Ferrero would see me as a good family man, she'd forget that I was a thief, and she'd mellow. Maybe the New World could wait. Maybe I could work for the chef, and if Francesca and I had a daughter, maybe we could name her Rosa. Maybe everything would work out, as the chef said, in its own time. But not that day. That day the lady glared at me with a look that could have singed pinfeathers, then she herded her daughters away at a quick irreverent pace.

I took two careful steps towards the chef and folded my hands across my chest like a penitent. 'Maestro, I've come to ask you humbly to allow me the same happiness you have with your family. You know how desperately I love Francesca. You know she's in a convent. I need your help, Maestro. I believe there's a love potion in your secret writings, and I beg you, in the name of love, to share it with me. If I lose her, I'll die.'

The chef rolled his eyes up to the heavenly scene painted on the church ceiling. He said, '*Dio.*' His head came down, and he said, 'After everything I've told you, this is still what you think about? This infatuation—'

'No, Maestro.' The firmness in my voice surprised even me. 'Not infatuation. Love. You have your secret writings and your wife and your daughters and your kitchen and your position in society. I have a cat and a dream. It's not fair.'

'Now he wants justice. Who told you life was fair?'

I almost sobbed. 'There's nothing wrong with what I want.'

'I know there's nothing wrong with it.' The chef sighed. 'But there's no potion to get you what you want.'

'I think there *is* a love potion.'

The chef raked his fingers through his hair. 'You've probably heard talk about an aphrodisiac, eh? And you think it's a love potion. Yes, there are aphrodisiacs, but an aphrodisiac won't make Francesca love you.'

I believed he was trying to trick me with words. 'Call it what you wish.'

The last worshippers had gone, and we stood alone in the cavernous church. The chef stared at me for a moment, then he said, 'I understand your obsession. I understand only too well. You really can't let her go, eh?'

'No, Maestro.'

'I see. But, Luciano, no potion will make her love you.'

'Then what's the harm in giving it to me?'

'You'll be disappointed, I'm sure of it. But I suppose you'll be disappointed no matter what I do.'

'Please, Maestro.'

'Perhaps the best way to convince you is to let you see for yourself.'

My heart leapt. 'You'll give it to me?'

'Only if you promise to remember this: No potion will make anyone love you.'

'*Grazie*, Maestro. *Grazie.*'

'*Va bene*,' he said. 'Tomorrow night.'

CHAPTER ✤ XXI

THE BOOK OF FORBIDDEN FRUIT

T HE NEXT NIGHT, I WIGGLED AWAY from Bernardo without waking him, slid off my pallet, and tiptoed down to the kitchen. The chef was asleep at his desk, and I shook his shoulder gently. 'Maestro, it's time.'

He yawned and stretched, then sleepily removed the key from the chain around his neck and shuffled over to his cabinet to collect the makings of my dreams. I expected him to assemble an elaborate array of secret ingredients, and I was mildly disappointed when he returned with only a small bottle of black liquid and a shrivelled brown disc, no bigger than a fingernail. It looked like a piece of dried mushroom.

He set them on the chopping block and tapped the bottle. 'Coffee,' he said, 'from Arabia. The Turks called coffee berries the Fruit of Lust.' He scratched the back of his neck and yawned again. 'But I don't think it's the coffee that does it.' He picked the bottle up, and we both stared into its murky depths. He said, 'You roast the beans and grind them in a mortar, then pour boiling water over the grounds and let it steep. I brewed this at home.' He uncorked it and my nostrils filled with that smoky smell, like burnt chestnuts. This was what I had smelled on his bedroom balcony. Finally!

He filled a cup with the thick, black coffee and dropped in the wrinkled button. 'We'll let that soften while we make the syrup. The coffee is bitter, and this addition makes it more so.'

'Is that a dried mushroom? Is it amanita?'

'Oh, stop that. This is peyote from the New World. It's from a plant called the sacramental cactus and its effect is something like wine. But too much can make you sick. We use it sparingly.'

The chef mixed sugarcane and water in a pan; he boiled it down to syrup and poured it into the coffee. He used a fork to mash the softened peyote button to a pulp, stirred it, poured it into a carafe, and corked it. Then he held the carafe out to me and said, 'Shake it before you drink, and, please, take only a small sip.'

'That's all?' I couldn't believe it.

'What did you expect, a soufflé?'

I took the carafe and examined it. Bits of mashed peyote still settled, drifting through the black coffee like magic dust.

The chef said, 'I don't want you to think I tricked you, Luciano. Let me be clear. I know you think this will induce love. It won't.'

'But it's a love potion.'

'No, it's a mixture of drugs. You'll feel strange sensations, but they're false, and they're temporary. Try to understand this: love is a ripening of honesty, a deepening of truths that people can tell each other. It comes with time. This drug will *not* make anyone love you. It might even make you feel unwell if you take too much. A small amount can be an aphrodisiac, but only for people who already desire each other. It will create nothing; it will only heighten what is already there.'

Love potion or aphrodisiac? Boh, *just words.* I imagined Francesca and myself being overcome by passion. I said, 'Is this enough for two?'

'That's enough for a crowd. One small swallow will be plenty. Now good night.' The chef lumbered out the back door, mumbling, 'Half a night's sleep wasted on nonsense.'

I stared at my dark carafe. There was more than enough for a test, so I shook it vigorously, pulled the cork, and tasted it. As he said, it was bittersweet, but not unpleasant. I tipped my head back and took a generous gulp.

Immediately, I felt a rush of panic, as though I'd accidentally swallowed poison. I wanted to believe it was a love potion but . . . could that dried bit have been amanita? Why would he do that? To teach me a lesson? Should I make myself vomit? No, the chef would never poison anyone. I laid a hand on my chest to calm the thudding there and forced myself to take deep breaths. I recorked the carafe, climbed onto the table near the back door, and pushed my prize into the recess over the lintel. I jumped down and peered up at the lintel from various spots in the kitchen to make sure my treasure was well hidden. I was craning my neck, looking up at the lintel, when I felt a numbness steal over my lips. Warmth spread over my chest while a chill rippled down my legs. I heard a sound like a loud vibration and looked around, but it seemed to be coming from beneath my skin.

A feeling of vertigo overcame me. The room swayed; the

warmth in my chest moved down to my stomach and turned sour. Nausea hit like a sledgehammer, and I doubled over groaning. I closed my eyes, and the world inside my head began to spin. I thought, *Marrone, he* did *poison me.* Then my thoughts turned chaotic. I retched, hoping to see the poisonous black fluid pour out of my mouth. I retched again, but nothing came up. I lay on the stone floor moaning. I don't know for how long.

As quickly as it came, the nausea subsided, and in its place I experienced a sense of intense clarity. I straightened up, feeling strangely alert and invigorated. The vibrating sound had gone, and instead I heard the footsteps of an ant crawling across the floor. Then the smell of boiled syrup walloped me so hard I tasted sugar on my tongue, and I swallowed a mouthful of sweet saliva. The taste mutated into the sound of an oar slicing through water, then into the gentle green fragrances of celery and thyme. I stared at a carrot top and watched it grow until it surrounded me like a feathery jungle. Carrot tops tickled my face.

The smell of simmering beef stock made me ravenous, but when I moved towards the stockpot, the kitchen turned upside down, and I fell on my backside. I pulled myself onto hands and knees, falling first this way and then the other, and finally, craving my bed, I crawled towards the servants' stairway. But the kitchen had grown immense, and the distance to the stairway seemed impossible. I watched myself crawl in someone else's dream, moving but not making any progress until, without warning, my hand hit the first stair. I thought the stairway had moved to meet me.

I hauled myself up the first step on my elbows, but I couldn't feel the stone beneath me. When I looked down to make sure it was there, I understood that it was not just cold stone but something warm and alive – rose and dove-grey and amber humming and melding as if it were breathing. I felt myself sinking into the rose, becoming the amber. I have no idea how long I reclined on that step. It felt like seconds; it felt like days.

The next thing I remember is lying on my straw pallet, staring out of a high window at a square patch of starry sky and a lemon moon. I felt I could rise in the air and fly out of that window, but I was content to stay there and watch the stars. Somehow, I was already among them. It must have been very late, but I wasn't sleepy. I wove through a sparkling universe filled with wonder. I blessed the chef – he'd been so good to me – and Marco, he'd been good in his own twisted way, and quiet, grateful Domingo, he was almost like another brother. I even felt sympathy for Giuseppe, that poor, sorry drunk. I loved my straw pallet, oh, and Bernardo, and all the servants snoring in the dormitory, and all the servants all over Venice. I loved life and everyone in it. Some small, drug-addled corner of my mind rejoiced: *Dio mio*, I love everyone! It *must* be a love potion.

A misty vision of Francesca gazed down at me from a corner of the window. She gave me her wicked-sweet smile and the stars sparkled in her pale hair. I wanted to call to her, but I had no voice. I smelled the mixed scents of her, and I imagined the lush, tropical feast I'd prepare for her on our wedding night.

I'd slip raw oysters between her lips. We'd share ripe figs and plump, dewy cherries. I'd offer her sweetmeats and honeyed milk, blood oranges peeled and ready, salty artichokes stripped down to the heart. I'd prise open a lobster shell and feed her tender morsels of meat, slowly, slowly. The flavours would mingle and mount and burst inside us like soft explosions. I wanted to believe it would all be possible.

I imagined her staring into my eyes while she dragged a buttered artichoke leaf between her teeth and sucked on the flesh. It was good. I rode through the long, lovely night on wave upon wave of pleasure, smelling her, tasting her, touching her . . .

I heard myself moan, and in that fierce embrace, I believed.

CHAPTER ✤ XXII

THE BOOK OF HALF TRUTHS

THE SUN ROSE, THE CITY plunged into another day of commerce, and the kitchen came to life like a spicy batter thwacked to a froth – all while I lay comatose on my pallet. One of the servants in the dormitory told me later that I looked so still and pale he thought I'd died, and he'd rushed down to tell Chef Ferrero. The chef waved him off, saying, 'Luciano isn't dead. Although later he might wish he was.'

The midday sun slanted needle-sharp rays through the high window, and I opened one eye with a careful squint. There was a nugget of pain inside my head that rolled when I moved; my eyes felt dry and scratchy, and my stomach ached. I sat up, tired and dazed, and wondered what I was doing in bed so late.

Then I remembered.

Marrone. A headache was a small enough price to pay. In spite of my discomfort, I felt cleansed, serene and sated. In spite of the headache, a light euphoria lingered. I confided in Bernardo, 'The chef says an aphrodisiac isn't a love potion, but you know what a perfectionist he is. They're just words.' I was convinced that when Francesca and I shared the magic black elixir, we'd bond for ever.

I knew instinctively that my tryst with Francesca must take place at midnight, when dull, ordinary people are asleep and it's safe to do magic. I'd find a place to share the star-shivering night without fear of disturbance. I'd croon soft reassurances through the initial sickness, and then we'd soar together and melt into each other the way I'd melted into colours and sounds. We'd wake up in each other's arms, affirm our love and make tender vows.

I walked down to the kitchen on wobbly legs and sidled up beside Dante, who was chopping leeks viciously. He said, 'You honour me with your presence?' He scooped up some chopped leeks and held them poised over a steaming pot. 'Is Your Highness ready to observe this preparation?'

'Sorry. I was sick.'

'Sick. *Boh.*' Dante screwed up his mouth and looked behind him, hoping to see the chef marching over to upbraid me. While his head was turned, I grabbed a handful of chopped leeks and stuffed them in my pocket for Domingo. When the chef failed to come over and reprimand me, Dante scowled and clicked his tongue at me.

He dropped his leeks into the boiling water and added a dash of salt, a pinch of sugar, and a splash of white vinegar. 'To enhance flavour and preserve colour,' he offered grudgingly. While the leeks cooked, he ordered me to slice long thin ribbons of scallions so that we could tie glazed carrots in attractive little bundles to arrange on each dinner plate. He said, 'Be sure the ribbons are long enough to make bows with generous tails. No dry ends. If that's not too much trouble.'

I sliced thin green strips of scallion, thinking about Francesca's demand: *Show me something*. Now that I had a genuine love potion, I could show her something all right, and I couldn't wait. The wild joy of the previous night made everything in the kitchen seem trivial. I couldn't bring myself to take scallion ribbons seriously. As Chef Meunier once observed, we are helpless in the grip of love.

I tried to pay attention to the scallions, but the peyote had left my stomach queasy, and there was a faint prickling under my skin. That alone would have been endurable, but a tremor in my hands along with frenzied thoughts of Francesca distracted me further, and I cut my finger.

'*Mamma mia*, you're bleeding on the scallions!' Dante pushed me aside.

'Sorry, Dante.'

'What's wrong with you?'

'I . . . I told you. I'm sick.' I wrapped my finger in a cloth.

'*Boh*. You're an idiot! Good for nothing. Hopeless.'

When the chef said I was his hope, that I had God inside me, and that I could be better, I felt encouraged to rise above myself. But Dante's attitude worked an opposite alchemy: if he thought I was a hopeless idiot, why try to please him? I cradled my bandaged finger and ignored him as he clicked his tongue indignantly and threw away the bloodied scallions. At that moment, I cared nothing for Dante and his ruined vegetables; I wished only to be away from him and his abuse. Now I see the childishness of my reaction, but that day, shaky, fuzzy-headed and aching to show Francesca something, I chose to wash my hands of ill-tempered Dante.

I reverted to the theatrical training I'd acquired in the streets. Marco taught me to feign illness in order to draw attention to myself while he stuffed his pockets with the goods of whatever merchant took pity on me. If no one came to my aid, we'd move on to another street and I'd 'take ill' again.

I doubled over, groaning and pressing my fists into my stomach. I wailed, '*Madonna!*'

Dante glared at me. 'Chef Ferrero,' he called. 'Something's wrong with the boy. He cut himself and now he's useless, as usual.'

With my head bent to my knees, I watched the chef's cordovan shoes approach. He stopped in front of me. 'Sick, eh?' He lowered his head close to my ear and whispered, 'I warned you, didn't I? Those drugs are probably too strong for a youngster, but you insisted, didn't you?'

'Oh, *Madonna!*' I produced a loud belch.

The chef whispered, 'You brought this on yourself. Now do your penance.' His shoes pivoted, and he walked away, raising his voice for everyone to hear. 'Dante's right, you're useless like this. Get out of here. Come back when you're fit to work.'

I walked across the kitchen half-bent, my hand over my mouth, cheeks ballooning in a pantomime of holding back sickness. Once up the stairs, I unwrapped my finger, shoving the stained cloth into one pocket and my soft toque into the other. I turned away from the passage that led to the servants' dormitory and pattered quietly through the Hall of Doges, and then through a series of elaborate rooms, all empty but for an occasional maid dusting a gilded chair or polishing crystal. I cut around to a stairway that led out to the street and I left the palace.

It was the hour of siesta, and as I ran through deserted residential streets, I heard music and murmurs coming from dim, half-shuttered rooms. At the convent, I hoisted myself over the wall using the woody, twisted jasmine vines for hand- and footholds. I dropped into a shrub hedge on the other side and, in a half crouch, scuttered across the deserted cloister and along the convent wall.

I dared a peek into each open window and saw sights I've never forgotten. In the first room, a thick woman in a white cotton chemise pulled a thorny vine tight around her waist until blood spots bloomed in a martyr's ring around her middle. She winced and pulled tighter. Through another window, I saw a bony woman, wisps of white hair pasted to her sweaty forehead, kneeling on a scattering of raw rice; tears trickled down grooves in her weathered face.

As I stared, openmouthed, a goose waddled around the corner of the cloister and started up a terrific honking. The nun turned her head to the noise. I dropped flat on the ground, dug some leeks out of my pocket, and threw them at the goose. The honking stopped, and I crawled on.

Francesca sat on her cot with a round pillow on her lap. Her nimble fingers moved over a complicated web of thread and needles as she tatted dragonfly lace. A lock of her hair had slipped over one eye, but she was so lost in her work she seemed not to notice.

Her veil hung neatly from a hook on the wall, but her habit lay in a rumpled heap on the floor. The cells had no chairs or tables, only a narrow bed, a clothes chest, and a prie-dieu. What else did a nun have to do but sleep and pray? Francesca's blond hair cascaded over her shoulders in soft waves, and I wondered whether such lavish length was allowed or whether it was her secret vanity. Her hair was so long and thick it would have been difficult to hide, and I supposed this extravagance must have been allowed until she took her final vows. Still, as a captive in that austere place, some indulgence in a sensual pleasure, whether allowed or not, would have been in keeping with Francesca's nature.

I watched fine strands of hair move in a slight gust from the open window, and then, slowly, I straightened up until I stood in plain view, framed by the stone casements of her window. She felt my eyes on her, looked up, and set the pillow on her cot. She stood up and we faced each other in silent surprise, she wearing a thin cotton chemise trimmed in lace, and I naked in my longing. The sight of her alone and half-undressed made my knees weak. I held onto the casement for support.

She grabbed her habit off the floor and held it up in front of her. She blinked a few times, then slowly relaxed her grip on the fabric and smiled tentatively. Her lips parted, revealing sweet white teeth, and the effect was like a dress slipping off one shoulder. My knuckles whitened on the window casement. She said, 'How did you get in here?'

'I climbed the wall.' I hoped my voice wouldn't crack. 'I have to tell you something.'

'More about that book?'

I nodded. 'I've tried one of the formulas. It works.'

'Oh?' Curiosity caused her to lower her habit and step up to the window. 'What formula?'

'It's amazing. It's, um . . .' I noticed a tiny bead of perspiration shimmering like a pearl in the hollow of her neck, and words died in my mouth. The shadow of one nipple and the undulating outline of her body were visible through her thin chemise. My throat constricted, and my mouth felt coated with plaster dust.

'Well?' She sounded annoyed. 'What does it do?'

I unglued my tongue from the roof of my mouth. 'It makes you feel, um . . . wonderful.'

After a tiny hesitation, she said, *'Boh.'* She turned her back to me and slid the habit over her head, shimmying to make it fall into place. I almost moaned as her ripe body disappeared under the grim brown robe. She said, 'You'd better get out of here.'

'No. Listen. It makes you free, Francesca. *Free.'*

'You know my name?' She glanced at me while she tied the rope around her waist.

'Sì. And my name is Luciano.'

'What do you mean, free?'

'It's a sweet black liquid. You drink one mouthful, and the world turns soft and bright. Confinements disappear.'

'It sounds like wine.'

'Better than wine. It's an adventure. You can fly. You can touch the stars. You want to . . . you feel nothing but joy.'

'Why do you keep coming here?' She stepped closer to the window and put her hands on her hips like she meant business. 'What does this have to do with me?'

I leaned into the window. 'I want to share it with you.'

'Why?'

'Because I . . .' Did I dare? 'Because I love you.'

A smile spread over her face, and then she laughed outright.

She sauntered back to her cot, sat down, and leaned back on her elbows. 'You love me.'

'I do.'

'You don't even know me.'

'I've watched you, oh, many times. I saw you feed that stray dog. You love life. You make dragonfly lace. There's something beautiful inside you.'

'You watch me?'

'Whenever I can. I want to take you away from this place.'

Her eyes narrowed. 'For what price?'

'No price. Only the hope that you might come to care for me.'

Her brow creased in disbelief. 'I don't . . . I never . . . Surely you want something.'

'Only your happiness.'

She was shaking her head. 'I don't know what you're up to, but even if I was curious about your potion – and I'm not saying I am – how could I try it?' She gestured at the walls of her cell. 'I'm a prisoner.'

'But you got out during siesta. Can you get out at midnight?'

She ran a hand around the edge of the tatting pillow and her voice became small and unsure. 'I'm not sure. I've never tried.'

'You could climb over the wall, like I did. Or I could come back tonight. We could drink it here in your room.'

She kept her head down while she played with her needles. When she looked up, a flush had blossomed on her cheeks, and her eyes were alive. 'It would be safer to stuff a bulge under my bed-covers and meet you some-where.'

'You'll meet me? Really?'

'But I can't go too far. I have to be back for prayers at dawn.'

Success! An idiot's smile stretched so far across my face I felt my ears push up into my scalp. 'I know where we can go.' Remembering the copyists, those strange Jews with their air of separateness, I said, 'Meet me in the Jewish Quarter at midnight.'

'The Jewish Quarter?'

'It's not far, and the Jews can't come out after curfew. It'll be deserted.'

'Oh, that's clever.' She smiled and the soles of my feet tingled.

I said, 'Until midnight.' Then I escaped across the cloister without feeling the ground beneath my feet.

I was so elated I almost forgot to stop at the fishmonger's stall and give Domingo what was left of the chopped leeks. I backtracked to the Rialto and emptied my pocket in Domingo's hands. I said, 'Fry them in olive oil with your fish tonight.'

Domingo barely glanced at the leeks. He stared at me with such excessive gratitude I had to look away. He said, 'You're a good friend, Luciano.'

'They're only leeks, Domingo.'

'You know what I mean.'

I did.

In the Hall of Doges, I encountered the majordomo picking his finicky way along the line of portraits, swishing a lilac-scented handkerchief at imaginary dust on the gilt frames. Instantly, I doubled over and 'took ill' again. I tried to shuffle past him gagging and mumbling, but he blocked my path. He tapped the curled toe of his slipper and said, 'The kitchen is the other way. Where are you coming from?'

Unable to invent a story fast enough, I whined, 'Sick.' Then I produced a magnificent belch, clapped my hand over my mouth, and pushed my cheeks out until the skin stretched to a shine. The majordomo squealed and jumped back to avoid the defilement of his hand-beaded slippers. 'Disgusting! Get out of here!'

I hobbled away. Behind me, the majordomo mumbled, 'Some days I can barely go on.'

I'd been dismissed from work and so I spent the rest of

the day stretched out on my pallet, pulsating with anticipation. Just as well. It would have been impossible to concentrate on leeks and scallions on the eve of my rendezvous with Francesca.

I stared out of the high window and watched the light on the sill change from afternoon glare to crepuscular glow to moon-shade. *Marrone*, the earth moved slowly that day. Eventually, exhausted servants straggled into the dormitory, and I pulled my knees up to my chest and emitted an occasional belch for effect. No one bothered me, and shortly before midnight, I stole away.

CHAPTER ✣ XXIII

THE BOOK OF SEDUCTION

I HAVE VISITED MANY CANAL CITIES that call themselves Little Venice, but it's an empty brag. Walk along the *Canal Grande* on a summer evening and see how the water cuts a glittering swath between two hundred moon-drenched palazzi; feel the exhalations of Venice's ancient stones releasing the spirits of infamous lovers and adventurers; listen for her treacherous voice in the whisper of a gondola slicing the water like a stiletto; walk into a fog-shrouded *calle*, and you'll know: There is only one Venice, and happy love stories are not in keeping with her character.

If Francesca and I had met in some innocent Little Venice – a pretty, well-tended village like Bruges or Colmar – perhaps the outcome would have been different. But the real Venice infects her inhabitants with the sin and pain in her own slatternly soul. We were doomed before we began.

I removed my magical carafe from the recess above the lintel and hurried through a maze of *calli* and *rii*. I crossed the bridge that separated the Jewish Quarter from the rest of Venice, hurried past a sleeping gatekeeper, and entered a dark Old Testament world. The streets were devoid of any Christian shrine – no tragic Madonna, no mutilated martyr – and the alleyways were so narrow that the houses appeared taller than normal. Hebrew inscriptions carved over the wooden doorways looked alien even to my untrained eye, and the high wall that encircled that place enhanced its sense of otherness. There appeared to be no right angles, no perpendicular lines; the huddled houses sagged against each other, listed over the street, and held in their tangled smells of sweet wine and queer foods. I felt a simultaneous sense of exile and confinement.

The Venice I knew was open and sea-swept, and so the dark, cramped ghetto roused my claustrophobia. My chest constricted; my breathing turned fast and shallow. The night felt more like a test of will than a romantic assignation, until the moment I arrived at a moonlit piazza and saw her standing beside an ancient, wide-mouthed well. She wore her brown novice's habit, but she'd left her veil behind. Moonlight burnished her hair to a silver sheen. I approached her with a confident smile, but when I held up the carafe like a trophy, my hand trembled. Her voice was as shaky as my hand. She asked, 'Is that it?'

I nodded. 'We might be seen here. Let's go into that *calle*.'

In the confinement of the dark *calle*, I again felt a twinge of panic. I tried to calm myself as the chef had taught me, but without him to steady me, I had difficulty slowing my breath. Francesca misunderstood. She said, 'I'm excited too, Luciano.' It was the first time she'd said my name, and hearing it from her mouth soothed me. She stepped closer and I saw that her breathing was as fast as mine.

She stroked my cheek. *Marrone.* Her fingers glided along

the line of my jaw, and then she reached up and touched my birthmark. I let her trace its shape with her fingertip and I felt branded. She said, 'I like this mark. It makes you look different. And you are. You're different from anyone I've ever met.'

'How so?'

Her lips pressed in a moue of distaste. 'Men leer and women treat me like a servant. But you . . . you're different.'

Was she saying she liked me? I was afraid to believe it and glad I had the love potion to leave no doubt.

As her hand fell, she let it skim over my chest. She said, 'This is the most daring thing I've ever done. I want to be free, but I'm afraid.'

'I'll protect you.'

She tilted her head. 'You would, wouldn't you?' And she sounded surprised. Then she pointed to the carafe. 'But I'm afraid of that.'

'I'd never hurt you.'

'No.' She gazed into my eyes. 'I don't think you would.'

My fingers felt numb, but I managed to prise out the cork and hand the carafe to her. As she brought it to her lips, I remembered that she needed to be back before dawn. I stayed her hand and said, 'Only a small swallow, Francesca.'

She watched me for a moment, then – and for some reason I remember this in slow motion – she drank without ever taking her eyes from mine, as if I were her anchor. I felt powerful and protective. I took the carafe from her and allowed myself a conservative swallow, less than I'd taken in the kitchen. I recorked the carafe and set it on the paving stones, and we faced each other in the dark, each hoping our separate hopes.

She said, 'Would you really take me to the New World?'

'Yes.'

'And would we be rich and have beautiful things?'

'Anything's possible in the New World.' I stared, enthralled by her eyes, the curve of her cheek, the mingled scents of her, the miraculous fact of her presence there with me. I cupped her face and leaned down to touch my lips to hers – they were warm and smooth – and she angled her head back and closed her eyes. I pulled her close to me and felt the length of her pressed against me, the swell of her breasts, the arc in the small of her back, and my body responded. Her mouth opened slightly and I tasted the smoky potion on her breath. Her tongue grazed my lip, and urgency gripped me. I crushed her to me, but she broke away. I started to apologize as she doubled over and hugged herself. She groaned, 'What have you done to me?'

I wrapped my arms around her and buried my face in her hair. 'This will pass.'

'Oh, my God.'

'It'll pass. I promise.'

'Oh, God.'

Then I, too, was overcome. Together, we sank to the ground against a crumbling plaster wall. I lost the ability to speak, but I managed to keep my arms around her and we suffered together. After some unknowable time, she relaxed in my arms. She said, 'Oh. Oh, my . . .'

Through my retreating nausea I said, 'I told you.'

'Oh. It's all crystal . . .'

As my stomach settled, I made a clumsy attempt to pet her hair, but she pushed my hand away. She removed herself from my embrace and pulled herself up, her palms climbing the wall for support. She looked around as if she were lost in an extraordinary place, then she stretched her arms wide and walked away. 'You were right. I'm free.'

'Francesca?'

'It's so . . .' She wandered away in the dark saying, 'Oh, my . . . goodness . . .'

I crawled behind her, calling weakly, 'Francesca?' but she disappeared in the deep shadows of the ghetto. I scrambled to my feet, lurched and fell forward with such force that I slammed my head on the paving stones.

I awakened splayed on the ground, face-up and staring at a striated moon, hovering between rooftops in a strip of night sky. Something was wrong; Francesca was supposed to be with me. I tried to focus, but objects moved and swam and blended in dreamlike sequences. Thoughts disappeared before I could take hold of them.

The smell of the Jewish Quarter surrounded me, and I tasted grilled flatbread and soured cream and bitter herbs. I reeled into doorways, bumped my face, and reeled back out. At some point, I found myself slumped in a deep entryway, trying to remember how I'd got there. I heard sap running through the wood, and looking up, I became fixated on the Hebrew inscription carved into the lintel. I floundered at the mercy of every sound and smell and texture, and some part of me knew this was not right. Francesca was supposed to be cradled in my arms. Where was she?

The night passed like splintered images in a broken mirror: a desperate search for Francesca in the crevices of a brick wall, exaggerated sounds and smells, a face in the moon laughing at me, the sinking feeling of having failed, and in between, falling, over and over, into black chasms.

When it was over, I found myself lying in the piazza, arms and legs flung akimbo, looking at a silhouette of rooftops against the first hint of dawn's uncertain light. I retrieved the

carafe from the pavement and went in search of Francesca;
I stumbled like a drunk, carrying last night's bottle by
the neck.

I found her curled in a doorway, half-awake and shivering
in the damp air. Her brown habit was streaked with chalky
residue, probably from the peeling plaster of walls she'd
walked into. Silky blond hair straggled over her eyes, and
when I tried to brush it off her face I found it stuck to her
cheek by dried saliva. She said, 'I'm thirsty.'

'There's no time.' I pulled her upright. 'Dawn is breaking.'

'But I'm . . . dawn?' She pushed the hair out of her face
and looked up at the ghost moon in the early sky. I saw
alarm in her face. 'Dawn?'

'We have to go. Now.'

'Dawn. Oh, *Dio*.'

We staggered out of the Jewish Quarter in morning
twilight, sea mist swirling at our feet. A tired prostitute on
her way home laughed when we tripped over a snoring
drunk who lay hidden in the low fog. The cry of an
infant sailed from an open window, and the smell of
fresh bread wafted from the street of bakers. I could hear
both of us breathing hard, trying to hurry. Still slightly
inebriated, we tripped on the cobbles and careened around
corners. I became aware of Francesca mumbling under
her breath.

'What did you say?'

She looked at me, and her eyes were wild. 'It *was* magic.'

'It wasn't, um, what I expected.'

'It was *magic*. What else is in that book? I want to
know more.'

Marrone.

'You said there were formulas for gold and eternal youth.'

'Those are just rumours.'

'But that's what you said everyone wants.' She paused and looked at me. 'I want it, too, Luciano. I want that book.'

'What?'

'If you got this potion, you can get the others. With those formulas we could go anywhere. Do anything.'

'But—'

'What's one night of freedom? I want a life. Don't you?' She moved away from me. 'If you love me, bring me that book.'

'Francesca . . .' I reached for her arm, but she yanked it away and ran ahead. At the convent wall, she smoothed back her hair with her fingers and beat the plaster dust out of her habit. 'We have to have that book, Luciano. It's our only chance for a real life.' She climbed like a boy over the jasmine-covered wall while the dawn bell sounded from the convent chapel.

From the other side of the wall, I heard her farewell. She said, 'The book, Luciano.'

CHAPTER ✤ XXIV

THE BOOK OF TEARS

MY LOVE POTION HAD INCITED lusts in Francesca that I couldn't satisfy. I had exaggerated myself into a corner and had no idea how to get out. I didn't know where the book was, and even if I *could* bring it to her, she'd find nothing in it but gospels and history lessons. Then she'd hate me for a liar, and rightfully so.

The next day, while the chef watched me prepare an artichoke for stuffing, he asked, 'Did you give Francesca your "potion"?'

'*Sì.*' I pared the tips off the artichoke.

'Indeed?' He nodded. 'And how did that turn out?'

I dug out the hairy centre, careful not to damage the heart. 'She didn't exactly fall into my arms.'

'Indeed. And what did you learn?'

I shrugged.

'I see. You need more pain to learn this lesson.

So be it.' The chef started to walk away, then turned back. 'By the way . . .' He held out a few coppers.

'Sì.' I dried my hands on my apron and took the coppers from him. 'What do you want me to buy, Maestro?'

'Whatever you want. These are your wages.'

Marrone. I'd never had wages before. 'That's for *me*?'

'You're a vegetable cook, aren't you?' He deposited the coppers in my palm.

I stared at the money. Five coppers! A modest week's pay, to be sure, but I had no need of food or lodging. I decided right there that I would save every bit and add to it every week. I'd let it accumulate until I had enough to marry Francesca. If I could provide food and clothing and a place to live, I could get her out of that convent and she'd forget about the book. I slid the money into my pocket. '*Grazie*, Maestro.'

'You earned it. Now don't ruin that artichoke, eh?'

I spent my days shelling sweet peas and grilling aubergine, and my nights counting my coppers. Using my fingers to add, I calculated that, at five coppers per week, I'd need twelve hands, or twelve weeks, until I could rescue Francesca. Some days, twelve weeks seemed impossibly long; other days, it seemed frighteningly quick. I opened a seam on the side of my pallet and hid my coppers in the straw.

Meanwhile, our syphilitic doge pursued his quest for eternal youth while Landucci and Borgia manoeuvred for power. It was an ugly time. Venice and the Veneto were overrun with soldiers, the streets and countryside teemed with the doge's guard, the *Cappe Nere* and Borgia's Swiss mercenaries – all of them ransacking homes, shops, schools and churches, taking prisoners and spreading terror. Mania for information about the book had created a police state where everyone professed ignorance while passing rumours and suspicions under tables and behind backs. Neighbours betrayed neighbours to save themselves and the dungeons filled with hapless suspects. Experienced torturers came from Rome and two black-hooded Inquisitors were summoned from Spain, one of them a student of the infamous Torquemada himself. The Bridge of Sorrows bore an unusual amount of mournful traffic.

One day, it was my unfortunate duty to bring food to the dungeon. Normally Giuseppe delivered those meals, but there were so many extra soldiers and killers to feed, it was necessary for me to help him carry the bags of bread and cheese. We were meant to leave it with the guard at the gate, but as we handed it over, a piercing scream assailed us from the bowels of the dungeon. The guard smirked. 'The Romans sent over a Judas Chair. Want to see it?'

Giuseppe beamed a rotten smile. 'Is there someone on it?'

'Sounds that way.'

They started off, and I said, 'I'll wait here.'

'No you won't, *bastardo*.' Giuseppe looked at the guard. 'This one thinks he's too good to get his hands dirty.' He grabbed me by the back of the neck and pushed me ahead of him.

We walked down a tight spiral of stone steps; it became darker, the screams became louder, and then they stopped abruptly. At the bottom, the guard pushed open a low heavy door and I saw a naked woman strapped to a throne-like chair covered in iron spikes. Shadowed figures moved around her, and I gagged at the stink of urine and faeces. The woman's head was slumped over so I couldn't see her face, but her whole body quivered. The only light came from tall candles shivering in the corners; the only sound was the skittering of rats. To prevent escape, the woman's arms and legs had been tied to the chair with leather straps. The cool voice of a *Cappa Nera* said, 'Wake her up.' A tall man in a black hood wrenched her shoulders tight against the spikes; he grunted as his thick fingers pressed hard into her flesh, and her head jerked up. Her eyes were round with terror; her face was bruised and swollen and twisted in agony. She howled, and blood dripped steadily beneath the chair.

Giuseppe picked his teeth and asked, 'What was her crime?'

'Her? Nothing.' The guard scratched his crotch. 'In a few minutes, when she's good and bloody, they'll bring her husband in to watch. He's the one they want; he's a librarian. She'll only last a few hours, but he'll talk fast enough. No one watches very long without talking. It's a good chair.'

When we got back outside, I vomited into the canal, and Giuseppe laughed. He said, 'I knew you had no balls.'

While Venice cowered under the watchful eyes of soldiers, the kitchen staff kept busy preparing foreign dishes for the inquisitive doge's steady stream of scholarly guests. We served professors from some of the oldest universities (pork and buttered dumplings for one from Heidelberg, and pasta with a creamy meat sauce for another from Bologna), a renowned herbalist from France (rich cassoulet), a noted librarian from Sicily (cutlets stuffed with anchovies and olives), a dusky sorcerer from Egypt (marinated kebabs), a Florentine confidant of the late Savonarola (grilled fish with spinach), an alchemist from England (an overdone roast joint), and monk-copyists from all the major monasteries (boiled chicken and rice).

During those long dinners, conversations became interrogations, and the Ugly Duchess always showed one blue eye and one brown. The most important guests were questioned politely and bid *arrivederci*. But there was an unexplained spate of highway robberies, and one heard rumours about many of the doge's guests disappearing on the road after leaving Venice. Guests of lesser consequence, like monk-copyists, were simply surprised over dessert by guards who appeared out of the wall to escort them to the dungeon for more strenuous interrogation.

I wasn't the only witness to those abductions. In a palace with so many servants, rumours circulated freely about new and grisly tortures in the dungeon: crushing, disembowel-ment, drowning, foot roasting and leisurely flaying. Torturers employed rats, saws, molten metal, thumbscrews and claws. Sometimes the stories were reported with disgust, sometimes with fear and sometimes, I regret to say, with relish.

During that anxious and brutal period, the chef appeared at work each morning with dark circles under his eyes. He walked around the kitchen massaging his temples and sometimes failed to test a sauce before it was served. Once, Pellegrino asked him to taste a mushroom sauce and the chef only stared at the pot. Pellegrino tapped his shoulder and the chef started. He tasted the sauce and nodded, but for the first time in my memory, the chef wore his toque at a sad tilt.

One day, we heard that Giovanni de' Medici had begun private inquiries into the book; Florence would vie with Venice and Rome for information and they had their own dungeons. This news so distracted the chef that he failed to complete his menus for the following day, and he stayed late in the kitchen that night, hunched over his desk.

I tarried over the stockpots until all the cooks left and then approached him. 'Maestro,' I said, 'when will we speak again about the secret writings?' I hoped for some crumb of knowledge, some interesting tidbit with which to pacify Francesca until I had enough money to rescue her.

The chef pressed a thumb and index finger into his eyes. 'Not now, Luciano. This is a volatile moment. Keep your head down and don't stir anything up. We'll talk when the pendulum swings back to calmer times.'

I decided to broach another sensitive subject. 'Maestro, do you think the doge really believes there's a formula for eternal youth?'

The chef laughed. 'Did you really believe there was a potion to make Francesca love you? People believe what they want to believe. Beliefs are stronger than facts.'

Was a more profound truth ever spoken? Many people believed the book had whatever they wanted most, but all of us wish to believe that the people we love are exactly who we want them to be. The chef saw my potential more clearly than my flaws; I saw Francesca's charm more clearly than her pragmatism. Were we so different from the doge, who saw the hope of rejuvenation more clearly than the certainty of decay?

Now, I sometimes imagine the doge in his private rooms, naked, gazing into a looking glass. He would have seen a shrunken old man with loose, sallow skin, sagging jowls, the bridge of his nose caving in from syphilis, fleshy bags draped under his eyes, and brown splotches dappling his bald head. His stringy neck would have descended into deep hollows behind his collarbones, and his concave chest would have drooped in a series of flaccid pouches dotted with pallid nipples and moles. The skin on his upper arms would have hung like crepe. His penis would have been a shrivelled worm covered with cankers, and his scrotum stretched and elongated, all of it dangling sadly between spindly, hairless legs distorted by swollen veins. He might have wept.

He would have turned away from the looking glass and lain down on his bed. He would have closed his eyes to see himself anew. In his mind's eye, his face smoothed out and his jaw firmed up square. His nose reasserted a strong profile, his eyes cleared and a thick shock of dark hair sprouted on his head. Sleek muscles defined his legs, his shoulders widened, his skin thickened, his biceps inflated, his chest expanded and his genitals regenerated.

Ah, if only. He'd feel alive again. Kumquats might taste sweet again and women's loins regain their clutch. He'd find his long-lost eagerness for challenge, and best of all, he'd have a second chance. Yes, of course he believed it, and no doubt he wanted it as much as I wanted Francesca.

Francesca's impossible demand wasn't my only worry. Since my promotion, Giuseppe had been finishing his days drunker and more belligerent than ever, and his animosity towards me had intensified. One inevitable night, I found myself alone with him. The chef hadn't hired another apprentice, so Giuseppe had been forced to take up most of my former chores in addition to his own. He did everything except oversee the stockpots. That task was too important to entrust to him, and it was still my last chore of the day.

While I adjusted the simmer under the pots and banked the fire for the night, Giuseppe loitered at the back door. It was unusual for him to stay one second longer than he had to, and his presence made me nervous. He leaned on the doorjamb taking long swigs from a flat flask.

Giuseppe walked towards me, unsteady and listing; he must have been drinking all day. I picked up my broom as a defensive measure. Giuseppe wasted no time on preliminary threats; he wrenched the broom out of my hand and pulled me up close to his face by the front of my white jacket. I smelled the sweat in his clothes, the oil in his hair and hard alcohol on his breath. He said, 'Vegetable cook, eh? You're really special, aren't you.'

I tried to pull away, and he slammed me against the wall.

'You know how long I've worked without a promotion, thief?'

The chef had told me to keep my head down, so I thought it best to let his rant run its course. I could defend myself if I had to. '*No, signore.*'

'Years! No one helps Giuseppe. *Boh.*' He spit in my face, then pulled the toque off my head and flung it away. 'Why should you get a promotion?'

I wiped the spittle off my face. 'I don't know, *signore.*' I stifled an urge to hit him.

'Filthy little bastard. Picked off the street for no reason. Clean clothes, three meals every day . . . now a promotion, and Giuseppe works harder than ever.'

'Sorry, *signore.*' I tried to push him off, but he shoved a knee between my legs and held it there. I dared not move.

'Sorry? Not yet, but you will be. That crazy chef thinks he can bring a thief into the kitchen? It's an insult. I'll get him, too. Giuseppe has ways. Giuseppe knows people.'

The pressure between my legs was more threatening than painful, but all he had to do was push up. I said, '*Sì, signore.*'

The network of spidery red veins over his nose and cheeks deepened to purple. '*Sì, signore, no, signore.* You don't fool me. I'm watching you, *vegetable cook.*'

I stood very still, hoping silence might defeat him, but it only seemed to enrage him further. Giuseppe drew back and hit me hard with the flat of his hand, and I fell on the stone floor. Before I could scuttle out of his way, he grabbed my hair and wrenched one arm behind my back. He was bigger and he had me off balance. With a drunk's reckless strength, he dragged me towards the fireplace. I tried to swat at him with my free arm, but he twisted my hair and yanked my arm up higher behind my back, forcing me nearer the fire. I felt heat on the rim of my ear and thought I was finished, but he jerked me back and hurled me against the wall. A vestige of sobriety must have reminded him he could lose his job and possibly more. I crumpled on the floor; my ear throbbed, and my arm hung limp and aching at my side. Giuseppe said, 'You're not worth it.' He spat in my direction, swayed while he swigged from his flask, and staggered out the back door.

I touched a wiry patch of singed hair near my ear. The ends felt crispy as *fritto misto*. My ear felt hot and sore, and my cheek stung from Giuseppe's blow. But I blinked back my tears. I wouldn't give him that. I resisted the urge to take up Enrico's bread paddle and follow him. He was bigger, but I could surprise him. I could smash his crude face, and he'd never see it coming. I really wanted to, but I heeded the chef's advice. *Keep your head down, and don't stir anything up.* I applied cold water to my ear and congratulated myself for my restraint.

If only the chef had heeded his own advice.

With daily reports of torture and executions goading him, my maestro couldn't restrain his culinary meddling. I knew he was planning something the morning he came to work with the old hop in his step and his toque starched straight up. I wanted to say, 'Remember, Maestro, don't stir the pot,' but a vegetable cook doesn't presume to counsel the chef. Alas, with hindsight, I know I should have dared.

We had instructions to prepare a dinner for a philosopher from the University of Padua, one Professor Pietro Pomponazzi, who had gained a controversial reputation with his essay 'On the Immortality of the Soul'. In it, Pomponazzi proposed the idea that after death a soul lingered in some ambiguous state, waiting to take possession of a new body. Exactly how it worked was the subject of many heated debates in Padua.

The chef announced that he'd personally prepare the main course, a special dish of his own creation. He said the preparations required intense concentration and he'd need complete privacy. This behaviour always preceded his most suspicious meals, and it made me uneasy. The chef said, 'This dinner is important. Our guest has the social grace of salami but he inspires worthy discussion. He has theories that deserve consideration.'

I couldn't believe he took Pomponazzi seriously enough to interfere. I said, 'Maestro, the man says we continue to be born over and over again in new bodies.' I opened my palms as if to say, 'Surely you jest.'

The chef smiled. 'Crazy, eh? But if you think about it, being born twice isn't any stranger than being born once, is it? Open your mind and don't be too quick to dismiss it. If nothing else, it should make you ponder our purpose. Now bring me a nice fat capon.'

He instructed Eduardo to prepare simple custards for dessert and added, 'I'll make the garnish myself.' The chef made an impromptu trip to the Rialto, and then he assembled his ingredients with a brisk efficiency. He made one foray into his private cabinet and shoved a handful of something into his pocket. I had a bad feeling.

That evening's special dish was Capon Stew in Mare's Milk. The chef boned and chopped the capon, brought it to a boil in reduced chicken stock, then added mysterious herbs and spices. He lowered the heat before adding the rich mare's milk, and the aroma of the sexless meat stewing in its well-seasoned sauce made my mouth water. The cooks sniffed curiously while Pellegrino, excluded from the preparations, simmered in envy. After ladling his masterpiece into a porcelain tureen shaped like a rooster, the chef brought a handful of dried leaves out of his pocket, crushed them to a fine powder over the stew, and stirred them in.

For the custard garnish, he boiled two dozen roses to make a scant cup of rose-petal jam. This, too, received a heavy sprinkling of the finely crushed leaves from his pocket. He placed a big pink dollop of the rose confection on each cup of custard.

The dinner began with an antipasto of *frutti di mare*. Pomponazzi speared a little squid ring and chewed. He gave a grunt of approval and said, 'Your chef has the touch. Very tender.'

'Sì, I have a genius for a chef, and it seems I also have a genius at my table.'

'Many in Padua would disagree.'

'Shortsighted fools. Tell me, *professore*, if the soul lingers, waiting for rebirth, does that mean that no one really dies?'

'Ah, you're a student of the soul.' The professor warmed to his favourite subject and quickly became bombastic. If one could tolerate his pedantic style one might contend that he made a plausible case for his implausible theory.

But the doge was not interested in dissecting the argument. He wanted to know about the professor's sources, the books he had read and where he had read them. Through the partially open door, I saw the doge tapping an impatient finger on the table, and I expected him to call the guards out from behind the Ugly Duchess at any moment.

But Pomponazzi was a fast eater as well as a fast talker. The *frutti di mare* disappeared quickly, and immediately a maid bustled in with the rooster tureen. She announced, 'Capon Stew in Mare's Milk,' then ladled generous portions into two bowls and bowed out of the room. The men examined the unusual dish and inhaled the fragrant steam rising in their faces.

Pomponazzi said, 'What's that delightful aroma?'

The doge shrugged. 'My chef is full of surprises. But tell me about your research. Is it the library at Padua—'

'*Madre mia!*' Tasting his first mouthful of capon, Pomponazzi appeared to be gripped by a culinary orgasm.

The doge looked into his own bowl. 'It's *that* good?' He tasted it, and his eyelids fluttered.

Conversation ceased. They ate greedily, licking spoons, sucking their fingers, and tipping the bowls to lap up all the sauce. After swallowing his last bite, Pomponazzi sat back with one hand on his belly. Suddenly, he looked bewildered, and then upset. He pointed to the rooster tureen. 'You realize,' he said, shaking a finger, 'for the pleasure of this food, we've become party to the castration of a proud animal. The mutilation of one of our own sex.'

'Well, I hadn't . . .' The doge looked appalled. He belched and laid a hand on his chest. He said, 'Abomination.'

'And mare's milk.' Pomponazzi shook his head sadly. 'Imagine the newborn colt, still wet on the ground, struggling up on trembling legs only to find that we've drained its mother's milk.'

The doge put his head in his hands. 'Poor little creature.'

Both men slumped over the table in despondent silence. The doge wiped the corners of his eyes. Pomponazzi sniffed, then snivelled, then sobbed. The doge shuddered and then wept openly. They planted their elbows on the table and bawled like large, overdressed babies. Wailing filled the room, and tears streaked through the powder on the men's cheeks. The maids and I watched in shocked silence, but when Pomponazzi held a handkerchief to the doge's nose for him to blow, we held our hands over our mouths to keep back the laughter.

One of the maids took a moment to compose her face before she served the custard with rose-petal jam. The chef had instructed her to announce that two dozen roses had been sacrificed for the garnish. He'd said, 'Be sure to use that word – "sacrifice".' She made her statement to the blubbering men and then bowed out of the room, barely restraining her giggles until she arrived on the landing.

After a few listless bites of jam and custard, both men put down their spoons. The doge wept with his head resting on his arms while Pomponazzi patted his shoulder, saying, 'I know. I know.'

The doge looked up and said, 'Life is so sad.' A glob of rose-petal jam hung off the tip of his nose.

Pomponazzi agreed. 'There's no mercy.' Custard rimmed his mouth.

The doge stood. 'I'm sorry. I must retire.'

'Of course.'

The men embraced. Pomponazzi blew his nose in a napkin while the doge sniffled into his collar. Then they limped towards the door, whimpering and supporting each other – invalids crippled by melancholy. Once they were well out of the room, we on the landing let our laughter go. The brown eye of the Ugly Duchess blinked, and we heard muffled guffaws from behind the wall.

Later that night, I carried a glass of ginger syrup to the doge's bedchamber to settle the old man's stomach. The next day, a depressed professor was allowed to return to Padua with red, swollen eyes. The chef heard that the man had left unharmed and said, '*Bene*. The man may be a dolt, but his debates at Padua have opened minds. We do what we can.'

Unfortunately, he shouldn't have done anything.

CHAPTER ❖ XXV

THE BOOK OF N'BALI

ON REFLECTION, I SUPPOSE THE events following that dinner weren't only the chef's fault for meddling, but also mine for telling Marco about it. I can see that now, but at that time I thought we'd laugh together at the spectacle of the doge and his learned guest weeping like babies and slobbering into their custards. I hadn't seen Marco in more than a month, avoiding both him and Francesca because of their demands, but I thought a funny story might ease the tension between Marco and me.

One Saturday, I brought Marco some boiled chicken necks I'd fished out of the stockpot – it wasn't a lot of meat but it was well flavoured – and while he sucked on the little round bones, I entertained him with the story of Pomponazzi. 'You should've seen it, Marco. The maids are still laughing.'

Marco put down his chicken neck. 'Weeping over a capon?'

'Wailing like babies. Howling like cats. Custard and jam all over their faces.'

'It sounds suspicious.'

'It was hilarious.'

'No. It's like everything else about the chef – suspicious.'

Marrone. What a pain in the neck. 'Marco, where's your sense of humour? The food changed their mood. So what? The chef has herbs that can do that.'

'He has more than herbs. He has opium.'

'For soup.'

'*Boh.*' Marco wouldn't be put off. 'He's up to something.'

'Oh, *Dio.*' He hadn't even cracked a smile over the ridiculous doge and his blubbering guest. 'The chef uses recipes to protect certain people.'

'*Certain* people? The chef chooses who to protect and who to sacrifice?'

That question gave me pause. Many of the doge's guests did end up in the dungeon, and only rarely did a meal turn the tide. The chef wanted Pomponazzi to go on promoting his wild ideas, but on another occasion, after the doge had sent a notorious forger to the dungeon, the chef mumbled, 'Good riddance.'

I said, 'The chef knows what he's doing.'

'Oh, I'm sure he does. I'm sure he knows a lot of things.'

I didn't like Marco's conniving tone. I said, 'Leave it alone, eh?'

'Never.'

That night, I lay on my straw pallet, petting Bernardo and listening to music and voices drifting in from the street. I narrowed my thoughts to Francesca's fingertip on my face, and eventually I dozed, but my sleep was light and restless. In the small hours, half-awakened by a dream of Francesca in her chemise, I reached for Bernardo, but my hand only skimmed the burlap of my pallet. The streets were quiet by then, and the dormitory rippled with snores. I swept my hand up and down my pallet, and then opened my eyes. 'Bernardo?' He was gone.

I sat up, rubbing my eyes, and then pulled on my trousers. On bare feet, I padded down the length of the dormitory, whispering. 'Psssst. Bernardo?' I found the dormitory door open, but that wasn't unusual. Often the last servant to bed was too tired to close it properly. Out on the landing, I called softly, 'Bernardo?' I stepped down a few stairs and saw him, midway down the staircase, crouched like a giant fur ball. He looked back at me and blinked. I said, 'What is it? Did you hear something?' Bernardo glided down the stairs and I followed.

Halfway down, I heard a click. Was it a door closing? A lock turning? I crept down farther and peered into the darkened kitchen. An oil lamp outside one window creaked and swayed in the wind and cast a dim, intermittent light on a figure moving towards the back door. I tiptoed down the stairs and through the kitchen and jumped him from behind. He cried out, and we both fell to the floor. Just as I raised my fist to pummel the intruder, he said, 'Luciano!'

'Marco?' *Marrone*, he was bold.

'Get off me, Cabbage-Head.'

'What are you doing here?'

'What you won't do.' Marco reached into his shirt and pulled out a small cloth bundle. He spread it open on a chopping block to show me what he'd stolen from the chef's cabinet – a few dried leaves, a shrivelled flower, a bean and a pod. He'd sprinkled a powder and some crushed herbs into two pieces of parchment and twisted the ends shut. It was nothing but herbs and spices, and to hide my relief, I kept my head down and fingered the dried leaves. I said, 'You turnip. What are you going to do, cook dinner?'

'I'm taking these to the Abyssinian. Tomorrow. I'll find out what he's up to. And I'm going to ask her if she knows where Rufina is.' He looked pathetically hopeful.

'The Abyssinian? How will you pay her?'

He jingled his pocket and jerked his head towards the spice closet. He had taken money from the silver box that I had told him about.

'Oh, *Dio*, Marco—'

'You said a few coins wouldn't be missed.'

I knew immediately that I couldn't let him go to the Abyssinian alone. He'd only stolen herbs and spices, but I feared what flights of fancy Marco might take. It's human nature for people to see what they want to see and hear what they want to hear. I had to protect the chef.

Even if I'd wanted to seek advice, I couldn't; the next day was Sunday, the chef's day off, and I'd have to handle Marco on my own. I said, 'This is foolishness, but I'm curious about the Abyssinian. I'll go with you.'

Marco smiled. 'I knew you'd come around, Cabbage-Head. I'll come for you in the morning. Save me some breakfast.' He thumped my back, then cantered out the back door.

After we served the doge's breakfast, I told Pellegrino I was going to Mass. I met Marco outside the back courtyard and gave him a slice of bread piled with sardines. I watched while he gobbled it down almost without chewing and then we made our way through the Rialto and into the hidden streets of Venice. When we arrived in the Circassian Quarter, that colourful district with its shifting, nomadic population, we stood in front of a *ristorante* and stared up at the gossamer curtains fluttering in the Abyssinian's tall, arched windows.

Rumour had it that N'bali was the daughter of an Abyssinian woman and an Italian sailor. The sailor had brought N'bali and her mother to Venice and left them with the Circassians. The man went back to sea and, as so often happened, he never returned. After her mother died, N'bali stayed with the Circassians because, like them, she resisted assimilation.

Unlike them, she did not have a reputation as a charlatan or a thief. Some people called the Circassians gypsies and scorned them for living on the fringes of society, isolated and answering only to their own laws. But even in that population apart, N'bali was an individual apart, for she was acknowledged as one of the true *adepti*, those who hold genuine supernatural power in their hands. It was said that she had the power to heal and to know simply by touch.

We walked through the noisy crowd in the Circassian *ristorante*, wading through smells of spicy goulash and heavy amber wine, and wondering at the dissonant music and the staccato language. When we ascended to N'bali's sparse room, with its high windows and agreeable scent of sandalwood, it seemed a short trip from chaos to calm.

N'bali sat straight-backed and cross-legged on the floor. She was honey-coloured and bald, with long, slim limbs and sadness in her languid movements. She wore rope sandals, necklaces of wood and bone, gold armbands and tiny gold bells around her ankles. She had a fine nose, a carved mouth and pagan eyes. Her small breasts were only incidentally covered by a simple red cloth that was wound around her lean body and thrown over one shoulder. She had a smooth buttery voice and spoke Venetian with a lilting accent. Amharic had been her first language.

Her sandalwood scent came from the oil with which she rubbed her body in an effort to be more like her mother, the true, full-blooded Abyssinian. Her sadness came from an understanding of her *mingi* – the Abyssinian word for all the bad luck in the world. N'bali's *mingi* was having her pure Abyssinian blood diluted by her father's Italian blood. Her mother taught her to keep herself separate from the debasing influences around her, lest they wither her Abyssinian spirit and leave her no better than a Venetian.

She was never seen in public and her room was decorated only with the few items her mother had left her: a woven floor mat, a bright yellow cloth thrown across the banquette under the windows, a cowhide stretched on the wall, a polished gourd to eat from, and a drinking cup made from a steer horn. Wooden figures carved from dark wood, and showing private parts in shocking detail, were displayed on a low, crook-legged table.

N'bali kept two watchful cats, one white and one black, who stared at her when she spoke to them. Some said the cats understood her purring words and did her bidding. No one ever said anything like that about my conversations with Bernardo, or about the doge's sugary speeches to his pets, but words took on special meaning when spoken by an *adeptus*.

Everything about N'bali was different. She didn't engage in any of the practices of witches or Circassians: no dimming of the light with heavy curtains, no incantations, no mysterious concoctions or decoctions. When we entered her airy room, she motioned us forward, saying, 'Come, sit with me,' as if she'd been expecting us.

We sat on the floor mat. Marco looked at me and said, 'First Rufina.'

'Sure, Marco.'

He said, 'Can you tell me how to find my sister?'

N'bali unfurled her long hand, saying, 'My mother told me that people do not value what they do not pay for.'

Marco took the coins from his pocket and placed them on her narrow palm. Open-handed, N'bali slid them into a wooden bowl, where they clinked against the coins of many nations. She said, 'You stole that money.'

Marco's jaw dropped. 'No—'

'That's not my affair. My mother told me I am not responsible for what others do. I am keeper only of my own deeds.'

Marco and I both let out our breath. He said, 'My sister?'

N'bali closed her eyes and a pained expression came over her face. She said, 'Your sister and your mother are together.'

'Where?'

She looked at him sadly and shook her head.

Marco looked stricken, and then angry. 'If you don't know just say so.'

'I don't know.'

I saw my opportunity. 'See, Marco. This is a waste of time.'

'No! I already paid.' Marco took the cloth bundle out of his shirt and spread it out before her. 'Here,' he said. 'Are things in this cloth magic?'

N'bali smiled, a big, white, generous smile. 'Of course they are,' she said. 'Everything in this aromatic world is magic.'

'But what kind of magic?' The set of Marco's shoulders told me he was a little frightened. 'What are they used for?'

'Just tell us what they are,' I said. 'That's enough.'

Marco shot me a warning look.

N'bali ran her fingers over the leaves, the bean, the pod and the dried flower, then she untwisted the ends of the paper packets and touched the grainy powders in them. She laid both of her hands flat on the open cloth and closed her eyes. After a minute, she said, 'Why do you ask me what you already know?'

'But we don't know.' Marco wrinkled his brow. 'That's why we're here.'

She studied me until I squirmed, then she said, 'I see.' She picked up a leaf and waved it under her nose. 'Valerian,' she said. 'It calms the nerves, makes you forget your troubles. Of course, if you take too much, you forget everything from one moment to the next.'

Sauce Nepenthes.

She picked up the other leaf and said, 'Henbane. A small amount is good for quieting high-spirited children. But too much can injure the heart and bring on a deep melancholy.'

Pomponazzi and the doge weeping into their custards.

She flicked a contemptuous finger at the shrivelled flower. 'Hibiscus. Some say it's an aphrodisiac.' I held my breath. 'But it's just a flower. Some use it to make tea.'

I blurted, 'Are you sure?'

She looked at me with a glimmer of amusement. 'You are perhaps fourteen? Fifteen?'

'Something like that.'

She leaned her head back and let her eyelids droop; a full throaty chuckle bubbled up from deep in her chest. She said, 'You're right, an aphrodisiac. Eat hibiscus, and you will make love again and again.'

There had been no hibiscus in the chef's potion. I wondered whether his potion might be an incomplete recipe. Maybe that was why things went wrong with Francesca.

N'bali took up the bean in one hand and the pod in the other. She said, 'Coffee and cacao. These are from the New World. They can be made into stimulating drinks and sinfully delicious confections.'

Behaim calling the coating on his biscuit delicious as sex.

N'bali touched her fingertip to the powder, and her face darkened.

Marco said, 'What is it?'

'Opium. This will take away pain and give you blissful dreams.'

Marco pushed. 'It's never used for cooking, is it? It's a drug, isn't it?'

'Of course it's a drug.' N'bali gestured at the herbs arrayed in front of her. 'All of these things are drugs.'

'I knew it.' Marco pushed the other paper packet at her. 'What is this one?'

She sighed. 'This is tiresome.'

Good, I thought, *she's anxious to be rid of us.*

Marco pointed to the money in the wooden bowl. 'We paid you.'

N'bali flicked a hand at the packet. 'That is amaranth.'

'I knew it!' Marco slapped the table of idols so hard they jumped.

N'bali growled. 'How dare you.' She scattered our herbs with a violent sweep of her long arm. Marco scrambled after them, but everything except the cacao pod disappeared into the woven floor mat.

Marco whispered, 'What have you done?'

N'bali moved her head from side to side as if loosening her neck. She said, 'I know what you think. Eat amaranth and live for ever. My mother told me that legend, and many others: the Gates of Alexander, the Fountain of Youth, salamanders who live in fire, and the priest-king, Prester John.' She sneered. 'He was nothing next to the illustrious Queen Eylouka. My mother told me everything. She knew about the book long before Venice started talking.'

I stiffened.

'My mother told me about many books, and about the fools and knaves who seek them.' She pointed a long, thin finger at Marco. 'You want gold.' Then she pointed at me. 'You want love. You both think the book can satisfy your desires.'

Marco jumped up and stood with his fists balled at his sides. 'What do you know about the book?'

I stood between Marco and N'bali. 'She doesn't know anything. Nobody does.'

N'bali looked up at me and said, 'Don't do that.' She waved an apathetic hand at me. 'You know your teacher has the book.'

Oh, *Dio*. The chef had never quite come right out and said it, but I did know. I'd known it for a long time, perhaps since Rome, but I wasn't ready to say it so bluntly, and certainly not in front of Marco.

Marco turned on me. He nailed me to the floor with a look. He said, 'You knew.' It was not a question; it was an accusation. We stared at each other.

N'bali said, 'You should never look anyone directly in the eye like that. Some people have the power to kill with a look.'

Marco said, 'You knew.'

I had no reply.

N'bali unfolded her legs and stood in one graceful motion. She reached out and touched my birthmark. I flinched, but she traced its outline gently with two fingertips. She said, '"*Mingi*" is the name given to all the ill fortune that befalls men. Certain things are sure to bring it about – twins, crooked teeth and birthmarks.'

A terrible thrill raced up my spine, and I pulled my head away from her hand. She smiled her generous smile. 'It's all right. Your *mingi* can be overcome by a simple sacrifice. Someone must die, but don't worry, someone will.

You have only to wait. My people say patience turns milk to butter.'

My mouth went dry, but N'bali simply sat down and laid her hands in her lap, palms up. She sat perfectly still, her clean gleaming head balanced on her stem-like neck and her eyes unfocused, a picture of otherworldly serenity.

Marco and I backed away. When we reached the door, N'bali raised her hand and said, 'It will be all right. Someone will die.'

Marco and I squeezed through the door together and clomped down the stairs. At the bottom, he hissed, 'You knew.'

'Marco, you don't understand.'

'I understand you're a liar.'

'Let me—'

'I'm going to get that book from him. Don't try to stop me.'

'Marco, listen—'

But he shoved past me and disappeared into a crowd of dancing Circassians.

Making my way through the *ristorante*, I kept hearing N'bali's voice in my head: *Someone will die.* My thoughts were interrupted by a prickle on the back of my neck, that sense of being watched, and I looked back to see Giuseppe staring at me from a corner table. What was Giuseppe doing in a Circassian *ristorante*? He was one of those people who called the Circassians gypsies and then spat. He stared directly into my eyes, and I remembered N'bali's warning about killing with a look. I turned away, but it was already too late.

THE BOOK OF IMMORTALITY

THE NEXT DAY, I STRUGGLED WITH how to broach the subject of N'bali with the chef. My preoccupation was obvious. All morning the chef snapped his most common admonition: 'Pay attention.' That morning I was so distracted he hit me with that phrase repeatedly, like a club. I was grateful when the time for my mid-morning *panino* came around. I took my bread and prosciutto out to the courtyard and sat down to eat with my back against the water pump. As I finished licking salt and crumbs from my fingers, the chef came out and stood over me. He said, 'All right, what is it? The girl?'

'No, Maestro.' I wiped my mouth with the back of my hand and mumbled, 'Something new happened. I'm afraid there might be trouble.'

'There's already trouble.' The chef bent over with his hands on his knees. 'But in my experience, trouble often brings opportunity.'

'There are soldiers all over Venice and everyone is under

suspicion. I'm sorry, but I don't see the opportunity in that.'

'It's an opportunity to practise an Indian method of menu preparation.'

'Menus?' *Marrone*, I thought, my maestro is too single-minded.

The chef squatted next to me. 'An Indian teacher named Deviprasad separated food into three types: root vegetables, which have the quality of inertia; meats and peppers, which promote excitement; fresh fruits and vegetables, which are ethereal. Every meal must create a balanced whole. Too much of one type can throw the meal out of balance.'

I spread my hands. 'What has that to do with anything?'

'In uncertain times, we must keep ourselves as level as a balanced meal; we mustn't become too apathetic or too excited or too distracted. Deviprasad instructed his apprentices to be patient and vigilant.'

'But—'

'Did you hear me? Patient and vigilant; that means paying attention.'

Patience and vigilance were fine, but he didn't know about N'bali. 'Maestro' – I thought it best to be straightforward – 'I went with my friend Marco to see the Abyssinian.'

The chef pressed his thumb and forefinger into his eyes. 'Why?'

'Saturday night, Marco broke into the kitchen. I caught him, but he'd already stolen things from your cabinet. You weren't here on Sunday, and he was going to take them to N'bali with or without me. I know Marco, I thought I could handle him, and I wanted to protect you.'

'What are you telling me?'

'Maestro, N'bali told him you had the book. How could she know that?'

The chef shrugged. 'She is an *adeptus*.'

'She said someone is going to die.'

'*Boh*. That's like saying the sun will rise.'

The chef didn't seem to grasp the gravity of the situation. 'I'm worried about what Marco might do.'

'Marco?' The chef's eyes tightened in amusement. 'There are more serious threats abroad than Marco, eh?'

'But—'

'Look, I appreciate that you tried to protect me, but you can't control every situation.' The chef put a hand on my shoulder. 'You need to learn how to stay calm through perilous times. Meet me in the kitchen tonight. Late, after everyone is asleep.'

That night, I stole down the stairs on bare feet. The stairway was dark and quiet, and I paused halfway down for no reason except that all things clandestine inspire hesitation. In the kitchen, the chef sat at his desk in a circle of yellow light like a puddle of melted butter, with his head bent over one of his cookbooks. I said, 'I'm here.'

He looked up. 'So you are.' He bade me come closer and pulled a chair around so that we sat facing each other. 'Luciano,' he began, 'you know about my secret writings.'

'*Sì*, Maestro, the book.'

'Well, there are many books. But I have a book of recipes that are the tools of the teacher. These recipes are code for knowledge that has come to us from many different places and times.'

'*Sì*, Maestro.'

'There's one recipe that's easily misunderstood, but its message is important.'

'*Sì*, Maestro.'

He flashed an odd little half smile. 'It's a soufflé made

with amaranth. Some believe amaranth to be extinct, but it's not, as you saw in the root cellar; it's only difficult to find and quite expensive. The amaranth gives this soufflé a nice nutty flavour, but amaranth has an inflated reputation, and the recipe has inspired tales of immortality.'

'But there's no immortality.' Confusion loomed. 'Is there?'

'Not in the sense that it's usually understood.'

'What does that mean?'

'We all die, but we all leave something behind. We achieve immortality by passing on knowledge.' The chef leaned forward until we sat almost nose to nose. I noticed new lines in his face and puffiness around his eyes, but he looked pleased with himself. He said, 'The soufflé teaches the folly of pursuing immortality. Life is death. A moment arises, and it dies. There's nothing but the present and you can't hold onto the present – you can only be in it. A soufflé awakens an awareness of the moment. It forces us to appreciate the rich and fluid now.'

I scratched my head. 'A soufflé?'

He sat back. '*Ecco*, look here.' He pulled a ragged cookbook across his desk. The cover was made of some inferior hide, ripped and stained from careless use. The leaves were torn and patched, and loose parchments stuck out haphazardly. As the chef turned the pages, I saw entries written by many different hands. The letters seemed to take a multitude of strange configurations, and some looked like the letters I'd seen inscribed on the doors of the Jewish Quarter. About midway through the book, he turned it around to face me. The page he pointed to was lovely: the parchment tawny with age, the edges embellished with gold leaf, the script flowing. Exquisite little vines and flowers decorated each corner of the page. He said, 'There it is: the amaranth soufflé. *Bellissimo*, eh?'

I said, 'This is . . . the book?'

'*Sì.*' The chef gazed at the page, and his expression grew abstract. He said, '*Madre di Dio*. Just the thought of immortality makes me tired.' He blew out a long breath. 'You know, one of the forbidden writings calls spiritual awakening "the elixir of immortality". Maybe that's where all the talk about elixirs began.'

'Wait. This is *the* book?'

'What's the matter? You knew I had it.'

'But it's so shabby. And it's right here in the kitchen. Out in the open? On your bookshelf?'

'*Sì*. Hidden in plain view. It's the best way. That's one of the advantages of being a chef – my books interest no one but me. Everyone is looking for a rare and handsome volume, an oiled leather cover and illuminated pages, carefully preserved and well hidden in a monastery. That would be too obvious. No, we Guardians take the bits of knowledge we come across, we encode them as recipes, and we pass them along. This book is a teaching manual.'

'So, this is the book.' *Marrone.*

He stood up. 'Come, Luciano. Now you'll learn something.'

The chef walked over to the table in front of Enrico's brick oven and selected a whisk. He said, 'Understand, soufflés are about technique.'

'But why are we making a soufflé? What about the Gnostic gospels, and Borgia and Landucci and Marco and N'bali?'

'The Guardians have always lived with the threat of discovery. That's why you need to cultivate patience and vigilance, and to do that you must be fully present. *Allora*, we make a soufflé.'

I scratched my head again.

'*Ecco*. Pay attention. A soufflé is magical. It rises out of the pan like a golden cloud, and it has an ephemeral nature.'

'A what?'

'It doesn't last, Luciano – like life. That's what makes it precious.'

The chef assembled sweet butter, cream, amaranth, flour, cheeses, eggs, a brown spice, a chip of salt and a white peppercorn. He said, 'Amaranth gives it a pleasant flavour, but the old symbolism has caused confusion. Forget all that; it's just a rare grain. Lovely flavour. Now prepare a fire. Very low and very even.'

Chef Ferrero separated eggs with one hand, dropping yolks in one bowl and whites in another, and then he set both bowls aside. He gave me a mortar and pestle to crush the salt chip and peppercorns. As I ground them down to powder, the chef said, 'Very fine. No lumps. Attention to detail makes the difference.'

I grated cheeses while the chef combined melted butter, amaranth and flour in a pan, whisked it to a paste, and set the pan on a high grate over the fire. He added cream gradually with one hand while whisking with the other. His face grew ruddy from the heat, and he looked basted in sweat, but he never varied his stroke. After removing the pan from the fire, he beat in half the egg yolks, sprinkled in the salt and pepper, and reached for the brown spice. 'Nutmeg,' he said. 'There must always be some spice.' He chuckled.

The chef stirred in the grated cheeses, then set the thick mixture aside. He added a pinch of salt to the egg whites, tilted a copper bowl in the crook of his arm and began whisking with a quick, steady rhythm. I'd seen him do this before and I enjoyed watching the egg whites thicken and expand into a fluffy cloud. He folded whipped egg whites into the cheese mixture and poured the whole concoction into a straight-sided dish. He slid it onto the highest grate of the brick oven and said, 'Gently. You can never be too gentle.' He wiped his hands on his apron, saying, 'Now we wait.'

I groaned at the thought of a long wait, and the chef said, 'Much of life is waiting. It helps if you can do it with grace.'

'Sì, Maestro.' I made a pillow of my arms on the table and laid my head down. The firelight, the quiet, the warmth, the gathering aroma, the whisper of pages being turned, all of it enfolded me in a sense of peace and I dozed. A soufflé takes an hour, but it seemed only seconds before the chef woke me with his announcement. 'Finito!'

The soufflé looked just as the chef said it would: a golden cloud rising magically out of the dish. He cradled the hot dish between two towels and lifted it off the grate tenderly. Keeping it level, he set it down on the table, stepped back, and said, 'Behold. A soufflé.' He looked like a proud father.

We admired the burnished crust, inhaled the rich perfume and wondered at the domed architecture. Then a dimple appeared at the centre of the soufflé. The dimple deepened to a crater, and wrinkles began to spread out around it. I said, 'Maestro, it's collapsing.'

'Of course it's collapsing. Just think, Luciano, that soufflé will never rise again, and you saw it. If you weren't paying attention, you would've missed it.' He shook his head. 'One of the silliest rumours I've heard is that the addition of amaranth prevents it from falling. As if that would make it better. Boh.' He gestured grandly at the shrinking soufflé and said, 'Impermanence. Exquisite, eh?'

I strained for the comprehension that would take a lifetime.

The chef handed me a spoon, but before we dipped into the soufflé, he said, 'Right here, right now, there's only us and the soufflé. The time is always now; we merely need to inhabit it. Can you do that?'

'I think so, Maestro.'

'*Bene*. Now we eat.' The chef broke through the delicate crust and scooped out a serving for each of us. He offered me a plate and a smile. 'Savour the crisp simplicity of the moment, Luciano.'

The soufflé was light and lush. The first taste burst inside my mouth, and I gave myself over to the smooth flavour and silky texture; the amaranth did indeed give it a rich nutty undertone. The second taste coated my tongue with luxury, and my worries retreated. The chef had been right – fully inhabiting that present allowed nothing else to intrude. The soufflé consumed me.

As the last bite slid down my throat, the chef smiled. He said, 'You know, Luciano, sometimes I think the rumours about alchemy might also have been started by this soufflé.'

'Because of the golden colour?'

'No. Because once you learn to live in the present, you're as rich as anyone can be. We must embrace each moment.'

'Even the bad ones?'

'Especially the bad ones. Those are the ones that show us who we are.'

While I tidied up, thinking about my lesson, the chef went to his desk and perused his book. The spine was broken; some of the pages were worn almost to transparency while others were so brittle they crackled when turned. The rest were loose, creased, stained, torn . . . the book had clearly been in a state of flux for many years, constantly being revised and enlarged. It came to me then that the book must have grown considerably as it passed through countless hands over the centuries. When I finished the dishes, I sat with him at his desk. I asked, 'What did the original book contain?'

He leaned back in his chair. 'Originally, there was no

book, only scrolls. Some believe undiscovered scrolls still survive in desert caves.' He thought for a moment. 'It's possible. Hot, dry deserts preserve things quite well. Some writings say there are royal tombs in Egypt where ancient kings are still preserved, along with piles of gold and even some of their slaves.'

'*Marrone.*'

'Our tradition started with a grain of knowledge that one person wanted to destroy and another wanted to save. Some wily scholar rolled up a controversial parchment, stuffed it into a clay jar, and hid it in a cave. Others followed his example, and the custom, along with the body of knowledge, grew like yeast. In time, certain scholars organized their effort and agreed to embed concepts in recipes so they could pass the knowledge along in the guise of cooking lessons. We preserve what we have and we also add to it when new ideas come to light. Much as you did with your cheesecake. That will be a fine addition to our book, and I wouldn't be surprised if it became a favourite.

'Of course, some recipes are more valuable than others. If I had to choose, I suppose I could select the ones I consider most important – the Gnostic gospels and the letters of Roger Bacon. But to do that would be like paring down an artichoke to the heart, and it would be a shame to lose all those meaty leaves, eh?'

'It's amazing,' I said. 'To think all these writings survived centuries of war and politics.'

The chef smiled. 'In times of crisis, people become clever about protecting what's important to them. But our first duty is to preserve the tradition and protect the Guardians.'

I imagined the ghostly image of a long line of chefs stretched out behind my maestro, their tall, white toques trailing away into antiquity, blurring and morphing into hoods and turbans and biblical headdresses. His was a clandestine lineage of chefs who were much more than chefs, each having preserved what was given and adding to that body of knowledge. I felt humbled to think I'd become heir to this ancient trust. I asked, 'How is it managed, Maestro? One book passing through so many hands over so much time . . . it seems impossible.'

'One book? That *would* be impossible. And foolish, don't you think? No, each Guardian has his own book, and none are identical because they're always changing and growing. Like life, eh? Each Guardian looks after his book until the time all things can be revealed safely. It doesn't matter how long it takes, no seed sees its flower.'

Excitement swelled in my chest and filled my head with a tumult of questions. 'Do the Guardians know each other? Are there others in Venice? How many are there? Are they all over Europe? Where do you get your knowledge? Do you have secret meetings?'

'Slow down,' said the chef. 'Patience and vigilance are our watchwords.'

'But do you know any other Guardians?'

'Each Guardian knows the names of two other Guardians in different countries. If a book is in danger of exposure, it must be destroyed.' The chef clutched at his heart. '*Madonna*, what a thought.' He shook his head. 'Sadly, it did happen once. A Sicilian chef came into possession of diagrams that showed how the Great Pyramid of Giza had been built. He was working on an elaborate recipe that encoded that incredible feat of engineering – I heard it used huge amounts of marzipan – but somehow he was discovered. The pyramids were thought to glorify pagan gods and the chef was arrested as a heretic. The diagrams were destroyed, but he died honourably without betraying the Guardians.'

'You should hide the book, Maestro.'

'Nonsense. This is the safest place for it. Landucci and Borgia have no reason to look at a dilapidated cookbook. And they think themselves too intelligent to consult reclusive *adepti* like N'bali. They leave her to superstitious peasants. As for your young friend, he's not likely to be believed by anyone. I think the Guardians are safe for the moment. In any case, the most important writings, like the Gnostic gospels, are recorded in multiple places. Threats come and go, but we remain quiet, and we wait.' The chef closed the book and passed his hand lovingly over its soiled cover. 'Well then, what have you learned?'

'To pay attention to the present moment.'

'*Bene.*' He held me with his eyes and said, 'It's time to be a man now, Luciano. No more games with Marco. When the doge dies and the rumours subside, you have to be ready to buckle down to a long, hard course of study.'

'I'm ready.' That book would make me worthy of both the chef and Francesca.

The chef shelved the book and said, 'First you'll learn to read and write – many languages. Then you'll study history, science, philosophy.' He smiled. 'But all anyone will see you learning is culinary art.'

'That's a lot of learning.'

'You can do it. You're better than you think. Let's have your first lesson now.' He took a parchment from his desk and wrote a word. '*Ecco*. See this? It says, "Guardians." Can you memorize the letters and their arrangement so that you'd recognize this word again?'

I considered each letter alone and then the pattern they made together. I ran my finger under the word, pausing at each letter. *G-u-a-r-d-i-a-n-s*. With the thrill of sudden literacy whistling up my spine I whispered, '*Marrone*, I can read.'

The chef crumpled the parchment into a wad and said, 'Don't be too impressed. You have a long way to go.'

He tossed the balled-up parchment into the fire. It blackened and disappeared with a whispery crackle, but I could still see that word – 'Guardians' – in my mind's eye, the word that would save my life.

CHAPTER ✣ XXVII

THE BOOK OF NOW

THE CHEF PULLED A HAND DOWN HIS tired face. 'That's enough for one night. Think about what you've learned, and we'll talk more after he's gone.' He glanced up at the ceiling to indicate the upper floors where the doge lived. 'Remember, Luciano. These are the times to be present and alert. Practise the lesson of the soufflé. Be here, not there.'

But that was easier said than done, for next came the time of chaos. I'd been in the palace almost six months by then, and the doge's obsession had escalated with his disease; his quest for immortality had reached a full rolling boil. The doge was finally succumbing to his syphilis, and in some quarters gossip about the book took second place to wagers about how long the old fellow would last. The chef said, 'The doge is like a flounder on a chopping block, thrashing for his life.' Indeed, his ruffians were running wild through the city while the *Cappe Nere* quietly observed and made arrests. Meanwhile, the Swiss mercenaries monitored the *Cappe Nere*. Everyone spied on everyone.

No doubt Marco and Francesca had seen the swarms of soldiers and were full of questions. For that reason, I stayed close to the palace and continued to avoid them. Before I left food scraps for Marco, I peeked out of the back door to be sure he wasn't there. I didn't miss him (especially since he'd lost his sense of humour) but, oh, Francesca. I'd saved twenty coppers by then; in a few more weeks I'd have enough to rescue her.

Fortunately, events in the palace kept me busy. As the doge deteriorated, I heard Teresa gossiping to Enrico about what she saw in his private rooms. Apparently, the doge urinated in corners and sat on the floor weeping. Teresa, Enrico's gossip-mongering counterpart, had taken to visiting the kitchen more frequently, and the two of them often conferred in whispers near the brick oven. Once, I stopped her at the service door, on her way out, and asked how long the doge might last.

'Who knows?' She blinked excitedly. 'He wanders his rooms naked and bewildered. The stains on his bed clothing would make you gag.' She pulled a face full of disgust. 'It can't be long now. At least we hope.' She winked and hurried off to gather more news.

We in the kitchen found ourselves preparing meals for a series of physicians visiting the palace. The first doctor, from the medical school in Padua, gave the doge a thrice-daily dose of sarsaparilla. When that proved useless he offered his apologies and moved away with his family to Milan. The next one, a Roman priest and the pope's personal physician, brought greetings from His Holiness and an offer to administer the last rites. He was sent back to Rome without thanks.

Then they began arriving from far-flung places: a herbalist from Paris; a professor of medicine from Frankfurt; an English physician who brought mercury that turned the doge's sores a deep blue; and from Persia, a hoary old man with a long white beard, dressed in purple satin and carrying incense and leeches.

Rumour had it that the syphilis had been contracted from a courtesan sent to the doge years ago as a gift from the chief magistrate of Genoa. Teresa said, 'I remember her. A buxom slut.' She pulled her eyelid to indicate that the diseased woman must have been sent either as a dark practical joke or for some political vendetta.

Talk of vendettas reminded me of Giuseppe, who appeared strangely disinterested in the virulent gossip. He was preoccupied with hating me, and since my promotion, his hostility had grown to single-minded obsession. The more proficient I became as a vegetable cook, the more he despised me. I felt his malevolent gaze on me while I chopped onions, while I salted aubergine, while I consulted with Dante over the stewed cabbage. When I hung a pot to boil, Giuseppe was there, poking the fire and muttering. He gave me the evil eye at every opportunity and some-times walked out of his way to brush by me, scowling and tapping the side of his nose. He was like a pot on the edge of boiling over.

Meanwhile, the doge stopped appearing in public. He'd always been a lusty diner, but now his meals were meagre and bland, only clear broth or thin porridge taken in his rooms. I often saw him, hunched and hollow-eyed, already looking like a ghost as he haunted the cavernous halls of the palace, an ermine-trimmed robe thrown over his night clothes, sagging on his diminished frame and trailing behind him like elegance forgotten.

One day, a Chinese doctor arrived at the palace and the

chef ordered me to prepare an assortment of vegetables, finely chopped and quickly sautéed over a high flame in a bowl-shaped pot. The ingredients and preparation of that dish were foreign to me: sesame oil, limp black mushrooms, squares of firm white curd, pale greens, and crisp transparent sprouts tossed in at the last minute. The chef ladled the mixture over steamed fish and fine rice noodles in a light broth. The doctor supplied his own seasoning, a fermented black liquid, and ate with two ivory sticks instead of cutlery. He scandalized the maids by picking up his bowl to drink the broth.

Every day, the inscrutable doctor treated the doge behind locked doors. The little ochre man, who wore a long coat of brocaded silk and a black braid sprouting out of an otherwise shaved head, inspired a good deal of talk among the maids. They described gentle chanting in a high-pitched, tonal language and obeisance offered to a smirking idol. What it all meant inspired endless speculation. A constant stream of rumours galloped through the servants' quarters by night and kept everyone expectant and titillated by day.

No one knew what the Chinese doctor was up to, but everyone wanted to find out. All the servants knew that the palace was honeycombed with secret passageways that led down to the dungeons as well as to spy posts behind the walls of certain rooms. The entries to those tunnels and the spy holes themselves were well concealed, and many, no doubt, long forgotten. I only knew about the one behind the Ugly Duchess, but other servants knew more.

Curious about the treatments administered by the Chinese doctor, Teresa came to the kitchen one day, fluttery and agitated. She stood near the service door and waved with her apron until she caught my eye; then she signalled with an urgent thumb at the door to the back courtyard. When I met her outside, Teresa said, 'I can't stand it another minute. I have to know what that heathen is doing.'

'But, Teresa—'

'There's a door.'

'A door?'

'In the Hall of Knights. You know the wall niche for that great, frightening suit of armour? Looks like a giant wore it, eh?' She shivered dramatically.

'What about the door, Teresa?'

She smoothed back her crinkled grey hair as her worn face turned smug with secret knowledge. 'The door behind the giant armour leads to a spy post behind the doge's bed. It's a small hole hidden in the shadows of a mural of fruits and flowers. You know that trick they do with paintings? Like the Ugly Duchess?'

'Sì, Teresa.'

'The doge never noticed the hole – it's very good – and now he's too far gone.'

'You mean you're going to—'

'Ooooh, not me! I couldn't squeeze through.' She patted her full hips. 'You, Luciano, you're small and quick. Next time the heathen goes into his room, I'll stand watch, and you just slip in and take a peek.' Her smile was full of expectation.

Just slip in and take a peek? Irresistible.

The next day, as soon as the Chinese doctor entered the doge's bedroom, a chain of maids passed the message along to Teresa. Minutes later, in the Hall of Knights, Teresa patted my cheek, saying, 'Go with God.'

I squeezed behind the armour and checked for evidence of a door in the stone block wall. When my fingers detected a slight draught from an unmortared groove, I put my weight against it and pushed with my shoulder. The door gave way with a grating of stone against stone, and a musty rush of cool air skimmed my face. I slipped through the opening and immediately felt relieved at the sight of a heavy iron pull on the inside of the door. Confident that I could get back out, I pulled the door shut.

Blindness!

I was enveloped in darkness so complete I couldn't see the hand I waved frantically in front of my face. I reached out and touched cold, rough-hewn walls less than an arm's distance away on both sides.

Trapped! In the dark!

Sweat erupted on my forehead and under my arms; my heart pounded in my throat. I couldn't breathe. I made a frenzied grab for the door's iron pull and heaved it half-open. I hung in the narrow shaft of light and gulped air. When my heart slowed, I took a deep breath and wiped the sweat from my face. My underarms felt soggy, and my hands trembled. I thought, *Marrone,* all the Chinese doctors in the world couldn't make me close that door behind me again. I stared at Teresa's broad back and imagined myself slinking back to her, shamefaced and mincing, admitting I couldn't walk through the tunnel. I vacillated, unable to step out or step back in. *Stupido.*

I thought about asking for a candle, but surely draughts blew through this tunnel like any other, and a flame might sputter out, leaving me stranded. I looked over my shoulder, hoping to see a torch hung on the wall, waiting to be lit. There was no torch, but to my happy surprise, the half-open door provided enough light to make out the walls and floor and even shadows. That light was more reliable than a candle, and the partially open door was a reminder of easy escape. As I peered down the dimly lit tunnel, I felt like a child who had lit a lamp in a dark room and found no monsters lurking. I remembered taking that deep breath in the root cellar, and I decided I could do it again. I took one step, then another, and it was all right. Soon I was walking at a normal pace.

Almost imperceptibly, the light began to diminish, and my breathing quickened. I stopped, closed my eyes, and reminded myself that I could turn around and walk out whenever I wished. There was no danger, only the fear of danger. Here and now I was fine. I steadied my breathing, then opened my eyes and discovered that the total blackness of closed eyes had made the tunnel seem lighter by comparison. I walked on, and when the light dimmed further, I closed my eyes again to help my vision adjust. But the next time I opened them, the shadows were gone: At that point, the dark looked the same whether my eyes were open or closed. I stretched out my arms, and the walls seemed closer than before. There wasn't enough air. An unreasonable terror rose in my chest. Aloud, I said, 'Breathe.' But it was no good. A scream stuck in my throat, and I choked. I whirled around to run for the door.

In my panic, I fell, and my head glanced off the rough wall. When I pulled myself up, I felt blood trickling down my face. I was disoriented. Which way was forward, and which was back? I ran, terrified, unthinking, stumbling and falling, getting up to run again, falling again, panting and weeping. Even though the ground rose like a ramp under my feet, I wasn't coherent enough to turn and go the other way. I smelled myself, the musk of animal panic.

I saw a light, and I blinked to squeeze the tears out of my eyes. Yes, a pinpoint of light! I ran for it, and it grew larger. It was a spy hole the size of a grape, the backside of another magnificent *trompe l'oeil*. When I reached it, I leaned my damp forehead just above it, allowing the scant light to fall on my face. I don't know how long I stood there, panting and trembling, but at some point I heard the doge mumbling. When I put my eye to the hole, the bedroom opened before me, and I saw the draped and gilded ducal bed only steps from where I stood. My breathing slowed as I took in the shocking scene.

The Chinese doctor was bending over the doge, who lay in bed on his back, naked as a plucked chicken. The doctor manipulated one of many long thin needles sticking out of the doge's legs and chest and private parts. The sight was morbid and bizarre, and my ignorance made it fascinating. I winced as the doctor slid a needle into the doge's groin, but the doge didn't recoil from what looked like a painful procedure. He lay on the bed, murmuring incoherently like a man locked in a dream of defeat. The doctor took another needle from a bedside tray and aimed at the doge's testicles.

I couldn't watch any more. I crouched under the spy hole, first trying to understand what I'd seen, then once again becoming aware of the dark tunnel and dreading the long walk back. I remembered what the chef had told me in the root cellar: Fear of the dark was fear of the unknown, an unreasonable fear of misadventure that might somehow materialize out of thin air. Baseless. It wasn't the tunnel that was frightening me, it was my own imagination, my own creative powers conjuring demons and disasters lying in wait.

I had already walked through the tunnel. I knew nothing lurked there, and I knew that the walls would not move in to crush me. It was merely my own fear rattling imaginary chains. I looked around at the quiet dark and murmured, 'It's just an empty tunnel.' Conquering panic was simply a matter of keeping that thought foremost, digging deep into myself and finding the ability to keep myself present and resist flights of fancy. I had only to stop my mind from running ahead of my feet. 'It's just an empty tunnel,' I told myself. I needed to keep myself grounded in the moment instead of allowing my mind to leap ahead into a terrifying future alive with ogres and calamities.

I wished the chef were there to ask me what I'd learned. I could tell him I'd learned to be here, not there.

I took a deep breath and said, 'It's just an empty tunnel.' The sound of my own voice reassured me. I stood slowly, then took a deep breath and began walking. 'It's just an empty tunnel.'

I said it over and over again. My voice grew stronger and the repetition provided a rhythm for my feet to follow. The tunnel ceased to exist; there was only the sound of my voice and my feet moving along, step by step. My breath quickened only when I allowed my thoughts to wander away from my catchphrase. I don't know whether the tunnel was long or short, curved or straight. I walked in a trance, chanting the soothing words, staying present in the dark but harmless moment.

After some unknown length of time, wan light began to define the walls. I felt cheered to think I was nearing the exit. I'd done it! But when I actually saw the slice of light coming from the half-open door ahead, my concentration cracked. I stopped reciting my mantra and ran for the light so mindlessly that I smacked into the door's edge and bloodied my nose. With sweat-slippery hands, I heaved it fully open. Light and air flooded over me, and I collapsed in a heap against the legs of the giant's armour.

Teresa gave a little scream and ran over to pull me out of the wall niche. She staunched my bloody nose with her apron, dabbed at my tear-stained face, and clucked at the bruise on my head. When I had recovered enough to speak, I sputtered a disconnected account of what I'd seen.

'Needles,' I said. 'Long, thin needles in the doge's body. All over. Even in his private parts.'

Teresa's eyes widened as she listened. When I mentioned the doge's private parts, she forgot my injuries and flew up like a bird startled from a nest. 'Ooooh,' she said. She pressed her hands to her cheeks and squealed, 'Needles down *there*? Ooooh.' She ran from the hall and disappeared through the tall double doors, mad to share her wonderfully indecent new gossip.

No doubt Teresa embellished – she always did – and in the time-honoured way of all gossip, the stories grew more salacious with every telling. Within days, all of Venice was recounting the barbaric acts being committed on the doge's person: needles in his private parts, yes, but also in his eyes and under his nails and pushed deep into his anus. Everyone agreed that this submission to such desperate methods must mean that the end was very near.

It didn't help that the doge, lying in his bed, incontinent and furious, sensed the futility of his situation and allowed his howls of frustration to echo through the palace. With what little pluck he had left, the doge made one last, death-rattle stab at salvation. He ordered his soldiers to search every literate corner of Venice and the Veneto and bring him all the old books they found – every last one. The soldiers gleefully embraced the opportunity to wreak havoc on the scholarly elite, because who did they think they were anyway? The doge lay in his grand bed, already buried beneath the dusty tomes piling up around him.

The general citizenry considered the doge's quest to be no more than the death throes of an addled old man, and the thick-necked soldiers confiscating books merely a passing inconvenience, but they wished it would pass more quickly.

One day, while shopping for the chef, I saw a rowdy bunch of the doge's soldiers upset a root merchant's stall, just because they could. The merchant held his praying hands up to heaven and rocked them over his scattered onions and carrots. 'Dio,' he prayed aloud, 'deliver our doge from his suffering. Soon, eh?'

When the greengrocer came over to help him restack his vegetables, they spoke not about the vandals, but about whom the Council of Ten might elect as the next doge. The root merchant said, 'The candidates are ancient and corrupt, as usual.'

'Sì,' said the greengrocer. 'Bandero walks into walls, and Clementi has blood on his hands. But did you hear about Ficino?'

'Ficino of Florence? Are you sure?'

'Don't get too excited.' The greengrocer pulled his eyelid. 'It's just for show.'

Marsilio Ficino, a humanitarian scholar under the patronage of Giovanni de' Medici, was a teacher of Plato and poetry and a theory he called cosmic love, which, he claimed, governed order in the universe.

The root merchant said, 'Ficino's a virtuous man. Too bad he can't be doge.'

The council had only named Ficino as a gesture of respect to the powerful de' Medici family (and probably as an overture to join their quest for the book), but everyone, even Ficino and his patron, knew he would never be elected. Although he was old enough and sick enough, he was neither stupid enough nor corrupt enough.

One day, while seasoning a complicated love-apple sauce for his stuffed pasta, the chef idly remarked, 'It would be interesting to stir a wicked pot with an innocent spoon.' He straightened his toque, and that odd half smile lightened his face while he stirred cream into the pot. *Marrone*, I thought, *he's at it again.*

Although the doge was not yet dead, the council decided he was dead enough to proceed with the election. On voting day, the chef prepared an elaborate menu for the council's dinner meeting and gave every course his personal attention. He rushed around the kitchen all day, sometimes serious, sometimes wearing his half smile, stirring this, tasting that, giving orders, straightening his toque. A huge, unidentified haunch of meat had been soaking in a pungent marinade all night, and that morning the chef hung it on the rotisserie. As he basted it with a dark, salty marinade, he mumbled to himself like a mad alchemist. Watching him, I had the uncomfortable feeling that my maestro was somewhere far away from the here and now.

CHAPTER ❖ XXVIII

THE BOOK OF BEASTS

THE COUNCIL OF TEN FILED into the dining room through double doors held open by white-gloved footmen. Oh, how rich and solid they looked – well-fed men with soft hands and rings on their fingers. They wore Oriental silks, Turkish brocades and fine Florentine wool. Some wore wide fur collars and heavy gold chains that lay on their shoulders as if carefully placed to balance the weight, front and back.

They all wore hats. The most stylish were a purple velvet cloche banded in gold, and a burgundy silk pouf with silver tassels. The others wore feathered caps, linen coifs, oversized berets, stuffed turbans and one rolled-brim affair with a cockscomb trailing over the shoulder. Marching into the dining room in their fabulous hats, they looked like an assemblage of fantastic poisonous mushrooms.

Dinner began with a simple salad of clover dressed in extra-virgin olive oil, balsamic vinegar and a drop of honey. Clover was believed to enhance sluggish appetites, and the chef wanted that important meal to be fully appreciated. When the plates of clover had been set before each diner, portly Signor Castelli, who fancied himself an epicurean, adjusted his blue beret, frowned, and pushed the leaves around his plate. 'Grass?' he asked. 'Are we rabbits?'

Landucci grabbed his fork and stabbed the clover. 'Don't whine about the food. We're here to do business.'

Munching a mouthful of clover, Signor Cesi flicked back the silver tassels of his hat and said, 'This is delicious.' When Landucci glared at him he shrugged. 'We might as well enjoy the food. Our business won't take long.'

Landucci grunted, 'I suppose it doesn't matter which of the two old fools we choose. They're equally pliable.'

As the maid cleared the salad plates, Signor Abruzzi addressed the table. '*Signori*, shall we save some time and simply put the two names in a hat?' He lifted the red fez off his head and offered it to the other men with a mischievous grin.

'Abruzzi, you dog!' Signor Bellarmino slapped the table with a hairy hand and laughed out loud. 'Are you suggesting we have so little respect for the office of doge that we make a game of the election?'

All the men laughed. Even Landucci smiled.

They were still laughing when the maids brought in the next course. As they set a plate before each man, the laughter dwindled to throat clearings and then silence. Each man examined the intricate creation in front of him.

Quail are very small – no more than a bite or two per bird – and one man can eat several. That's why quail were usually served headless and heaped on a huge platter that needed two maids to carry it. But that night, each man found himself facing one tiny quail, head intact and beak open as if to warble, with wispy wings spread as though it had just that moment alighted on its airy pastry nest.

I'd watched the chef construct the nests himself. He pressed out pastry circles with a wineglass and then overlaid them with pastry rings that fitted precisely. He brushed his creations with madly beaten eggs and watched them closely while they baked. The instant they puffed up, golden and glossy, he pulled them out of the oven amid a rush of steam. He monitored each step as the cooks assembled the other elements on the dish. He tasted the pâté as if he were meditating, examined and sniffed each sprig of thyme, then sliced the quail eggs three quarters through and fanned them out. For the clear brandy sauce, he banished the sauce cook and stirred the pot with frightening intensity.

Bellarmino said, 'First grass and now one quail? Is this a joke?'

'*Madonna!*' Signor Castelli had tasted the pastry nest and its sauce. He spoke with a full mouth. 'This pastry could float on a breeze. And the sauce! Taste this sauce.'

As the men took their first bites, a round of appreciative murmurs and hums filtered through the cracked-open service door. A few paused to admire the artistry on their plates. The quail, boneless except for the outspread wings, was stuffed with a rich goose pâté. Each little bird sat atop its own eggs, which were sliced and fanned out around it to create a scalloped platform. The buttery-light pastry nest had been drizzled with a clear sauce that glistened like dew. On the sky blue plate, sprigs of fresh thyme had been arranged to resemble a forked tree branch supporting the nest; selected thyme leaves shimmered under carefully placed droplets of sauce.

Castelli licked pâté off his fork. 'The presentation is delightful. Like a poem.'

Signor Gamba pointed to a tiny wing with his fork and said, 'Looks like he's about to take flight. Puts me in mind of my prized falcons.'

'Makes me think of music.' Castelli poked at the open beak. 'Like the little fellow died singing, eh?'

'Sì. The chef is clever.' Landucci frowned and prodded the body of his quail. 'Somehow he managed to remove all those little bones the way he does with mullet. This chef takes the bones out of everything. He must have a miniature catacomb in that kitchen.' Landucci pressed his finger into the boneless quail, and his frown deepened. 'I've never understood the catacombs. Why keep the bones of the dead?'

Signor Gamba answered absently while he chewed. 'A priest once told me they keep the bones to remind us.'

'Remind us of what?' Landucci's complexion darkened.

Gamba raised a forkful of quail to his mouth. 'He didn't say.' Chewing with his eyes closed, he murmured, 'Mmmm. A very clever chef.'

'Indeed he is,' said Landucci. 'I have a fellow in the kitchen who tells me suspicious things about that chef.'

He had a fellow in the kitchen? A spy? A sense of dread gripped me.

Landucci gestured at the elaborate quail. 'Why does he go to such lengths? It's only food.'

'He's an *artiste*, Landucci.' Castelli was irritated. 'Can't you enjoy a good meal? Our business isn't pressing. You said it yourself – one old fool is as good as the other. I like the idea of names in a hat. The irreverence is appealing.'

'Sì.' Gamba smiled. 'Let's take a lesson from our excellent chef and do things differently for once.'

'Indeed.'

'One's as stupid as the other.'

'Why not?'

Conversation stopped abruptly when the chef himself surprised us all by appearing with the next course. A maid held the door open, and Chef Ferrero, a man on a mission, marched into the dining room bearing a tray with his enormous haunch of roast meat still on its skewer. After the fanciful little quails, the brutishness of the dripping joint of meat impaled on an iron skewer was jarring, as was the presence of the chef acting as a waiter. The chef said, '*Signori*, this joint is too unwieldy for the maids. It will be an honour to serve you myself.'

The chef flourished a wickedly glinting carving knife, then wrapped a towel around the top of the hot skewer and hoisted it off the tray. He planted the point of the skewer on one plate at a time and, just inches from each man's face, he sawed off large, uneven strips of meat that fell onto the plates in ragged heaps. While the council watched this shocking presentation, the chef explained, 'It was my good luck to be in the Rialto just after a ship from East Africa arrived. This animal was alive and snarling just yesterday. It was supposed to be delivered, still breathing, to His Holiness and butchered in the Vatican kitchen. But a mistake was made, and they butchered it right there on the docks.'

'But what—'

'I was fortunate enough to acquire this cut for you,' the chef continued. 'The rest of the beast was put on ice for the trip to Rome.'

'But what—'

'Lion meat. I know you gentlemen must become bored with the same lamb and veal dishes all the time. *Signori*, I'm pleased to present you with the symbol of our own Most Serene Republic. Who better to eat this powerful beast than the most powerful men in Venice?'

I remembered the leopard in the Vatican kitchen. The chef knew perfectly well of Borgia's taste for exotic meat. He must have paid dearly to find out when that animal would arrive, and even more to have it butchered in Venice.

Signor Farelli watched bloody hanks of meat fall onto his plate, and he pulled his green wool cap down more securely on his head. He said, 'I don't think I—'

'Lucky is the lion that the human eats, for thus will the lion become human.' The chef beamed as he carved. 'Jesus said that.'

'He did?' Farelli looked around the table for confirmation, but everyone looked as blank as he.

'Tastes something like beef, but better. It has the flavour of power.' The chef kissed his fingertips. 'It's especially delicious with the heavy red wine I've selected; it's a rare vintage. Be sure to enjoy it.' The maid poured great goblets of wine while the chef hacked thick strips of meat onto the last plate. Then he bowed to the table, said, '*Buon appetito,*' and took his leave.

As he rushed past the maids, he mumbled, 'Keep the wine flowing,' and then he bustled down to the kitchen.

Signor Gamba fingered his wineglass and said, 'That quail was uncommonly filling. I don't think I want—'

'Coward!' Castelli stabbed a piece of lion meat and held it up. Blood and grease dripped onto the lace tablecloth. 'The chef said it tastes like beef.'

'But it's a lion.' Signor Cesi diddled his tassels and stared at his plate with distaste.

'*Boh.* Look at you. Cowards.' Castelli took a bite. The other men watched him chew and swallow. He looked Cesi in the eye and said, 'Excellent. Tender, flavourful, plenty of garlic, nice and salty.' He gulped his wine.

'All right . . .' Signor Gamba picked up his fork. 'If it's seasoned well enough . . .'

'Nice and salty.'

One by one, they tasted the lion meat. Owing to long marination, the lion meat was tender and flavourful. The council ate with zest, exhilarated by their culinary daring. They drank the robust wine, joked about their barbarism, and drank more. The maids kept the glasses full to brimming, as the chef had instructed. Some men put down their forks to hold the meat with greasy fingers; they roared before tearing into it with bared teeth. Only Landucci nibbled the food in a brooding sulk, but he, too, drank heavily. The meat was quite salty.

By the time the lion was finished, a wild sort of hilarity had come over them. They called each other savages, laughed and demanded more wine. Signor Perugini flung his stiff, dome-shaped hat merrily onto the table, where it wobbled before coming to rest like an upended bowl. Bellarmino called for parchment and ripped off two strips on which he wrote two candidates' names. He dropped the grease-smeared scraps into the hat, and they laughed. They had eaten a lion. They felt powerful. They *were* powerful.

Landucci reached out to draw a name from the hat, but – 'Wait!' Castelli held up a greasy hand. 'Let's make it interesting. We eat wild beasts. Why should we shrink from a decrepit old man who drones about love?' He wrote the name of Marsilio Ficino and held the third strip of paper in the air for approval.

Signor Cesi laughed. 'Why not? Should we fear a weak little philosopher?'

'We fear no one.'

'Of course not.'

After Ficino's name had been thrown in, Landucci put his hand in the hat of nominees and withdrew a scrap of paper. With noisy, high spirits prevailing at the table, the councilmen didn't immediately register Landucci's mute displeasure as he stared at the piece of parchment in his hand. Gradually, the laughter shrank to unsure chortles. Landucci reached for the hat to draw another name, but Signor Abruzzi said, 'Ah, leave it. He'll be dead in a year.'

Landucci sat back and looked around the table.

'*Sì.*' Castelli slapped the table and his potbelly jiggled. 'Leave it. We eat wild beasts. Should we worry over a sick old man?'

'No.'

'Ridiculous.'

'Here's to Doge Ficino.' Bellarmino raised his glass.

I looked at the maid standing next to me on the landing. Her mouth hung slack, and her eyes were wide and fixed. I whispered, 'Doge Ficino?' She laid one palm on her cheek and smiled. I could hardly wait to tell the chef.

Landucci shrugged and picked up his glass. 'I suppose we can dispose of him if we need to.'

As the council toasted their new doge, the maids served lemon meringue tarts for dessert.

'A lighthearted finish,' sang Castelli. 'Delightful.'

I rushed down to the kitchen shouting that the council had elected Marsilio Ficino. The chef sank onto a wooden bench and nodded. '*Bene.*'

'Maestro, please tell me.' I offered him my praying hands. 'What magic herbs did you use to sway them?'

'Magic herbs? They were drunk.'

'They weren't *that* drunk.'

'They were relaxed.' The chef patted the bench for me to sit next to him, and he put his arm around my shoulder. 'Luciano, I told you, what looks like magic is skill. The lion reminded the council of what they already know, that they need fear no one in Venice. Also, the lion was sinfully oversalted, which made them drink too much. Of course, with their stupid method it could easily have gone another way.'

'But you gave Ficino a chance.'

'We do what we can.'

'I don't know, Maestro. Meddling in the election seems dangerous. Landucci said he has a spy in the kitchen.'

'Spy? What spy?'

'I don't know. He only said he has a man down here.'

'Well, then, luck was with us.'

But luck must have been elsewhere when, later, a more sober Landucci came into the kitchen to question the cooks about the properties of clover, the deboning of quail, and the acquisition of lion meat. The cooks answered carefully, saying, 'Sì, signore. It was a clever meal. Our chef is a magician.'

'A magician?'

'Only an expression, signore. Our chef is skilled.'

The chef and I watched closely for the man who was too helpful, too familiar, but all the cooks were cool and polite. I'd begun to doubt what I'd heard when, as Landucci walked towards the service door, Giuseppe caught his eye and they exchanged a look of collusion. Landucci nodded curtly and left quickly. The chef and I exchanged our own look. Minutes later Giuseppe slipped out of the back door. The chef tapped the side of his nose and motioned me out after him.

Giuseppe walked through the courtyard and around the front of the palace. There, under the Byzantine arcade, Landucci waited in the shadows. Giuseppe's shoes rapped a sharp tattoo on the marble floor, so I took my own shoes off and left them behind a pillar. I glided silently from behind one post to the next. I needed to get closer than I would have wished to hear their hushed conversation.

Giuseppe's voice floated on the night air: '. . . it's more than just skill. I told you about that locked cabinet and his strange garden. And don't forget he took that thief off the street. He even promoted him.'

'Yes, yes. He's odd, but he's just a cook.' Landucci sounded impatient. 'Do you know anything I might care about?'

'Why did you come down to the kitchen tonight, *signore*?'

'A lion? I didn't like that meal.'

'Yes!' Giuseppe stepped closer to Landucci, shaking a finger in his face. 'His meals have unnatural power over people.'

'Step back, will you?' Landucci pressed his scarf to his nose. 'What are you getting at?'

Giuseppe's voice turned coy. 'A few weeks ago, the little thief stole things from the chef's private cabinet. He and his dirty friend took their booty to the Abyssinian.'

'A fortune-teller? *Boh.*'

'People tell her things. You told me to keep my eyes and ears open, so I followed them. After they left her room, I went up to see her.' Giuseppe sounded obscenely self-satisfied and I was shocked. I thought he'd only been following us to harass me.

But Landucci sounded bored. 'And?'

'The chef keeps opium in the kitchen.'

'A painkiller? So what? Maybe he has headaches.' But Landucci stood a little straighter. 'Anything else?'

'I asked her if the chef knew something about the book. Boom! She shuts her mouth and shows me the door.' Giuseppe's voice turned oily and insinuating. 'Have you ever seen her? Bald and skinny, little chicken bones. I twisted her arms behind her back to . . . um . . . persuade her to talk. But she smiled at me. Stubborn. I got a hand around her throat; I squeezed just enough to show her I meant business. When I thought she'd had enough, I let her speak. She was coughing and gasping, but the black *strega* smiled again. She said, "You'll never get the book away from that chef." *From that chef!* He has it!' Giuseppe gave a mean snort. 'I tried to get more but . . . *boh.* She died too easily.'

'She died?'

'Of . . . persuasion.'

I felt sick. N'bali had said someone would die. Had she known it would be her?

Landucci stroked his neat little beard, and Giuseppe danced nervously from one foot to the other. Finally, Landucci said, 'The word of a fortune-teller isn't worth much, but I suppose you want something for this.'

'Justice, *signore.* Although if there's a reward—'

'Justice?' Landucci barked an ugly laugh.

'Will you arrest the chef?'

'I'll have him questioned.'

'And his boy, too. They're in it together.'

'I'll send the *Cappe Nere* for them both.' He glanced out to the squadron of *Cappe Nere* on patrol in the Piazza San Marco.

Oh, *Dio!* It was all I could do not to cry out and run. I swallowed hard and forced myself to stand still and hear the rest.

'*Bene!*' Giuseppe looked as if he might levitate. '*Signore*—'

'Yes, yes, if this yields anything, there'll be a job for you in the dungeon.'

'*Grazie, signore.* But the senate seat—'

'Don't be ridiculous.'

'*Sì, signore.*' Giuseppe offered an obsequious smile of fear.

'Pity.' Landucci seemed to be talking to himself. 'You don't find such a clever chef very often. It'll be a waste if he, too, dies of persuasion.'

CHAPTER ✤ XXIX

THE BOOK OF FUGITIVES

I FLEW BACK TO THE KITCHEN ON bare feet, imagining I could already hear the *Cappe Nere* sharpening their knives. I charged through the back door panting, wild-eyed, breathless. 'Landucci . . . *Cappe Nere* . . . they're coming.'

The last two cooks in the kitchen, Enrico and Pellegrino, stopped tidying their stations to stare, first at me, then at each other. The chef lunged for his bookshelf, pulled out the battered cookbook, and said, 'Let's go.'

'Where, Maestro?'

'Follow me.'

We dashed out of the back door. Bernardo caught a whiff of our excitement and shot out after us. The uneven cobbles of the courtyard hurt my bare feet, and I cursed myself for losing my shoes, but there was nothing to be done. When we opened the courtyard door, we saw Giuseppe coming around the corner. His eyes cut to the book under the chef's arm, and he flashed a brown, malicious grin.

We wheeled around and fled back into the kitchen. Running past Enrico and Pellegrino, the chef shouted, 'Giuseppe's coming. Stop him.'

They smiled. Every cook in the kitchen would have welcomed an opportunity to manhandle Giuseppe. Enrico called out, 'With pleasure, Maestro.'

The chef called over his shoulder, 'Landucci might be behind him.' He headed for the service door, but that door didn't lead to the outside, it led up into the palace. We pushed through the door and the chef peered up the stairway. He rubbed his chin and said, '*D'accordo*. We go.'

As we mounted the stairs, we heard Enrico and Pellegrino hailing Giuseppe like an old friend. 'The maestro's gone. Have a drink with us, eh? What? When did Giuseppe ever refuse a drink?' Then came sounds of a scuffle.

I knew it would only take minutes for Landucci to order the *Cappe Nere* out of the piazza and into the palace. We climbed as fast as the chef's middle-aged legs would allow, which was not fast enough for me. Only moments after we passed the landing to the palace's main rooms, we heard voices on the other side of a door. Landucci said, 'The chef is still in the kitchen, but the boy might be in the dormitory. Arrest them both.' The door opened, and we heard boots on the stairs – the *Cappe Nere* went down to the kitchen as we went up. I said, 'Maestro, where are we going?'

The chef was winded. 'Come on,' he panted. 'Don't stop.'

I don't remember how many doors we passed, but I remember thinking we should open one of them and find a way out of the palace. When we finally stopped, I was winded, but the poor chef was flushed and gasping. We were standing in front of an arched door with a wreath of flowers painted around the handle. The chef eased it open a crack, peeked in, then swung it wide and motioned me in ahead of him.

It was a bedroom. The chef went straight to the wardrobe and flung open the door. While he rummaged through the clothes, I scanned the room. The bedchamber was well appointed, with a soft satin coverlet on the single bed and a collection of porcelain kittens on a night table. A swath of ivory silk tented the head of the bed, and a man's shaving things lay in tidy array next to a washbasin bordered in pink rosebuds. Every detail in the room appeared carefully chosen and precisely arranged. It was the sanctuary of a lonely man.

The chef said, 'The majordomo takes his evening stroll at this hour. We have a little time.'

The wardrobe was filled with neatly hung clothing: richly embroidered robes, silk doublets, velvet cloaks and a row of beaded slippers, some with curled toes. A faint whiff of lilac came from the clothes. The chef grabbed a white shirt with puffed sleeves, a simple vest, and a pair of black trousers and tossed them to me. For himself, he chose a magnificent violet doublet with gold piping and matching trousers. The fit was not perfect for either of us, but the clothes buttoned on him and didn't fall off me. Good enough. Over his fine suit, the chef wore a long, sweeping cloak of royal blue wool with a crimson silk lining. It hooked at the neck with a gold clasp and draped generously down his body, leaving plenty of room to hide the book. He topped off his grand outfit with a hat bearing an extravagant ostrich plume. When he set that hat on his head, he became a different man. He handed me a simple green-hooded cape.

The chef closed the wardrobe and shoved our kitchen clothes under the bed; then he sat down on it and bade me do the same. He still wheezed from running up the stairs, and his words were halting. 'Tonight, I'm a saddened dignitary come to pay respects to our ailing doge. You're my page.'

'Sì, Maestro. But I have no shoes.'

He noticed my bare feet for the first time and said, 'Dio.' He went back to the wardrobe and pulled out a pair of green silk slippers beaded in a pink floral motif. 'Here. They'll have to do.'

Unhappily, I slipped them on.

He sat beside me. 'Now, what happened with Giuseppe and Landucci?'

'Giuseppe told him you have the book.'

'How could Giuseppe know?'

'When I went to N'bali, Giuseppe was there. After I left, he talked to her.'

'Dio.'

'I didn't know he would talk to her. I thought he was only there to harass me.'

'Dio.'

'Maestro, Giuseppe killed her.'

'Scoundrel!' He grimaced and blew out a long breath. 'But there's no time for regret. We have to get out of here.'

He pressed his fingers into his eyes. 'Luciano, do you understand what will happen if we get caught?'

'I think so, Maestro.'

'We'll be killed the Venetian way – beheaded. But first, the dungeon.'

I swallowed hard. 'Sì, Maestro.'

'You could disappear. Leave this room now. Go back to your friends on the street. There are so many like you out there, you'd be invisible.'

I never thought going back to the street could sound so appealing, but I said, 'I'll stay with you.'

The chef squeezed my shoulder. 'I knew I chose rightly.'

His eyes filled, and he turned away. After a moment, he said, 'Luciano, if we end up in the dungeon, remember this: in the end, you'll die no matter what you say or don't say. Use your rage to win.'

'Win what?'

'If you tell your torturers nothing, you die victorious. They'll have nothing, and you will have died for a purpose – to protect the Guardians. That's as good a death as any man can hope for.'

Sweat broke under my arms. 'I hope I can do that.'

'I hope you won't have to.' He stood up. 'Pull up that hood and keep your head down. We can't have the servants recognizing you.'

'Maestro?'

'What?'

'Won't they go to your home? What about your family?'

'My wife knows that if I don't come home when I'm expected she must take the girls and go to her sister's house. If she doesn't hear from me, they will flee to Aosta.'

'You already had it planned?'

'Of course.'

We went down to the palace's main floor, and the chef swept into one of the public halls like the noble man he was. He affected a haughty expression, which transformed his face, and he tapped his lip as if in deep thought. No one interrupted him. I walked behind him with my hood up and my head down, as always, the invisible servant.

There would be no skulking around corners for this chef who hid his precious book in plain sight. He marched boldly up to the palace's main entrance and stood there, brazen as a gold tooth, tapping an impatient foot and flicking a finger at footmen who hurried to haul open the heavy doors. He strode out into the Piazza San Marco with me three steps behind, and I brimmed with secret delight as two *Cappe Nere* stepped aside to let us pass.

We ambled around the piazza for as long as we dared. I assumed that the chef was trying to think of a place to go. He was not accustomed to hiding in the streets and unwilling to put his friends at risk. After we'd covered the perimeter of the piazza three times, people glanced our way, apparently noticing that we were walking in circles. We went down a side street, crossed a bridge, and wandered into increasingly narrow *calli*. There, people stared at us because of our elaborate costumes. The magnificent clothes had served us well for escaping the palace, but if a nobleman were going any distance in Venice he'd travel by private gondola. We ducked around the back of an inn, and the chef removed the royal blue cloak and the plumed hat. I shed the green cape and vest, but I still needed the flamboyant beaded slippers.

While we stuffed our grand accessories under a pile of refuse, we overheard the innkeeper announcing that a couple of *Cappe Nere* wanted to question them. The inn went instantly quiet, and we listened. The *Cappe Nere* kept their voices low, which somehow sounded more threatening than shouts would have done. A man and a boy – criminals, they said – had stolen expensive clothing from the majordomo. 'They think they're clever, parading around disguised in fine clothes, but we know exactly what they took. The majordomo is very upset. The doge has his guards on the lookout, too.' He described the ostrich-plume hat, the blue wool cloak, my green cape, and my beaded slippers. The *Cappa Nera* said, 'These criminals might be carrying a book.' The mention of a book caused a rush of whispers (I could imagine their pulled eyelids), but everyone spoke over each other in their rush to denial.

'No, *signori*.'

'We've seen nothing.'

'We're all regulars here.'

'Sorry.'

Our one advantage against the *Cappe Nere* was that every-one hated them.

We crept away from the inn and scooted across a bridge. Without the wool cloak, the book under the chef's arm, shabby though it was, looked to me like an announcement of guilt, but the chef had a plan. He said, 'There's a church around the next corner. In the sacristy I can exchange my clothes for a cassock and surplice roomy enough to hide the book. We'll get a choir robe for you.'

'That's smart, Maestro.'

'It's ironic. Let's go.'

We turned the corner and came face-to-face with two tall, broad-shouldered *Cappe Nere*.

There are so many things I could have done. I could have called the chef Papà and complained about my school lessons; I could have pretended we were not together, clumsily bumped into the *Cappe Nere*, excused myself, and walked away; I could have done *something*. But the anxieties of that night converged in that moment and made me freeze. I stood rooted to the spot, staring at the *Cappe Nere* with a slack mouth. They looked at the book under the chef's arm, then at my beaded slippers. They blinked, and I ran. The chef cursed and ran after me.

The *Cappe Nere* pursued us with knives and pistols drawn. We fled through the darkest, most convoluted *calli* I knew, but every time I thought we'd lost them, the next moment brought the sound of shouts and heavy boots close behind. We ran down a *calle* that looked deserted, and a dagger, seemingly out of nowhere, whizzed past my head and thwanged into a wooden door only inches away. I spun around and pushed the chef in the opposite direction.

If I'd been alone, I might have outrun them. I was younger, smaller and quicker, unencumbered by heavy pistols and swords banging against my thighs. But the chef held me back. His breath became laboured, and he lagged farther and farther behind me. The *Cappe Nere* were gaining ground, and it was only a matter of time before they caught us.

The chef had got us out of the palace with his daring and cleverness, but now, in the street with dark coming on, we were in my element, and it was my turn to be clever. I knew all the best hiding places in Venice. I called, 'Maestro, this way.' I would take him to the thieves' quarter, where everyone was accustomed to minding their own business. I led him through a street of prostitutes, where Marco and I had often gone looking for Rufina, knowing the girls would delay any soldier who came within an arm's length.

To take a shortcut to our destination, I pulled the chef into a cul-de-sac and kicked aside a pail of rubbish to reveal a jagged hole low in the brick wall. 'Through here, Maestro.' He put his head through, but his shoulders stuck in the narrow opening. I said, 'Give me the book so you can wiggle through.'

He backed out of the hole and looked at me over his shoulder. I said, 'Maestro, I know where to go, but we have to get to the other side of that wall.' After a moment, he handed me the book, then cursed as he squeezed through the hole, tearing his clothes on broken bricks.

I lobbed the book through the hole and scrambled after it. By the time I pulled myself up to the other side, the chef had the book tucked under his arm. I reached through the hole to pull the pail of slops back for camouflage, and we ran through *calli* so dark they reminded me of the tunnel in the palace. This time, the threat was real, and oddly it was more manageable than my flights of fancy. My breath came fast, and my senses buzzed, but not because of panic. It was the familiar thrill of the chase.

I led the chef to a disreputable street where women sold themselves for sour wine and criminals met to plot their crimes. Those people wouldn't look twice at a couple more *banditi* who carried the scent of the fugitive. I hoped to blend in that unsavoury crowd long enough to decide where to spend the night.

But I miscalculated. When I peeked around the edge of a tavern to check who was on the street, I saw *Cappe Nere* everywhere, busily rounding up scheming thieves and ruthless murderers, not to arrest them, but to provide descriptions of us and offer a reward. I had taken us to the one part of the city where anyone would gladly sell us for the price of a bottle.

I pulled the chef in the recess of a deep doorway. 'Maestro, we have to get off the street.'

'Where can we go?'

'I know a place, but you have to trust me.'

'Let's go.'

We dashed out of the thieves' quarter and along a narrow *rio*. I heard footsteps behind us, so I rushed onto a certain humpbacked bridge that had saved Marco and me many times in the past. The chef hesitated when I ran over the crest of it in plain view but, *grazie a Dio*, he followed me. At the far side, I jumped down and scurried underneath. In the dark and confusion, it must have looked to the chef as if I'd disappeared into the canal.

'Luciano.' The chef sounded desperate. 'Where did you go?'

I poked my head out from under the bridge. 'Hurry up.' I

pointed to where the irregular stones of the canal wall jutted out like stairs and ran down to a narrow ledge underneath the bridge. He climbed down clumsily, trying to get a handhold on the slimy canal wall while clutching his book. 'Maestro, hurry.' He tried, but the ledge was covered with slippery algae, and he lost his footing. I caught his arm barely in time. I remember thinking he would have made a poor thief, and in the same moment, I understood how utterly his death would devastate me.

We stood on the ledge under the bridge and pressed our backs against the muddy canal; sludge squished and moulded itself around my body. I sucked in my breath as the big-booted *Cappe Nere* stampeded across the bridge and stopped directly above us.

A rough voice asked, 'Did you see which way they went?'

'Too dark. They just disappeared.'

'We have to split up.'

'*Sì.*' This one sounded irritated. 'Landucci wants them alive. What a nuisance.'

'Cut them down, but try not to kill them.'

'*D'accordo.*'

'*Andiamo.*'

Even after the sound of their boots faded to nothing, we remained motionless, pressed to the wet wall like weird outgrowths. I heard a cat meowing in the shadows, and I hoped it was Bernardo. The chef let out a long, slow, whistling breath. He sagged but held the book fast to his breast. The damp seeped into our clothes, the night deepened, and fog curled under the bridge. The chef shivered. He said, 'Where do we go from here?'

'Don't worry, Maestro. I know a place in the street of fishmongers.'

'The fishmongers?'

'I have a friend there.'

I climbed out from under the bridge and pulled the chef up after me. Our once splendid outfits were spattered with canal filth, our hair was wild, and our faces were streaked with sweat and grime. The chef looked at me, then down at himself. He said, *'Dio mio.'*

I said, 'The dirt is good, Maestro. We'll blend in with the street people. Just get that book out of sight. Will it fit under your clothes?'

He undid the buttons on his doublet and stuffed the book under his shirt. The mud-covered doublet gaped open, and the book made a bulky, unnatural bulge under his shirt, as if he had some freakish deformity. He said, 'This won't fool anyone.'

'It's all right. We're so filthy now we're just two more poor people no one wants to look at.'

We made our stealthy way, listening and looking in every direction before choosing the most deserted *calli*. We crept along in the shadows and at the slightest sound of voices or boots we melted into the opaque dark of the nearest doorway.

We sneaked along a cobbled footpath beside a narrow canal, where three old women had stopped for a spot of gossip. We strolled along casually, but just before we reached the women, a pair of *Cappe Nere* appeared at the far corner and walked toward us. We pivoted in tandem to go the other way, but after a few steps, two of the doge's guards, strutting and wielding halberds, turned the other corner and walked towards us from the opposite direction. I felt close to panic, but the chef turned his attention to a gondolier poling by, looking for a fare.

Gondolas are expensive and very slow, not a good choice for outrunning anyone. Yet, the chef stepped up to the canal's edge and hailed the gondolier. I shifted from one foot to the other while the *Cappe Nere* approached from one end of the footpath and the doge's guards from the other.

The gondolier leaned on his pole and looked the chef over: clothes smattered with stinking mud and clearly hiding something under his shirt. He wagged his head and started to pole away. The chef summoned him with a demanding voice: *'Venga qui! Adesso!'* The voice of the maestro giving an order. The gondolier looked at him again, and the chef raised his chin and held up a shiny gold ducat. The gondolier shrugged and then manoeuvred his boat against the canal wall. The chef scolded him for dawdling as he stepped in the boat and waved me aboard.

I hesitated. The chef was accustomed to travelling in gondolas and didn't realize what a suspicious scene two filthy street people would make climbing into such a luxurious means of transport. I glanced at the *Cappe Nere* closing in from one side and the doge's guards on the other. They were looking for a man and a boy, and at that moment the best strategy would be to split up. As the chef widened his eyes, wordlessly urging me to join him, I lunged at one of the gossiping women and ripped the purse from her belt. She shrieked, and the *Cappe Nere* came at me.

CHAPTER XXX

THE BOOK OF STRUGGLE

AS THE GONDOLIER PUSHED HIS pole against the canal wall to get clear of the commotion, I darted left and right, then dashed between the two men in a well-practised move. The gondola glided away, and I fled into the tangled embrace of my old city with the *Cappe Nere* clamouring at my heels.

I dropped the purse immediately after turning the first corner, hoping the *Cappe Nere* would be content to return it to the woman and let me go. That night they had more important prey than a common street thief. I ran a mad, senseless route until I was sure I had lost them. It was a relief to slow down, but as I made my way to the street of fishmongers I prayed that the chef would remember where to go.

He did, and as usual, there would be no cowering in alleys for him. I found him seated out on the docks, hunched over to hide the irregular bulge under his shirt, holding out a dirty, palsied hand and pestering passersby for alms in a wheezy voice. I helped him up, saying, 'Time to come home, Grandfather,' and I led him to the house of Domingo's fishmonger.

The fishmonger had given Domingo a small storage room at the back of his house in which to sleep. Sleeping indoors was a great luxury for Domingo, who could sprawl out on his dry, wood-plank floor wrapped in as many burlap bags as he wanted for warmth. In that room, the fishmonger kept extra canvases to cover his stall, sturdy wooden crates full of straw to hold the precious ice on which he displayed his fish, and an assortment of knives for scaling and gutting. Domingo kept the knives clean and sharpened with the devotion of a future owner.

High on one wall, a small, glass-paned window that opened like a door allowed Domingo to come and go without disturbing the fishmonger's family. He could lie there at night watching the stars through that window, drowsing and lulled by the liquid sounds of Venice. Even better, sometimes he could watch cold rain pelt the glass and listen to it pound the roof while he snuggled, warm and dry, under layers of burlap. Some nights, he watched the moon-glow play on the shiny surfaces of the fishmonger's knives and dreamed of the day he'd be master of his own fish stall, perhaps even have a wife and family. Domingo loved his little room and he was happy.

I said, 'My friend Domingo will help us.' I reached up and tapped the window with my fingernails, but Domingo, who was fast asleep, didn't stir. I rapped with my knuckles, but still he slept on like an innocent. When the chef boldly pounded on the sash and shouted, 'Domingo!' I gasped. The chef said, 'A name called out once in the night attracts less attention than an eternity of knocking.' He stood on his toes and peered into the little room. 'And it's more effective.'

Sleepy Domingo had crawled out from under his burlap. He stood rubbing his eyes as he unlatched the window. I hopped onto the crate Domingo used to reach the window, pulled myself up onto the sill, and climbed through.

Domingo and I tried to drag the chef in, tugging on his shirt while he strained to lift his own weight, but he was already worn out from the night's exertion, and the cumbersome book got in his way. Domingo reached through the window, saying, 'Give me that book.'

The chef said, 'No,' and swatted Domingo's hand away.

I said, 'It's all right. Give it to me, Maestro,' and he handed it over without hesitation. I set the book down, and Domingo and I stood on crates to brace the chef under his shoulders. We hauled him halfway through the window, far enough for him to get one leg over the sill. Then he swung the other leg up and over and jumped down into the little room. I picked up the book, wiped some dried mud off the cover with my sleeve, and gave it back to him.

He tucked it under his arm, saying, '*Grazie*, Luciano.'

In that tiny, cluttered room, the three of us were forced to stand uncomfortably close to each other. I smelled stale fish on Domingo's clothing and rank canal slime on the chef and myself. I saw tension in the chef's face and worry in Domingo's eyes. This time, I was not bringing food; I was bringing trouble. I started to explain, but Domingo held up his palms to stop me.

He turned an imaginary key at his lips. 'I don't want to know,' he said. 'I'll help you because you're my friend. Let's leave it at that.' His eyes moved skittishly from the chef's face to the book under his arm. He'd heard the same rumours everyone else had heard, and he talked often with Marco. No doubt he'd already guessed the truth.

The chef said, 'We have to leave Venice.'

'We want to go to Spain.' I said it so impulsively that I surprised myself. But Marco and I had so often planned to sail for the New World from Spain that it was the first place that came to mind.

Domingo nodded. 'Spain is a good idea. From there you can go to the New World. No one will find you there.'

'I'd like to take my family.' The chef shifted the book to his chest and hunched his body around it. 'By now they'll be at the home of my sister-in-law. Domingo, you could go there and—'

'No.' Domingo shook his head emphatically. 'It'll be hard enough to arrange an escape for two. A whole family? Never.'

The chef's face seemed to cave in on itself, and his eyes sank deeper into their sockets. He whispered, '*Dio*. What have I done?'

Domingo said, 'Give the book to Luciano. He'll take it to Spain.'

'I can't do that.' The chef tightened his arms around the book. 'He doesn't know how to use it yet.'

I felt a surge of relief to think we wouldn't be separated. I said, 'The chef can't go home anyway. The *Cappe Nere* are looking for both of us. We both have to get out of Venice.'

'*Cappe Nere? Merda.*' Domingo rubbed his pimpled forehead. 'All right. A freighter sails for Cádiz in one day. You can stay here till then, but be quiet.'

I said, '*Grazie*, Domingo.'

The chef turned away. It took a moment, but he said, '*Sì, grazie.*'

I was glad to hear we had one day. That would give me time to see Francesca. Perhaps I could . . . maybe she would . . . I didn't quite know what to expect from her, but I couldn't just *leave*.

Domingo said, 'How much money do you have?'

'Enough.' The chef spoke quietly. 'I'll meet my wife tomorrow at her sister's house. Luciano, you'll come with me.'

'I can't. I mean, you don't want me around when you see your wife.'

The chef turned a serious face to me, and I saw an angry edge in his look. 'You have some other plans for tomorrow?'

Marrone. I couldn't lie to him. 'I'd like to say goodbye to Francesca.'

'Oh, *Dio*, Luciano.' The chef rubbed his face like a tired father.

'But, Maestro—'

'We're in enough trouble. You want to make it worse? You want to put her in danger, too?'

'I won't get caught if I go alone.'

Domingo stepped between us. 'Don't argue, someone will hear. I can't do anything for you tonight. We should all get some sleep.'

The chef gave me a stern look and turned away.

Domingo balled himself up in a corner and pulled a burlap sack up to his chin; he closed his eyes tight, determined to see nothing. The chef sat on the book and leaned his head against the wall, but he didn't close his eyes. Since there wasn't enough room to stretch out, I sat with my knees pulled up to my chest and pretended to sleep while I watched the chef through slitted eyes. After he yawned for the third time, he bunched a burlap bag between his head and shoulder for a pillow and closed his eyes. I waited until the buzzes and snores became regular, then I rose, silent as smoke, and slipped out of the window.

I ran along the docks, feeling safe without the chef and his book. As he said, one more dishevelled boy was nothing special on those streets. By then, my beaded slippers were torn and so caked in mud they looked like the miserable, broken-down shoes any downtrodden boy would wear. A moist wind ruffled the water and cooled my brow. For some reason, that light touch on my face gave me hope that Francesca might . . . she just might come away with me.

The irony of the chef's willingness to leave his beloved family while I still schemed to be with Francesca didn't escape me. But I bit off that thought and swallowed it whole. Guilt, like a rich meal eaten too quickly, lay heavy inside me.

The hour was late, and the only noise – raucous laughter in the distance – came from a sailors' bar. When I turned into a dark *calle*, the street curved unexpectedly, and I ran along a canal I didn't recognize. The moon multiplied itself in the black water of the canal, and the angle of the light made me question whether I was going in the right direction. I never got lost, but that night, guilt confused me. I turned another corner; the convent should have been just another turn to the right – but no. A gaming house spilled light and noise into a small piazza. Through the open door, I saw men drinking and gambling while *Cappe Nere* walked among them, asking questions.

I backed away and tripped over a pile of rags; the pile groaned and moved. A blind beggar sleeping in the street sat up, and the light from the tavern illuminated his blank eyes. He held out a withered hand. I turned and ran, but the beggar called after me. 'Alms,' he wailed. 'Alms.'

I walked on, whispering, 'I can't. I just can't.' The beggar couldn't hear me. I was talking to myself, and to the chef.

At the convent, I climbed over the jasmine and scrabbled along the convent wall. When I reached Francesca's open window, I stood and softly called her name. She stirred immediately and sat up in bed with tousled hair. She slept more lightly than Domingo; perhaps she was less innocent.

She came to the window in her flimsy, lace-trimmed chemise, and it took a mighty effort for me to speak with composure.

I said, 'I have the book.'

'The book?' She was instantly alert.

'I leave Venice tomorrow, and you can join me later. I'll send money.'

'You really have the book?' She tossed her hair in a nimbus of moonlight. 'The book of magic?'

'It's not magic, Francesca.'

'But you said—'

'Francesca, it's a cookbook.'

'A cookbook?' She stepped back. 'What are you playing at?'

I leaned into the window. 'It's not an ordinary cookbook. It has recipes used to teach things. There are gospels—'

'Gospels?' I watched her eyes go dull.

'I can't explain, but the book is important.'

'So there's no magic?'

'No.'

'But there is a reward.'

'Yes.'

She picked up her brown habit and swung it lightly on one finger. 'Where are you going?'

I hesitated. If she didn't want to come with me, would she turn me in for the reward? I searched her face and saw curiosity, enthusiasm, desperation for a better life, but no malice and no treachery. I said, 'Spain.'

'Really?'

'Tomorrow night.'

She kept swinging the habit on her finger. 'I've heard things about Spain. The sisters say it's full of Moorish castles and gardens with reflecting pools. Orange trees and fountains.' She glanced over her shoulder at her solitary bed, the tragic crucifix and bleak bare walls. 'I'd like to go to Spain.'

'Yes!' I said. 'We could be married in Spain.'

'But first you'll get the reward.'

'No. I'm taking the book to Spain.'

'What? Why?'

'It's not my book. I'm going to Spain with the chef.'

'Wait.' Her lovely eyes narrowed. 'It's a cookbook and you're going to Spain with a chef? You're still going to be a cook?' She was shaking her head, backing away. 'That's not the kind of life I want. I could stay here and catch a rich cardinal.'

'But—'

'I used to be poor. I know how people treat you when you're poor. I can't go back to that. I can't be a cook's wife.' Her chin trembled and her voice came out strained. 'You said we'd be rich.'

'But we could be together in Spain. I thought you—'

'Yes, Luciano.' She came back to the window, and moonlight bathed her face. 'Yes, I'd rather be with you than some fat old cardinal. But we can't always have what we'd rather, and you're asking too much. I can't be poor again. I can't.'

'We wouldn't be poor—'

'No? Are vegetable cooks wealthy in Spain?'

'I already make five coppers a week—'

She looked incredulous. 'Five coppers? Five *whole* coppers?'

'But someday I'll be a chef and—'

'Sell it. So what if it's a cookbook? They all want it. Offer it to the highest bidder. Then we could go to Spain and really live. We could have a pink villa by the sea. With servants!

We'll give ourselves titles and be invited to the Spanish court. I'll make the most beautiful lace mantillas, but only for myself. I'll have silk gowns, and you'll have a carriage with white horses. We could—'

'Francesca.'

She stopped, then she leaned over the windowsill and placed her palm on my chest. My heart thudded so hard I knew she could feel it. She said, 'Don't you love me any more?'

'Of course I love you.'

'I love you, too, Luciano.' She stood on her toes and pushed her upper body over the sill until her cheek grazed mine. She moved easily, supple as a cat. She kissed me, oh so gently, on the lips and murmured, 'Do you like that?'

The chef's voice came into my head. *Dig into yourself and find strength.* I closed my eyes and said, 'Please don't.'

She kissed my closed eyes so tenderly I moaned. She said, 'Isn't that nice, Luciano? Hmmm?' She traced her fingertip around my lips, brushed her lips over my neck, and breathed a humid breath into my ear; the thrill rippled down to my toes.

Dig.

'I love you, Luciano. We can have children, if you like. We can have a wonderful life together.' She touched her lips to my ear and nipped at the lobe. She stroked my hair and whispered the words I'd longed to hear since the first day I saw her. 'I'll go with you and give you everything you want.' She laid her head on my shoulder, and the scent of soap and baking unleashed memory and desire.

I said, 'Then you'll come with me?'

'Yes.'

Marrone. It was really happening.

Her voice had a velvet undertone. 'Just sell the book.'

I began to imagine how it might be done without hurting the chef. Why should I care whether Venice or Rome prevailed? I knew I could get my hands on the book. After all, he'd freely handed it to me twice that night. He trusted me. The difficult part would be getting him on that ship and out of harm's way without it. Perhaps Domingo would help me; he might hold the chef while I tied him up. Maybe Marco would help us carry him aboard the ship if I promised him part of the reward. We'd have to gag the chef to keep him quiet. It was a painful thought, but at least he'd be out of danger. Then I'd go to his sister-in-law's house and tell Signora Ferrero where he was. His family could join him in Spain instead of disappearing into the mountains of Aosta.

Once they were all safely away, I could make a deal with Landucci. Of course, he couldn't be trusted. I'd send word through a string of anonymous couriers. Maybe a nun could deliver a sealed message thinking it was church business, a message offering to sell the book. Yes, a note telling Landucci to bring half the money to a ship bound for Spain. No – can't let him know our destination. Have him bring the money to a ship bound for Constantinople, or to some bar in the thieves' district. I could agree to have the other half payable after he took possession of the book. I'd have to check the shipping schedules; it must be perfectly timed.

After that, a sailor could deliver another note telling Landucci where to find the book and where to leave the rest of the money. Francesca could write the notes, and I could hide the book in an obscure corner of Venice. We wouldn't try to claim the rest of the money – that would surely be a trap. But half would be plenty. By the time Landucci found the book, Francesca and I would be out at sea, bound for Spain and then the New World. Yes, it could be done.

The silence of that moment was almost total. Only the voice of Venice, the whore, lapped at my ears, whispering, *Sell. Sell.* Then I heard the voice of the chef: *You can be better.*

I looked into her hopeful, luminous face. 'Francesca.'

'Yes, my love.'

'I can't.'

She stiffened and then stamped her foot. 'No!' She stamped again. 'No! No! I can't stand this! You have a way for us to be together and you won't take it.'

'But I *will* send for you.'

'To live like a peasant in some Spanish hovel? If I wanted to settle for that I wouldn't have joined a convent.'

'You wouldn't be a peasant.'

She clasped her hands, and her voice turned soft and imploring, but I heard an edge of desperation, too. 'It's just a book, Luciano. *Dio*, it's a cookbook. Sell it, and I'll go anywhere with you.' She looked up at me, begging. 'We could be so happy.'

'Francesca.' I took her face in my hands and my fingers tangled in her hair. 'We don't need to be rich. I love you. I'll take care of you. I'll protect you.' I reached behind her neck and pulled her to me. I kissed her hungrily, ferociously. When I finally let go, I stared into her face. Her lips had a swollen, softened look, like bruised fruit. I said, 'We can be happy just as we are.'

She tried to shake her head but I held her fast. She said, 'You're trying to confuse me.' We stared at each other for what felt like a long while. Moonlight touched off flecks of copper in her eyes and I saw comprehension glimmering there. She had never considered the possibility of finding happiness in a simple honest life, and she was trying to envision it. I watched possibility quicken in her, flit across her face, and then disappear.

'You're a dreamer, Luciano. Poor people are not happy. But if you sell that book for me, I'll love you for ever.'

I remembered the chef insisting that nothing could make someone love me. I groaned. 'Oh, Francesca.' The flawless creature I adored existed only in my mind, just like the demons I feared in the dark. The pleading girl standing at the window was beautiful, but not brave. The perfect creature of my imagination was no more real than the formulas for gold and immortality.

For the third time in my life, I felt the urge to pray. I looked up, because that's what people do, and I saw only the empty night sky. Then, I remembered, *Don't look up; look in*. I thought, *Please* – but this time I closed my eyes and summoned strength from inside myself.

Letting go of her face felt like ripping away a part of myself. I dropped my hands and walked away.

'Luciano . . .'

I could hear her weeping like a child, and the sound burned where she had touched my face. I walked across the cloister with no thought of being seen. I climbed over the wall and walked north, then south – it didn't matter. An eerie sense of sleepwalking blocked the full impact, until, in the middle of a stone bridge, reality engulfed me.

I would never see her again.

Grief brought me to my knees. I pressed my forehead to the cold stone and clasped my hands over the back of my head. My sob echoed in the night. I didn't know it was possible to feel such pain; physical injury would have been a welcome distraction. I must have looked small – a boy huddled in the dark, convulsed with mourning. After the last shudder, I crouched there, hollow and spent. After a while, I rose and wiped my eyes with a listless wrist. I plodded towards the street of fishmongers, wondering who I would be without her.

Dawn had just begun to dilute the inky night sky when I slipped through the window. Domingo still slept, but the chef was sitting up with his book, awake and haggard. He said, 'You went to her.'

'Yes.' I hung my head.

'She rejected you.'

'Not exactly. She wanted me to sell the book. I refused.'

'*Bravo*, Luciano.' The chef stood up and embraced me. He hugged me tight, so tight. 'You found your manhood, and it's formidable, as I suspected. Your pain will pass.'

I wanted to ask when. How long must I feel this way? But the chef sat back in his corner and closed his eyes to give me privacy. I curled against the wall and wept silently until Domingo began to stir. I wiped my face on my sleeve and pretended to come awake.

Domingo looked at me hard. 'Luciano? Are you all right?'

I didn't answer, afraid my voice would give me away. I feigned a yawn, and Domingo said, 'I'm going to work. The ship leaves tomorrow at dawn, but I need the money as soon as possible. Ten ducats for each of you, and five more for the captain to let you sneak aboard tonight.'

The chef said, 'I'll get the money. We'll meet you here later this morning.'

Domingo hoisted himself through the window without another word. He was so anxious to get away from us and from that book that he cracked his head on the window frame and didn't even stop to touch the scrape. I heard his feet hit the ground, and he ran.

CHAPTER ❖ XXXI

THE BOOK OF OPIUM

WE TOOK A CIRCUITOUS ROUTE TO the chef's rendezvous with his wife. By then, we looked like the worst of the street people – dirty, smelly, beaten and bone-weary. The chef carried the book under his shirt in much the way many street people carried their meagre possessions. He kept his head down and one arm across his middle as if he had an ache in his stomach. I dawdled, keeping a good distance behind him so that we didn't appear to be together. Although we blended in with the roving poor, we still turned away whenever we saw the *Cappe Nere* or the doge's guards. We kept to little-used footpaths and half-deserted streets, always stopping to look around corners before venturing forward.

We detoured through a poor section of the city, the Cannaregio, a desolate wharf area where caulkers repaired derelict boats. Balcony railings hung loose over a sluggish canal congested with rotting vegetables and soggy straw from discarded mattresses. Everything spoke of abandonment and wretchedness, and the sombre people there, preoccupied with the business of survival, ignored us.

In the twisted Calle del Capitello, we walked between tall, forbidding walls that towered over a constricted alley known as the street of murderers. Most people went out of their way to avoid that street, burdened as it was by the spirits of outraged victims. Wherever a murder had occurred on that street, a small shrine to the Virgin had been placed in a wall niche. A grimy Virgin smiled down on us every few steps.

We emerged from the Calle del Capitello in front of a tumbledown palazzo swaddled in an air of quiet decay. We walked along the footpath in the shadow of the palazzo, and I looked through the wrought-iron gate. I glimpsed a well-tended garden, pensive and secluded, full of oleanders and roses glowing in morning light. There's something hopeful about Venetian gardens, oases of life blooming courageously while everything else is slowly licked away and worn down by salt water and time. I took the garden as a sign that somewhere in this dangerous maze of events we might yet find salvation.

At his sister-in-law's home, a respectable house similar to the chef's, he told me to wait in the back courtyard while he went inside. He said, 'Rosa will be frantic by now.'

I saw them, the chef and Signora Ferrero, and even heard scraps of their conversation through an open window on the main floor. White curtains billowed inward in a sea breeze, and a pitiful scene unfolded in the soft flashes revealed by the panels, which opened and closed like a slowly blinking eye. I allowed myself to watch the sorrowful tableau.

The chef spoke first. I saw apology in his expression and helplessness in his gestures. His face was destroyed. Signora Ferrero's face, at first frightened and confused, soon darkened with a powerful rage. The chef bowed his head and allowed her harangue to go on without interruption until, abruptly, her anger crumbled. Her fierce look dissolved, and her arms, upraised in mid-tirade, fell around her husband's neck as she collapsed into his arms. They wept together, and their unconstrained sobs reached me clearly and cut deep.

She stopped weeping first. She wiped her eyes with a handkerchief and caressed his cheek with gentle resignation. They talked, touched each other's faces, wiped away tears, and then slipped into the comfort of a familiar embrace. They stood like that for a long time.

When finally she drew away from him, they went about preparing for his departure. He slid the book into a flour sack, and I was surprised to see him also pack a quill and a blue ink stone. Then I remembered; his daughters would be in school at that hour to keep up an appearance of normality. No doubt he'd write them letters, perhaps while we waited to board the ship. I wondered whether they could arrange to be reunited in Spain. Perhaps he would write a father's reassurances.

His wife helped him into a clean shirt and brushed dried mud off his knees. She put a loaf of bread and a wedge of cheese into another sack, and she tucked a fat purse into the pocket of his trousers.

They came to the back door together, holding hands like young lovers. The chef looked as though he wished to speak but had no tongue. Signora Ferrero pulled herself up straight. When she spoke, her voice was steady. 'We've been happy, Amato.'

'Sì, cara mia.'

'But now we must be more than happy.'

He caressed her cheek. 'Now we must be brave.'

'Go.' She looked away. 'I'll gather the girls and leave for Aosta today.'

The chef was about to speak when he heard a loud pounding at the front door.

'Maestro.' I tugged his sleeve. *'Cappe Nere.'*

He looked crushed and shrunken. *'Cara—'*

'Go,' she said, sweeping us away with her hands. 'My sister will be slow to answer the door. Go!'

But the chef didn't move until she closed the door in our faces.

At the docks, we rounded the corner at the street of fishmongers and stopped short at the sight of four *Cappe Nere,* milling around outside the home of Domingo's fishmonger. We backed up along the side of the nearest house and watched as the *Cappe Nere* tried the fishmonger's front door, peered into his windows, and circled around the back to peer into Domingo's room.

Giuseppe was there, too, holding Bernardo up like a squalling prize. He shook my poor cat by the back of the neck, and Bernardo swiped at the old drunk's eyes with his claws extended. Giuseppe held Bernardo up to a *Cappa Nera* and whined, 'I told you they'd come here, and they did. This is the thief's cat. He'll come back for his cat.'

The captain said, 'Bruno, stay here and keep an eye out.'

Giuseppe scurried after the captain. 'You're only leaving one man?'

The captain turned on Giuseppe and produced a small knife from his sleeve. He held the point under Giuseppe's chin and pushed up until Giuseppe's head strained backward. 'You think one *Cappa Nera* can't handle a cook and a boy?'

'Yes, *signore.* I mean no, *signore.'*

The *Cappa Nera* pushed the point of the knife just hard

enough to draw a bead of blood, then withdrew it with a casual wave of dismissal. 'If you think one man isn't enough, stay here yourself. You and the cat will be a big help.' The *Cappe Nere* laughed mirthlessly and then moved off like a single, many headed animal. Bruno posted himself at the side of the house so he could watch the front and back at the same time, and Giuseppe squatted on the street with Bernardo.

The chef and I communicated with a look, then crept back to the poverty-stricken Cannaregio. We walked down a street that was deserted save for a woman in a third-floor window who was hanging dingy laundry on a line stretched between buildings. There were no other people about; it was a neighbourhood where men left early to do hard labour for other men, and women kept to themselves, busy with household drudgery performed without help and often with a babe at the breast. Only in the evening did those people pull rickety chairs out onto the narrow street to share gossip and homemade wine.

That day, the silence in the street seemed deeper because of the solitary sound of the clothesline creaking at regular intervals as the woman pinned up her clothes and let out the line . . . pinned up her clothes and let out the line . . . pinned up her clothes and let out the line . . . No faces looked out from any of the run-down houses, no sound reached us but the monotonous, repetitious squeak of the clothesline.

The chef led me to the parish church, and we slipped in through a narrow side door. We walked up the aisle past black-clad widows with bitter faces who mumbled rote prayers for the long-gone husbands who had left them impoverished. The church was antiquated and as dim as a cave, with the smell of mildew and incense permanently embedded in the wooden pews. The place was as poor as its parishioners – the altar cloths were threadbare, the gilding on the saints' halos was wearing thin, and the Virgin's mantle had faded to grey. The domed ceiling picked up sounds, expanded them in an acoustical heaven, and sent them crashing down onto the bowed heads below. We heard the amplified click of rosary beads and the rustle of skirts as the widows shifted arthritic knees on the stone floor. They prayed in voices lowered to a deathbed hush.

We sat in silence, and I wondered how long we'd stay there. I wondered how we'd get back to Domingo's room. I wondered what he'd do if we didn't get the money to him on time. I wondered why the chef had agreed so easily to Spain. I wondered whether he knew another Guardian there. I wondered what other recipes like the soufflé he had to teach me. And I wondered, for the hundredth time, what exactly the chef did with opium.

Votive candles sputtered in dark corners and enlivened the features of gloomy martyrs. Narrow shafts of light, furred with dust motes, bisected the shadows. The crucifix over the altar looked blunted by time, and the pale face of Jesus was blurred and burdened by decades of dust. I thought, *Well, if there are more secrets to tell, this is the place to tell them.* I whispered, 'Maestro?'

'I'm thinking.'

'There's something I need to ask you.'

'What?'

'What do you use opium for?'

'*Dio*, now?' He sighed. 'It has to do with one of the writings in the book.'

'What writing?'

He raised his eyebrows. 'You want to know now?'

'We're not going anywhere.'

The chef stared at the crucifix for a while and then said, 'Sì. Maybe this is exactly the right place to tell you about opium.'

Out of nowhere, Bernardo streaked up the aisle and leapt into my lap. 'Bernardo!' I stroked his back, and he purred. 'You got away from Giuseppe, eh? Good boy. Smart cat.' I kissed his head and laughed. A widow turned and glared at me, but I was so relieved to see Bernardo, I glared back at her.

The chef clucked his tongue. 'Are you finished playing with the cat?'

'Sorry, Maestro.'

'*Bene.*' He leaned towards me and whispered. 'There's one very simple recipe in the book – water, vinegar and opium.'

'You don't use opium in your white-bean soup?'

'Where do you get these ideas?' He ran a hand through his hair. 'Well, once in a while, maybe just a pinch if circumstances call for it. You can't detect it in food. It's a painkiller, but it has some powerful side effects. Too much can even kill you.' He shook his head. 'It's not a benign herb to use with abandon. Opium must be handled carefully. We keep opium as a memento of one of our most important writings – an account of the crucifixion, by a Roman soldier who was there. It's an unusual account that reminds us to be open to alternative explanations of, well . . . everything. The soldier said he gave Jesus a sponge soaked in vinegar and water, but first he mixed opium into the water.'

'Why?'

'It was an act of compassion. After all, Jesus was suffering. The soldier knew the opium would either ease his pain or kill him mercifully.'

I was confused. 'But the Romans are the ones who crucified Jesus.'

'Sì.' The chef smiled ruefully. 'They crucified Peter, too. And yet the church of Jesus is centred in Rome, and no one questions it.' The chef shook his head and sighed.

He continued, 'Not all Romans wanted Jesus dead. That soldier was a secret sympathizer, one of many who dared not speak up. The same soldier pierced Jesus's side. See the wound in the statue?' The chef pointed at the dusty crucifix, and I noted the slit between two ribs on the wooden Jesus. 'He made a shallow stab so that he could declare Jesus dead and prevent the soldiers from crushing his legs as they did to the other two. Of course, the water that came from the wound meant nothing. Hanging on a cross will cause water to collect in the lungs. Some say the fact that there was blood with the water proves Jesus was still alive, because dead men don't bleed.'

'So opium killed Jesus?'

'Maybe not. A certain amount of opium will put a man into a state resembling death. Accounts say Jesus suddenly "expired" after taking the sponge, but the soldier says Jesus lapsed into a deep opium sleep and later awoke in his cave tomb. His disciples started a rumour about resurrection in case he was seen.'

'Jesus survived the crucifixion?' It was difficult to keep my voice low.

'According to Thomas, Jesus returned to his disciples more than a year after the crucifixion. He told them he'd been in hiding and that they could join him if they wished. Jesus may have lived a long time and died a natural death.'

'Do you believe the soldier's story?'

The chef leaned back in the pew and stared hard at the crucifix. 'Jesus was a young, healthy man. He was only on the cross for three hours. Most people lingered on crosses for days. The two crucified with him had to have their legs crushed to hurry death. Why should Jesus have died so quickly, and immediately after receiving a drink? Yes, I believe the soldier's account.'

'Marrone.'

'This business of resurrection is not an unusual story, really. It's not surprising that the disciples would come up with that. Centuries before Jesus, there were at least three pagan god-men who died around the time of Easter – the spring equinox – and were resurrected after three days. Is that a coincidence? Or did the disciples simply adopt a tired old story to protect Jesus?'

'What do you think?'

'I think the soldier's story is one of those writings that could be true, but that threaten the church, and that's why we Guardians need to preserve it until a time when it can be examined and discussed openly.'

'When will that be?'

'I don't know.' The chef cupped his hand on the back of my head, and it felt like a blessing. He said, 'But right now, you and I can take comfort in knowing Jesus was a man, like us. Jesus didn't resurrect himself like some trickster of death. If he knew he could do that, what value would his death have? Jesus was purely and divinely human, and that's the good news. What do human beings need with the example of gods? You have the same strength in you that Jesus had in him. Whatever happens, remember that.'

'But, Maestro, Jesus was one of a kind.'

'Sì. One of *our* kind. Jesus said, "All I have done, so can you do also, and more." Perhaps we're all *adepti* in the making.'

'Like N'bali?'

'Like all those teachers in sandals.' He gave me his enigmatic half smile.

The widows ticked their beads, the chef bowed his head,

and I considered this while I stroked Bernardo. That's when I realized that Bernardo had found us when the *Cappe Nere* had not. I whispered, 'Maestro, Bernardo outwitted them all.'

In spite of our circumstances, or perhaps because of them, this twist seemed like the most splendid comedy. Frayed nerves snapped and we laughed out loud. The black-clad widows turned and fixed us with furious stares. One shook a tiny fist, and that made us laugh louder. We haemorrhaged laughter. Uncontrollable spasms without lightness or joy rocked us to the core. I fell sideways on the wooden pew, shaking with laughter that surged over the razor's edge we'd been walking for too long. The chef threw his head back and roared in a sumptuous, luxurious, overdue easing of tension. A cathartic explosion poured from our mouths, leaving us breathless and coughing, weeping and gasping, holding our ribs against the tearing pains in our sides. Eventually it subsided, *grazie a Dio*, and finally, *finally*, it stopped.

We sat in purged silence. Bernardo nuzzled his head into my chest and the chef once again bowed his head. The widows had long since shuffled out of the church, marvellously scandalized. Our sacrilegious laughing fit would make a good story that night on the street.

I said, 'You told your wife about the Guardians.'

The chef nodded. 'I'd hoped she'd never have to know, but after the doge began his campaign, yes, I told her everything.'

'Will she join you in Spain?'

'I hope, someday, that will be possible. But there is much to do before we think about reunions.'

'Won't people ask questions when she turns up in Aosta?'

'She'll say she's a widow. My Rosa would give her life

before she'd betray me. As I would die before betraying the Guardians.'

'Aren't you afraid to die?'

The chef seemed more tranquil than I'd seen him in weeks. He said, 'Staying alive for its own sake has no more meaning than a ticking clock.' He shrugged. 'To die is nothing, but to live with purpose and integrity, that's something.'

CHAPTER ✤ XXXII

THE BOOK OF ILLUSIONS

WE FOUND DOMINGO AT THE FISH STALL, and the chef handed over a purse full of ducats. Domingo had seen Giuseppe and a *Cappa Nera* watching his house when he went back to meet us, and he was jumpier than ever. He dug his hands into his armpits, stared at the ground, and mumbled a promise to make our arrangements. Then he turned away.

The chef touched Domingo's arm. 'We need a place to stay until tonight.'

Domingo chewed his bottom lip, and I sensed the urgency of his wish to be rid of us. I wondered how much loyalty bread and leeks and fennel really bought. How well did I actually know silent, solitary, sullen Domingo? I'd always assumed that all he wanted was to become a fishmonger, but what if he wanted more? Apropos of nothing, the chef said, 'You can live a long, peaceful life selling fish once we're gone, Domingo. It's in everyone's best interest that we board that ship tonight.' Perhaps it wasn't necessary, but I was glad the chef had said it so I didn't have to.

I said, 'Domingo, you've been a good friend to me in my trouble. *Grazie.*'

Domingo nodded. 'There's a sailors' bar called Vino Venezia on the docks, near the crabbers' boats. It's a clearinghouse for smugglers, and there's a cellar. Tell the barkeep you need a place to stay until tonight.' Domingo jabbed his chin at the chef. 'Do you have more money?'

The chef jingled his pocket.

Domingo nodded. 'The barkeep gets his cut of everything that goes in or out, especially people. He runs slaves and hides criminals. Give him four ducats. I'll come there tonight, late.'

'*Grazie*, Domingo.' The chef stepped away from the stall and turned to go.

I started to follow him, but Bernardo was squirming under my arm. He missed his regular meals in the palace, and the smell of fresh fish was too much for him. He leapt from my arms, clamped onto a fat mackerel, and made off into the crowd. The fishmonger bellowed and chased him with a scaling knife. I wanted to go after him, but the chef held my arm. Domingo said, 'Get out of here.'

I looked for Bernardo on the way to the crabbers' boats, but he'd vanished with his mackerel. So there it was – Bernardo and Francesca both lost for ever.

Vino Venezia stank mildly of fish and spilled wine. The smell might have been stronger, but the front and back doors had fallen from their hinges and not been replaced. A steady, salty sea breeze sailed through the place and freshened the air. The broken doors served as tabletops, and three-legged wooden stools stood scattered around them.

The bar and barkeep made a good pair, both crude and greasy. The barkeep looked up when we entered, but he didn't stop wiping a smeary glass with his wine-stained apron. His eyes didn't match his dull, meaty face – they were piercing blue, sharp as steel under black eyebrows. His eyes gave him the look of a man who could produce a stiletto from his sleeve before you saw him move.

The chef spoke to him quietly. The barkeep put down his dirty glass and watched the chef place four ducats on the bar. He slid the money off the bar and into his pocket in one move, then made a lazy gesture for us to follow him. He hadn't spoken a word.

In a small room behind the bar, the barkeep grunted as he lifted a wine crate off a stack in the corner, then another, and another. When he kicked aside the last crate, we saw a trapdoor in the floor. He knelt clumsily, sweating as he bent over his soft belly, and pulled the door open by a rope handle. I saw the top half of a long ladder; the lower half was swallowed in darkness. The barkeep lit an oil lamp and turned the wick down to conserve fuel. Holding the lamp, he started down the ladder, and we followed.

He led us into a musty cellar stocked with crates from which the stamp of the winery had been roughly scraped off. The only ventilation came from a small, open window up at street level. I could hear the slow drip of water behind the walls, and the earthen floor felt slimy underfoot. We were below sea level. First my skin crawled, then panic gripped me, and my breathing turned fast and laboured.

The chef said, 'Steady, Luciano. Here and now you're safe. Breathe.'

I remembered the tunnel. 'Sì, Maestro. *Grazie.*' I focused

on my breath – breathe in, breathe out – and the fear subsided.

The chef took the oil lamp from the barkeep and turned up the flame. The man pulled his eyelid to indicate that we were all thieves and could therefore trust each other. He lumbered up the ladder, pulled it up after him, and slammed the trapdoor shut. I heard the scraping of wooden crates being replaced.

'Find a dry spot,' said the chef. 'Rest while you can.'

I sat on a wine crate and concentrated on my breath moving in and out, slow and steady. When my thoughts strayed to the window, or the ladder, or the fear that Domingo wouldn't come, I refocused on my breath. I closed my eyes and synchronized my breathing with a drip of water behind the walls, in and out, regular as a pendulum. At some point, I heard a tearing and rustling of paper.

The chef was barely visible in the guttering lamplight, but I made out the shape of him bent over his book and scribbling away with his quill. I remembered seeing him take the blue ink stone and quill from his house, and I thought it must wrench his heart to have to write to his daughters. Could he assure them that he would find them again, or did he have to say goodbye?

I said, 'I'm sorry you have to be separated from your family.'

'So am I.'

'If you're writing notes to your daughters, Domingo can deliver them for you.'

'Do you mind? Can I have some privacy?'

'Sorry, Maestro.'

I went back to my breathing. The scratch of quill on parchment receded, and just as I began to a feel a melancholic peace, we were disturbed by the sound of footsteps and crates scraping overhead. The chef and I looked at each other – it was much too early for Domingo. We watched the trapdoor open; a dusty ray of daylight slanted into the cellar and the ladder was lowered. Then one worn-out shoe stepped onto the top rung. It wasn't the boot of a soldier, *grazie a Dio*. The chef put the book on a crate and stood in front of it with his quill dangling from his hand. The next foot came down the ladder, then the legs and torso. A young man with a bundle under one arm climbed down. I said, 'Marco?'

The trapdoor slammed shut with a bang. 'What is this?' The chef's lamp-lit face wavered between anger and surprise.

Marco stood at the foot of the ladder, and even in the cellar gloom I could see that he looked jaunty and pleased with himself. He said, 'I brought you something.' Marco opened his bundle and revealed a loaf of bread. 'I went to the kitchen and heard you two had run out like madmen with *Cappe Nere* after you. Domingo told me where you were when I showed him the bread I stole for you. You're hungry, aren't you?'

'*Merda.* What do you want, Marco?'

He laughed. 'That Domingo. He didn't want to talk to me. So I asked him, "Do you want Luciano to starve?" How often did he feed you?' Marco pushed my shoulder with his. 'What's the matter, Luciano? You weren't planning to run out on me with the book, were you?'

'There's nothing in the book for you, Marco.'

'Sure. That's why everyone is so crazy to get their hands on it.'

'You don't understand.'

'I understand that you're not going to cut me out.'

'*Madre di Dio.*' The chef ran his fingers through his hair and cursed under his breath. I was afraid Marco might try to take the book by force, so I moved in front of my maestro and stood with my feet apart. He'd have to come through me.

A mean smile spread over Marco's face. 'You think you can fight me?'

The chef stepped beside me. 'There are two of us.'

Marco boosted himself onto a short stack of crates. 'No one's going to fight. You think I haven't thought this through? Luciano, you should know me better. They'd never give someone like me a reward – much less a senate seat. If I brought them the book they'd only take it, and maybe even kill me.'

The chef said, 'That's right. So what are you doing here?'

'Same thing you're doing here.' Marco pushed his chin out. 'When Domingo comes, I'm going with you. There's a formula to make gold in that book. I know there is, and I want it. I go where that book goes.'

'Marco,' I said, 'you don't know what you're doing.'

The chef shook his head. 'You really don't, boy.'

'I'm staying. What are you going to do about it?'

I stepped towards him. 'What about Rufina?'

Marco snorted. 'If I haven't found Rufina by now, I'm not going to. N'bali said what we've all known all along. My sister is dead.'

I nodded. I hadn't realized that he had allowed himself to accept it.

'Anyway,' he went on, 'even if she were alive, what could I do for her when I can barely feed myself? That book is my only chance.' His expression fluttered between rage and despair and I knew there was no way to make him leave.

I said, 'All right, Marco.'

'Oh, *Dio*.' The chef sat down and put his head in his hands. 'I have to think.'

Marco smirked. 'Think all you want.' He scooted back to make himself comfortable on the crates. 'The three of us will just relax and wait for Domingo. I hear we're going to Spain.' He lay on his back with his feet against the wall and his fingers laced behind his head.

I didn't want to look at Marco, and I didn't want to know whether the chef was looking at me. I sat on a crate and closed my eyes. I struggled to go back to my breathing, but minutes later we all came alert at the sound of heavy boots scuffling on the wooden floor above us. The voices of the *Cappe Nere* sailed out of the open back door of the bar and in through our high window. One said, 'Keep your stolen wine. We want the people you're hiding.'

'People?' The barkeep sounded bored. 'What people?'

'That's your business, isn't it? Hiding people.'

'What are you talking about? I'm a barkeep.'

I took some comfort from hearing the barkeep remain so calm, as if this sort of raid was routine.

A *Cappa Nera* said, 'They were seen coming in here.'

'*Boh.* Someone made a mistake. But since you're here, how about a drink? On the house, of course.' The sound of breaking glass made us jump. The barkeep yelled, 'What the hell are you doing? Are you crazy?'

A *Cappa Nera* said, 'Crazy enough to cut your throat with this.'

'*Madonna mia!* What do you want? Money? Here, take it. What are you *doing*?'

I cringed under a horrendous crashing of glass. They must have pushed over all the shelves behind the bar. My heart leapt in my chest at the sound of upended tables and wood splintering against the walls. Marco jumped off his crate and stood staring up at the trapdoor. The chef took the purse from his pocket and stuffed the letters to his daughters inside it. The tread of heavy boots pounded overhead and a man shouted, 'Hold him!'

Another said, 'I've got him.'

'All right,' said the first voice, 'this is simple. I take one finger for every question you don't answer. Let's start with a thumb. Like this . . .'

The barkeep screamed; it was a raw howl of pain and horror. He sobbed, 'They're in the cellar.'

'That's it,' said the chef. 'It's over.' He pointed to the ladder and made a sweeping movement. I moved it away from the trapdoor and set it under the window. We heard boots above us clomp into the storeroom.

The chef picked up the oil lamp and smashed it against a crate of wine packed in straw. Slender flames leapt from the straw and blackened the wood. A spark jumped to another crate, and the chef pushed the burning crates together.

Marco yelled, 'Are you crazy?'

Above us, we heard crates being moved to expose the trapdoor.

The oil-soaked wood exploded into a conflagration, and we shielded our eyes as wine bottles burst and smoke rushed to the ceiling. Under the whoosh of flames I heard the chef say, 'God forgive me.' He held up the book.

I shouted, 'No, Maestro!'

'*Figlio di puttana!*' Marco leapt forward and tackled the chef just as he flung the book into the blaze. As the trapdoor opened, Marco tried to reach into the fire but instantly pulled back with a hiss of pain.

The chef saw my horrified face and said, 'The Guardians are more important than one book.'

The dry parchment caught immediately and curled away while the leather blistered and blackened. Orange light danced crazily on the rough walls as if the cellar had come alive with dancing shadow demons. *Hell*, I thought. *We're in hell.*

A voice above us cried out, 'Fire!'

'Get them out. Landucci wants them alive.'

'Get a ladder.'

The chef shoved his bulging purse into my pocket and prodded me towards the ladder under the window. Marco already had a foot on the bottom rung, and the chef grabbed him by the hair and threw him to the ground. 'Continue the tradition,' he whispered fiercely. He pushed me roughly onto the ladder, slapped my backside as if I were a mule, and said, 'Go!'

While the *Cappe Nere* cursed at the barkeep to hurry with the ladder, I crawled out through the high window, knelt on all fours, and peered down into the inferno. The cellar was filling with smoke and I barely made out the movement of another ladder dropping through the trapdoor.

Marco had climbed halfway to the window. He stretched out a hand to me, then his face opened in shock and he slid down into the roiling black smoke. I thought his foot might have slipped on a rung; it did not occur to me until later that the chef could have plans for him. I watched Marco's frightened face drop away from the window and disappear in the smoke.

I flattened myself against the side of the building and stood tight against the wall. The cellar was sludgy and damp; after the initial blaze, the burst wine bottles wetted the straw and there was more smoke than fire. The billows puffing out of the window were already diminishing. A *Cappa Nera* hollered, 'Smother it!' Another one cried, 'The boy's on the ladder.' I heard a scream, the smack of a fist on flesh, groaning, and everyone coughing and coughing . . .

Someone yelled, '*Merda!* I burnt my fingers for nothing. Nothing left but the binding.'

'I can't breathe.'

'Get out now.'

I wanted to run, but I thought the chef and Marco might somehow still escape. Maybe I'd have a chance to help. I looked around for a place to hide and saw an overturned rowing boat waiting for new caulking and paint, a derelict little vessel with gaps between the boards. It would do. I scrambled out to the dock, and as I started to raise the rowing boat, a couple of fishermen, who'd left off mending their nets to watch the commotion stared at me. I met their eyes, one at a time, and each of them nodded. They saw nothing; after all, it was Venice. I heaved the rowing boat up and crawled beneath it.

Through the gaps in the boat, I watched men stumble out of the bar. They came out clawing at their throats, choking and coughing, and then they sat down or stood bent over while they sucked greedily at clean sea air. A few sailors and fishermen tossed buckets of seawater into the cellar, and the smoke dwindled. The wet, muddy cellar had kept the blaze from spreading, *grazie a Dio*. One *Cappa Nera* kept a tight grip on the chef's arm, and another held Marco by the nape of his neck. The barkeep knelt on the ground, cradling one hand wrapped in a blood-soaked bar towel.

The chef's clean shirt was streaked with soot and splotched with wine. His face and hands were blackened, whether from dirt or burns I couldn't tell, but he held his head up. Marco staggered in a daze, wiping a bloody nose. The *Cappe Nere* led them away with their hands bound behind their backs.

It would be many years before I learned the details of their fate.

CHAPTER ✤ XXXIII

THE BOOK OF REVELATIONS

THEY'D HUNTED FOR THE CHEF and a boy, and they'd caught the chef and a boy. Fate was whimsical that day. With nowhere to go, I remained crouched under the overturned boat. I had no doubt the chef and Marco had been taken straight to the dungeons, and try as I might, I couldn't think of any way to help them. If I'd had the book, I would have tried to trade it for their lives. That would have been foolish as well as pointless, and I've often felt thankful that I didn't have that choice. I huddled under the boat and wondered whether only the *Cappe Nere* would interrogate them, or whether Landucci himself might take part. I don't know which scenario horrified me more.

I imagined the chef, silent and stoic, and Marco, cringing and crying, swearing that he was the wrong boy. It had occurred to me by then that the chef had kept Marco in the cellar to take my place. In the dungeon, the chef would keep silent, and the *Cappe Nere* would laugh at Marco and call him a coward. Poor Marco. Torture and death seemed like a disproportionate punishment for ordinary human weakness. The chef knew what he was dying for, and he was willing. But Marco, my poor hungry brother, would never know that his death served a purpose. Did that purpose give his death meaning even though he wasn't aware of it? I wanted to think so, but that was no comfort for him. Oh, Marco, why did you have to follow me? It seemed monstrously unfair. They wanted *me*, and the notion to surrender myself and save Marco seemed right. But I knew they'd only take me and keep him, too. I remembered his face dropping away in the smoke and I wept.

I had thought that losing Francesca was the worst that could happen, but under that boat, the pain of losing her merged with the pain of losing everything – the chef, Marco, the book, all our hopes and dreams – and I despaired. In that terrible moment, I remembered a corpse Marco and I had once found hanging under a bridge. The man had tied one end of a rope to the stone balustrade and the other around his neck, and then he had simply jumped. It looked as if his neck was broken, but he may have strangled to death. His tongue protruded from his mouth, his face was blotched purple and blue, and a putrid stench surrounded him.

Marco and I recoiled at the sight of him, but later we talked about it and wondered over it. Filled with plans for our future in the New World, we couldn't understand how he could throw away everything in one quick leap. How could anyone stop hoping so utterly?

That day under the boat, I understood. It was possible to despair and to crave oblivion if for no other reason than to escape the crushing guilt. Why should I be allowed to carry on while the chef and Marco could not? Wasn't it I who excited Marco with talk of alchemy? Wasn't it I who brought Marco into the chef's life? I considered filling my pockets with stones and jumping into the lagoon, but I knew I couldn't do it, and I despised myself anew for cowardice.

I considered turning myself in to the *Cappe Nere* simply to let them do it for me, but I remembered the Judas Chair and I feared I might break under torture and betray the Guardians. I remembered the chef's last words to me: *Continue the tradition.*

Perhaps that could be my redemption. I could carry the secret of the Guardians and find small ways to spread the chef's respect for knowledge. I wouldn't learn all the lofty things the chef could have taught me, but I could keep his message alive. Anyway, I wasn't fit to be a Guardian. In that dark and cynical moment I castigated myself for having believed I could ever have been part of something so grand.

Then I remembered something else the chef had said: *You're better than you think.*

This then would be my mission – to be better. I would be the man he wanted me to be. I would honour the chef's belief in me by staying alive and becoming the best man I could be. And that was my moment of resurrection.

I stayed there, huddled under the boat, hoping Domingo would come to the bar as we'd arranged. I curled into a foetal position and waited. After a while, my legs cramped and my head ached, but any thought of crawling out to stretch was quashed by a frigid wind that swept in from the sea at dusk. It rocked my shelter and whistled through gaps in the boat. I saw a gondola caught in a squall; a sailor's hat blew by and wind ransacked the water. Then the rain came in sheets, in torrents. It pummelled the little boat, leaked onto my head, splashed around me and soaked my clothes. It went on for hours. My teeth chattered and my empty stomach gurgled. I wrapped my arms around myself and squinted through the gaps. I wasn't sure I could trust my eyes when Domingo appeared, loping along the dock, holding a scrap of canvas over his head. He stopped in front of the burned-out bar and stood in the rain, staring at the blackened frame of the cellar window.

I crawled out from under the rowing boat and darted up behind him. I said, 'The *Cappe Nere*—'

He held up his hand. 'We have to hurry. The captain is waiting.'

There were few people out in the storm – only a prostitute with dripping hair huddled in a doorway and two sailors who buried their chins in their collars and hurried past us. Domingo's black eyes flashed beneath his wet lashes, but he didn't look at me. Rain streamed down our faces, wind whipped our hair, a jagged vein of lightning flashed, and a crash of thunder rolled over Venice like a lion's roar.

We came to a massive old freighter rocking unsteadily, waves chopping at her barnacled hull. Domingo ran up the gangplank and waved me aboard. Just then, Bernardo appeared out of the rain, soaked and bedraggled but running straight at me. He pushed himself between my legs, purring, nudging me with his wet nose, and looking up at me with enormous eyes in his small, rain-slicked head. Bernardo had followed me faithfully into the kitchen, out of the kitchen, into the church, and now to the boat. He broke my heart. I folded him in my arms and trudged up the gangplank.

The captain couldn't keep still. His head swivelled back and forth and a muscle jumped spastically in one cheek; he made frantic gestures to hurry me along. He peered down the rain-darkened gangplank and asked, 'Where's the other one?'

Domingo said, 'If you were expecting two people, you should give back half the money.'

'No, I remember now. One is right. Go on, get out of here.'

But I held Domingo's arm. 'Thank you, Domingo. You saved my life.'

'*Niente.*' He tucked his hands in his armpits and looked at his feet. 'Good luck, Luciano.'

'I said get out of here.' The captain shoved him, and Domingo clomped down the gangplank and disappeared in the rain.

The captain had no time for sentiment. 'Get down in the hold before someone sees you.' He pushed me towards a stunted door, and only then did I remember the chef's letters in my pocket. I should have given them to Domingo. The captain said, 'Are you waiting for the *Cappe Nere*? Move!'

That night, I sat against acrid-smelling barrels banded with metal so biting cold they burned to the touch. I was drenched and chilled to the bone, trembling from head to toe. The tips of my fingers were numb, and I blew on them while I recalled my childhood fantasy of stowing away, warm and dry, between sacks of Florentine wool as the vessel rocked me to sleep. There were no soft surfaces in that hold except for my own breakable body and Bernardo. The cargo had been efficiently packed for sea travel in wooden barrels sealed with tar to protect against salt and damp.

The boat rolled and bucked in the storm; it threw me back and forth, banging me first on one barrel, then on another. The motion made me sick, and I retched, but there was nothing to bring up. A bitter, metallic taste pooled in my mouth and I swallowed it.

I managed to move some barrels into a haphazard circle and then jammed Bernardo and myself into a space in the centre. It was tight, the barrels stank of damp, and the cold metal bands stung, but at least the ship couldn't toss us about like rag dolls. At the first squeeze of claustrophobia, I inhaled deeply and came back to the moment. It was an uncomfortable moment, but I survived it.

The captain, steady on his veteran sea legs and quite friendly once I was stowed and hidden, climbed down to bring me a hunk of bread and a half bottle of wine. He left it in my lap and bid me a cheery good night. I knew I should eat. I needed to eat; I wanted to eat; and I tried to eat. But thinking about the chef and Marco and the lost book, I couldn't swallow. I chewed a mouthful of bread into a pulp for Bernardo, and he licked it from my hand. I braced myself against the motion of the boat and laid my cheek down on the plank floor. Bernardo snuggled against me, fastidiously licking his wet paws. I smelled brine and wine, wet cat and wet wool. My cheek chafed against the splintery wood under my face, and I could still taste my own bile. Exhaustion brought the small mercy of a fitful sleep.

When I woke the next morning, the storm had passed, and the boat moved easily over soft swells. Bernardo and I found our way above deck, and I wondered for a moment whether I was meant to remain hidden. I quickly decided that, no, I had paid for my passage – or Chef Ferrero had. I stepped out onto the deck, and the light blinded me. The captain greeted me with a friendly smile, congenial now and free of his nervous tics. It was only in port that he'd been afraid; it would be bad for him to be seen pocketing money for unscheduled passengers. Once we were at sea, I was free to roam at will.

I'd never seen so much bright blue space. The green canals of Venice are lined with buildings that block the horizon. The port, congested with the ships of all nations, obscured the open sea with a forest of masts and riggings.

Out at sea, ocean merged with sky, and blue stretched to a three-hundred-and-sixty-degree for ever. I felt giddy in the novelty of such openness. I stretched out my arms and turned in a slow circle. Balancing on the gently rolling deck, I walked to the rail, hooked my arms over the side, and took my first look at the world beyond Venice. I reached out one hand to touch the unbroken blue and felt the sky ripple between my fingers. For an instant, my world was peaceful and infinite. Then Bernardo mewed and moved against my leg, and everything came back in a mournful rush. The perfect peace of an infinite heaven was an illusion.

The captain came up behind me and clapped me on the back. He said, 'Go down to the galley if you want some breakfast.'

In spite of my downcast mood, the crisp sea air and the mention of breakfast made hunger rear up. It felt traitorous to want food under the circumstances, but I did. I went below and followed appetizing smells to a room with a low ceiling and a long table. The galley cook, a toothless old salt, handed me a bowl of steaming porridge while Bernardo pounced on a mouse, and we both settled in to eat. Though the porridge was hot enough to scald my mouth, I felt nothing.

I remained numb for the entire voyage, which was brief, uneventful, and marked chiefly by sadness. Blue became the colour of defeat and salt air the smell of loss. After we docked, I walked the streets of Cádiz with no destination and no plans. I carried Bernardo under my arm, and he purred contentedly in ignorant bliss.

Cádiz is deeply rooted in Africa, and even then I recognized the city's exotic elements as Moorish. I'd often heard 'Africa begins at the Pyrenees', and I saw that it was so. The Moors left enduring footprints on the soul of Cádiz.

I strolled the wharf area, a rough, seedy port swarming with sailors; bars and whorehouses lined the docks. I didn't speak Castilian, but Cádiz was a busy place, ringing with all the languages of the world. I walked along asking, 'Nessuno parla italiano?' Now and then someone would answer, 'Si, paesano,' and I'd ask about ships bound for the New World. The answer was always the same: No one goes there any more. Colombo made his last voyage from Cádiz in 1493. One man suggested I go to Lisbon and seek out a captain named Amerigo Vespucci. Where on earth was Lisbon?

I wandered farther into the city, hoping to find someone with more knowledge than common sailors. Cádiz proved to be no more than a maze of cramped alleyways where residents lived in stone houses with narrow slit windows, little fortresses of ignorance where doddering grandmothers barricaded themselves against the evil eye. One grizzled hag said, 'What New World?' Her tiny eyes squinted, and she shoved a fist behind her back for protection from the devil.

Cádiz reeked of superstition, yet everywhere, I saw incongruent hints of the recently departed Moors – flowery courtyards carefully paved with hand-glazed tiles, keyhole windows, and ornately carved lintels. Cádiz had a poetic underside, and I began to think I could live there.

Guitar music floated out of a high window. The four-string Arabic instrument sounded one-dimensional compared to an Italian lute, but it was just as evocative. The haunting music followed me as I headed back to the docks. It snaked through the twisting alleys, mingled with the smells of roast lamb and sweet sherry, swirled around the tile frieze of a whispering fountain, and faded slowly, like a memory.

Outside an old church, I stepped aside to make way for a

sullen procession of hooded penitents wearing long, red robes. They were weighted down with heavy chains and bent over by life-size wooden crosses on their backs. In the people's dark eyes, I saw glints of religious fanaticism and a cruelty more raw than any I'd seen in Venice. I decided then that I did *not* want to live in that place. I thought again about Lisbon and wandered on.

I came to a street of *bodegas*, like a small Rialto, with stalls offering octopus tentacles hung overhead like laundry, suckling pigs with tails gleefully curled, and fat smoked hams swinging from wooden beams. Merchants called to me in Castilian, but I had no reason to inspect their wares, no chef to shop for and no cooks waiting for peaches or cheese.

I walked until the sun dipped into the bay and beckoning lights came on in the bars. The sounds and rhythm of the workday yielded to the laughter of sailors prowling the docks for pleasure. They streamed into the bars and whore-houses like the tide. I stopped in the open doorway of a crowded bar and watched a young woman ascend a small stage. Her blue-black hair was folded into a sleek chignon at the back of her neck. She had pinned a red rose behind one ear, and she wore a long satin dress, snugly fitted over her body until it flared, like an impulse, at the knee.

She walked the perimeter of the tiny stage with eyes full of contempt. She seethed as a young man in tight black pants and a white shirt joined her on the stage. He faced her, stiff backed and challenging. They circled each other like animals smouldering with barely restrained lust. From the background came an occasional world-weary *'Olé.'* A man sang a plaintive *canción* that conjured sad fellahin souls, and soon the singer was joined by guitars and syncopated clapping to an ancient, percussive rhythm. With a primal shout, the woman lifted her flounced skirt above her knees, her thighs flashed, and her heels beat a furious tattoo on the wooden floor. She snapped her fingers and released the snake-rattle of castanets. The young man responded, inflamed and enraged. Their dance was a duel, and they taunted each other to a frenzied climax.

I thought of Francesca and I won't deny my regret at losing her. Like Marco and me, she lived on the edge and had no solid reason to put her fate in my hands. We both did what we had to do. If the chef could ask me what I'd learned I'd say that unrequited love does not die; it's only beaten down to a secret place where it hides, curled and wounded. For some unfortunates, it turns bitter and mean, and those who come after pay the price for the hurt done by the one who came before. For me, this has not been the case, *grazie a Dio*. Time has dulled my pain, but now and again something sparks the memory of her antelope eyes, the scent and feel of her, and in those moments I love her still.

At least I had Bernardo. On our first night in Cádiz, Bernardo and I found a bar whose shingle showed a hand-drawn picture of a bed, an advertisement of rooms to rent for illiterate travellers. I went in and pointed to the shingle. The crone behind the bar kept a slim, black cheroot clamped between her stained teeth while she rubbed her thumb and forefinger together – money first. I reached into my pocket and pulled out the purse the chef had given me. I hadn't yet looked inside or opened the letters to his daughters. I wouldn't have wanted to read them even if I could; after all, not delivering them was yet another way I had failed him. I opened the purse and I worried briefly that I might need Spanish currency. Then I remembered that Cádiz was an international port, like Venice, so any currency would be welcome. I wondered, absently, whether I might have enough money for passage to the New World.

I extracted the folded sheets of paper and saw there was, indeed, plenty of gold, but more astonishing were the papers themselves. I saw immediately that they were not letters but selected pages from the book – the chef's most valuable writings. He had peeled the artichoke down to its heart. Most surprising of all, written across the bottom of each page, in blue ink, was the one word I could read, written the way I'd learned to read it: 'Guardians.' Under that word were more words, also scrawled in blue ink, which would prove to be the names of two chefs and where I could find them.

CHAPTER ✣ XXXIV

THE BOOK OF BONES

M Y MAESTRO WASN'T ABLE TO give me years of instruction, but he led me to another teacher who could. He also left me an excellent blueprint for life – his own example. Am I his son? Does it matter? A father and son aren't made of anything so fragile and corruptible as flesh and blood. What is that but soft fruit and turning meat? No, a father and son are forged by effort, will and heart. I had all that; there's nothing more.

I paid a Spanish copyist to read the names of the two Guardians. One lived in the far north of France and the other in the ancient city of Granada, only a few weeks' journey from Cádiz. That's why the chef had agreed to go to Spain. I later learned that *'granada'* means 'pomegranate' – and thus my journey came full circle.

The Spanish Guardian was the chef to Queen Isabella the Catholic at her residence in the Alhambra. I will simply refer to him as my teacher, and if I appear reticent about his precise identity or my present whereabouts, you will appreciate that there are still many who would silence us.

I walked for twenty-three days, and when I arrived in Granada, I made my way through the Arabic casbah, the Albaicín, a labyrinth of narrow streets and whitewashed houses with secluded inner gardens. At the highest point of the Albaicín, a panoramic view of the Alhambra, the magnificent Moorish citadel, took my breath away.

Massive cream-coloured walls, turrets, towers and crenellated battlements rambled across a plateau covered in tufted green. Moorish poets describe the Alhambra as pearls set in emeralds. For centuries, the Moors who resided there ruled over a diverse kingdom of Muslims, Christians and Jews. After the Spanish conquered Granada for Isabella the Catholic, the Moors converted to Christianity and the Jews were expelled from Spain.

I climbed up to the citadel and joined the pilgrims, petitioners and merchants streaming through the gate. The severe exterior of the compound is intended to heighten by contrast the splendour of the interior. I wandered dumb-struck through a series of genteel courtyards and marble halls with domed and fretted ceilings. Everywhere, I saw fluid arabesques and filigree walls like stucco lace. The effect was one of airy lightness.

When I found the main kitchen, I entered by a side door and stepped around an army of busy cooks while I searched for the chef. I was curious about the foreign foods I would come to know as chorizo, fire-roasted piquillo peppers, La Mancha saffron sealed in blue clay jars, Serrano ham, and pickled aubergine. That kitchen smelled like a cross between my maestro's kitchen and Borgia's. It had the clean airiness I was accustomed to, but a tang of briny olives and smoked meats flavoured the air.

The chef was a tall, angular man who moved with arrogant grace. When he noticed me wandering in his kitchen, he walked towards me at a brusque, businesslike pace, and I knew who he was by the way the cooks parted before him to clear a path. He was a head taller than I, and I felt cowed by his bearing and his stony expression. '¿Quién es usted?' he asked, holding his head back and his neck stiff. I shook my head dumbly and produced my maestro's hastily scribbled note, on which the Spaniard saw his own name. He brooded over that for a long time, rubbing his clean-shaven jaw and eyeing me suspiciously. The kitchen staff continued work at a steady tempo and paid us no attention, an indication that this chef did not tolerate idle curiosity. He folded my note carefully and slipped it into his pocket. Then he took me outside.

We stood in a tiled courtyard next to an orange tree growing from a massive ceramic pot. He crossed his arms over his chest, saying, '¿Qué quiere usted aquí?' I didn't understand, but I named Chef Ferrero of Venice as my maestro, and a glimmer of interest came into his eyes. Fortunately, Castilian and Italian are close enough in vocabulary and syntax that I was able to communicate the dismal news that my maestro had been arrested and most of his book lost.

The tall Spaniard studied me a long time. His gelid stare and aloof manner did not reassure me, and I pressed my fingernails into my sweaty palms. Eventually he said, 'Bueno, venga.'

His body language conveyed an order to follow him into the kitchen, which I did, but he didn't acknowledge me. He took provisions from a food locker and set a pan on a wood-burning stove. I waited while he melted butter and added a smooth white slab of meat to the pan – fresh calf's brains. I assumed he meant for me to observe, so I watched him sear the brains, add wine and stock, and then reduce the skillet liquid to an aromatic liqueur. I clasped my hands behind my back and sniffed at the air as he folded in beaten egg yolks and cream. He covered the pan and tempered the fire to let the delicate meat poach in a smooth sauce.

While the meat simmered, he turned his dispassionate stare on me, and I began to wonder whether I had misunderstood, whether I had been dismissed and should leave. But I had nowhere to go, so I stood there, hoping to meet his measure, while his unblinking stare chilled my marrow.

After a minute, my teacher removed the pan from the heat and laid sliced calf's brains in cream sauce on two earthenware plates. He set one plate on a table and handed me the other. The tall man motioned me into a chair opposite him and said, 'Usted ha venido a mi para conocimiento. Bueno. Empezamos compartiendo estos cerebros.' He nodded decisively and cut into his meal.

I didn't understand his words, but he clearly wanted me to dine with him. The dish was rich and satisfying, and after we finished, he sat back and smiled. He had opalescent teeth and a friendly overbite that nipped his bottom lip. When I saw that smile I understood that our sharing of brains had affirmed the beginning of our joint quest for knowledge. Guardians love culinary metaphors.

It took twelve years for me to become a Guardian, and every day with my teacher was a privilege. After I became a master chef, I married. As it was with Chef Ferrero, maturity brought me an appreciation of qualities beyond flaxen hair and caramel skin. Even with her hair turning white, my wife is a light-footed goddess with a knowing smile. I have three children, including one son who was never interested in culinary art. He's a bookish fellow who likes numbers. Although I was briefly disappointed, I learned that allowing him to show me where his natural talents lay is more rewarding for us both. But I taught my daughters to cook – and more. Their husbands feast and are beguiled. Ah, those lucky men. I never taught my children what to think, I taught them *how* to think. I never made them go to church either; I made them go to school.

Bernardo found a mate, too, a silken, sloe-eyed minx, and after he died, I adopted one of his daughters. Now his great-granddaughter Marietta prowls my kitchen, flirting shamelessly for tasty morsels. Chef Ferrero would have liked Marietta; she's impossible to resist.

The chef would also have liked to see that *stamperie* and quick-books have spread across Europe; printing methods are continually improving. More books mean more literacy, which will in turn mean more books. Even now, hand-copied books are beginning to be regarded as quaint. It looks promising.

Chef Ferrero anticipated the success of printing, but he never saw it. I discovered his fate ten years later, after the danger had passed and I was able to return to Venice for a visit. Those ten years were tumultuous. The doge died in 1501, Castelli killed Landucci in 1502, and Borgia was murdered by one of his many political rivals in 1503. After Borgia and the twenty-six-day papacy of Pius III came Pope Julius II, a warrior-priest determined to extend the power of the papacy through battle. Hearing of his election, I remembered the chef saying, 'Beware the man who uses the words "holy" and "war" in the same sentence.'

Pope Julius joined the League of Cambria for military support against Venice. Castelli, feeling threatened and desperate, redoubled his efforts to find the elusive book that might discredit Rome. It was not until 1509, when Castelli was killed at the battle of Agnadello, that Julius turned his attention to defeating France, and the search for a mysterious book passed into legend. Finally, it was safe to return to Venice.

I went to the chef's house, hoping Signora Ferrero might have come back, but she was gone – dead or retired to a cloister for widows, I never discovered which – and the girls, I suppose, all married and dispersed. I stood in front of the house, staring at the blue front door, remembering my Sunday dinners with the family and the night I spied on their balcony. Without the chef's family there, it was just another house, so I strolled around the neighbourhood noting that nothing had changed but the people. The same fruit cart stood on the same corner overseen by a different man. In a nearby *trattoria*, I stopped for a glass of wine. The barkeep was an old man, and I asked him whether he remembered the chef to the last doge. He poured his wine, saying, 'The last doge died, what, ten years ago? I barely remember him, much less his chef.'

He started to turn way, but I held his arm lightly, saying, 'He lived right around the corner, in the house with the blue door. He had four daughters.'

'Oh, *that* fellow.' He set the bottle down. 'That fellow was beheaded.'

I swallowed hard. 'What was his crime?'

'Probably no crime.' He pulled his eyelid. 'They said he knew something about a book of heresy and dark arts. But if he did, he didn't talk. He was in the dungeon three months before they gave up on him. *Sì*, now I remember. He was an ordinary fellow. I don't know why they thought he knew anything about sorcery. It was a treacherous time. That chef and his apprentice were beheaded together.'

I murmured, 'The apprentice, too.'

'Sì, I was in the crowd and I can tell you that boy was terrified, weeping and trembling. He kept sobbing, "You made a mistake." I have to admit, he pulled at my heart. He was young, eh? But he was raving. Why would they care if they made a mistake? He was nobody. Poor boy. They had to hold him down.

'But that chef, he was dignified to the end. He was skin and bones, no teeth, a broken man in shackles, and yet before he put his head on the block he said, "I die victorious."' The barkeep shrugged. 'Maybe he was raving, too.'

'It sounds like he didn't tell them what they wanted to know.'

'Could be. But a man separated from his head doesn't look victorious to me.'

'There are many kinds of victory.'

The barkeep gave me a cynical look, then shuffled off to attend another customer.

On that same visit, I went to the convent and asked after Sister Francesca. A new and equally formidable Mother Superior said they had no such nun in that house. I said, 'She was a novice here ten years ago.'

'Novices come and go, signore.'

'This one tatted dragonfly lace. I understand it brought a good price.'

The nun's face closed up tight. 'I told you, signore, we have no Sister Francesca.' She went to the door and held it open for me. 'Goodbye, signore.'

I walked through the cloister and paused there, remembering the times I'd come to that place to meet Francesca. As I made to leave, a priest entered and stopped short, surprised to see a man in that female bastion. 'Signore,' he asked. 'May I help you?'

'Sorry to intrude, father. I came to visit a nun, but she's not here. A Sister Francesca.'

'Nuns don't keep their given names. How else might she be known?'

'I have no idea. I only know she tatted dragonfly lace.'

'Ah, you must mean the beautiful widow of Verona.'

'Widow?'

'I understand she was a novice here once, but she ran away with a young nobleman from Verona.' He chuckled. 'I think the nuns were not so scandalized as they were envious. But, alas, her young man died soon after the wedding and his family turned her out. She sold the jewellery he'd given her and opened a lace shop. She has an endless series of suitors and, I'm afraid, a rather wicked reputation as the maker of, well, shall we say provocative lace undergarments. Her costumes are popular with noble ladies all over Europe, though few will admit it. The widow of Verona is quite shameless.'

I had to smile. 'Perhaps not shameless, father. Perhaps only practical.'

'Perhaps.'

From the convent I went to the Rialto and saw Domingo, heavier and happier, supervising a thriving fish stall. I bought a smoked trout from him and as I laid the coppers in his hand, the light of recognition came into his face. He smiled and I nodded. He handed me the trout, and I said, '*Grazie*, Domingo.'

'*Niente*, Luciano.'

I left Domingo to his happy life and went back to mine. I've been a master chef for many years now. With the aid of my Spanish teacher, I've built on the kernel of knowledge the chef gave me and I believe he would be proud to see my book. I've had several apprentices, one not smart enough, one too smart for his own good, one dishonest and one too frivolous. Recently, I found my heir. He's a local boy, a salami maker who, though already gainfully employed, came looking for something better. I liked that. I'm happy to say he's intelligent and inquisitive, and he has a spontaneous sense of humour, indispensable qualities that cannot be taught. One day, I caught him just as he was about to throw away the skeleton of a magnificent salmon. I grabbed his arm and said, 'Are you out of your mind?'

He said, 'Maestro?'

'The bones, my boy, they encase the essence. We'll extract all the flavour and nourishment this fish has to give. We'll make soup.'

He handed over the skeleton with its fleshy bits clinging here and there. I filled a stockpot with fresh water, then added the salmon bones and hung the pot over a high flame. While it heated, we chopped onions and carrots and celery. He added them to the pot and I called his attention to the harmony of colours and the music of the boil as the vegetables danced in the water. When the boiling water started to render the bones, the broth took on substance and the aroma engulfed us.

'Pay attention,' I said in my most tutorial manner. 'The bones provide a noble base to which we need only add a soupçon of salt, a dash of dill and a handful of parsley. Thus we create a full-flavoured nectar through which the strength of this fish may pass into our own bones.'

A careful look in his eyes and the stillness about his face told me he understood that we were talking about more than soup. My bright apprentice watched the broth simmer, pensive and wondering. He doesn't quite know what to make of his lesson yet, but he's thinking. *Bene.*

I, too, have been thinking for a long while now. I considered writing this memoir as early as 1521, when a fiery German named Luther used *stamperie* and quick-books to expose the corruption in Rome. Luther was a hard man, but my maestro would have enjoyed his plain-talking comparisons between Rome and Babylon. Emboldened by the success of quick-books, as well as by the freethinkers who have flourished in recent years, I dared to write this account. Perhaps it will find its way to a *stamperia* soon, or perhaps not until the new age. Everything comes in its own season.

For time's pendulum swings, and always, the teachers are the torchbearers. Thanks to my teachers, I've abandoned superstition and embraced an unfettered quest for knowledge. Now, I live every day alert to discovery. Only yesterday, I overheard a German traveller discussing a new idea called celestial physics and I turned, as if the chef had called my name.

ACKNOWLEDGEMENTS

Like most authors, I'm indebted to more people than space allows me to name, but first among them are my teachers, especially Drusilla Campbell, who taught me how to write a novel. This book would not have found a home without my extraordinary agent, Dorian Karchmar, and it would not have found its final form without my equally remarkable editor, Emily Bestler. Also indispensable were the thoughtful readings and insightful comments of fellow writers Seré Prince Halverson, Chelo Ludden and Laurie Richards. I'm grateful to my husband, Frank, for his patience and support, and to my father, the chef, for the inspiration. To friends and family who cheered me on through this book's birth pangs, thank you all.

AUTHOR'S NOTE

THIS IS A WORK OF FICTION, and the astute reader will notice that I have taken artistic licence with certain details. The famous Bridge of Sighs was constructed between 1600 and 1603, significantly later than the events of our story. However, it seems likely to me that there must have been some lesser bridge roughly in the same place and used for the same dark purpose. With that in mind I created a fictional bridge named the Bridge of Sorrows.

Marsilio Ficino was never a doge of Venice, but he was one of the most influential humanist philosophers of the early Renaissance. I used his name in order to demonstrate Chef Ferrero's sympathy with the humanist movement of the period.

Although the heliocentric theory was not widely appreciated until later than 1498, Copernicus made his first observations in 1497, and they are recorded in his epochal work, *Six Books Concerning the Revolutions of the Heavenly Orbs* (*De revolutionibus orbium coelestium libri vi*). It was my feeling that the chef, as one of the enlightened elite, would have been aware of the heliocentric theory, which had also been recorded by Muslim astronomers centuries earlier.

Pietro Pomponazzi wrote his famous treatise, *On the Immortality of the Soul* (*Tractatus de immortalitate animae*), in 1516. However, I think it would be safe to assume that he was vocal about his theories long before he published his opus, and that his opinions were widely known. Again, as an enlightened and well-informed person, Chef Ferrero might well have heard about Pomponazzi's theories.

It seems, to my surprise, that my use of the word *marrone* needs some explanation. I had an Italian grandmother from Bologna who used *marrone* as an all-purpose exclamation. I can still see her entering a room that my sister and I had strewn with toys, throwing up her arms and saying, '*Marrone*! What a mess!' On reflection, I see that the word might have been peculiar to her native Modena, or perhaps simply peculiar to her. I don't know. Throughout my childhood, I heard this word used exactly as I have used it in the book. If this has a strange ring to the Italian ear, I can only say that it must be the spirit of my grandmother manifesting through Luciano.

As for the presence of New World foods such as potatoes and tomatoes in an early Renaissance kitchen, I hope the reader will understand that Chef Ferrero was not just any old cook. In his fictional kitchen of marvels and magic, this chef knew many things that others of his time did not. It seems likely to me that Columbus brought back a few potatoes and tomato seeds and some ever-vigilant Guardian chef saw an opportunity to expand his culinary repertoire. Over time, I believe the tubers and seedlings made their clandestine way through the underground network of educated chefs and into the capable hands of Chef Ferrero. How else could it have happened?

I take full responsibility for any other historical inaccuracies and beg my readers' kind indulgence. My primary objective was to tell a good tale.

Grazie and *buon appetito,*
Elle Newmark